INTERGALACTICA

Intergalactica
by F. P. Trotta

Translated by Fernanda Poltronieri
Edited by Andrew Hirst
Layout by Franco Poltronieri
Art by Raiane de Almeida
Amanda art for final chapter by Bruna Polonia

This book is a work of fiction. Names, characters, places and incidents are the product of the author's imagination. Any resemblance to actual events, locales, or persons, living or dead, is coincidental.

Copyright © Franco Trotta 2023

First published in Brazil in 2016 by LIVROS ILIMITADOS LTDA., Rio de Janeiro

All rights reserved. In accordance with the U.S. Copyright Act of 1976, the scanning, uploading, and electronic sharing of any part of this book without the permission of the publisher is unlawful piracy and theft of the author's intellectual property.

ASIN: B0C9R6TW5M
ISBN-13: 979-8850916749

Introduction

This is the first English release of Intergalactica: previously released in Brazilian Portuguese, Intergalactica and its sequels were born out of a love for exploration and the unknown - a much-needed return to an optimistic view of the space opera genre, but leaving some of its sanctimonious aspects behind. I have always enjoyed intricate stories that took their time when cooking up their twists. Hopefully, the sequels will also be translated in the near future. It all depends on whether you enjoy this trip to the stars.

F. P. Trotta

Chapter One - The Realm - 6
Chapter Two - Jaded - 34
Chapter Three - Set-Up - 44
Chapter Four - The Lair - 51
Chapter Five - Wanted - 69
Chapter Six - The Plot Thickens - 81
Chapter Seven - Masks & Shields - 91
Chapter Eight - Sessions - 99
Chapter Nine - Infiltration - 112
Chapter Ten - The Firm - 127
Chapter Eleven - Undercover Nights - 133
Chapter Twelve - Energy - 160
Chapter Thirteen - //hypersleep - 170
Chapter Fourteen - 2051 - 172
Chapter Fifteen - Gliese - 208
Chapter Sixteen - Plethoreae - 231
Chapter Seventeen - The Palace - 239
Chapter Eighteen - Utopia's Puzzle - 256
Chapter Nineteen - Visions of Anyara - 276
Chapter Twenty - Through the Stellar Door - 284
Chapter Twenty One - Reign of Fire - 296
Chapter Twenty-Two - Bells of Heaven - 314
Chapter Twenty-Three - The Beyond - 341
Chapter Twenty-Four - Alienized - 357
Chapter Twenty-Five - The Belladonna - 376
Chapter Twenty-Six - Kratik - 383
Chapter Twenty-Seven - Frost - 393
Chapter Twenty-Eight - The Other - 407

Chapter Twenty-Nine - Pleiadians - 416
Chapter Thirty - Home? - 434
Chapter Thirty-One - Judgement Day - 447
Chapter Thirty-Two - Sky Gods - 467

Chapter One - The Realm

MAY 3, 2041

An intense storm took over the skies of Chicago. Cars were stuck in traffic, honking and making no progress in the pouring rain. The grey, electric clouds swallowed the skyscrapers. Raindrops thudded against the streets and windows, drenching the city in a deep chill. In Saint Barth's hospital, however, hundreds of workers co-existed oblivious to the storm that raged outside, and, inside the white-stoned walls, an even colder atmosphere reigned over room 406.

"What if she doesn't come back?" asked Ripley.

"But she will," assured Stryker.

"It's been eight days. She used to glow. We knew she was here. Now it's as if she's an object, Stryker. Look at her. She's lost her vivacity," said Ripley, pointing.

"I don't know how to deal with it. It makes us feel powerless and useless. There is absolutely nothing we can do except hold on and wait," said Stryker. "You know it - I know it," Ripley and Stryker looked at the window and saw their reflection as the rain beat on the glass from outside: her short, curly brown hair and Stryker's light brown hair both seemed dark blue as more and more raindrops collapsed against the window and their faces became less distinguishable.

"I know," said Ripley, still looking outside. "But she's in a deep coma. They said the part associated with higher functions was inactive. Should we prepare for the worst?" asked Ripley.

"No. It's her. She's a tough one. Please stop filling my head with this. It doesn't help,"

Ripley sat down on one of the visitor chairs and started zapping the TV. The controls were built into the arm of the chair.

"I wish remote controls would make a comeback," said Ripley. She clicked through channels until settling for a news channel broadcasting a NASA announcement.

"So, they're really going to Jupiter, huh? My grandma's still alive and she saw man's first landing on the moon! I wonder what these people think about this. You know, people who never thought they'd live to see it. This is huge!" Stryker seemed genuinely excited.

"Want to bet on what they'll find there?" asked Ripley, smiling.

"Hell, I just want them to find something! Do you have any idea how much of an achievement for humanity it would be? Enough hoping for disclosure! One discovery, whether it's microbial or marine, can revolutionize humanity's perception and understanding of itself. It's the single biggest discovery ever and we'll live to see it. I'm telling you, I'm going to be all over this soon. They'll broadcast the ship, right? That is so cool, Ripley. We can watch it at home as they land!"

"Would you go? If you had the chance? asked Ripley. "'Cause you know they might not come back."

"Hell, yeah! Wouldn't you?"

"Oh, absolutely. I'd be terrified, though,"

"Who wouldn't?"

"I mean, to come back. That must feel incredible," said Stryker.

Ripley and Stryker looked at each other in agreement, and the silence in the room was broken by a loud breath coming from their left. Both looked at the bed and saw Amanda's eyes were wide open. She then reached in for a second breath, and in what seemed like a fraction of a second, Ripley and Stryker were up from their chairs and by Amanda's side.

"Amanda!" yelled Ripley, as Stryker ran into the hallway, screaming for a nurse. Ripley hit every alarm and the room quickly filled with medical staff. Amanda's breaths deepened as she regained consciousness. She blinked her eyes and, as she closed them beneath the oxygen mask, Ripley could see a faint smile.

The medical staff permitted Ripley and Stryker to re-enter the room a few minutes after Amanda's heartbeat stabilized. The rain had not stopped and there was a sense of adrenaline as they eagerly waited to greet her.

Both seemed to tip-toe to the bed, slightly in awe of what had happened. Her disease had taken enough of her and its advanced spread didn't seem to give her much chance of ever coming back from the coma.

"How...how are you?" asked Stryker. Ripley already had tears in her eyes.

"I saw you smiling, girl. I knew you'd make it," she said, touching her hand.

Amanda had a peaceful look on her face, but was visibly weak. She looked at the both of them smiling and then said:

"I remember everything."

"What?" What do you mean?" both asked, intrigued.

"I need to tell this to someone...thank God you're here. Please sit down."

"But...how are you feeling?" Ripley asked again.

"I'm fine. But..," Amanda's eyes started to tear up. Ripley and Stryker pulled their chairs together and sat down next to her bed. As raindrops fell, Ripley held Amanda's hand, both of them listening. Then she began:

"Please keep in mind that I've spent ten years of my life studying brains. To you, it may sound delirious... it will seem impossible. To you, this will sound... like I want pity, even. But I need to tell you because I want to keep it fresh - I saw... I saw many..," then she sobbed and inhaled a deep breath.

Ripley and Stryker looked at each other, confused.

You could hear a pin drop: they hadn't expected this dialogue with their friend, nor did they understand what point she was trying to make. Still, they sat down and listened carefully, as Amanda chose each word thoughtfully and started her account.

"Please imagine darkness. It was dark, but visible - like a shade of dark that is slightly green and brown, because you can see it - it is palpable, like mud, like dirt. It felt claustrophobic, suffocating. I was conscious, but I didn't know who I was. I didn't know my name, I just knew me, myself, you know, this dominant voice that's in our heads all the time, the main one. Listen to me..," Amanda said.

Ripley and Stryker were gripped and intrigued.

"I was in this void for so long. There was a vibration in the distance - a pulse of some sort that was ever-present. I didn't have a body. Not one that I was aware of. But I was there, in this pulsating, beating darkness. I can't tell you how long I was there, but it seemed like an eternity. As I seemed to linger in that void, I sensed that, by my side... there were little shapes and patterns forming, even though my eyelids were closed. I noticed blurry, root-like lines in the darkness. I felt like I was buried underground, yet I could see vines that would show me the way. It is incredibly hard to picture, but trust me, this is the hardest part. But I loathed being stuck, and I became more and more uncomfortable in that place. And then... "

Amanda's blue eyes filled with tears as she looked at the storm raging outside the hospital windows. She continued in a mournful tone:

"I swear I remember this vividly... and then, from above, something so beautiful, so, so perfect, you couldn't believe how familiar it feels. Yet you're in awe of this presence, this glowing entity that came floating towards me, as it shone through the darkness...and I remember vividly once I focused on the light - which was often very white, but with these golden shades coming through it - once I focused on it, it pulled me up...like magnetism. It attracted me to it, floating towards it effortlessly... The darkness seemed to fade before me as I went through the beam of light and a whooshing sound came from it - and there I was. So, I wanted to tell you this - I remember it so vividly..."

"I could give you all the adjectives in the world to describe the beauty of this place I found myself in... It was stunning, vibrant, and alive. It felt like my entire body was floating in ecstasy. Below me, there was a countryside. It was lush, so green, and so Earth-like. But it wasn't Earth.

"It feels like being in your favorite childhood spot, but you only realize it now as you reminisce about the nostalgic experience, causing you to feel overjoyed. I could fly. I flew over trees and fields, streams and waterfalls, rivers and flowers - flowers which were so colorful, like Monet's paintings...

"And there were people, there were children... they laughed and played, sang and danced around in circles. I saw dogs jumping and running, as full of joy as everyone else. They wore these simple garments, almost like peasants, Ancient Greece-like, yet less refined, with an ease and flow, prettier.

"On top of the mountains and above a waterfall, there was the most intricate, awe-inspiring palace I've ever seen. I wish I had gone there. I wish I could know what was in there. It was so high, as if it were built of pale, purple emeralds...

"Then I remember hearing the flapping of butterfly wings as I saw dozens approach me. I wasn't a physical being; I don't know what I looked like to them... but I realized, I was floating on one... and her colors were so detailed - she flapped her wings so effortlessly... and then I floated up.... towards these pointed, gigantic mountains up in the sky... I remember we were so high... and all the butterflies flew around me, and as we flew into the clouds, everything became white. And then, from that brightness, I felt conscious of my body again. The first thing I remember feeling were my eyelids... and when I opened them, I breathed in and I was here." Amanda looked down, closing her eyes and smiling again. Ripley and Stryker could see how deep within herself she searched to remember what she had experienced.

It was such a beautiful, incredible dream-world. "

"Except it wasn't a dream," Stryker said.

Amanda looked at him and smiled.

"Exactly. The most riveting sight of all, though... was right after that. I looked up and this winged being came floating towards me. She shone in an astonishing light, moving graciously as she slowly approached me, dressed in simple clothes... powder blue, indigo, and pastel. She had the most peaceful look on her face, and big, expressive blue eyes. Her silvery hair resonated with everything in the place. Everything follows an effortless pace - it's indescribable, really. And when she looked deep into me, you could sense your whole life, everything you've felt and experienced suddenly being worth it. It wasn't a romantic look, not a look of friendship. It was beyond that. Beyond the love we have on Earth. It was higher, and, using no words, she spoke to me. The message went through me like a wind, and I instantly knew it to be true,"

"What...what did she say?" Ripley asked.

"It was more of a message. An incredible way of communicating that felt obvious, yet I couldn't believe I could really understand her. Her love was so strong I could communicate without words." Amanda's voice shook as she remembered, a tear rolling down her cheek. She paused for a second and then went on.

"This message had three parts. If I was to translate it to words, it would go something like... "We are all cherished and watched, deeply and forever. The second part would be that fear plays a crucial part in evolution... but it is useless, for there is no need to fear anything. I remember finding it such a revelation...but you can't do it justice by translating it into words...it's so hard to explain."

"And the last part? What was it?" Ripley sat up in her chair and stared at Amanda with an unblinking gaze, just like Stryker.

"The last part was the most important one of all...it asked me to remember. The last part felt more like a suggestion, and it would soon be revealed why. I remember it would translate into "The more you remember, the more you will understand...""

"Do you believe that your soul was floating through the afterlife? Choosing whether to come back?"

"It wasn't a matter of choice, I think. It always felt as if I was meant to come back. I can't even believe what I'm saying. But it felt as if I was being given that... tour...on purpose. I'm a woman of science. I'd only listen to facts. But... but I was there... and that will never be taken away from me. So, I have to deal with this. It has to mean something."

"The doctors told us your brain was completely shut down. You couldn't have dreamt these things even if you wanted to," Ripley added. Stryker nodded in agreement.

"I... I believe you!" said Stryker.

"So do I, but I don't think she's really looking for us to believe," Ripley stated, letting out a small laugh.

"I'm glad you do, but I'm just so certain. It doesn't really matter to me if people believe me or not. I know what was there..."

"We're so happy to have you back," Ripley added. "Stryker and I have been here back and forth, non-stop. Just hoping, and it didn't look good, Amanda. But how do you feel? Are you genuinely okay?"

Amanda shrugged her shoulders and replied: "Yeah, I feel... fine. Weak, of course, tired, but... I'm fine. I need to rest... I need to write this down. This goes against everything I've studied!"

"Yeah, wait till you hear the news. They just announced they're manning for Europa. Jupiter's moon. 8-man op searching for extraterrestrial life. Deep space, baby. They're launching in six months," Stryker said gleefully.

"Are you serious? Do you really mean that? They're really going?" asked Amanda. The announcement seemed to affect her more than the average person: she leaped forward in her bed and, as Stryker nodded, she asked more questions:

"Did they give any information about who's funding it?"

Ripley and Stryker looked at each other confused and Stryker replied: "Hm, isn't NASA the one who funds it, or SpaceX?"

"No, they stamp their name on it, but the cash doesn't really come from them."

"When you walk out of here, you'll see. It's everywhere. It'll be the worldwide topic of the year for sure - maybe of the decade, depending on what they find there."

"I need to find out more about this," announced Amanda as she clicked on the table beside her and a thin computer screen came out of the arm of her hospital bed. She typed on the screen and started to browse and fill herself in about the expedition. Amanda opened up dozens of screens and typed faster and more frantically by the minute. Their friend's sudden burst of energy and concentration astonished Ripley and Stryker. Amanda was like this, though, so Stryker and Ripley felt reassured that she was fine.

"Listen, you need to spend the night today, so-" Stryker spoke, but Amanda interrupted him, saying, "Shut up! I'm reading about Europa! Hush!"

So, Stryker asked: "Hm, is it okay for you if Ripley and I go, then? It's past visiting hours. We'll come back first thing in the morning, though,"

"Yeah, sure. Thanks for coming," Amanda replied mechanically, staring at the screen in front of her as she continued typing and scrolling down pages without looking at them.

"Wow, I didn't think you'd be so interested in this," Stryker added. Ripley let out a small laugh.

Amanda looked at them and said:

"I'm sorry. It's just that..," she paused, clearly withholding information, and then continued: "Never mind. I'll see you both in the morning, right?"

"Absolutely," said Ripley. They hugged Amanda and made their way to the door.

DECEMBER 18, 2019 - 22 YEARS AGO

It was a chilly afternoon in a secluded area inside the grounds of Hallormsstaður, Iceland. The winds blew a polar rush of wind announcing winter - and on the far end of a big, open field stood a secluded wooden mansion. To the home's left there was a long lake whose nascent was inside the woods and where transparent blue waters frosted alongside the shore. The isolated setting fostered an atmosphere of seclusion, which was only disrupted by the sound of flames crackling inside the fireplace of the mansion. It was there that a young girl pondered.

"Daddy, do you think you can invent something for me to fly?" asked nine-year-old Amanda to her father, as she sat down to eat her lunch in their country home's kitchen. The maid, Shirley, assisted Amanda in serving her food. Oswald Rose Collins, who sat on the far end of the table, looked up at Amanda while going through a pile of files and documents, smiling at her ambiguously.

"Oh, but you see, Amanda, that is not exactly what Daddy does,"

"But I want it as a gift!" said Amanda, eating a spoonful of casserole. "Maybe in the future, then?"

"Yes, child... maybe in the future," Oswald smiled at his daughter and focused back on his papers.

"It's snowing, Daddy!" yelled Amanda, pointing outside. She could see a few snowflakes falling down from the sky onto the grass that covered their porch. Amanda got up from her chair, leaving her lunch behind, and stormed out of the kitchen, excited.

"Amanda! You must finish your meal first!" yelled Oswald, watching his daughter disappear as Shirley ran to her aid.

"Just a few minutes, Shirley!" pleaded an agitated Amanda, with one hand already clutching the front doorknob.

"Fine, but if it gets too strong, you must come back immediately. Let's go," said Shirley, stepping out with Amanda. From inside, Shirley heard Oswald call out:

"Don't encourage her, Shirley! She must eat first!"

"She loves the snow, Mr. Oswald. I'll bring her back to finish her meal in a few minutes - it hasn't snowed in so long!" Shirley answered back, cheerfully. She saw him go back to his papers without answering her.

Shirley turned around to see an energetic Amanda already at a distance, spinning around with her mouth wide open as she attempted to eat the flocks of snow. Every time she succeeded, she would let out a loud belly laugh. Shirley rejoiced in watching the little girl's liveliness.

***

August 8, 2020 - 21 YEARS AGO

Amanda woke up in her bedroom in the middle of the night and looked around - it wasn't sunrise yet. She lifted her sheets and got up from her bed, making her way out into the hallway. Her father was away on business, so all she heard was Shirley's snoring... It had been a quiet five months - the world was undergoing the pandemic and barely anyone would come over to the house. She crept to the front door, longing for warm milk, and felt a car rumbling outside.. She checked the curtains but saw nothing - except the empty fields of a snowy Icelandic winter, with her father's lab to the far right and the lake to the left. Her dad's workplace had the lights on - could Oswald be back so soon?

Amanda looked at the clock near the kitchen wall and saw it was 4:40 a.m. She was curious, so she took a snow coat and headed to Oswald's lab. As Amanda crossed the field, the grey clouds let the moonlight shine through, reminding her that winter wasn't over yet..

The grass, wet with dew, silenced her footsteps and, after what seemed like two minutes, she reached the metal door that opened to her father's personal place. Behind the lab started Hallormsstaður, Iceland's largest forest. Usually, Amanda stayed away from Oswald's lab, unless she had a reasonable explanation.

She touched the metal bars on the door and it slid open - "so someone could have left the lights on, after all," she thought as she stepped inside.

Amanda had not visited her father's lab for a considerable time, and was initially taken aback by the abundance of silver gadgets that filled the room from floor to ceiling, each possessing a similar, silvery-gold hue. She knew her father was famous for manufacturing all sorts of robotic engineering - and that's how his entire career had blossomed - he'd always been a master of creation. But she only remembered seeing a few scattered items–other than those, it seemed his lab remained the same: dozens of long, white concrete platforms, used as tables, divided the room. On them were dozens of items Amanda still didn't quite understand the purpose of - but she knew they were for research, since she could recognize microscopes and syringes alongside boxes of samples.

She made her way across the lab to switch off the lights, but as she got closer, she noticed another open door on the left-hand side - also with the lights on. After a few seconds of walking towards it, Amanda heard the alarming, grating scream of someone in terror coming from inside. Next to the door stood the first of the twelve columns that filled the room, and on top of it, a shiny purple item in the form of a spiral. Amanda observed a beautiful glowing spiral inside a transparent bubble, visible only up-close, which was neither big nor small. It mesmerized Amanda: what sort of gadget was Oswald building now? The mystical, enticing object caught her attention, making her forget the scream and walk towards it in a trance.

"Oh, wow..," she said as she got even closer to it. She was now only a few feet away from the door, and before reaching out to grab the object, Amanda focused on the door next to her. As she took it out of its place, Amanda kept her focus on the path home, ready to bolt if anyone appeared: but what set off chaos wasn't nearby; it was in her hands.

The moment she touched the item and examined it, a loud alarm sounded and the room went into emergency mode, with red lighting and a message blaring on a loop throughout the entire space.

ITEM UNSECURED - ITEM UNSECURED - ITEM UNSECURED - ITEM UNSECURED

As soon as she ran away, a shadow covered her line of vision and she saw her father emerge from the room that stood only a few meters away. His red and dark silhouette held a gigantic needle in his hand: "AMANDA!"

She sprinted away as fast as possible and then connected the needle to the agonizing scream, concluding that her father might be the cause of the pain in the other room. She used this fear, intensifying her will to run, clutching at the unknown item as the alarm repeated on an endless loop.

Oswald called out for her again: "GIVE ME THE ORBIT NOW! IT'S DANGEROUS, AMANDA!"

Despite the unbearable repetition of the alarm and her racing heart, she ignored him. She held the Orbit, not because she wanted it, but because she was angry and would only give it back if he answered her questions. Amanda stepped outside the lab and ran across the field back to her home again. The sun rose from the mountains and glinted on the lake. As she ran across the field, Amanda looked back again and saw Oswald from the distance emerging from the laboratory door:

"PUT THE ORBIT ON THE FLOOR, NOW!!! OBEY ME, AMANDA! IT WILL SELF-DESTRUCT IF YOU DO NOT COMPLY!"

She looked down at the item she'd been clutching and saw the spiral vines seemed to shine in a different tone of purple now. Darker, redder - she looked at Oswald and then at the Orbit as a strong current of wind blew. The little girl then left the Orbit on the ground and made a run for it - since it was so dangerous, she didn't really want it anymore. She saw two enormous attack helicopters off from somewhere in Hallormsstaður, while Oswald ran towards her, frantically waving his arms at the helicopters and shouting for them to abort.

"IT'S SAFE - RETREAT!!"

Despite the blaring alarm inside the lab, Amanda was stunned by the chaotic scene unfolding outside. Oswald was running towards the helicopters, flailing his arms and shouting, while the sun rose higher and illuminated Amanda's face. In the commotion, the Orbit slipped from her grasp and fell to the ground with a loud crash. It fell from her hands aggressively, reacting negatively towards sun exposure.

"COVER IT, AMANDA!" Oswald threw his coat at Amanda, but the item suddenly burst apart - exploding and sending shattered glass pieces everywhere. Amanda covered herself with her arms and felt four or five cuts tear through her skin as Oswald screamed, "NO!"

The Orbit was now shattered in pieces, with grey smoke coming out from its center - Oswald ran towards the object without taking even a quick glance at his daughter. Amanda removed a few glass shards from her right arm, wincing with each pull, while her father remained unaware. The helicopters landed next to them and three men came out from each, dressed in military uniforms, wearing face masks and holding firearms.

"Sir!" One of them called out, running towards him. Amanda seemed to go unnoticed.

Oswald stood up to talk to the first of the soldiers, and soon the other five joined them. Oswald spoke to them, but there were too many voices speaking together for Amanda to fully comprehend what they were saying.

"Arlo, it is done, tell everyone to retreat," said Oswald.

"Sir, did it self-destruct?" asked the man apparently named Arlo.

"Yes. Sunlight again. Tell Ops that Mass Manufacturing is now Priority One."

"Dad!" called Amanda.

All men became silent, turning and walking away. Oswald, however, was the only one with an angered expression - the only one of his faces Amanda feared:

"Go back home, Amanda. *Now*. We'll talk in the morning."

Amanda looked at him, baffled and heartbroken, filled with questions racing through her mind. She decided not to answer anything back, feeling intimidated by the soldiers. Amanda turned to her left and strolled back home without uttering a word. She went into the corridor and opened Shirley's door - then, Amanda gently tapped Shirley twice and, when her eyes opened, she silently revealed her bloody arms. Shirley's eyes bulged out of her face and she instantly sat up on her bed, asking Amanda what had happened. As Amanda filled her in, Shirley proceeded to clean her cuts with care.

"So he's home and didn't warn us, then? Oh, dear…don't worry, sweetheart. It will be fine. You know how he is with his research. You shouldn't have gone in there..,"

***

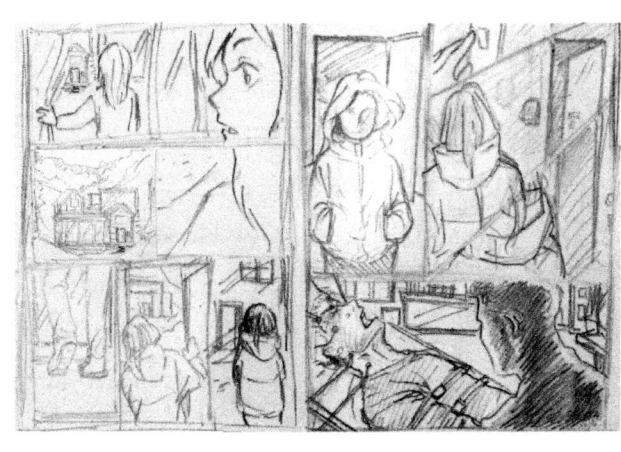

March 11, 2024 - 17 YEARS AGO

Amanda opened her eyes and saw herself in a white room with a corridor ahead: she immediately recognized that she was inside the far left room of her father's lab. The last time she'd been close to that place, five years ago, she'd destroyed her father's Orbit. She tried to move but realized she was strapped to a chair: she tried to open her mouth but realized her lips, too, were strapped.

By her side, she saw Oswald walking towards her, smiling. He focused on her and said, as he went through items on a desk set up to her right:

"Don't worry, Amanda. I just can't let you move for this, dear."

She tried to scream as her eyes filled up with rage as she looked at him without blinking and tried to jolt from the chair, protesting.

"You won't get out - stop trying to," he said. "It's just for a few minutes."

Amanda clutched at the arms of the chair, carving her nails into the cloth as she felt tears stream down her face with no possibility of wiping them. She tried to regain her breath as she cried and still tried to free herself from the straps.

"I am only giving you a gift, dear. You're old enough now to be a crucial part of your father's life - and you can finally represent the company as intended," he said, tapping a dripping needle twice.

"You know very well how these go. Starting today, you'll think clearer than ever before, my dear - oh, how excited I was for you to turn fourteen. As of now, your judgement centers are fresh and ready to thrive, my dear. Thrive, do you hear me?" he screamed, excited. "I see how terrified you are now, but you will soon understand it all, dear. I've waited fourteen years for your recognition!"

He placed round metal sensors on each side of Amanda's skull and strapped her up with dozens of red and white wires. He glued one on the center of her forehead and three alongside her jaw and throat. Amanda's fingernails dug so tightly into the cloth of the chair, she felt them tear the seam between the cloth and plastic.

"All the issues and troubles you've had to endure in your life were because of wrongful emotional thinking, Amanda. You know that to be true. Tell me if you've ever seen one of my employees falter, or struggle! Of course you haven't! I have built them, prepared them to excel in what they do. Now let's get started."

With the flip of a switch, she felt a jolt of pain surge through her entire body, as if hit by an invisible truck. Then, she trembled with the electrocution as nothing made sense for a few moments - and her mind and body seemed to go numb. Oswald typed and clicked away on his desk - and then strapped more wires to Amanda's head.

"Every day I think of the time I've been given in my life and how it'll be by the end - someday you will understand the bigger picture," he said, calmly.

Amanda regained her breath and closed her eyes. She ferociously tugged at the cloth and continuously ripped it the most she could - she could now fit her fingers beneath it entirely. She made sure to only move when Oswald moved - so if any ripping sounds came, his clicks silenced them. He flipped another switch and started typing on his keyboard, copiously taking notes and focusing on multiple items that showed up on the log screen.

Amanda experienced excruciating pain as another jolt pulsed through her brain, making her question the worth of the procedure. She had never despised him more: an unstoppable rage grew within her with each passing second, as she felt her heart skipping beats whenever the shocks ended - and she ripped the cloth more, allowing her to loosen one of the straps. As her father looked away and typed, she retrieved it quickly. By ripping one off, she noticed another one was accessible to her grasp, this time in her arm. She tore it open and saw Oswald still hadn't glanced her way. Freeing her arm, she quickly tore off the other straps, only to be electrocuted by a sudden jolt. Amanda howled in agony, causing Oswald to turn his attention to his fleeing daughter. She yanked off the fourth and fifth straps while shrieking, and as Oswald hurried towards her, Amanda flung herself to the ground. This action pulled all the wires with her and caused his desk to flip over, disconnecting everything and causing it to crash to the floor.

"GET BACK ON THAT CHAIR, AMANDA!" He grabbed her, but she quickly kicked his stomach with all the strength she could muster, making him fall to the ground. She stood up and quickly grabbed a knife that had fallen on the floor and stabbed him in his left thigh.

Pain caused Oswald to scream as he threw his right arm towards Amanda's face, attempting to punch her. Amanda swiftly dodged and fell to the floor, but quickly got up again.

"You will get nothing you want from me," she said, storming out of the room. She ran past the lab and burst through the doors, running onto the open field.

She looked back again and was reminded of the night, a few years before, when she'd taken the Orbit from her father. There was no alarm, no rising sun, and no helicopters in sight this time. She saw only the lab roof shining in the moonlight during the dead of night. She ran away when she spotted Shirley's car parked next to her home - she quickly burst through the doors of her house, screaming for Shirley.

"Shirley! Where are you?"

Shirley immediately came running in her direction. Amanda took her by the arms and screamed:

"We have to leave now and I need you to drive us," she stared at Shirley deep in her eyes. She knew that time wasn't a luxury and she needed to get away as fast as possible, so she had to convince Shirley of the gravity of the situation. "I promise I will explain everything on the road,"

"Sure, Miss Amanda! Why are you trembling so much? Please, calm down!" Shirley picked up the car keys and headed for the door. When she opened it, she saw the door to the lab open as well, but with no one in sight. She didn't think Oswald could make a run for it in his condition - and that's exactly why she'd stabbed him where she did.

"Run, Shirley, run to the car please!" Amanda yelled as they made their way out of the house.

Shirley and Amanda got in the car and Shirley sped away, only holding her and Amanda's bags in her right arms.

"What happened, Miss Amanda?" asked Shirley as she drove away from their home.

"You know the procedures he runs? He tried them on me,"

"The experiments, you mean? Because I am sure those aren't safe! I can't believe it! He wouldn't!" Shirley looked at Amanda, flabbergasted. She stepped harder on the accelerator and sped away, now entering a road next to their house. "Why isn't he after us?"

"I stabbed him in his thigh," Amanda answered.

"You didn't!" Shirley looked at her, startled, but her open mouth was slightly smiling.

"Why are you smiling, Shirley?" said Amanda, involuntarily grinning as she felt the wind blow through her hair.

"Oh, well, good riddance! About time someone stood up to him, I say! It's getting completely out of hand!" she said, staring at the road. Amanda felt closer to Shirley than ever before; she knew the maid had always cared for her in a motherly way, and it was right of her to test that sense of protection by asking Shirley to run away with her instead of disappearing on her own - she knew Shirley would be there for her. The two drove off into the night.

Chapter Two - Jaded

Lina Rafn woke up to the sound of her alarm clock and immediately punched it with her right hand. Reluctantly, she groaned as it failed to halt its grating, impenetrable sounds - she had to remember to change that sound. Waking up to those piercing sirens was the last thing she needed in the wake of her 29th birthday.

Every day after her unchallenging job typing encryptions and computer logs, she returned to her empty apartment and repeated to herself that she was the unlucky one with a cursed life. From the outside, Lina didn't seem to have many issues: she still earned good money every month from her job, no matter how repetitive it was - so she couldn't say she was struggling in her finances as much as some of her friends seemed to be.

Her job demanded minimal effort, and her love life was fading away due to the dumbness of every guy she met, leading her to believe that her standards for life were too high. This realization had a non-negotiable outcome. The more she thought about whether her life seemed doomed to boredom and repetition, the more repulsed and obsessed she became.

"Stryker, I'm telling you, I'm losing my mind over this," she told her friend on the phone that morning, not yet knowing of Stryker and Ripley's situation in the hospital. Lina spoke while combing her blonde hair in the mirror, noticing her blue eyes looked brown in the darkness of her poorly lit bedroom.

"But you're the smartest, most ambitious person I've ever met. You're so quick with the jokes, Lina. Maybe you should go to LA - maybe you should try comedy! Acting, who knows? Maybe this just isn't the city for you," he replied with a worried tone.

"I'm on the verge of my 30s and I really can't tell you why this affects me so much, but you can't help but feel a bit *cheated*, you know? God, I sound crazy."

"No, you don't. I know what you mean. We all thought it was going to go somewhere. It's the adult life, it's the boredom. Demeaning jobs, no love life. It's like you're always about to get that big break, but it never comes."

"Yes. Nothing ever happens. I can't take this anymore."

"But Lina, honestly…," asked Stryker. "What did you expect?"

"I…," she mumbled a few words, thinking out loud. "It's as if we at least expect our life's path to be clearer, you know? I feel like I live in the twilight zone and the world has forgotten about me. It's been five years since the last time I truly hoped and aspired to become something, you know? It's been five years since I last had that naïve feeling about the future. Now I just feel stuck in a rut. I'm sorry. I shouldn't be babbling about my life on the phone with you."

"Hey! No worries. I'm here for you and you know Ripley is, too."

"Where are you two?"

"Well, you wouldn't believe the night we had. Did I tell you about my psychiatrist?"

"Sure! Wasn't she in a coma for months?"

"Yes, and she just woke up."

"Are you serious? Oh, I'm glad! But what about her meningitis?"

"You know what, Lina? We should arrange for you to meet Amanda," said Stryker, suddenly with an eager tone of anticipation in his voice. "You wouldn't believe the things she's saying. It's bound to at least give you something to think about."

"What are you talking about, Stryker?" asked Lina, curious.

"Well, are you ready for this? Okay. So, she came back this morning and as soon as she opened her eyes, she seemed so calm. We were right there by her side, and it happened in a fraction of a second. But the thing is, she's telling us she remembers a lot of when she was out. She's got intricate images - it's so fascinating, Lina, about dying and coming *back*! I'm telling you, it's insane. The way she tells it, even I believe her now. And you know how I am with stuff like this."

"Wait, what do you mean? Dying and coming back?"

"I mean she has the most believable descriptions and details about what her... *soul* went through when they didn't know if she would make it or not. It's insane, but the way she tells it, Lina... she's finishing all the procedures to check out and she says she wants to write it down as soon as possible."

"And you don't think she's crazy? You let this woman prescribe you drugs and treat you?"

"You need to meet her and you'll understand. Look, this woman's studied years and years; she's majored in everything you can name on neuroscience, yet the look in her eyes now, Lina. She seems more alive than ever. Ripley and I heard her last night, and we just got here again this morning and she seems even more vital and energetic. It's a miracle, really. Tell you what, let's arrange for all four of us to go to a bar on Friday. Sounds good?"

Lina obliged and, after hanging up the phone, she headed towards the bakery at the end of her street to pick up groceries. She lived in a two-bedroom apartment in Forest Park, Illinois, where the winter weather was gradually becoming milder, paving the way for the spring leaves to flourish. A fading sun shone between two buildings and warmed up the snow-covered street as Lina snuggled into her snow coat and walked down her street. Everyone in the bars and restaurants she passed seemed to be talking about the Europa expedition announcement. She could hear a few comments in between her quick steps towards the bakery, and, intrigued, took her phone and searched for an article to fill herself in. A middle-aged woman was counting bills on the bakery counter as Lina entered the shop, still reading the article. Immediately, the woman looked up and spoke to Lina:

"Did you hear, child?" She pointed at the mirrored televisions on the walls. "They're going to Europa!"

"Yeah, I just saw it. At last I have something to be excited about!"

The woman seemed to turn whiter as she opened her eyes wide and started talking back to Lina as if she'd taken offense at Lina's support. Lina struggled to keep from laughing as the woman went off:

"Excited? They shouldn't be messing around with that, I tell you! What if there are... beings there? What if they come here? We need to learn to mind our own business, that's what!"

"There...there can't be the sort of aliens you're talking about there. If there's life there, it's marine life, or microbiological. No people. It's a planet covered in ice, with water inside. Didn't you *read* about it?" Lina asked in disbelief. She couldn't believe what this woman was saying and couldn't help but notice that she stood for everything that Lina was against.

"Still, they better pray they find nothing there!"

"Why not?" Lina asked. "I sure hope they do!"

The woman looked at Lina and then started counting bills again. She then spoke in a strong southern accent, one she didn't seem to have until now: "Well, I guess we'll just learn to disagree won't we?"

Lina rolled her eyes and made her way to the groceries. As she crossed things off her list, her phone rang again. It was Stryker.

"Yo!" he greeted her. "Punch Bowl on Friday - be there at 8, okay?"

***

"Cheers!" said the four of them as they toasted. They sat at the second of six small booths in a small coffee-shop in downtown Chicago. The bar wasn't busy for a Friday night at

8, but Amanda picked it for its vintage wooden 70s cabin interior and dim lighting.

"The moment I saw you, Lina. What is it about you? You have this way of making people feel very comfortable around you," began Stryker.

"Thank you."

"Yes, Lina's very easy-going, that's true," Ripley added. "She's like a comedian. Her timing is spot-on every time."

"Aw, thank you for sending a small spark of love through my cold heart," said Lina, laughing. "No, Amanda, really, I'm like this because I have to be. Haven't you noticed how it's easier at least, if you can be funny, to use it as a way to get everything?"

"Oh, absolutely," Amanda said. "But I don't have that, unfortunately. It comes as a reflex, right? My father taught me a lot about this."

"Yes! I can't tell you the joke before-hand, it's really like a reflex. It's funny you've noticed that."

The four of them sipped their drinks and went on with the conversation.

"But, really, since we're all friends here, I can say the legend about most comedians being depressed a lot of the time during their lives is absolutely true. The sarcasm and pessimism of the person's inner-self gets reflected in their razor-sharp sense of humor."

"But what do you do so you don't say what you think every time? Since it's so instant, what if you say something that offends people?" asked Ripley.

"Oh, but I do it all the time. And then I start backtracking, and trying to make up for it. It's always *miserable*, really," Lina sipped her drink, put it down and then said: "I wish I cared!" and smiled. They all laughed.

"Shit, yeah, I don't care either. We sound like the douche-bag table, you know," added Stryker, laughing.

"I am not mean, I feel just... jaded," said Lina. "I can't tell you how many times I've heard stupid stuff lately and finished those conversations thinking "Oh, God, seriously? What's this guy's game plan?"

"Also, going a bit off-topic here, but let me just say I'm dying to know about your odyssey into the beyond, Amanda." Lina touched Amanda's hand while saying this.

"I sense some sarcasm?" Amanda asked.

"No, not at all. I mean, you'd think that, given my snappy banter, but I'm truly intrigued by stuff like this. Please fasciante me."

"Well, this is really not the place. I've already written all I could remember about it," Amanda answered, sipping her drink. "I'll show you."

"I see now why they wanted me to meet you, Lina," she continued. "I couldn't agree more, though. We are reasonably smart people, though: we're all pretty successful, right? Stryker's one of the most infamous hackers of all time; Ripley is tough, and she's had a rough past, yet she pulled through in a way that, frankly, I never could," explained Amanda. "But I've noticed how many people I meet are so oblivious to their issues. A woman I saw while grocery shopping appeared to be experiencing a moment where all her personalities had come together to give her a talk-down: she moved her arms frantically and talked to herself as if she could see them. It was so insane!" Amanda laughed as she told her story. "I mean, how crazy can you be? How unaware?"

Everyone laughed at Amanda's anecdote. She then went on:

"So I approached her-"

"Of course you did," said Ripley. A server went by and took their order for food. After they'd all chosen their meals, they began talking again.

"What did she do?" asked Ripley and Lina. Stryker drank his beer and giggled.

"She started crying, explaining all of her problems to me, obviously. I knew she'd do that," said Amanda. "I think I approached her because, seriously, when I see shit like that, I'm genuinely curious, being a neurosurgeon and all. Because that's all in the brain, really. When you're at the point where you're talking to yourself in public as if you've multiplied... I mean, if I didn't intervene there... I just couldn't ignore it."

"Okay", Lina started. "I may be going off-topic here but I have to ask: what's the deal with you guys? I mean, how can she be your psychiatrist, yet still a close friend?" Lina asked, looking at Ripley and Stryker.

"Well, she has been incredibly helpful," said Ripley. "And she knows me - us, really - so well."

"But isn't that a barrier you shouldn't cross, Amanda?" asked Lina.

"Look, the thing is, no one knows. None of my other patients are aware and we don't flaunt it around. There's no harm to it and it doesn't affect their treatments. I started caring about Stryker and Ripley because, out of all my patients, they're the most similar to me. Or at least, versions of my past self."

The door of the bar burst open and a team of six policemen entered it, fully armed.

The police officers came forward. The one who spoke was tall and still extremely muscular, even though he seemed to be in his mid-60s.

"Amanda Collins. You're under arrest for treason and for conducting illegal experiments on a US-Military Base Unit."

Chapter Three - Set-Up

The other five men approached Amanda, and in a few seconds, pulled her from her seat. It all happened in such quick succession that neither one of them had time to react properly. Lina noticed they were dressed like city police officers but sported a different badge on their chest. This badge was silver, in the shape of an inverted triangle.

"*What the fuck*? Get your hands off of me!" screamed Amanda, reluctantly being pulled up. Lina, Ripley and Stryker stood up and screamed:

"Hey! This has to be a mistake! What the hell?" Ripley yelled. The entire bar looked stunned and most people didn't know what to make of it - the bartenders stood like gargoyles holding their trays.

"No! You can't do this!" screamed Stryker, coming forward and standing up to the lead police officer. Meanwhile, another officer spun Amanda round in order to handcuff her. In a split second, Amanda kicked the chief officer's elbow and disarmed him. With the gun airborne, she twisted her back to Stryker and the police officers. In a fraction of a second, with her right hand, she shot the officer trying to handcuff her in the foot.

As all remaining five officers quickly went to retrieve their guns, Amanda shot the first man while they all looked down at their weapons. With precision, she shot the second, third, and fourth officers while the others aimed their weapons. She was then shot in the shoulder by the fifth officer, but she shot him back in the thigh. She screamed in pain and gripped her wound tight - not a single person in the coffee shop moved or made a sound. Lina, Stryker and Ripley stood flabbergasted, as if waiting to hear a dropping pin. Amanda looked at the three of them and said:

"Through and through. Goodbye," she turned around and stormed out, ignoring the five dead bodies on the floor as the customers began to scream and reach for their phones.

"I'm coming with you," said Lina, getting up to follow Amanda. As Amanda ran to the door, she looked back quickly to smile at Lina as she got up.

Stryker and Ripley exchanged a glance, then bolted together as Lina and Amanda neared the door.

"Hey! Hey!" screamed the manager. But it was too late.

Amanda stormed outside and made for her car. While frantically grabbing her keys from her pockets, she warned the other three:

"They weren't regular officers. Didn't you see their badge? That's why I shot them. I can explain everything. Get in my car, everyone." She showed complete focus on getting out as soon as possible, without a single expression of remorse or shock. Lina couldn't help but feel enthralled by her control: she wanted to get away as fast as she could, but not out of panic or fear. She wasn't running away - instead, Lina noticed, Amanda seemed strangely more aware, or as if she had been waiting intently for such an incident.

"Why did you shoot them?" asked Lina, as all of them, with no option, climbed into Amanda's dark grey SUV. She immediately noticed the weight of the bullet-proof door as she pushed it open. She closed it with a thud, joining Amanda in the front while Stryker and Ripley slammed the back doors and Amanda stepped hard on the gas. Lina noticed she slightly bit her lip when putting pressure on the pedal.

Lina glanced behind her and saw a group of people taking pictures of Amanda's car as it drove away, the flashes becoming smaller and fainter as Amanda accelerated into the night.

After a few seconds, Lina addressed the overwhelming silence that took over the entire car.

"So, treason?" Lina asked.

"Illegal experimenting?" Stryker added. "You're my fucking psychiatrist! Have you ever done anything to us?" asked Stryker.

"Oh, come on, Stryker! None of that was true. They're framing me for all the shit my father's done. He's doing this to me, actually. I told you I can explain everything. Also, will you stop pretending you're friends with your psychiatrist because I'm fully aware you're in this for the drugs!"

"What? Well, *fuck* me then, right? If you wanna discuss boundaries, then start by explaining *the shooting*!" yelled Stryker.

"Those weren't real cops. They're from The Firm. They worked for my father...and that was my way of saying *sorry, but I won't be going to his jail any time soon*. I'm telling you, you have no idea how big all of this is. Congratulations to the three of you, because now I'm going to have to spill the dirt and it'll start tonight. I *knew* this would happen. I knew it!" said Amanda, punching the car panel lightly as her other hand gripped the steering wheel with such strength that Lina noticed her long, red fingernails starting to rip the covering leather.

"Wait, The Firm? I've heard about them. Aren't they supposedly a major underground... *cult* of sorts? But who is your father?" asked Ripley.

"He's a *monster*. The biggest scumbag to set his disgraceful being on Earth. And, of course, one of the most powerful magnates in the world," said Amanda, sighing. "It's not a cult, it's a firm. A major geopolitical alliance run by greedy, powerful men who have absolutely no concern for anyone's well-being but their own. But it is underground. It's supposed to be invisible, untouchable. And you'd never believe the major parties that are associated with it."

"So, we're breaking out another World War?" joked Stryker, nudging Ripley on her shoulder. "Us?" he asked, laughing.

"You must be joking because you're clueless and unaware of the stakes," Amanda said, gripping the wheel as she headed towards Downtown Chicago on Highway 311.

Lina raised her eyebrows and asked:

"Still, why were they there, Amanda? Why would fake cops close in on you in a bar? If they wanted to catch you, they certainly would have planned it better. I mean, not that anyone was truly expecting you to kill..."

"I'm too well-connected. I run a major company that specializes in neuroscience, Lina. I own an entire network of patients communicating and depending on me all day, every day. Their plan works if you consider if I came along and then disappeared. He's been onto me since the day he knew meningitis didn't take me. I will shoot his bigoted ass, mark my words."

"But why?" asked Lina.

"Because I'm the only one who knows what he's about to do. What he's been building, planning, financing and structuring over the last two decades to make it happen. As soon as we reach my house, I'll tell you everything,"

"Holy shit," said Ripley and Stryker together. "So I guess we can kiss our sessions goodbye, then?" asked Stryker.

Amanda looked at Stryker through the mirror and said: "Well, that's exactly where you're wrong." She got off Highway 311 and onto another freeway exit, turning left.

"What do you mean?" asked Ripley and Stryker, yet again together. Stryker yawned and went on: "Well, what do you know, our psychiatrist, who is our close friend, is also a Russian Matryoshka doll!"

"Stryker, I am *not* kidding" - Amanda cut him off - "I can sense that superior tone to your voice and you better come to terms with everything. That's the third lame-ass joke that bombed, and this is no laughing matter."

They all remained silent. After a few seconds, Lina broke the ice:

"How long till we get there?"

"A few minutes left," Amanda replied. "You know what?" she said, as if an idea had just come to her. "He's obviously setting me up. This way, I'll contact him and ask what's wrong and why I'm being framed for what he's done. Oh, God, it was so obvious. How couldn't I see it before?" she asked, looking at Lina quickly.

Lina replied: "How long have you been out of contact with him?"

"Too many years to count. Ever since I left his wing, he's always wanted me back, and he always took it personally. If those charges were real, I mean," she proceeded to make a U-turn ono another avenue.

After what seemed like ten minutes, they stopped at the garage of Amanda's building. Lina noticed as the car went in it didn't seem like a residential building, since the last floors weren't even visible in the night sky. Lina noticed the garage was practically empty, with only two other compact cars on their far left and one on their right. They got out of Amanda's SUV and made their way to the elevator.

"Who lives here, Amanda?" Lina asked as they walked.

"Just me. This is a corporate building. You'll understand it once you see where I live."

The elevator doors opened wide and the four of them stepped inside its marble floor. Amanda clicked on number 44 and the elevator doors closed shut.

"It's a long way up," Amanda said, smiling.

Chapter Four - The Lair

"Don't those cops know where you live, Amanda?" asked Lina.

"No. No one knows I live here. Even Stryker and Ripley have never been here before. Again, you'll understand once we reach the top," Amanda looked at Lina and then continued: "I seem like a fugitive, but I *have* to hide, at least during my downtime."

"Why didn't you ever tell us this before?" Ripley asked.

"A little heads-up would've been nice," Stryker added.

"I never, *never* thought he'd send men after me. I never figured you'd be around, either. Put yourself in my position," Amanda answered calmly.

"Sorry," said Stryker. "So your dad's a Godfather, huh?"

"What is it with you that you either say something stupid or go to a lame joke when you're nervous, Stryker? Don't worry. *Nothing's* going to happen to you," Amanda looked up at the floor markings, which changed from 27 to

28. Amanda then added: "I think." Lina looked at her and asked:

"Do you think we'll be able to go home tonight?"

Amanda pondered for a few seconds and replied: "The three of you are free to do what you want. However, I wouldn't recommend you going home ever again. Not until we solve this."

The three of them looked stunned and blasted questions at Amanda, confused.

"What do you mean?" Ripley said.

"What the hell, Amanda? He'd send guys after us now? How would they even know where to find us?"

"Oh, please. You don't get it, do you? The Firm can track us anywhere. Footage from the restaurant, traffic cameras on every road and freeway of us escaping - everything! It's highly unlikely that they will locate us here, since I've put in many months of hard hacking work and made some connections to render this place virtually invisible. We're safe here, but if you're out on the street, they will find you if they want to. And they'll use you to get to me. Again, *if* that's what he wants. I'm not sure yet."

"What the fuck, Amanda?" Stryker screamed. "You can't be serious!"

"I told you to put yourself in my position, Stryker. I didn't know this would happen," Amanda replied. Lina looked at the floor count and saw they were now on floor 40.

She remained silent and thoughtfully considered every option in her mind.

"And what do we have to figure out? How to clear your name? You want me to hack into federal documents! That's what you want, don't you?" yelled Stryker. "I'm so screwed."

"Partly, yes. But it's more than that. Believe me, you still haven't heard a tenth of it, Stryker. Save it," ordered Amanda.

The elevator came to a halt, and the doors slid open, revealing a small corridor, which led to a tiny, circled room. The four walked towards the room in the center, which was empty except for a half-filled bookshelf and a magenta painting of a little girl dancing ballet at the end. Lina looked at Amanda as she opened her jacket and retrieved a small silver ball with two buttons.

She pressed the first button and placed it on the side of the frame of the painting - Lina hadn't noticed there was a side-spot which fitted perfectly round the small silver ball, and soon the entire wall moved to the side to reveal a secret entrance which led to a gigantic, abandoned ballroom.

"I told you it's hiding - in a way," Amanda commented as the door opened.

"In a way? This is superhero-level hiding, Amanda," Lina commented, giggling. Amanda let out a small laugh and the four of them went in.

To their left and right, the room had gigantic windows that went all the way to the ceiling. The windows were tinged with a dark bronze hue, a result of the accumulation of dust and lighting emanating from the stone walls. As Lina approached the windows, the sound of her every step reverberated through the room, producing a loud yet muted thud. Gazing out of the windows, Lina beheld a panoramic view of the entire city. The sheer vastness of the space evoked a feeling reminiscent of being inside a cathedral. The elegant ambiance and timeless quality of the setting captivated Lina. She felt the space gave you a cozy sense of being on top of the world, safely isolated. Two dark-red couches in the shape of a boomerang were positioned with a glass table at the center, next to empty walls on the left. On their right, a dozen mirrors were displayed, of varying shapes, sizes, and frames.

At the end of the room, a tiny bookshelf seemed to hold only electronic devices and a massive, advanced computer system lay on top of a metal desk.

"Welcome to The Lair," Amanda said, crossing her legs as she curved herself forwards for a light, refined bow.

"You're aware this is like a playground to me, right?" said Stryker, approaching Amanda's tech station, even more amused than Lina. Ripley looked at Lina and added:

"First, he was complaining. Now, you know he won't leave. That is some impressive hardware, though," Lina laughed.

"Well," Amanda said. She clapped her hands twice and from the far left corner next to the dark-red sofas, a tiny lady in her mid-60's appeared from the corridor. "This is Shirley," said Amanda. Shirley smiled at all of them and Lina was overjoyed by how bubbly and kind this lady seemed to be.

"Hello!" Shirley said, in a sweet, fragile voice. She wore a dark blue maid's outfit, held her hands together and tilted her head forward to each of them, as if greeting them in an oriental fashion. "What is it you require, Miss Amanda?"

"Bring us some tea, please, sweetheart. And something to snack on. These three will be with us for a long time."

"Oh! It's been some time since we've had guests. I will be delighted. Let me cook up something for you," Shirley announced as she turned around and disappeared into the corridor again. The corridor was now lit: Lina figured Shirley had entered the kitchen and turned the lights on.

"Yes, that's where the kitchen is," Amanda said. "It seemed like you were wondering about that." Amanda's sharp perception surprised Lina.

"Oh, yeah - I was. Shirley is adorable."

"She's been with me for two decades. Can you believe that?"

"And she lives here? With you?"

"Oh, no. Shirley can come and go anytime she wants to."

"But wouldn't your father...?" Lina asked, but Amanda cut her off again.

"She won't anymore, though."

Lina frowned and looked at Amanda, puzzled. This was the second time she'd completed her sentences:

"I can't read minds, if that's what you're thinking," she answered playfully.

"But please, *spill*. I can't wait anymore," Ripley added. "Explain everything that's going on. It wasn't at all smart of them to approach you in the bar like that. Why would your father order that?"

"No, to me, the real question is not the way they approached it, but why he's *framing* you for what he did!" Stryker said.

"Because of what he does," Amanda replied.

"He's still conducting experiments on people?" Stryker asked. "But exactly what does he do to them?"

Amanda sat down on her chair and the other three sat alongside each other on the sofa closest to Amanda. She opened a window tab on the arm of her chair arm to reveal a set of buttons. She clicked a button and the blue wall behind the sofas lit up: a hologram appeared on a computer screen attached to the arm of the chair.

"As I explain this to you, watch the show. It's better if you learn it this way. *This is important work we're doing.*"

Shirley came back from the kitchen with a tray of teacups and snacks and laid them on the glass center table.

"Is there anything else I can do for you?" she asked.

"Shirley, you won't be able to leave for some time, I'm afraid," said Amanda as she picked up her teacup and gave her first sip.

"Why not? Is everything okay? Is it him?" Shirley asked. Amanda sipped her tea again and then laid it back on the glass table. She crossed her legs, put her hands together and inclined forwards, replying with a casual tone: "It is, Shirley. It's him."

"Miss Amanda!" Shirley said, loudly. "Did he find us?" she asked, terrified.

"No, he didn't. He won't find either of us here, Shirley, which is why I need you to stick around for a few weeks until I say it's okay to go out, right? Make sure you order everything correctly, using your alias, please, and we'll be fine." She smiled at Shirley reassuringly and Shirley turned back, giving a nervous goodbye-smile that lingered on each person. Until she finally made her way back to the kitchen.

"When my father was young, he was a brilliant young boy," Amanda started. "He grew up in Stockholm for twenty years before he fled to London and met my mother - but once he was in London, he was already a millionaire. Not nearly as wealthy as he is today, but he had already taken his first steps."

"And he's...Oswald, right?" Stryker asked.

"Yes. His name is Oswald Rose, and at the prodigious age of 13, he figured out how to create a lamp that didn't require any batteries. All you needed to do was touch it, and your body's heat would light it up. It may seem small, but it was huge. He used the warmth to create energy. All he'd ever do was sit around in his bedroom with chemistry sets, an infinity of books and he'd... learn."

"That's impressive," Ripley added.

"At first he seemed to be on the right path, they said. His lamp turned into lightbulbs, which sold like candy in Europe, and he garnered some media attention and headlines for his achievement. My mother is the one who told me all this. She says that Oswald always had this attitude about him, that he was meant to create those things. He never seemed excited, pleased, or content, but he'd always be thinking about the next one. He always wanted to build something bigger."

"And then what happened?" Lina and Stryker asked, curious.

"Then, my mom says she met a wealthy man in his early 20s with a passion for building gadgets, equipment and anything and everything that revolved around energy - my mom always said he'd talk about how there is energy in everything... how we could harness it, pull from it, use it, anything. My mother found him fascinating. He was a genius, really. He still is. I have to give him that. I also know you're waiting to see where it goes wrong," Amanda announced, sipping her tea again.

She looked at the three of them, and then at the screen projected on the walls. Flashes of corporate logos popped on the screen, and images of what seemed like group pictures popped as Amanda explained each.

"In London, this is the first major corporation he worked with. He formed a close alliance with the owners after he sold what was a gigantic amount of the advanced light bulbs to their buyer, lending him his first big break. From that, he went to other companies" - the pictures flashed, always showing corporate symbols and logos that were widely recognizable worldwide. After close to forty pictures had flashed, Lina recognized who was the same man on each of them. He didn't look very much like Amanda, with aggressive facial traits and an ambiguous half-smile in every photo.

"My mom says he never had time for her," more pictures continued to flash "and during all that time, he was still working on perfecting his masterpiece. He was connecting with people, garnering the cream of the crop and working together with even bigger alliances each time, be it with politicians or regular city employees."

Lina noticed the pictures changed to show a war-zone and weaponry. "He aided the military government against the war on Iraq by manufacturing most firearms, as you can see. He then began selling to Russia when they invaded Ukraine," Amanda continued zapping the pictures. Lina pieced together what Amanda's point would be.

"He was once a major industrialist who had close ties with powerful men and owned factories. He announced a global launch of his newest creation. And during that time, my mother became pregnant with me." Amanda's gripping story of her father's rise to the top fascinated Stryker, Ripley, and Lina. They listened carefully as she went on:

"Over a quarter of a century after he invented his quirky lightbulb, he perfected a new structure, a new gadget, which was now an even bigger achievement in the scientific field. This little gadget, known as The Orbit, could now harness energy through radiation. It was small and simple, yet if properly charged, it powered enough energy to light up an entire neighborhood. All you had to do was point it at the sun. Which still seems fairly mediocre to us, I know. But keep in mind that was the 2010s, and we're now in 2041. His empire was only a blip on the radar then, and as each invention and gadget had the rights bought by mass manufacturers and the public went insane over them, his profits multiplied. Today, every kid in the world already has heat-ignition lanterns, portable metal propulsion also charged through our energy that lifts you from the floor for close to a minute, water-gliding roller skates, video-chatting through complete body-scan holograms: you name it - every revolutionary gadget that surfaced during the last three decades came initially from my father's mind."

"But, wait, you lost me. What was it, exactly? Not the toys, but the Orbit? A gadget the size of a soccer ball?" Stryker asked.

"Yes," Amanda answered.

"But what's wrong with that? I don't see where this is going," Stryker sighed.

"I do," Lina added. "I assume he didn't stop there, right?"

"No, he didn't. Are you ready for the catch? Thirty-one years later, Orbit 2.0 has been perfected. Or, as he likes to call it during his pitches - Orbit: *The Next Generation*. It's seven hundred times bigger, more potent, and his ultimate masterpiece. His carefully chosen, ever-growing network of powerful men allowed him to oversee all this before they even announced it. For thirty years, my father and The Firm have been responsible for the main funding of NASA's recent deep space exploration ventures. Because, do you know what he wants to do?" Amanda asked. She smiled and then said, ironically:

"He wants to take his baby into orbit and, while the ship lands to explore and dig Europa's icy oceans, Orbit will harness the astoundingly high levels of radiation in Jupiter to into energy. And that energy will be brought back to Earth.

An astounding amount of energy, the biggest concentration of particles ever gathered, and he's the one who gets to pull the trigger or not. Because, with that he can start World War III in a fraction of a second."

The four of them remained in impenetrable silence. Ripley and Stryker looked at each other astounded and Lina asked: "But do you think that's what he'll do? What would he gain from war?"

"Control," Amanda answered. "But I must warn you, this may not be completely correct - I also don't see the game-plan of going through all this only to get the energy," Amanda said. "The only thing I fear is what he'll do with it. I fear the answer," Amanda looked down and then raised her eyes and focused on Lina: "Because I also suspect it's not just war,"

"You said there's always a bigger reason, right?" Lina asked.

"Yes, but what could be bigger than this, Lina? What's his limit? What does he truly want? I never knew that."

"Where's your mother now, Amanda?" Lina asked.

"Amanda's mother died a few years ago, Lina," Stryker said.

"Oh, I didn't know that. I'm so sorry," Lina apologized. "You should have told me!" She slapped Stryker's knee. "Amanda, I didn't know."

"Lina, please. It's fine. I always knew this, but I never figured he'd go all the way. I never thought he'd perfect it. But when I woke up and Stryker told me of the NASA announcement, I immediately immersed myself in the most information I could find on it. I knew he had his dirty prints all over this operation, and it turns out I was more than right. He's not only funding it, like I asked you, Stryker, but he's managing and overseeing the entire expedition. His name was one of the few big, recognizable ones you could find on it, though. All his other contacts and partners, people just as powerful as he is but on major political parties or positions of power in the world, they're faceless because they can't stain their names if it turns to crap. But he's always been fearless."

"But is it known that the funds come from The Firm?" Stryker asked.

"Of course not. Oswald poses as a corporate magnate and only speaks on behalf of NASA on this. The Firm's name's never been mentioned. No one really knows it even has a headquarters."

"Say what?" Lina asked.

Amanda then looked back at her and went on: "Yes, it has a headquarters, hidden just outside the city borders of Reykjavík, Iceland. If you think this is isolation, you're in for quite a surprise once you try to find The Firm. It is designed to be invisible,"

"I'm sorry, I don't want to interrupt or annoy you, Amanda" Stryker interrupted, "but aren't you worried about the repercussions of the bar incident? You shot five men. They're probably dead."

"Oh, please, they're not dead. Most shots went through and out. I couldn't even aim right. I went for thighs and feet. All I needed was a way to escape, and that was the only one. Ask me another."

Stryker remained silent. Ripley then pertinently asked:

"They charged you with conducting illegal experiments on a U.S. Military Base. So that's what your father did, right? Did he experiment with those people we saw with him in the pictures? On his partners, personnel and soldiers?"

"He tested on selected subjects. People who didn't have much of a life to go back to, who seemed to him to be... disposable,"

"But what did he do to them?" asked Ripley.

"The more he got to know the soldiers, the more he saw in his mind that these people shouldn't falter between rational and emotional thinking. He was sure a soldier could only achieve his full potential in the horrors of war if his emotions weren't accessible - if they weren't driving them anymore. He spent decades searching for a way to split the judgement centers in the brain so a soldier could engage in the horrors of war and return home in the flip of a switch. The emotional scars would be locked safely away. You could say he wanted to stop post-traumatic stress disorder. I'd say he wanted to prevent it, permanently, so as to gain control over them. For the right amount of money, those people would then work as his first loyal followers and workers, as he secretly founded The Firm and started to build his fortress."

The room was illuminated by a sudden bolt of electricity, signaling an approaching thunderstorm. The sound of distant thunder grew louder and more intense, particularly on the top floor of the building. Soon, Lina saw Shirley walk across the room, turning up the heater near the kitchen. Lina failed to understand why she felt so at home at Amanda's lair, but dismissed her thoughts, deciding to focus on the ongoing debate.

"If you think about it," Ripley stated, "it's like he's always been preparing and arming for *war*. Maybe he'll sell the energy or use it as a power source to expand his manufacturing endeavors. Orbit 1, *The Original Series* could light up an entire neighborhood, right?"

"Yes, but you're talking about an enormous amount of energy. The radiation levels around Jupiter are colossal. He could go nuclear - and let us not call it that," Amanda pointed out.

"Nuclear? Do you really think he'd go for that? What would be his goal?" Stryker asked.

"But that's the thing, isn't it? He could use it as leverage. With that kind of power, he'd have the world at his feet. No one would want him to pull the trigger," added Lina.

"After what I saw, it makes me despise him more. To think someone's drive is only directed towards something that will bring so much destruction and chaos,"

"On that topic… " Lina remembered, "I'm dying to read what you wrote about your near-death experience, Amanda - I have to know what you saw!"

"You've been on a roller-coaster ride for the past week," Ripley added. "How are you handling it?"

"It's on the computer, Lina," Amanda pointed at her high-tech station. "You'll find the file once you look at the screen. Or you can ask the AI to give you a full lowdown on what I have so far. And Ripley, I've been spending most of my time trying to make sense of what I saw. I'm afraid I'll spend my whole life wondering and I might never fully comprehend it. I'm sorry about the trouble this news may cause you. As I've said before, I wasn't aware that such an… *altercation* would happen tonight."

Lina made her way to the computer as Amanda spoke. She sat down and started carefully reading each word Amanda had written.

"Amanda, those people you mentioned he experimented on. Did his experiments succeed?" asked Ripley.

"Some. Those who didn't were... cancelled," Amanda answered. "Those who did... still work for him today,"

"At this... Firm, you mean? With him?"

"Yes. I can't tell you exactly how many people there are. It doesn't matter, really. He can build up his army any day. All he needs is to get you in his chair," Amanda answered, with a sinister tone to her voice. Lina listened to every word as she read Amanda's writings. For the first time in a long-time, it felt good to multitask on such a riveting occasion.

"What do you think were the main reasons behind the funding for this Europa mission? Because this is the first attempt to send humans into deep space, ever. SpaceX was supposed to do Mars next year! The module needs to be built to withstand Jupiter's colossal radiation levels," Stryker asked.

"Well, it started around 2011, when better satellite images showed that beneath the icy surface, there were red spots that showed heat. If you've got an ocean with these heat levels beneath the ice, it means the temperature ranges from extreme heat - which probably emanates from deep underground volcanoes, just like on Earth - to extreme cold. It's entirely water, so what else do you really need? Close to the end of the first decade in the 21st century, we found out Earth's deep sea was an ecosystem more alive and home to many more species than we ever thought. If you transfer the same conditions to Europa, even the most skeptical of subjects is forced to admit that marine life on Europa is not only possible, it's probable," said Amanda. "To me, it's a no-brainer."

Chapter Five - Wanted

"Could you feel anything while you were experiencing this, Amanda? Or would you say it was the sort of experience where you'd just watch more than anything? I mean, did it feel you could alter it? Did it feel like reality? Or an ongoing, never-ending dream? Do you get the point I'm trying to make?" Lina asked.

"It felt more real and intense than anything I've ever experienced. But each moment didn't feed into the next. It felt more like an unfolding. Each sight would amaze me with so much information that, in pure awe, I'd follow it into the next moment. It didn't feel like a dream. It felt as if I was in... a ride. A rush. A high of sorts."

Lina continued reading Amanda's intricate depictions. "This is incredible," she said before finishing reading.

"And yet you couldn't have imagined it," Stryker noted. "We've told you this before, right, Lina? Her brain was completely shut-down. The cortex responsible for imagery, identity, the notion of reality, wasn't there. Amanda wasn't there."

"Not to go out on a limb here," Lina said. "But supposedly this is evidence of an *afterlife*. Have you considered how you feel about this? Because you seem entirely vindicated and confident in what happened, so a part of you can't help but have to deal with this realization: what changed in you?"

Amanda took a deep breath, as if recharging one last time. She inhaled slightly, and then let out a small sigh. Her eyes opened, and she began:

"It's been...haunting me. Whenever these thoughts race back, a small part of me can't help but loathe humanity. I feel as if a part of me has awoken, yet I still can't tell you how to use it. All I know is I don't believe in coincidence, and never have," said Amanda, with a soft tone in her voice. "I mean, isn't it astonishing how most people still don't believe? How they can truly overlook all the statistics, throw the big picture away all-together but still believe that maybe it'll work out in the end. Most people are so afraid to act. I despise conformity. Yet it plagues us."

"What do you mean by that?" Lina said. "You know we all agree with you."

Amanda looked down for an instant, closed her eyes again and pouted her lips slightly. Her eyes then opened up, now looking up, and she continued:

"I know now there are so many more worlds. There are so many more oceans and so many more forests. An infinity of types, races. I cannot see how we've come so far as a society with such narrow-minded, mind-bending stupidity. It is truly the equivalent of really thinking as an animal. I see how most people are so frustrated, depressed and come to such drastic decisions all the time - why everyone is so fueled by violent emotions. It's because they are all so, so incomprehensibly oblivious," Amanda said with disgust.

Seeing Amanda express her concerns made Lina feel like she had found a kindred spirit to face whatever came next. Despite carrying the weight of the world on her shoulders, Amanda impressed Lina by maintaining a perfect, unshakable public demeanor.

"But I say that with the greatest of care," Amanda continued, now looking at them and smiling. "Because the potential is there. It's always been there. I never imagined how selfishness could mislead anyone into never-ending cycles of self-destruction and complacency. I mean, by the time you're repeating the same mistake for the tenth time, I assumed anyone would start feeling like a lab rat. But no one ever assumes they're the ones who are wrong. The issue is never internal, and it's never done intentionally." She paused and smiled slightly. "Because they're so proud to live in the bubble."

All three of them understood exactly what Amanda meant.

"Maybe something dumbed us down. There seemed to be better synchronicity between rational and emotional thinking before technology,"

"So, Europa's a given for you, then," said Lina.

"Of course. I mean, how could you even...ugh," said Amanda. "Consider the odds. If you multiply the number of stars in our galaxy by the number of galaxies in the Universe, you get approximately a gazillion stars. That's a 1 followed by twenty-four zeros. And there could be even more! The chances that we are the only living organism in the universe... To me, thinking we're unique is pretentious. It's a matter of time. I'm sure anyone who doubts this is in for a rude awakening soon. Even though we've just started the fourth decade of the 21st century, there are still many people who are oblivious to these truths."

"They're probably the same ones that still believe in the supernatural," said Stryker, laughing ironically.

"I figured of all people you would believe in most of these things? In the paranormal, in the spirit world, I mean," commented Ripley.

"Oh, please," answered Stryker. "With all the technology available today, millions of digital cameras and video cameras, billions of photos and millions of hours of recorded footage, yet not one real image of a being or anything remotely paranormal has ever been confirmed. Nothing, zilch."

He looked down, shaking his head slightly in disbelief.

"But some people want to hold on to a belief in the paranormal as though it's any different from believing in goblins, angels or wizards… none exist, but people still believe in this tripe. We have simple people wandering around abandoned facilities at night with EMF and digital recorders, trying to convince themselves that a tapping sound is a lost soul back from the dead, or the scratchy inaudible sound recorded is a voice from beyond the grave," he laughed.

"If you believe in ghosts and spirits, you truly have a child's view of the world."

Ripley seemed thrown off by Stryker's skeptic speech and immediately stood up, talking back at him:

"How can you say that, Stryker? After what you witnessed Amanda go through?" she asked, looking at him incredulously.

"Oh, Stryker," sighed Amanda. She then looked at him, squeezing her eyes as if she could see through him. "You're attempting to approach a nonsensical subject with strict rationality. The world isn't so black and white. Your clinical view of everything is your downfall. As much as science has advanced, we're still in the dark about most of life's mysteries and not one human soul on this planet can tell you what actually happens after you die," she said.

Amanda then stood up and started prancing around the room, talking to all:

"Once you accept that you're an insignificant, inconsequential blip on the radar of time—one of billions of people who have come and gone in a few million years—and humble yourself with the idea that all you truly know about the universe is what other, greater men have told you from their own observations, then maybe you won't act so pompous as to declare you know all there is to know about a subject that has stayed in the forefront of society's concerns since time immemorial."

She paused for a moment and went on. "It isn't just country kooks and attention-seeking nutters that believe they've seen a ghost or had a paranormal experience. There are many learned men who would stand up to scrutiny as upright characters, like presidents, who have claimed to have seen spirits. Trying to lock down such a persistent, widespread phenomenon into this "*This is this and that is that*" rationality is just silly. We exist in a world where we don't know why we're even here, and things in your daily life operate on a scale of normality that you've grown accustomed to - never mind that several centuries ago, many things you do would be considered "magic" or "abnormal." The torchbearers who brought us electricity, telephones, and computers have pushed the darkness of ignorance back only so much, but you're making the mistake of thinking you can see the entire cave beyond your *small circle of light*," said Amanda.

Stryker remained dumbstruck, staring stunned as Amanda laid out her insights, verbally putting him in his place.

"Your knowledge—humanity's gadgets and all their little toys— like my father's, no matter how advanced they are - these objects you rely on to disprove this topic are all just small steps to illuminate the dark cave we have always lived in in terms of our existence. Don't assume that, just because we're in the 21st century and have cell phones and computers, we're "above" things now. Your pride is arrogant and many arrogant men have come and gone, not realizing how *smug* they are in the face of their insignificance to this world. You're making the mistake of thinking you—and me, and many other "learned men"--are above what we are."

"May I add my two cents?" Lina chimed in, raising her hand. Amanda, Stryker and Ripley looked at her. Ripley smiled slightly and Amanda answered instantly:

"By all means, Lina, please do."

"While I admire both your conviction and... *erudition*, I have to disagree with...both of you," she announced. She could sense the other three weren't expecting this. "While I have no problem with people believing in ghosts and spirits, there is zero scientifically verifiable evidence to suggest they exist. Although investigations have been taking place for hundreds of years, with ever more sophisticated technology, there has not been a single case which has even gone beyond the level of 'Unresolved'. That means, the null hypothesis (the reasonable stance) is to accept that ghosts likely don't exist."

She licked her lips, formed her next sentences in her mind and went on.

"This is supported by not just a detailed understanding of the natural world, which explains how natural phenomena can be misconstrued as paranormal activity, but a growing understanding of the wonderful tricks our minds play on us, in terms of things like pareidolia. These shift mundane occurrences into something quite different. Using the argument that 'So many non-kooks have had paranormal experiences, therefore there must be something to it' is a logical fallacy which can't be reasonably accepted. All we know is that we don't know," Lina finished explaining her thoughts and instantly looked at Amanda, who was looking at her like a proud mother.

"What?" asked Lina. "I'm sorry if I said anything offensive," said Lina. "It wasn't what I meant at all."

"That's not the case, Lina. That's not the case at all," replied Amanda, smiling. "I'm just glad to have you with us, since that wasn't even the best part. God, that was just the tip of the iceberg."

"What do you mean?" asked Ripley and Stryker at the same time.

"Today, we're a faceless mass of one." She said. "You may say we're constantly interconnected. You may say we're more united than ever. To me, as a society, we've never been more bound by invisible chains."

Amanda stopped, licked her lips, and breathed in. She then went on: "I don't mean everyone, certainly. Some people are astonishingly aware of how a great mass is oblivious to the truths of the universe, like all three of you. So, thank you for that and the wonderful company. You wouldn't comprehend how I relish arguing with smart people," complimented Amanda.

She smiled at all three and Stryker broke the silence: "You don't have to thank us."

Faint footsteps grew closer and closer and Shirley came out of the kitchen with a startled look on her face, yelling: "Miss Amanda! You must turn on the news stream!" Amanda clicked on a couple of arm-chair buttons and a streaming news channel projected onto the walls in front of them. Instantly, you could read the headline, and Lina felt a tug in her chest as she read:

"SHOOTING AT DOWNTOWN CHICAGO BAR - 4 WOUNDED, 1 POLICEMAN SHOT DEAD AS CRIMINALS REACT TO ARREST"

"...still unsure at which point the altercation began, as Amanda Collins, 31, renowned local psychiatrist, reacted to the arrest and refused to accept her charges - Amanda was charged on Tuesday with treason and allegations of conducting illegal experiments on a US-Military Base Unit. With her at the scene of the crime were recently identified as ex-marine Ripley McGee, 32, computer analyst Stryker Pendarvis, 30 and financial executive Lina Rafn, 29. All four, authorities warn, are very dangerous and could be armed. If anyone has any sight or encounters with any of these four people, we ask you to report immediately to your local authorities---"

The bar's camera footage displayed still frame images of all four faces, which were now exposed to global media attention and branded as rogue individuals on the loose. Ripley and Stryker stood up and started moving around the couch, pacing back and forth as they went online. Stryker switched between looking at his phone screen as he read the breaking news and back at Amanda. She filled another cup of tea, crossed her legs and sighed.

Lina, instead of reacting, settled for staring at her friend's reactions to the news. She didn't really mind (knowing herself to be innocent) being framed for the time being. Amanda's story was still more captivating than concerning to her, and she believed this remarkable woman had much more to offer her than if she ignored it altogether.

This insane night seemed re-assuring: maybe Lina's life wasn't doomed to conformity after all.

Lina was lost in thought when she suddenly snapped back to reality upon hearing the voices in the room getting louder.

"Our faces have been broadcast to the global media! They're framing us! I didn't want to be dragged into this, Amanda!" screamed Stryker, pointing fingers and with his face flushed. Lina could see the sweat on the tip of his nose - Ripley remained with her hands in her hair, staring at the news report which was now showing the bar manager screaming fanatically at the news reporter: "It happened within a second and they were gone! To us, it seemed like they were expecting the cops to do it, since they got out of it so easily!"

"Did you hear that?" Stryker yelled. "Now we're a fucking gang, Amanda!"

The tension in the room was palpable, and Lina could feel the hostility growing.

"We'll come up with a plan, Stryker. Most people won't give a shit about it, anyway," Amanda said, coldly.

"Amanda, this is *bad*," Ripley pointed out. "This is terrible. We *really* can't leave your lair now,"

"I am aware of the situation," Amanda replied.

"We need to clear our names," said Lina.

"This is exactly what he wants," spoke Amanda, as soon as Lina finished her sentence. "This way I can't help but surrender to him. If I don't contact him, these charges will never be dropped. The only way to clear our name is if I come to him,"

Chapter Six - The Plot Thickens

Lina, Stryker and Ripley looked at Amanda, waiting on edge for her to continue. "So what are you suggesting, exactly?" asked Stryker.

"I'm saying, I think I just had an idea how to solve this." She got up from her chair and stood in front of the projected screens on the wall. "I'm saying I'll have to come *to* him. And I'll tell him that after two decades of intense research and academic achievements, I've come to terms with the fact that the only way to become even bigger is if I *join* him. It makes sense, it's what *he* wants. He's always wanted me by his side, and that's the only flaw in his plan and I should twist it for our own benefit."

"So, what do you mean? You're coming to him and sentencing yourself to eternal emotional slavery by his side as you watch him do something you're completely against? All by yourself?" Stryker asked. He looked at Amanda, baffled.

"No. You're all coming with me. Hear me out," Amanda announced.

"What?" Ripley asked. "How could we?"

"My resignation from my life's work is conditional on my three closest co-workers being able to join me in The Firm's new chapter with him. I'll say it's been a long time planning and studying for this possibility until there came a day, which would be today, when we all agreed it would be the appropriate next experience for us. Together," Amanda explained. She smiled apathetically, looking at the three in front of her and added: "Think about it. The four of us combine everything we need to take all of his operations down. Inside The Firm, we'll be there when Orbit 2.0 and the crew come back from Europa. We'll be in the heart of the beast. He's my father. This is the *only* weapon I have against him and Hell, I can play this game too,"

Lina fully comprehended Amanda's idea. It worked on paper and it could work practically. Their relocation to the heart of The Firm *could lead to* achievements and prevent Oswald's plans after Europa's successful landing.

"It makes sense," said Lina. "You're the hacker, Stryker. Ripley's got the strength and the toughness and years of combat experience. Amanda's his daughter and his sole emotional connection. I plan on doing something useful with my life and stopping this man seems like a big priority at the moment! Soon this guy will have the biggest nuclear bomb ever known to man in his hands. We can't go on with our daily lives after tonight's shooting, since everyone's seen our faces. Our only chance is if, *truly*, we ask him to clear our names and, in repayment, we'll sign a decade-long lease or something with that longevity to work by his side," said Lina. She could feel her adrenaline levels rising.

"Won't he know something's up, though? You said he's a genius. Suddenly you're back and willing to join his side," asked Ripley.

"Except they have framed us for something only he can clear up. And he'll want something in return. But yes, that is why we can't strike now. We'll have to prepare and create cover stories which we will go through so many times we will end up actually believing them," Amanda answered vehemently. "It's the perfect plan."

"But the world doesn't know about Orbit 2.0? Won't the crew on the spaceship know about an energy harnessing operation going on while they explore Europa? Who's conducting it?"

"I'm not sure," answered Amanda. "No one knows about it, obviously. However, I'm not sure how he'll make it work. The operation might have classified assignments and three or four crew members could be Firm moles, planted by Oswald to work solely on the energy harnessing. He has the men to do it, and none would mind losing their lives either. Each one would eagerly volunteer for a one-way trip without thinking twice. He'll have his loyal assets by his side, always," Amanda answered. "This is one reason why we have to do this. We have to find out more about *how* he's hijacking Europa to get his way. We have to do it because it's the right thing to do," added Amanda.

"I agree. We can take it out if we work together. What's a few years focusing on bringing down something this major? I'm with you, Amanda," assured Lina. She smiled and felt an intense tingle of anxiety rising in her brain.

Ripley shrugged her shoulders and smiled, saying, "If the two of you are in, I'm in."

Stryker looked up at Ripley, surprised: "Seriously? You're in for this?" Stryker asked her.

"Why not, Stryker? It's the only way to clear our names! Plus, I don't know if you've noticed, but Oswald's a monster!" Stryker looked at Ripley incredulously for a few moments and then looked down, closing his eyes. He sighed and looked up, raising his eyebrows. Then, he sighed again and said:

"It seems we're in for a ride."

"If we're doing this," explained Amanda, "we need to prepare you. Forget Oswald for a second, because every worker for the Firm is also a highly skilled and well-trained professional who can see through you and smell anything fishy. For instance, you're too on edge, Stryker. In The Firm, such behavior becomes unacceptable when your limits are pushed. If you scream at anyone there, those are grounds for immediate cancellation. Remember most people there don't *feel* - all they do is react rationally because my father's screwed with their brain's judgement centers. You have to refine your movements, learn to control yourself in extremely stressful situations. Until the day I contact my father, I'll teach you all everything I know about this. When you're ready, we'll strike."

"Also, we'll need specific codes between us so we can communicate without raising suspicion. We can come up with gestures and keywords," Ripley added.

"Do you have any idea how hard this will be? Also, have you ever considered how slim our chances are of succeeding?" asked Stryker. "I don't want to be a drag, but we have to know this, Amanda,"

"Are you trying to lecture me on how high the stakes are?" asked Amanda, with a defiant tone in her voice. She raised her eyebrows and continued: "Because if I remember correctly, I was offering you reality checks just a few moments ago."

Stryker and Amanda stared at each other for a few seconds without speaking. Lina worried as she watched their escalating tension.

"Nothing worth doing is ever easy, Stryker," said Amanda, turning her back to them and walking towards the hallways. "You'd do well to learn that soon if you want to become someone in life". Her footsteps echoed as she walked away, and Lina looked at Stryker and Ripley when Amanda left sight.

"We can do it, Stryker," she reassured him. Stryker looked at her and then at Ripley. He then sat down next to Lina on the couch, took her hand and said:

"I'm sorry for dragging you into this, Lina. We didn't know, either. None of us had an idea how this night would turn out,"

Lina looked at him and let out a laugh. "Oh, please, Stryker. You don't have to apologize to me. I'd say I'm the one who's enjoying this the most, actually! I seem to be the only one of us genuinely pumped to take this guy down."

"But...aren't you worried, Lina? We could... die over the next few years! I don't know! Anything could happen and we can't blow our cover!"

"I look at it differently. I know that if we give our very best at each moment, then we will succeed - and in a few years I'll forever have an incredible achievement in life to hold on to, knowing I played a crucial part in bringing down these people and their conspiracies."

Stryker looked at Lina and smiled. "Thank you, Lina," he said.

Amanda's footsteps grew again as she came back, with Shirley walking by her side. Shirley carried a tray with two steaming pots.

"Shirley's going to set up dinner for us so we can rest later," announced Amanda. "There's a guest room with three single beds just at the end of this corridor. It is very welcoming."

"Thank God! We're starving!" said Stryker, sitting up and readjusting his position on the couch.

"Oh, Shirley!" said Lina. "Thank you so much!" She smiled at Shirley, who finished placing the pots on the table and smiled back at her.

"I'll go get the rest," said Shirley. She left and came back in a few seconds with another steaming pot and everyone's cutlery. They dined together and used their time wisely, choosing lighter topics and anecdotes for the dinner talk. The group brought Lina a sense of familiarity and happiness, allowing her to momentarily forget the stakes and cherish the small moments of bliss they created.

***

"Good morning, Lina," said Amanda, already fully dressed and eating breakfast at the main glass table. Lina had just gotten up and was still downloading her soul back to her body as she made her way to the kitchen for breakfast. Amanda had accumulated a wardrobe of clothes over the years, which she never got rid of. She gifted them to both women, including nighttime gowns, social and vintage clothes, and several winter coats from Icelandic winters. Since they were confined to Amanda's lair, Stryker had been dressing with what he could find that he didn't classify as too girly.

"Morning," said Lina, still with a raspy, sleepy voice.
"Sleep well?" asked Amanda.
"Yeah. Hard to associate everything and still wake up in one piece, though," said Lina.

Amanda giggled and added, while pouring sugar in her coffee: "I'm glad you came through so easily," said Amanda. "Here, sit down, have some breakfast." She pointed at the table, which as Lina approached, she noticed had been filled with food and warm drinks. Stryker and Ripley soon joined them, and breakfast seemed to go by smoothly. No-one mentioned The Firm or seemed shaken anymore by the framing.

"Hey, come check this out, everyone!" said Ripley, air-dropping a video from her phone to the bigger screen. It was footage of a news channel transmitting an Europa expedition segment.

"People from all around the world have shown their support online as the Europa mission is the most talked-about topic online globally for the past week - and some even took to the streets! We have exclusive footage of demonstration occurring in the Middle-East, Asia and, most recently, Russia, where the people marched to their respective chiefs of staff with signs that said, "We are not alone", and "Soon". What's ironic is how these protests seem to emerge mainly from third-world countries

or extremely religious countries and governments." The broadcast then started streaming videos from small demonstrations around the globe, reacting to the news.

"That's expected," added Amanda. "The world is reacting to the *possibility*. Some people are awaking. Reality is setting in."

"But what kind of backlash are we talking about, here?" asked Stryker. "I mean, suppose it's confirmed."

"Any kind of life is enough to prove we're not alone," said Amanda. "That completely changes the entire foundation of the way our society and humanity perceive themselves - our galaxy is way grander and vaster than we could ever imagine. That is bound to shake up even the most outdated of groups."

"But what will happen to those people? I'd pay to see the look on their faces," said Stryker.

"What if some don't understand?" asked Lina. "Or simply refuse to."

"What do you mean?" asked Ripley.

"Consider some people truly won't understand. They'll refuse to - and some will label it as a conspiracy. I can see bigots claiming all of this is Satan's doing. Can't you?" asked Lina.

"Well, certainly. It remains to be seen, my friend..," said Stryker.

"Maybe that's exactly what Oswald's hoping for," noted Amanda. "If you think about it, we aren't truly considering the aftermath of any announcement that will come from this expedition. What if the first blow of violence comes from an enraged mass of ignorant people?"

"It's something to consider, right?" asked Lina.

"Certainly," answered Amanda. Ripley remained focused on the news when she suddenly pointed at it, saying:

"Look! They're going to announce the expedition crew's names next week."

The broadcast continued showing images and details that they already knew about the mission. It became obvious to all how much the global media would squeeze out of this story: this would truly be the major topic until they made any discovery. The entire world seemed to be in an adrenaline rush - not just them, living in the shadows.

"When the three of you feel you're ready to start your day, let me know. I'll be finishing up some research I'm doing and we'll get ready for your sessions right away," announced Amanda. She got up from her seat and walked away.

Chapter Seven - Masks & Shields

"In order for me to mold you successfully and enable you to become an undisguised member of The Firm," began Amanda, "there are some things you must learn."

Lina, Stryker and Ripley sat on the couch as Amanda stood in front of the screened walls, which showed them the paused still frame of an animation of a brain. It felt like a neuroscience lesson.

"Miss Amanda," said Shirley, walking into the room. "May I watch this with them?"

"Of course, Shirley," Amanda answered kindly.

Lina smiled at Shirley and tapped the couch for her to sit by her side. Shirley happily obliged and joined Lina.

"There are crucial tricks I can teach you that will serve you well on many occasions inside The Firm - because these are the reaction triggers that distinguish you or anyone else on Earth from anyone my father has altered."

Amanda clicked on a remote in her hand to alter the images being screened. An animation of a pendulum appeared, with a black pointer on top standing on a white spot. The pointer could either fall to the left, becoming red, or to the right, becoming blue.

"This is our emotional range," explained Amanda. "It may seem double-sided to you, but it's much more intricate than it seems. Consider the last blue pointer to be the happiest a person can be, and the last red pointer depicts the worst, the angriest, most devastated."

"Stryker, will you put your finger here, please?" Amanda retrieved a wire with a tab for an index finger, which opened. Stryker placed his finger inside it and it lit up to a neon blue color, reflected in the stream on the wall, which now revealed his pulsating heartbeat. "This is Stryker's emotional range now."

"It's a matter of perceiving the entire scope of a situation," explained Amanda. "Say I first look at Stryker and tell him that his choice of clothing today is awful and he looks like Pennywise," Stryker's pointer dropped from white a third to the left, becoming orange.

"Now, after I've said that, if I ask you to give me a compliment right now, the best you can think of," asked Amanda. "Do you want to?"

"Obviously not," said Stryker, instantly.

"Yes, because I just offended you," added Amanda. "Now, if I told you that you shouldn't have believed me when I said you didn't look good, and you should have remembered that, in fact, I was the one who gave you those clothes as a gift two years ago, so I think you look incredibly presentable," smiled Amanda, giving him a daring smile. "What would you say?" Stryker's pointer bounced back from red to its exact opposite position, now one third blue.

"And now the crucial part: doesn't it seem easier to compliment me now that you are in the blue area?" asked Amanda.

"Very much so," said Stryker. "I can't believe I didn't remember you gave me these clothes. Still, I wouldn't know what to say to make you happy," said Stryker.

"That doesn't matter. What matters is how much easier it seemed to do good to me after I boosted you up. This is the point and the main trick for you to succeed in The Firm," added Amanda. "It is always fundamental to be aware of what is being asked of you and to react to it in the best way possible - at all times, no matter if your emotions tell you otherwise. They are impeccable and excel because they don't react emotionally to anything. You *must* master this to have an edge over anyone inside The Firm. This is the only way we can fight fire with fire."

"But wait, I get the gist but not the entire scope. How should I act on it?" asked Stryker.

"No matter what situation is thrown at you, how you react to it is the key to everything - every Firm employee reacts in extreme logic and reason because their emotions are completely blocked away. Yours are not, so think of it as a muscle you must exercise. Any time you sense something has been thrown at you, imagine this graph," pointed Amanda, "and understand within yourself how you'd react to something at your highest blue level. Because this is your best behavior, your best self. It'll seem demanding, but, like every muscle, it needs persistence and perseverance. Otherwise, they *will* see you're reacting negatively to an altercation and sense the violent emotion brewing inside you. Start seeing yourselves as the machine you were built to be, where each action involves processing and reasoning, not abrupt decisions and instant reactions," said Amanda.

"This is how you manage to do it, isn't it?" asked Lina. "This is why you're always on, with the best answer at the tip of your tongue and it seems effortless to you."

"I've perfected this for decades. At first you don't truly comprehend the benefits of it, but once you master this...," said Amanda. "You can do anything."

"How would it go in a conversation with a stranger, though? What would you suggest? I'll have an easier way to grasp this if we start from scratch."

"You *should* start off with a compliment," said Amanda. "That will ease your way into the conversation.

Always show yourself to be interested in anything that is solely about them. Let them go on without interrupting them, always taking an interest until their own alarm goes off and they tell you "enough about me, what about you?""

"But that's when the issue strikes. What should I tell them about me? That's when I choke," confessed Stryker.

"It depends on what you wish to get - if it's romantic, impress them. If it's someone you want something from, never outshine them. You can't ever let your story impede how fantastic that person seems to you. But you shouldn't see these as situations where you either choose a or b, Stryker. It all depends on the moment. That's why you must coach, tame your mind. That way, it'll always show you the way, especially with all of you."

***

"WRONG!" buzzed Amanda as the alarm went off again. "BODY LANGUAGE! You cannot adjust your clothes!" screamed Amanda at Stryker, who stood in the middle of the ballroom as all four looked at him. Amanda had suggested an exercise where each of the three would stand in front of all and sell the act as an icy, unshakable presence.

"You want us to talk like you, right? Polished and refined, with this assuredness behind every word," said Lina, while Stryker struggled, walking around the room in circles while thinking to himself how to play this.

"If it helps you capture it through that point of view," said Amanda, "by all means, be me."

"Stryker," said Lina "you have to talk like her! You know she's mastered this technique, so just sell the act as a male version of Amanda!" suggested Lina.

"Easy for you to say! I can mumble up a few sentences, but not forever! Eventually, something will give me away. This is the work of a character actor."

"And that is exactly what we need to perfect," said Amanda. "You must learn to control your mind, Stryker. It is your mind that sends you the trigger to readjust your clothes for the one-hundredth time when there is nothing to be adjusted. It is your mind that combs your hair and tries to distract us with those gimmicks."

"I can't. I can't really do it now. Can we switch?" asked Stryker. "I'll get it soon, I promise."

"Lina, do you want to go?" asked Amanda.

"Yeah," Lina got up from her seat and made her way to the middle of the room.

She reached the middle of the room and turned around to face her friends. Lina focused on her breath and state of mind until she felt a stable vibration run through her body. She opened her eyes, more aware of the room's smell and temperature.

"What do you think sets you apart from anyone else here?" asked Amanda.

"I am aware of my convictions," replied Lina, apathetically. "I know once I put my mind to something how far I can go - it's up to you to question its extension and if that sets me apart from anyone." Amanda tilted her head slightly to the right, interested.

"If I told you it shows that you're not ready yet,..." said Amanda.

"I'd say you're lying," replied Lina, instantly. "I know it doesn't."

"Why is it you think you're not showing any signs of weakness?"

"Because I don't have a reason to feel weak in front of you."

Amanda raised her eyebrows and let out a half-smile.

"Very good, Lina," said Amanda, breaking character. "It astonishes me how each of you truly has key characteristics that, given the right amount of training, can blossom to let us succeed with flying colors. It seems we might succeed, after all."

"What did you do?" asked Stryker. "How were you able to talk back to her questions so instantly? I can't pull that off."

"It's just a switch I can turn on, that's all," said Lina "and I cannot see why you couldn't. I truly brought out the worst in me, because that's when I get the sharpest - when I despise something, when I bring myself to feel those negative emotions. I thought that was something everyone could do."

"He might," answered Amanda. "but I still enjoyed seeing how easy it came to you."

***

Chapter Eight - Sessions

"I'm afraid of what you'll say," said Ripley as she entered the room and sat down in front of Amanda. "I mean, I'm used to opening myself up to you but not for you to tear me down. Stryker went straight to the bedroom."

"Did he?" asked Amanda, scrolling down a page in her pad without looking at Ripley.

"Yes, and I gave him a little smooch on the cheek to cheer him up and -"

"I'm sorry, 'smooch'? Let me just stop you right there. What is that? Why would you choose that word?"

"What do you mean?"

"Did you just use 'smooching' in a sentence? You need to drop that act, Ripley. This won't do anymore."

"But, Amanda ..."

"You've been through too many things in life to think you can sell this kind exterior. You must stop putting all this blame on yourself for having lost your parents."

Ripley looked at Amanda for some time, saying nothing. She opened her mouth but still didn't say a word.

Then Ripley closed her eyes and breathed in. She said, with closed eyes:

"I can't be funny like Lina or dry like you, Amanda," said Ripley, almost in a whisper.

"No one's saying you should. I'm saying this kind act is not genuine for you. Your eyes will give you away every time. You deserve to be better. You are better than this."

"What are you suggesting, then?" asked Ripley, now staring at Amanda.

"I'm saying you should let your tough skin show through - it would do wonders for your love life. Why is it you hold back so much?"

"I've always been repressed and neglected, Amanda. You're very aware of that."

"But you're also aware of the anger pent up inside you, yet where you fail is at connecting this anger with a purposeful goal. Why do you think that is?"

Ripley hesitated for a moment and then answered.

"I guess it's a mix-up of all the stages of fear we can subject a person to - when you grow up holding yourself back, you create this wall. A silent exterior that works as a filter between you and the world. It's easy to get lost in it... it's always easier to not say anything. But when my parents died, it simply took control of me... effortlessly."

"You see, that's where you're getting it wrong," interrupted Amanda. "By not expressing yourself, you're only building up the numbers of situations in which you stay silent. That will easily multiply over the years until the moment you realize how many of the choices and consequences in your life were not your choice - yet you could have acted then."

"Are you saying I should risk myself more?"

"I'm not only talking about risks. I'm talking about your entire outer personality, which is stupendously submissive to anything. You *must* find your voice, Ripley," said Amanda, fixing her eyes on her. "Soon it'll be too late to save yourself,"

"But how can I do that?" asked Ripley.

"All you have to do is wait. You know well every time your mind wishes to speak up. Except this time, you'll let your opinion come through, no matter what it is - I don't care if you babble from now until infiltration day. If it comes out stupid, no one will care or judge you - remember that. Search for your voice. Once we get to the Firm, I need you to be in the best shape possible, because there I want to use this filter of yours. It'll do wonders in The Firm. You're also just as perfect for the program..."

***

"What about you, Lina? What created this sharp exterior?" asked Amanda.

"I suppose I've always had my expectations for life set way too high. And then, as life started to unfold, all I could do was make jokes about it, because it was so far away from anything I'd expected, and not in a good way. Everything let me down."

"Do you mean successive events or your own interpretation drained the color of life?"

"At first there were events. I've always felt like an outcast, and that intensified after my parents got divorced - and then I had a terrible relationship happen to me, which outweighed the pain I was going through with my parents. Then it became a situation of one bad altercation being worse than the last, time after time, because after the break-up I couldn't go anywhere with my professional life. Then a few bad choices with friends and... yeah, it starts to get to you."

"Get to you in what way, Lina?" asked Amanda.

"Well, in how I noticed life would be a longer, harder road, it seemed. And as I accepted that, I understood how many things were wrong in the foundation of everything I knew myself to be - I identified just a few close friendships to be of completely mutual benefit and noticed how many people were only friends with me because I was the clown. That's when the isolation hit."

"And how did you come out of it?" asked Lina.

"Like who I am today. To quote your words, 'with this sharp exterior'," Lina smiled. "I've grown to accept it, almost like it,"

"That's good to hear," said Amanda. "What would you say is your biggest disappointment with the world today?"

"That most people still aren't aware of the stakes. I'm disappointed that not everyone is as smart as I am. I'm disappointed because, to this day, most people still obsess about useless things instead of doing something that will leave a legacy behind. I'm sometimes disappointed in myself for labeling these people as creatures, but I can't help it. Some don't seem to comprehend the value I give to being alive."

"And what value is that, Lina?" Amanda asked. "I'm curious to know."

"It may sound drastic to you. But when I made sense of my place in the universe and took the time to understand what it means to be alive, and how we have thrived as a society to this day... Every time I look at the night sky, I realize we still have a long way to go. I wonder why we still aren't eight billion connected souls; working together to figure out what to me is a smothering mystery: are we *alone* in this universe?"

"I know the answer to that," added Amanda. "Half of the world isn't as smart as you, Lina, and they never came to such questions of self-identity at such a young age. And the other half, well, most of them are afraid that maybe we will find out that the answer is that we are *not* alone. It takes people like you and me to push it forward. That, we have in common with Oswald," said Amanda. Lina locked eyes with her for a few seconds. "I believe there is a special reason why I met you," added Amanda.

"Thank you, Amanda," said Lina. "If you were to foreshadow the next decades of humanity... what would you say will happen?"

"Well, I may be wrong in many of my assumptions, but," began Amanda, "the last month has led me to suspect that maybe it's already brewing. I have to confide to you that on the day we came here, a part of me was...glad. Not that I would ever want any of us near any danger, but we share the same drive, don't we?" asked Amanda, looking at Lina. "We seem to share a similar purpose."

"You said it yourself," noticed Lina. "If you think about it, no one else in the world can right this wrong, except us. To me, it wasn't even a question of whether I was revolted at being framed - I was in from the moment you told us your story."

"Exactly," agreed Amanda. "And, in doing so, I believe we'll prove successful - but I think the mission will come back with many consequences to us. When we raise the suspicion of an awakening mass of people that were oblivious until then - I mean, if the entire structure in which we perceive ourselves as a society... you can't help but think there will be fallout. And the more and more I think about this, I know he's planned this, I know he's controlled the narrative on this situation before...," said Amanda.

"Not being able to figure out his goal, being stuck in this haze, is what frustrates me. It prevents me from trying to foresee anything, because I *need* to know what he'll do."

"We'll find out," said Lina, reassuringly. She sat up on her chair and looked at Amanda, giving her a cheerful smile. "You can count on me."

***

As a month went by, Lina found herself closer to Amanda, Stryker and Ripley. After each morning, they'd check the news on every platform they could, always on the hunt for more details of Europa's mission. They would search every news article for a trace of what The Firm's next goals and purposes were. Stryker hacked into Iceland's import and export systems, hunting the database for every item Oswald made an import into the facility. This included fake registries for entries of potential firearms or weapons of mass destruction. Ripley and Lina worked together, helping Stryker fake new passports for each of them, as Amanda supervised each operation, adding her knowledge to trace someone whose identity they would replace. Once they decided their aliases, Stryker and Amanda began working on cloning their fingerprints, as they 3D printed, after dozens of failures, fully functional prosthetics. Given their limited workspace, Amanda made the best out of her tech station and any outlet of communication from the Lair - they'd call via phones, online, radio and hack through broadband and Wi-Fi connections.

They created their own language, assuming The Firm's facilities to be fully recorded and secured by advanced AI. Whenever they'd need to branch into anything involving Orbit 2.0 and Oswald's yet unknown goal while inside The Firm, they'd refer to it as "Ripley's condition", to have an alibi for speaking more privately and anywhere needed. Whenever Amanda felt one of them wasn't contributing much to the work during a certain moment, Amanda used the time to invite them into her therapy sessions as she continued to mold each of the three, teaching them how to portray themselves inside The Firm, how to behave in unexpected situations, how to trick them into rational thinking without listening to pent-up emotions, and any intel she had on The Firm's operations and tests. On the morning of the fourth Friday after they'd arrived at the Lair, Amanda called everyone in the main room early to catch up with a recent newsflash:

"I have just received some very important information that will aid us tremendously," she announced. "Though the Europa Mission shuttle is scheduled to launch at

Cape Canaveral, Florida - it's programmed to land back in Hallormsstaður, Iceland. The Firm's HQ."

"So, this just adds more fuel to our fire, really. We *must* be there," said Lina.

"Tomorrow, they will announce the crew to the world. That's the last we'll hear from this until they launch," said Amanda.

"This also means Oswald's really expecting something to be brought *back*," suggested Amanda, "except we must understand how they'll design the ship to harness the radiation and bring it back here. What is the machine it will be attached to? A giant *battery*? What does it do? Because that *is* his weapon!" asked Amanda. "We need to search for every entry in their system about the design of the ship and the Orbit 2.0. To do that, we need to be inside of The Firm, as soon as we can."

"Also, I'd like to announce" said Stryker "that our new passports are *ready*, my ladies," he said, proudly. "Amanda, to go through customs and the flight there you'll be Esther van der Werf," he threw Amanda's passport towards her. She grabbed it in the air and laughed. "Lina, you're now *Alma Rohleder*, I'm *Bjarmi Fannar* and Ripley, I've saved the best for last." He threw Lina's passport in the air and then held onto Ripley's, announcing her new alias: "Nice to meet you, *Birta Björk*."

"We won't actually have to go by these names, right?" asked Ripley.

"Not really, it's just that it's certainly safer to be returning home to Iceland, with no business, than to be tourists. We don't want to draw any attention, remember," added Amanda.

"Shouldn't we go separately, though?" asked Lina.

"Yes. I'll come first, and you can come with me, Lina. Stryker and Ripley, wait until the Oswald situation is over with. When I've safely sold the plan to him, you'll catch the first plane there and a Firm team will meet you at the airport. But it is safer if you stay behind and we add *comms* to our ears, talk all the way through it without him knowing, just so we're safe. Because in case it goes wrong, we need to have a place to come back to," noted Amanda.

"That's true. I don't mind. What about Shirley, though?" asked Stryker.

"Shirley will stay here for the time being. With us gone, she's safe to go back to living her life for a few years. She has a son that lives in Montana and she asked me if he can move in here, with her, for the time being,"

"That's good to know. At least if it turns to crap out there we can come back here, in any case," said Ripley.

"Do you think he'll buy it, Amanda?" asked Lina. "I mean, now that it's closer and that you're about to see him again. Are you ready for it? I have to ask!"

Amanda hesitated for a moment. "It's a gigantic place. You'll understand it when you see it. What worries me is all of you. I hope you understand the severity of the situation. You are all about to meet very dangerous people and most are invisible to the world. They have no life to go back to and they will stick to my father's orders. But I know that we're doing it because we have to. We don't have the option of ignoring this and going back to our lives. So yes, I'm ready. I have to be. I'm ready, but wary."

Amanda walked out of the room and headed towards the corridors. As she left, she announced she'd be back shortly.

"Give me ten minutes. I have something to do," she said, stepping out and heading towards her bedroom.

Amanda's bedroom was a spacious, white room with white satin curtains that hung from the ceiling to the floor, and a round, blue, king-sized bed at the center. The floor was the only one in the Lair that was fully covered with a smooth carpet, and in front of a door that led to her bathroom stood a beautiful nightstand with an oval porcelain mirror. Amanda walked over to her nightstand and sat down. She looked at herself and closed her eyes.

She focused on what she'd been imposing on the group and assured herself they were strong enough to handle whatever was thrown their way. She knew actions always led to consequences, yet she couldn't help but feel a little guilty for leading these three raw soldiers into her saga. For years now, she'd known if she'd ever had the chance to take on Oswald, it certainly wouldn't be alone. Amanda had noted potential in the three, but her energy had a significant impact on them as she helped them overcome their challenges, strengthened their moral compass, and molded their character. She'd always been a leader, a force you wouldn't stand up against - people always had a hard time saying 'No' to her. Amanda knew her energy was infectious, even insidious, and her perseverance and persistence rubbed off on whoever she worked with, as if her blood were feeding them - if she was in a position of control, it could be done. All she ever needed were the extra pairs of hands, the ones who'd paddle as she announced which direction to row for.

"No one thinks we can," she said to herself, as she opened her eyes to stare at her reflection. "That's exactly why we have to do it."

Chapter Nine - Infiltration

"I'm not worried about today," said Amanda, pouring herself some coffee as Shirley finished setting up the table. "I'm worried about what we'll find out *after* today," she told Lina and Stryker as Ripley sat on the computer, browsing through news coverage.

"There aren't many alternative scenarios for today, after all," said Stryker. "If you think about it, even if he says "No" to us, at least you two will be around, because he won't let you leave, right?"

"Exactly," added Amanda. "But the best scenario is if we can all work from there. We'll still be able to meet at nights because I know it's a gigantic place these days, since the workers don't even need to go home."

"Listen, I just found something," said Ripley. "There are lots of articles and discussions online about the design and technicalities of the ship," said Ripley. She cleared her throat and continued: "and in one it clearly states that while all manufacturing has been carried out in Washington, multiple separate modules which will work as add-ons are being built in… Iceland." Amanda looked at Ripley with a stunned expression on her face and then blurted out:

"That just means we need to get a move on. If we see the Orbit ourselves before the launch, we'll finally have a better understanding of what it is he's really planning."

The afternoon seemed to go by quicker than Lina expected. As the ballroom became filled with the orange tones of an approaching sunset, Stryker and Ripley sat on the tech station and carefully placed ear comms on Lina and Amanda's ears. That way, they could communicate with each other all the time via audio, as Ripley and Stryker would stay behind for the time being, remaining on the lookout for them.

Amanda and Lina prepared a few emergency bags in case they could not reach Hallormsstaður, or Hallo Woods as they'd been calling it for ease of pronunciation. After collecting their new passports from the tech station counter, they changed their appearance by wearing radical wigs, colored contact lenses, and prosthetics. They also wore snow coats that largely concealed their faces before descending downstairs.

***

After safely landing in Keflavik, Lina and Amanda left the airport by taking a cab. Amanda ordered the cabdriver to take them to a rental car store, where they could then drive off to Hallo Woods. Once they'd picked a car and were on their way out, Lina shut the door, getting in as Amanda took the driver's seat.

"How long 'till Hallo?" Lina asked.

"You'll see on the GPS that the actual name is *Hallormsstaður*," said Amanda. "Let me type that in for you," Amanda typed on the GPS of the car while Lina finished throwing their bags and packs on the back seat. Amanda located their destination and then clutched the wheel and turned on the car keys.

"It's *three hours* away," she announced as she sped away.

"So, let's go through it again," Lina added.

"As soon as we reach the border of the woods, we'll cross it until I know we're on their land. They're going to trace our faces through the stream feeds from the security as soon as we approach the headquarters. It'll only be a matter of time until a handful of men come for us, but they won't kill us or shoot on sight because they'll see it's me. Once we're in, I'll handle it. Once he agrees to it, we'll give them the stats on how to pick up Ripley and Stryker at Keflavik. They'll come as soon as we know we're in the clear. Are you there, by the way?" asked Amanda.

"We're here," a voice came from the bugs on their ears. *"Five by five,"*

Amanda sped up through the highway - they drove away, passing through small towns with very few houses in each. Lina marveled at the sight of a gigantic waterfall with geysers, only a few miles away from a small volcano with hot mud bubbling out of the earth. Amanda rushed through the landscape with little regard for her environment, whereas Lina was completely fascinated by the multitude of sights she came across. After what seemed like less than two hours to Lina, Amanda slowed down and announced:

"It's right up there." She pointed at a road sign that read *Hallormsstaður Forest*.

She parked the car a minute later, and they headed out, picking up their bags and heading heading for left-most edge of the woods. They crossed a small, barbed wire fence, throwing their bags first.

"We're in the woods, guys," announced Amanda to Stryker and Ripley, as she inched down to arch her body between the barbed wires.

"*Copy that. Good luck, girls,*" replied Stryker and Ripley at the same time.

Amanda and Lina picked up their bags from the ground and crossed a clearing among the trees that seemed never-ending. Lina observed that, without Stryker's tracking, it would be easy to get lost in the dense woods, as the trees all seemed identical and the branches were highly concentrated.

"Let's push through. Come on," Amanda said, holding onto two big bags. "I know they're heavy."

Lina breathed harder as the terrain inched upwards: even though they weren't climbing anything close to steep, they were still going up. A half-hour passed until Amanda pointed out in the distance the back of a house with a lake nearby, which she had instantly recognized as her childhood home.

"There it is! We're here! I can't believe the house is still standing!" said Amanda. "I was sure he'd have had it demolished by now."

"It's beautiful, Amanda. But that's not the headquarters, right?"

"Oh, no," said Amanda, catching her breath as they walked on. "The headquarters used to be right across from the house. You'd just have to cross a field, and you'd get to a small lab..," she said. She then stopped and said: "It's not a small lab anymore."

Amanda looked at Lina and said: "Hey, Lina," Lina stopped and looked at her.

"I need you to be extremely aware of everything from now on. Be extremely careful when we're inside, please. I won't be able to focus on what's going on, but the true reason I wanted you to tag along is because I trust your mind. The whole time I'll have my focus on getting the point across to him - so we can safely do this. So use your focus to snoop - look around. Find as much information as you can. Try to listen to what they're saying - we can use everything you see."

Lina nodded, and both women went on walking, soon leaving the woods and reaching the back of the house. As they passed the house to the front, Lina noticed Amanda looking through windows whenever she could, trying to catch a glimpse of whether anything was going on inside.

"As soon as we reach the end of the house, you'll see a gigantic open field, Lina. They'll probably be able to track us once we're in the middle," announced Amanda.

They finished passing the house and arrived at the front. Immediately, Lina and Amanda found what they looked for.

Across the open field stood Oswald's lab. The laboratory remained unchanged, except for a mammoth structure situated deep within the Hallo Woods. Oswald's small laboratory paled compared to the sheer magnitude of the building, to which it merely served as an entrance. Despite its monumental appearance, the headquarters of The Firm lacked towering ceilings. As they descended the building, it became apparent the entire structure was covered by a transparent ceiling, resembling a glass shield that extended out of sight. A giant living organism thriving in the middle of nowhere.

It didn't take them long to hear an alarm go off - and a robotic voice announced repeatedly at a deafening volume *"INTRUDERS"*.

"All that money and he couldn't change the robot's voice," said Amanda, with a disgusted look on her face. "They're coming, Lina," she said, looking at her.

After a brief period, a few outlines became visible from the woods, and before long, they realized that the initial group of outlines had grown to a formidable force of almost a hundred heavily armed men who were pointing their guns at them. Both Lina and Amanda's bodies were covered in red dots.

"Stay silent. They'll see it's me."

"STAND OFF!" a voice came from the lab door, and Amanda recognized him as Arlo. "IT'S OSWALD'S DAUGHTER!" All the men, who were now approaching the middle of the open field, lowered their weapons and Arlo ran past them, towards Amanda and Lina.

"What are you doing here, Amanda? As soon as Oswald saw it was you, he sent me."

"I must speak to my father. That's why I came, Arlo. I have decided to join him." Amanda knew Oswald would have a speaker on Arlo's ear, so she didn't react by tilting her head back like Lina when Arlo placed his hand on his ear and started talking to himself:

"In? Okay, sir," Lina connected the dots and saw Amanda was smiling. She'd already gone straight to the point and Oswald was now ordering them in.

"Very well," said Arlo. "Come with us."

"This is my friend, Lina," said Amanda. "It's *crucial* that she is with me in every step of this." She held Lina's hand and both walked alongside Arlo towards the entrance to the Firm.

Lina noticed the army remained frozen in position. As soon as they passed their line of fire, they retreated and started walking back with them, as if escorting them back in. Lina noticed how robotic their behavior seemed to be: threats who became protectors at the flip of a switch.

They crossed the laboratory door and, before stepping in, Amanda stopped in her tracks. She immediately noticed the inside wasn't spacious anymore - but instead, seemed more like the entrance to a cave, as all she could see was a way forward ahead - like a dark tunnel, but its sides weren't visible – only, if you reached out to touch them, you could feel the concrete walls.

"We've rebuilt the lab, Miss Amanda, if that's what you're finding odd," said Arlo, noticing Amanda's reaction. "It now works as a passageway as we go underground and then inside, straight into Mr. Oswald's office,"

"Straight into his office?" asked Amanda, curious. She then realized she and Lina wouldn't be able to glimpse into anything from The Firm to tell Stryker and Ripley in advance.

"Yes. Mr. Oswald ordered me to take you to him immediately." They went down a dark path, following Arlo.

The tunnel was lit by round, artificial lamps in the floor that guided the way.

"If we were to reach the facility," said Amanda, "which way would we go?"

"Oh, I'm not allowed to divulge that information," said Arlo.

Amanda looked at Arlo with an impatient look as they walked on and asked: "Why not?"

"Only if you work here can you know anything," answered Arlo.

"Well, hold on to that thought, will you?" Amanda said, sarcastically.

"Here we are," announced Arlo, as the lightbulbs in the floor suddenly stopped and continued to their right, leading into an elevator door. "This elevator will take us straight into Oswald's office.

The elevator had red doors that made a macabre contrast to the blackness of the tunnel. The three of them got in as soon as the doors slid smoothly open. There were no buttons inside. The elevator started to vibrate and move upwards. After only a few seconds, it came to a halt and the doors slid open again. Arlo left and Amanda followed him as Lina quickly followed her outside.

They found themselves in a refined business room with an elevator at each end. Every object in it seemed to be made of gold. Lina immediately noticed the brightness of many golden surfaces, including the table and chair outlines and every shelf bracket in the room. Each shelf showcased many intricate miniatures, all in different sizes, and the shapes of many objects, from animals to globes. An entire wall to their right was filled with accolades, awards, diplomas and achievements framed in gold, and, at the center of the room there was a round silver desk, which Lina assumed was Oswald's.

"You can wait here, he'll be with you shortly," said Arlo, leaving almost immediately. Lina and Amanda looked around when they heard the elevator farthest from them open up. From it, two men dressed in black suits came out, also wearing The Firm's badge on their chests. After them, a man in his late 60s appeared, dressed in a grey suit and tie, who Lina immediately knew to be Oswald. He held a silver cane in his right hand and only after he'd walked past his security men did he glance towards Amanda. Immediately locking eyes with her, he let out a half-smile and opened his arms, saying in a cheerful tone:

"I can't *believe* my eyes! My dear Amanda! It's been, what, twenty years?"

Amanda ambiguously hugged him, but she didn't press his arms against her or anything - as he held her, he quickly looked at Lina across the room. She felt her entire body shiver in anxiety, fearing to lock eyes with him. He then let go of Amanda and asked, holding her hand: "What brings you here?" Amanda remained silent and then turned her back and walked away for a few steps. She stopped again, and turned around to face Oswald. She then said:

"This would be slightly easier if you didn't pretend to be entirely happy, Father. It's almost as if you hadn't framed me for your actions," she said.

Instantly, she saw Oswald's tender expression turn cold as he looked at her and said, this time with a different, more serious tone of voice:

"Forgive me for indulging, Amanda. What brings you here?"

"You can smile now. I've decided it's best if I join you, after all. It has been brought to my attention recently that our fields and interests are very, very similar," she said. Lina couldn't see her face, but she could only imagine how penetrating her stare was at that moment. Oswald smiled again, but not as vividly as the first time - and answered, in a tone of disbelief:

"Oh, Amanda," he said. "And may I ask what caused this sudden... *change* of will?"

"I know you're behind the Europa funding and you know how much this fascinates me. You've done it. I want to be following each step closely and the only way for me to achieve that is through you. I can either stall my professional life or I can make amends with my father and thrive at home. I failed to see, during all this time, what you meant by the bigger picture. I understand it now," she assured him, with a razor-sharp tone of decisiveness in her voice.

"That is fantastic news," Oswald said.

"There is one thing I'll ask of you, however," Amanda said. "In order for me to dedicate all my time to being here in Iceland, with you and focusing only on this new goal, I must ask that you allow Lina," she looked back at Lina and smiled, "and two other friends to join you, as well. They have been the heart of my professional team for the last decade and each of them has specific and distinct qualities which they can contribute. It is in your *best* interest to have all four of us. I understand it's a lot to ask after two decades of nearly no contact and I ask you to please take your time as you---" Oswald interrupted Amanda, immediately answering:

"It is done, Amanda."

"What?" asked Amanda, surprised by how easy it had seemed. "Do you mean it?"

"I knew this day would come, Amanda. I know you better than you think," said Oswald. "And, forgive me saying, but it truly was only a matter of time. You are doing the right thing, my dear. I knew it. Dad knew you'd understand."

Lina seemed thrown off by the kindness he expressed in his words and at how gently he looked at Amanda. His actions towards his estranged daughter were so genuine that no one who witnessed them could accuse him of being evil. Lina knew she'd have a few questions to ask Amanda as soon as they left, but for now she knew Amanda also had to play her part the best she could. Oswald's security stood frozen in their place, without moving a muscle.

"As soon as I heard about Europa, I knew you were the one who had made it possible," said Amanda. "You *must* meet Lina, Father," Amanda said, turning back again and signing with her hand for Lina to come forward, as they graciously swayed across the room towards her.

Lina thought she could hear a hint of British in their accents, as the father and daughter conversed like business magnates at a charity event. Oswald and Lina shook hands.

"Nice to meet you, Lina," he said.

"Nice to meet you, sir," answered Lina.

"May I ask what you hope to achieve once you've joined us?" asked Oswald.

"Lina can assist you with any PTS subjects or testing," Amanda immediately chipped in, answering for her. "You wouldn't *believe* how much she's been through. I've perfected each of my colleagues and taught them everything I know. They are just as skilled as Arlo. All they need is more combat training. Lina is the perfect candidate for shaping each new subject of yours. I see much of myself in her," she said, smiling at Lina. "Also, we can't wait to get to know the entire facility, Father. *Such fun!*"

"Yes, about that..." said Oswald, standing up from his desk. "Why don't I have a team escort you to our dormitories and we'll have a meeting tonight, the five of us, at 8?"

"That sounds perfect," said Amanda. Lina nodded.

"Where are the other two?"

"You can have a team pick them up in Keflavik by 7 tonight," Amanda added.

"Are these Ripley and Stryker?" asked Oswald. Lina seemed surprised by him knowing their names, since that meant he knew hers as well.

"Yes. Ripley and Stryker" replied Amanda. "You've figured it was only a matter of time before I surrendered to your help, didn't you?" asked Amanda.

"Yes. After you attacked my men, I had underestimated my little girl," he smiled. Lina sensed an ounce of malice in his tone, and he went on: "You've always been quite... intense, Amanda. We figured arresting you was the perfect way to bring you here forever with no questions asked, my dear... I did. I'm glad you figured it out on your own."

Oswald pressed a button on a set of speakers that laid in his desk and said: "I need a team to escort two new grade A employees to the dorms," he said to the speaker.

He lifted his finger from the buttons and crossed his arms. He then shook his head as if saying "No" and said:

"I just can't believe you're finally here, my dear. What a great time to have you back." He said, "I'll see you at 8."

immediately, the elevator doors opened. Four men in black clothes with the Firm's inverted triangle badge on their chest came out. Oswald shifted his gaze from the women to the guards and said:

"These are recent additions to the team. We'll introduce them in the roundup. For now, take them to their new dorms."

Oswald shifted his focus onto his desk and, before Lina could assimilate, they were already inside another elevator. The elevator closed doors and started moving upwards and soon Oswald was already far away from them. Amanda stood by Lina's side and locked eyes with her as the elevator rose. She nodded with her head, re-assuring Lina all was well.

Chapter Ten - The Firm

Lina and Amanda continued to stand silently inside the elevator, until it finally stopped. The door slowly opened, and the guards went out, gesturing for them to leave next. Amanda and Lina emerged from the shaft to find themselves on the top floor of the facility, with the protective glass dome just a few feet above their line of sight.

It was an ample and airy space, with an adjacent metal platform in front of them that crossed over the building, leading to a new wing filled with doors and corridors. Lina quickly peeked down the metal platform, seeing all the Firm's floors from above, as if standing on top of a monumental colosseum. She glimpsed many Firm employees walking about their business, from the first floor to the one just below her. Lina then looked up to see a few raindrops falling against the glass bubble, crashing against the impenetrable structure. Lina and Amanda tried to assimilate as much detail and information as they could as they began crossing the metal platform.

As they arrived at the first doors and openings to their side, they stopped at the fourth door to their left. There were still many ahead, but the guards stopped and turned to inform them.

"I'm Chase and he's Keith. Welcome to the program. This will be your dormitory. Please make yourselves at home before our nocturnal gathering at 8." Chase and Keith, both bald men who seemed to be opposites of each other - Chase had barely given them time to think, yet Keith seemed to be bored and uninterested - then walked to the white door in front of them, which was locked by a black sensor in place of a handle. "To open these, you must press the red button and then look straight into the detector so they can scan your retina,"

Amanda and Lina thanked Keith and Chase, who left soon after, as they opened their doors and went into what would be their new room. They walked into a rectangular bedroom with white carpet floors. The walls were silver, and the bedroom had four king-sized beds on each side, perfectly aligned to point to the center of the room. The wall facing the bed had an entrance to another shaft on the left and a bathroom door on the right. In the center of the room, there was a glass cylinder connected to the floor and ceiling, with a computer screen and a built-in keyboard below it. Pinned on the wall next to each bed, there were five silver handles that, when pressed, opened to reveal drawers. The room's design was minimalistic, but efficient.

"Apart from the beds, the only other thing in the room is this cylinder. I'm surprised at how there's an elevator in each room," Amanda noted, walking around. She chose the bed between the bathroom and the elevator. Lina took the bed closest to the door, leaving the middle two for Ripley and Stryker. Despite a chilly and distant atmosphere, Lina and Amanda noticed a delightful fruity aroma that seemed artificial. Taking advantage of the cooler temperature in the room, they took a moment to unwind.

"I'm thinking there's an entire underground tunnel where the elevators glide through. I'm glad there are four beds, though. We'll all be together this way," said Lina, sitting on hers. The elevator by Amanda's bed then slid open, with their bags delivered but no one inside. On top of the luggage they'd brought with them, there were now four small suitcases which Amanda assumed would be The Firm's uniforms. Amanda and Lina got up from the bed and picked everything up. They laid everything on their respective beds and opened their suitcases. Amanda's suspicions were confirmed when the first thing she saw shining through the case were golden inverted triangles.

Arlo's face flashed onto the glass cylinder and a hologram of his face was projected onto each side of it.

"*This is your personal panel during your stay here. Use it to communicate and answer mass orders and announcements. We'll notify each recent occurrence through here,"*

Stryker's voice emerged through the comms and spoke in their ears:

"Yo, girls, next time you're with any of the big bosses, let 'em know we'll arrive at the airport at 7. We're boarding now."

Amanda and Lina sat up on their beds, startled, and quickly ignored the shock, so as not to let Arlo notice they were communicating through an ear bug. Even though a team would pick up Stryker and Ripley, it was best to not start things off on the wrong foot. Arlo gave them an intrigued look and asked:

"Is everything okay, ladies?"

"We just weren't aware you would show up there," answered Amanda instantly. Arlo dismissed her answer and then went on:

"Well, I am also here to ask you about your missing duo. When shall the other two arrive? Should we send a team to pick them up and if so, at what time."

"At 7. You can send a team to pick them up. Their names are Ripley and Stryker," answered Amanda. She replied as fast as she could.

"Very well. Tonight at 10 there's the nightly roundup. We expect you in the Roundup Room. Board the elevator at 9:55, and it will take you there. Your bathroom is on the right

and to request lunch and dinner, type either lunch or dinner on the keyboard below me and then place your request. Welcome - and see you at 10."

Arlo's face then logged off and Lina and Amanda saw each other again through the reflection of the glass.

"Guess now we know what that thing's for," commented Lina.

"They're surely making it seem… practical," said Amanda.

"I wonder what specific functions they'll assign to each of us. I'm still not sure what this place does, after all," said Lina.

—

Lina and Amanda talked little while waiting for the afternoon sun to fade and nighttime's roundup to arrive. They unpacked and chatted lightly, wary of being overheard by Oswald or anyone else who might be listening in. Lina took a shower in a bathroom that looked more like a futuristic *onsen,* with a rectangular wooden tub, white marbled floors, and golden handles on the sink. She was left befuddled once again, after the sun had gone down, by the design of the room.

Lina took a relaxing shower for what seemed like a half-hour, when she heard two voices knocking on the door and announcing:

"We're here, Lina!" yelled Stryker.

"Lina, we got here!" said Ripley from outside the door. She heard their voices and closed her eyes, relaxing under the hot water. She smiled while taking in that Ripley and Stryker had made it safe - and then felt a fire ignite inside her. A potentially hard part of the plan was done and over with, gone by *easily*. It was now up to them to play their cards right.

Chapter Eleven - Undercover Nights

Lina, Amanda, Stryker and Ripley heard the elevator doors close in front of them and then move down. The four stood inside in silence staring straight ahead, on their way to the Nightly Roundup, sporting their badges on their chest. Stryker and Ripley also weren't the most talkative of the bunch upon their arrival. Although they were all glad to see each other and joked around while dressing for the Roundup, there was a palpable sense of adrenaline and awe in the air: no one mentioned any plans or schemes to each other, but each knew they wanted to. Amanda's preparation was clear: being in a large, monitored place heightened the importance of non-verbal trust and safety cues. Any question, idea or suggestion couldn't be addressed immediately like it would be would back in Amanda's Lair. Instead, it had to be remembered until they found a later opportunity to be alone together.

"Do you think we'll already get task assignments?" asked Stryker.

"Yes," answered Amanda, flatly. They remained in silence for a long period as the elevator continued moving -

not only vertically but horizontally, they felt, as Lina's hunch at an underground network of elevators seemed more pertinent with each moment they lingered inside.

After a couple more minutes, it came to a halt, and the doors slid open. They stepped outside into a crowded circular hall that seemed like the inside of a conference room, unsure where exactly it was located inside The Firm's facilities. In front of them, close to twenty rows with dozens of bronze chairs were aligned impeccably, pointing at a big balcony at the end. Every person walking around wore the same black uniform, with the same badge on their chest, so it was no surprise to them they didn't attract any attention, blending right in. The room was only half filled, but on each side, more and more workers popped out of the elevators next to them, all seeming to be in a slight rush.

"Let's sit there." Lina pointed to four empty chairs on a middle row. They made their way over and sat down. Soon after, their row was filled and Lina and Ripley, who sat at opposite ends, had Firm employees next to them. It was Lina's first encounter with Oswald's PTSD-trained soldiers and Lina felt her curiosity spike, wanting to stare at the person next to her and see how they differed from any other human being. The entire concept of being next to an emotionless person was intriguing to her, but she looked at Amanda - who whispered in her ear:

"Remember, be cool. Most will come talk to us when they announce we're new."

At 10 pm sharp, the entire room filled and the volume of talking died down. From the balcony, an enormous screen rolled down through an opening in the ceiling and the lights dimmed. Oswald projected onto the screen, sitting at his desk in his office as he greeted the entire packed hall.

"*Good evening,*" he said. Every man and woman in the room stood up from their seats immediately and arched their heads forward in silence, greeting Oswald. Amanda, Lina, Stryker and Ripley looked at each other as they all got up a few seconds late. Once they were standing, everyone sat down - and the quartet became exposed as newbies.

"*Oh, there they are already, yes! Everyone, these are Lina, Stryker, Ripley, recent additions to the team. And, my dear daughter Amanda, a notorious psychiatrist who just today has graced me with the news that she and her team will now join us in our quest to move forward.*"

Every face in the room looked back at them, almost in sync. Amanda, Lina and Ripley greeted everyone with their heads forward and Stryker awkwardly waved to a few people who stared at him. Amanda stepped with her pointed heel on his foot and he immediately lowered his hand and arched his head before he sat down.

"*Tomorrow, starting at our usual working hour of 10 a.m., Amanda and Lina will join me and my team in our*

Experiments Lab as she will aid me with all of her insight and knowledge as we further perfect our techniques alongside her. Ripley is an ex-marine, which immediately suited her as the perfect choice as our new supervisor in Combat Training, and Stryker will show off all it is he can do to advance our programs in Ops."

Lina said quietly to Amanda, "I can't believe we'll work alongside him. Is he clueless or what?"

"He's hardly clueless... but this is good for us," whispered Amanda.

"*We are also proud to announce the names of the crew that will board Europa One on our incredible expedition,*" announced Oswald. All four sat up in their chairs, interested.

"I didn't remember it was today!" Lina said.

"Well, it's only tomorrow for the general public, but it's 10 p.m. so it makes sense he'd announce it early for his employees," answered Amanda.

"*From the selected six, four are now in the Washington, DC HQ, overseeing the final spacecraft changes. Two of them, however, are still here, and will be announced now,*" Immediately, you could hear the excitement building in the audience. "*Our mission commander will be Andrei Gustav, chief science officer Yukito Kinomoto, chief officer and marine biologist and oceanographer Charles Randall, chief engineer Nadine Nikolav,*" Oswald announced.

"I've heard of Yukito and Charles!" said Ripley.

"So have I. They were at the top of the list," whispered Amanda.

"Pilot and archivist Sergei Lee," Oswald announced and a man in one of the front rows stood up and inched his head forward again, as if thanking Oswald. Lina expected him to jump out of his chair screaming "YES!", or throw his chair away in excitement, but nothing else happened. Instead, the man sat down again and Oswald went on *"and finally, as our chief engineer, Madzia Wozdecka,"* A woman in the row in front of them stood up, also bowed her head and then sat down without uttering a word.

"Starting tomorrow at dawn, you will fly to Washington as you prepare for launch day. Congratulations," said Oswald. *"And, last but not least, an update to Restricted Level workers. With the approaching completion of the spacecraft starting tomorrow, all restricted level operations are at Priority 1. The reactor's propulsion tests and isolation chambers must be secluded and I am counting on each of you to see progress. Good night. Onwards,"*

The entire auditorium then belted out, in unison: "*ONWARDS!*" and the quartet jumped up again on their chairs from the sudden fright. The screen turned black and everyone stood up. Before Lina could turn to Amanda, she heard a voice from behind talking to them:

"Welcome to the team," said a man with blonde hair, tall and scrawny, in his mid-30s. He shook hands with Lina,

Stryker, Ripley and Amanda. Next to him soon appeared a younger-looking woman with dark hair. She approached Amanda and said, "Welcome to the team." The four of them noticed then a line was forming behind each, as everyone from the auditorium made their way to greet them.

"Welcome to the team," said a second woman, shaking hands with Stryker. Each Firm employee was presentable, but apathetic. After what seemed like ten minutes, Lina and the gang greeted the last of the employees, as she noticed the blonde-haired man and the dark-haired woman remained by their side, waiting to talk to them.

"I'm Carlos, this is Sarah," he said. "Sarah and I both work half-time each on Combat and in Programming. So we shall see more of you, Stryker, and Ripley," he said with a sympathetic look on his face and a part of him seemed to look forward to making new acquaintances. Lina couldn't help but stare at him, on the lookout for any behavior that lacked emotion, but his words seemed to come from an honest place.

"How does it feel to have Oswald Rose as your father, Amanda?" asked Sarah. She looked at Amanda curiously. "I ask because we all look up to him, so having you here is very odd."

"It's no different from having a regular father," said Amanda. "He's certainly made a name for himself."

"Indeed, he has" answered Sarah. The room was now starting to feel more spacious as the workers made their way to the elevators in groups.

"Well, it's been nice meeting you. I look forward to working together," said Sarah, turning around to leave.

"I also must be on my way" said Carlos. "I'll see all of you tomorrow."

Lina, Amanda, Stryker and Ripley still stood in front of the chairs they'd sat on, looking around at an increasingly empty hall.

"They seem... *welcoming*," commented Stryker, walking towards the end of their row of chairs.

"That was so freaky - how they all lined up to greet each one of us," commented Ripley.

"They seem to work together in perfect harmony, though," said Stryker. "I'm also glad I got Programming. That Carlos guy seems alright."

"Yeah, Sarah seems nice as well. I didn't expect any restricted levels, though" added Ripley. Amanda then took advantage of the fact they were still in public, walking back to the elevators, as she whispered to them:

"Our first step is anything regarding the restricted levels." As soon as Amanda finished speaking, the four heard someone calling her name.

"Amanda?" asked a deep, throaty male voice. They turned around to see a muscular, bald man in his 40s standing next to them. Amanda remembered shaking his hand a minute before, but she didn't know his name. "I'm Peter. I work on Experiments."

"Hello," said Amanda.

"I had heard about Oswald's daughter, but it's nice to put a face to the name," he said. "If you need anything, feel free to ask me. Lina, Stryker, Ripley, the same to all of you. It's been two years since we've had any new additions to the team - everyone is interested in you now," he said.

"That's nice to hear. In fact, since you're so helpful, we would certainly benefit from knowing how we can get a better overview of each sector's designations."

"Well, I'll escort you back to your premises and fill you in. Shall we?" asked Peter. The four nodded almost simultaneously and Peter walked on.

"How do we know which elevator to take?" asked Amanda. "They don't have any buttons."

"Oh. I see you really don't know many things about this place yet," said Peter.

"What do you mean?" asked Lina. "How do they work?"

"Well, we don't call them elevators; we call them shafts, since they move horizontally as well.

"But how do you select where to go?" asked Lina.

"They're programmed through The Firm's AI. If there's only one person in the shaft and assuming the shaft's not on event hours or start-of-work shift, the system identifies you and takes you back to your dormitory, always. If there's more than one from different dormitories, it'll stop at each. Or you can just say the name of where you want to go."

"What's event hours? Like this one?" asked Lina.

"Yes, if there are any special events, morning announcements, press conferences, news coverages, nightly roundups or emergency meetings, all elevators are instantly re-programmed to take you to the place where the event happens. It's often here, but it's not always in the halls," said Peter, as they got in the elevator.

"So I assume it'll also take us to our respective work shifts?" asked Lina, as the doors closed shut behind them and the shaft started moving.

"Yes, at precisely 9:55, when the doors open," said Peter.

"And apart from our assigned sections, what other ones are there?" asked Amanda. The elevator moved swiftly through, on their way to their dormitories.

"Well, there's Oswald's central floors, from 9 to 13 which are mostly for mass manufacturing and gadget production. The Restricted Areas take up the first four floors as well. Then you've got Experiments on 5 and 6, Programming and Operations on 7 and Combat Training on 8. On the 14th floor, you've got a cleared floor that holds anything temporary, such as meetings. It also stores many archives," said Peter, who seemed very sympathetic towards everyone and would often smile at all four, to reassure how he was addressing this to the entire quartet. "I'd say the 14th is the most social of all floors, since most people often come and go from it. And starting on the 15th up until the 20th are the dormitories," All four painted mental pictures of what their map of The Firm looked like. Peter seemed outgoing and spoke fast, as if he'd done this for every new recruit.

"We eat exclusively at each dormitory, as well. Do you know how to order your meals?" he asked, interested.

"We do," answered Amanda. "Thank you for filling us in, Peter. Do you think most people will welcome us?"

"Surely," answered Peter. "That is one of the many benefits of being in this place, Amanda," he said, with his expression turning slightly. Lina focused on him as she noticed Peter suddenly changed the nuance of his expression from curious to an ambiguous, empty stare.

"Why is that, exactly?" asked Amanda.

"In a regular facility, in the outside world, the start of new work relationships usually works by instinct, as either you or someone would approach you, claiming to like you. It's a standard survival procedure pattern of human beings, to attach to people we sympathize with. Every single person here will talk to you when they find an opportunity, out of our only mutual interest - our motto."

"What is that interest, exactly?" asked Amanda.

"*Onwards*, of course. Every one of us has created a working atmosphere in which we thrive," said Peter. "Every new member is always welcome, as they become a fundamental part of our process of growth."

The shaft stopped, and the doors opened back to their room. Amanda, Lina, Stryker and Ripley stepped outside. Peter then said, from inside:

"Well, I'll see Amanda and Lina tomorrow at 10! Stryker and Ripley, nice to meet you."

"Thank you, Peter," said Amanda.

"Good night," said Lina.

"Nice to meet you!" said both Stryker and Ripley.

The elevator door closed, and all four looked at each other.

"Apparently they follow their motto religiously," said Amanda, who started going through her bags and taking off her jacket. "I gotta tell you, I found it to be quite an intriguing choice of wording."

On the next day, the four of them made their way to their designated positions and started their shifts for The Firm. Much to their surprise, the procedures weren't too complicated. Amanda and Lina found the Experiments floors were top-of-the-line tech labs, divided into dozens of small and large glass chambers where, during the entire first week, they supervised tests and experiments from neuroscience. The research theme was held as a debate, where the group aimed to identify patterns in cognitive functions of the brain and would then veto or approve going forward with new experiments. Each was solely designed to improve and enhance the specified function of the mind. At first failing to grasp certain names and terms that were tossed around, by the end of the week, Lina felt like she'd heard the name of every drug available on the market.

Stryker struggled during the first few days, assimilating the cryptograph patterns and programming software, but soon found some spare time to blossom with his first hack, creating a private IP-sealed chatroom log connecting Lina, Amanda, Ripley and his work computers. This way, they became able to speak to each other freely, at least during shift hours. Ripley would reply the least, but she was the one who showed the most joy and delight in being within The Firm, claiming to have found her calling in Combat Training. She repeated many times that she had an epiphany during her second day, when she knew quitting the Marines was a mistake, since it was her only way to exteriorize her pent-up emotions. Any mention of the restricted areas was immediately addressed on the chat; however, they knew that because the elevator programming was controlled by higher powers, overriding the systems to access the lower levels would prove trickier than expected.

On the eve of the launch of Europa One, the four reunited in the dorm before descending to one of the Halls for a small conference streaming the event from Florida. They dressed quickly and boarded the shaft, which led them to a Hall they hadn't been to before, designed to look like an ancient, sleek Greek palace. There were six white stone columns, three to each side, with a stream of water near each middle column. The room emanated a peaceful and ethereal atmosphere which could almost make you forget it belonged to a Firm facility.

"This is the Royal Hall," said Peter, coming out of the shaft next to theirs. "It's on the opposite side of the Roundup Hall floors. I don't understand why they still use it. It's much nicer here."

The sound of the running water created a soothing ambience, and the Hall was lit by cold cathode lamps on the ceiling. People were noticeably more agitated this time around - workers talked to each other as everyone once again sat down to watch the transmission feed when the central screen lit up.

They all focused as they saw, for the first time, the spacecraft ready to launch. Designed like a gigantic torpedo, the white ship had a massive black platform encircling its base that more than quadrupled the ship's width. After a few minutes, they counted down to launch and watched as the shuttle's engines started and the ship slowly moved upwards with increasing speed, becoming faster and faster the more smoke it left behind on the ground, rising until it finally disappeared from the camera's range. Everyone burst into cheers as the reporter praised what an incredible achievement and step forward this was for humankind. Lina, Stryker, Ripley and Amanda processed the moment in slow-motion, as they smiled observingly, watching each Firm worker greet each other, displaying the most emotion and vivacity they'd ever seen. Amanda would often switch from smiling and looking around to focusing on the screen, as she clapped along but couldn't take her mind off of the encircling black platform which she knew was Oswald's contribution - now up in space, on its way.

Sarah and Carlos approached them, beaming with excitement.

"Can you believe it?" asked Carlos, smiling from ear to ear. Sarah stood by his side, just as pumped. "Now it's only a matter of months before we potentially discover life!"

"Everyone's taking their chances betting on a game of what the discovery will be," added Sarah. "Microbiological life, marine life, you name it, and the closest to figuring out will take home all the money from the pot. You're all welcome to place your bets as well, it's on our Global Panel on the 14th floor," she said.

"I'll take that bet," said Stryker. Carlos and Sarah then left, and the gang made their way back to the shaft. The doors opened up to their room, and Stryker immediately made his way to the panel, opening up a window log for their daily dinner meal order and testing a few keyboard tricks on it.

"I get the first shower tonight, right?" asked Amanda. Lina nodded a "yes" with her head and Amanda made her way to the bathroom to the sound of Stryker hitting every key on the keyboard.

"Can I go after Amanda, Lina?" asked Ripley. Lina replied, "Sure" and, as she finished saying it she jumped up in her bed when Stryker screamed "YES!" He clapped his hands and pointed at the screen with a smile on his face.

"What?" asked Lina. She looked deep into his eyes and tugged at his hand, as his sudden screaming behavior could be seen as suspicious by anyone watching their room.

"There's a new... *option* for Chinese food," answered Stryker. He went back to typing frantically. A few minutes later, when Amanda came out of the shower drying her hair, but already fully dressed, he yelled "I got it! Amanda dearest, you will bow down to me once I tell you what I just did," Amanda looked at him suspiciously. Lina and Ripley also seemed puzzled by his teasing. Stryker then said:

"Oh! We can *talk* now. I've shut down our audio and video. Switched it to footage of us sleeping safe and sound."

"Are you serious?" asked Amanda.

"I've never been more serious, baby. What's being sent to their feed is actually configured from this panel. Now if I could just hack the elevator programming to take us to a restricted level, no one would even see it."

"Stryker, that's unbelievable," said Amanda, smiling. "Can we really talk about anything?"

"Yes! Yes! Why is it so hard to believe that I'm *awesome*? I told you if I played around I'd pull some tricks out of the hat."

"How hard is it to get into shaft programming?" asked Lina.

"It's on the other hardware. I'm already inside it, but the AI is way trickier than I expected," said Stryker, scrolling down an endless list of scripts.

"Oh, Stryker, if you get it, now's really the perfect time!" said Lina. "Tonight's the only night no one's going to be focused on the restricted levels! They're all so hyper about the launch!"

Stryker remained focused, clicking and typing on the panel. "Damn, I wish I could sit down."

"But you can keep that footage being sent for an unlimited amount of time, right? Even if we don't sleep tonight and you only stop at 3 a.m., we can still go!" said Amanda.

"Yeah, but I'm not sure I'll break this tonight, ladies," His eyes were fixed on the screen. "This is way, way harder, oh - no it's not!" said Stryker. He frowned his eyebrows and smiled at the screen. "Okay, the hard part's over, sorry for the negativity, ladies. I get like that when faced with a challenge."

"Why does he brag when he's doing things right?" asked Lina, looking at Amanda.

"You're worried about bragging? I'm worried about this weird ladies-man vibe he's giving off," answered Amanda.

"Go, go, go!" yelled Stryker. The shaft's doors slid open.

Stryker yelled, gazing at the screen :"You three can go, I have to stay here! Don't take long, one hour tops! Deal?"

"You got it," said Lina, getting up from her bed. She got in and was quickly followed by Amanda and Ripley.

"Are you *sure*, Stryker?" asked Amanda, already inside. The shaft's doors closed.

"Well, I guess you're just gonna have to wait to find out, aren't you, Amanda?" gloated Stryker, as the doors shut. The shaft moved down and Amanda whispered to them:

"If anyone's in there, we remain inside,"

The elevator continued to move for a minute, until it stopped and the doors opened up. Immediately, they noticed the entire place was lit by a bright, purple light, which they later identified to be UV lamps attached to the ceiling. There was an impenetrable silence which all three women took as encouragement to step out.

They found themselves in another large laboratory, which shone in dark purple and black. At first, there was nothing special about it: it merely seemed like the Experiments level under emergency lighting. Amanda, Ripley and Lina silently walked around the room. The floor then led to a spiral staircase leading to a lower and wider level. Knowing there were four restricted floors, they walked down the staircase to the lower level, finding themselves in a room stacked with computers on each side. This floor was also lit by ultraviolet lamps and Amanda noticed the two first computers on the row next to them were turned on. At the end, another staircase led to another lower level.

"Quick, let's search the logs for anything on the Orbit," said Amanda to Lina. "Ripley, check if there's anyone on the third level down," Ripley made her way to the spiral staircase as Amanda and Lina sat down in front of each screen. Ripley quickly turned around and made her way back to the computers.

"What is it?" asked Amanda.

"I hear voices downstairs," said Ripley.

"Stay close then to see if anyone's coming up, please," said Amanda. Ripley tip-toed back and listened in.

"I've got an instant hit by just searching Orbit," announced Lina. "They're audio files, thirty of them. They're numbered from *Meeting 001 Orbit.wav* to *Meeting 030 Orbit.wav*"

"Play them," said Amanda. Lina looked at her, confused.

"What, *now*? *Here*?" asked Lina.

"The voices are gone," announced Ripley from near the staircase.

"See? So, yes! Play it! We need to go back with something! Let's listen in for a few minutes. If we hear anything approaching, we'll go."

Lina played file 001 and Amanda took some ear plugs from one desk. She gave one to Ripley and then to Lina, placed hers in her ear and they listened in. At first all they heard was static, but soon a familiar voice spoke in what seemed to be an open room:

"But how would that work, Sergei? Convince me you can do it using Earth's technology," asked Oswald.

"A warp drive would manipulate space-time itself to move a starship, taking advantage of a loophole in the laws of physics that prevent anything from moving faster than light. A concept for a real-life warp drive was suggested in 1994 by Mexican physicist Miguel Alcubierre; however, subsequent calculations found that such a device would require prohibitive amounts of energy. With the advancements in 2025 in the field of dark matter and the breakthrough in 2027, the only thing standing between the approval of this project today is, well, the fuel."

"How would that work? Energy is certainly my specialty," said Oswald's voice, in the same tone she'd heard in his office.

"An Alcubierre warp drive would involve a football-shaped spacecraft attached to a large ring encircling it. This ring, potentially made of exotic matter, would cause space-time to warp around the starship, creating a region of contracted space in front of it and expanded space behind. Meanwhile, the starship itself would stay inside a bubble of flat space-time that wasn't being warped at all. Everything within space is restricted by the speed of light," explained the instantly recognizable voice of Richard Obousy, president of Icarus Interstellar, a non-profit group of scientists and engineers devoted to pursuing interstellar spaceflight.

"Except space-time, the very fabric of space, is not. It is not limited by the speed of light. With this concept, the spacecraft would be able to achieve an effective speed of about ten times the speed of light, all without breaking the cosmic speed limit. White's colleagues began experimenting with this around two decades ago, with a mini version of the warp drive in their laboratory. They set up what they call the Interferometer, at the Johnson Space Center, essentially creating a laser interferometer that instigates micro versions of space-time warps. They tried to see if we can generate a very tiny instance of this in a tabletop experiment, to try to perturb space-time by one part in ten million. In 2038, it was perfected in the shadows," Sergei said.

There was silence in the audio and then his voice spoke loud again.

"The only problem, surely, is that such a drive is estimated to require a minimum amount of energy about equal to the mass-energy of Jupiter."

"It seems our interests dovetail perfectly. I admit you seem qualified enough for our standards," answered Oswald. "By 2041, Orbit will be in the skies, harnessing the fuel necessary for our successful warp."

"There's also a potential for energy reduction realized by oscillating the bubble's intensity. That is an interesting conjecture that we will enjoy looking at in the lab," said Sergei.

"My colleagues are more than prepared to treat this as Priority 1. With our combined forces we can perfect it in less than two decades," answered Oswald. "And you know exactly where it is we'd go to."

"Gliese 581G? Well, I thought so," nodded Sergei.

"Is that what you're calling it?" asked Oswald, letting out a brief laugh.

Immediately, Lina looked at Amanda and saw the color drain from her face. She had a suspicion of what this meant.

"Only seventeen light-years away. A close neighbor when traveling faster than light," answered Oswald's voice.

"Very well, Mr. Oswald. And how many subjects would you intend on transferring?"

"We'll consider our options carefully. I'm sure we can select the cream of the crop as we marvel at the imminent self-destruction. It seems there are great things we can..."

The lights suddenly switched from ultraviolet to the regular cold cathode lamps of The Firm. Without missing a beat, Amanda and Ripley made their way to the staircase at the center of the room towards the upper level. Lina closed the file and every window she'd left open and started to climb the staircase after them. There weren't any approaching sounds, but they assumed someone was close because of the change in lighting. They reached the laboratory, which also wasn't in ultraviolet anymore - and ran towards the shaft.

***

"If anyone was looking at the cameras from the restricted areas," said Stryker as all four reunited in their bedroom. "Then they've seen you and it'll get pretty ugly *soon*,"

"Why didn't you remind us of that?" asked Amanda.

"Well, Lina did say no one would be there, and there weren't any people, were there?" asked Stryker.

"Only on the floors below," answered Amanda.

"So, chill," said Stryker. "We're probably in the clear."

"I can't work with probabilities, Stryker," answered Amanda bluntly.

"Well, you'll have to for now. Our room is still safe," he said. Lina, Ripley and Amanda all sat on the edge of their respective beds, talking to Stryker who still typed away.

"Gliese 581G is an Earth-like planet located seventeen light-years away in the constellation of Libra," said Amanda, who still looked pale-white. "Everything makes sense now."

"So you know what Oswald was talking about?" asked Lina. "That's why your face went pale! Tell us, Amanda!"

"It's obvious to me now," she answered with a serious tone. She looked forward but her eyes were unfocused: she stared into nothing as she came to terms with Oswald's true plan. "It was discovered in 2010. Back then, it attracted attention because it is near the middle of the habitable zone of its parent star. That means it could sustain liquid water on its surface and could potentially host life similar to that on Earth. Ever since then, everyone has known it to be among the greatest recognized potential planets for having life and, in 2017, its existence was confirmed. In 2019, we got confirmation that it is a rocky planet with liquid water, perfectly habitable and we only haven't confirmed life there because we haven't reached it yet. That's what the Orbit 2.0 is for. It's the fuel to reach it."

"They talked about how many subjects Oswald intended to transfer. Do they really mean... there?" asked Ripley.

"I think so," said Amanda. "Now, everything fits. All this time, he was only getting the energy that would allow him to warp there,"

"But it's a one-way trip, isn't it?" asked Lina. "Which people would he deem as worthy to go?"

"Don't you see it?" asked Amanda. "He talked about the "imminent self-destruction". He'll select whoever he wants to and he'll ship away to Gliese as he wreaks havoc on Earth and we stay here to die," she announced. "We have to stop him," Stryker backed away from the panel and sat down on his bed, befuddled.

"Therefore, the only module the Firm meddled with was the energy-harnessing one," said Lina. "The energy will enable him to time-warp successfully. They perfected it with small objects years ago and the technology is surely evolving quickly. Who knows in how many years he'll be able to turn this into reality?"

"It's his master plan," said Amanda. "And it's about to come to fruition. He's always aimed to be the man who'd achieve this. He won't hesitate to sacrifice anything to get it."

"And he'd give up all he's built for this?" asked Stryker.

"Wouldn't you? For all we know, all that he has created was just a means to get to this."

"Are we sure it's only a one-way trip? They talked about energy reduction. If he goes but then comes back, and he brings something, *anything*, *back* along with him, his empire would only continue to thrive. But what can *we* do, really?" asked Lina.

"We could expose him," suggested Ripley. "Figure out which attacks he's planning before he launches off and warn people before-hand. We can spin this in a way they'll be seen as terrorists."

"Yes, that works," said Amanda. "As long as we're inside this place, we have the means to find out what he meant by imminent self-destruction."

"And what about when the Europa crew lands back with the energy harnessed in the vessel?" asked Stryker. "Why don't we destroy it?"

"Because we *can't*. If we try to destroy something with that magnitude of energy we'll explode along with it," replied Amanda.

"But I can guarantee you that as soon as the crew lands, things in this place will go ballistic," said Stryker. "Because as soon as he has it in his hands, he'll want to speed the process along and surely will only focus his time towards achieving this goal."

"That's true," said Amanda. "We need to have this place *forever*, Stryker. How long do you think you can hold that hack?" asked Amanda.

"I wouldn't suggest us overriding the shaft programming *again*. But the camera feed is easier. Whenever we need some privacy, I can switch the visual feed that they get. Don't worry about that."

"It's too big and massive for us to figure this out quickly…" said Lina. "We need to sleep on it and by morning we'll think clearer,"

"I agree. As of now it's just been expanded to many other possibilities," said Amanda. "But it doesn't matter what his plans are if he's planned something much shorter for anyone who stays behind."

Chapter Twelve - Energy

Amanda, Lina, Stryker and Ripley rolled around in bed all night as they mapped in their minds every scenario to Oswald's faster-than-light travel. The Firm's facilities were dead silent during the night, as all workers slept - the departments were left alone. All you could hear were the winds of Iceland outside the glass dome and the beeping and processing of the panel's system. Amanda considered anything she deemed plausible to explain why her father would plan this.

Her memories of him would always depict a distant, mysterious and hard-working man. As much as she despised knowing his plans to break out violence and destruction on Earth also involved him shipping away from harm to a planet far, far away, she couldn't help but feel intrigued and curious about Gliese 581g. Amanda knew that even though Stryker and Ripley might be on the fence about this, Lina wouldn't be.

The sun rose and 9 a.m. approached - all four of them stretched reluctantly, fighting to wake up early and still adjusting to the schedule of The Firm. Amanda groaned Stryker's name, so he'd run to the panel and change the feed again so they could be free to start fresh and discuss anything that had come to their minds during the nighttime. After a few seconds, Stryker got out of his bed yawning and made his way to the central panel.

"You know what came to my mind late at night?" whispered Amanda.

"Hold on to that thought for a minute, will you..," asked Stryker with a raspy, throaty, early morning voice. Amanda understood it to mean he still wasn't finished overriding the feed and, as he signaled an okay with his hand, she explained:

"I know the time-warping is hard to figure out but, after Europa, Gliese was one of the next in line for humanity's search for life. It's always been up there with Europa on potential planets, Europa is just closer and easier. My father's always been greedy and ahead of his time. It would only make sense that his master plan would speed up this process,"

The group started their morning routine and, as each brushed their teeth and took showers in turns in the bathroom, some made their beds and ordered breakfast on the panel. Soon after it was delivered, most of them finished getting ready while eating, as they rushed towards the shaft. Now they knew what to search for, they couldn't wait to see what they'd find by playing the right cards in each department.

The shaft drifted down. Amanda tapped her foot anxiously as she waited to arrive at the Experiments department. Stryker looked at her incessantly, tapping her feet against the floor of the shaft and said:

"Hey, will you chill for a moment?"

"This shaft is taking too long. This is wrong. They should have dropped Ripley on Combat Training already," she said.

"Hey, relax, maybe it's just going down to leave you on Experiments first," replied Stryker.

The shaft continued to move for what seemed like a minute and the doors opened to reveal they had arrived at Oswald's office. Amanda breathed in as she felt her adrenaline levels rising. Stryker, realizing what was happening, switched between looking at the three women and Lina closed her eyes, sighing. Amanda put on a brave face and stepped out into Oswald's office, followed by Lina and then Ripley and Stryker.

"Hello," said Amanda. His office looked the same as before: except this time his chair was turned around facing the wall. He answered from behind it as they heard the thud of the shaft doors closing.

"There's a flaw in your plan, Amanda," said Oswald's voice. This time there wasn't a soft tone to it, instead he spoke with a deep, rough voice.

"I'm not sure I understand," answered Amanda.

Oswald's chair turned around and he glanced at all four. He tapped a button on the panel of his desk and every screen in the room lit up with footage from a security camera showing Lina and Amanda sitting down at the restricted level computers and Ripley near the spiral staircase, looking down.

"It astonishes me how after I clothed you, I fed you and welcomed you and your friends with open arms, only a week later you'd betray my trust. Have you got any idea how I received this news as I got here this morning? Do you know how last night a giant leap for humankind was taken and, as the world marveled at this accomplishment, you were breaking into...our restricted areas? Do you have any idea how much we can help Earth *evolve*? Why would you do this to me, Amanda?"

"We only wanted to find out more information about the spacecraft," she lied. "We found the module built here so fascinating. Your Orbit 2.0 is truly astonishing,"

"Did you? And how did you arrive at the restricted levels? You're willing to hack into our systems just to find out more? Why not come to me and ask, Amanda?" asked Oswald. He talked to her in a paternal tone, as if he was still speaking to a child. Lina couldn't be sure if he was doing it on purpose or out of genuine concern.

"We didn't hack anything," said Amanda. "There was a problem with the shaft and it just left us there."

"You see, you keep lying," said Oswald. "I am so disappointed in all of you. This is why I do what I do, so I shape my soldiers and it horrifies me that you'd come in here and in *one week* break this harmony of loyalty we thrive on. *Never* has an employee of mine broken into the restricted areas without permission. Ever!" he yelled, opening up his arms. "Arlo traced your actions on the computer and it seems you spent exactly six minutes listening to an audio file. Is there anything you'd like to ask me, then?" asked Oswald. "I see there is some frustration," he said, in a cruel tone. Lina looked at Stryker and Ripley, who were just as surprised as she was and had also noticed the change in his voice.

"Why the selection? What do you gain with this?" she asked.

Oswald gave an ambiguous smile to Amanda. Lina felt a sinister energy emanate from him, as his laugh turned from ambiguous to sinister as he shook his head in disbelief, looking at them with disgust on his face.

"In ten years, a selected few will experience the discovery of another Earth. That is the trip of a lifetime."

"But why destroy what you'll leave behind?" asked Amanda.

"Silly you," answered Oswald. He shook his head negatively again. "I won't touch the anthill. My issue is with the ants. What's being brought back by the Orbit 2.0 is harnessed radiation converted to energy - enough to successfully send a spacecraft seventeen light-years away and enough radiation to expose and contaminate the planet. Marine life will survive, and so will nature. As I told you, my problem is with the ants."

"That's *pitiful*," said Amanda. "You don't get to make that choice,"

Oswald raised his eyebrows and answered: "Oh, but yes, I'm afraid I do. I'm reaching my 70th, dear daughter. I've worked my entire life to achieve this and I deserve to spend my last decades enjoying what I have always intended for myself."

"Yet you're willing to sacrifice everything else to get it!"

"Not everything else. Only what I believe doesn't deserve to go on," said Oswald. The shaft doors opened and four guards came out, fully armed. "Which is why I'll be glad to have all of you with me on launch day to Gliese," he said, as the four men walked in their direction. Amanda, Lina, Stryker and Ripley backed away, reaching for the shaft they'd come in from, but it was welded shut. Oswald then went on: "But until then, I'm glad to introduce to you four... one of our most recent achievements. An incredible new chamber in the first of the restricted floors, capable of suspending the body's autonomic functions while maintaining the health of each individual cell during stasis."

"Stasis?" asked Amanda. "Is that what you're going to do with us? Answer me!" she screamed as the first Firm guard took a hold of her arms. The other three successfully grabbed Lina, Stryker and Ripley, while Oswald continued:

"You can relax, child. You'll remain alive and breathing."

"You're sick!" protested Amanda.

"You can't take us!" screamed Lina.

"Oh, Lina," said Oswald, finally looking at her. "How disappointed I am in you. Don't worry, in ten years you'll be up for your last day as you witness our launch," he said, then let out an arrogant laugh. The guards held a tight grip on their arms and walked towards the shaft they had just emerged from. All four tried to break free and reluctantly moved around trying to set themselves free from the guard's grip.

"If you hadn't meddled in the restricted levels, none of this would have been necessary, you see," said Oswald. "Enjoy."

"NO!" screamed Amanda as the guards took each of them into the shaft with them. "LET GO OF ME!" she screamed as she tried to kick the guard on the leg.

"Let go!" screamed Lina and Stryker as they were dragged into the shaft. The doors started to close and Ripley butted her head against the guard's and he loosed his grip. As soon as she'd freed herself and kicked him again, the shaft closed and started to move up.

Just a few seconds later, Amanda, Lina, Stryker and Ripley were led into a round chamber, considerably smaller when compared to other Firm departments. The walls had five seven-feet tall white porcelain pods attached vertically to each side, marked in black from A to J, and a central mainframe system on the center. Two men sat at the desk in front of it, typing away on the panel.

"Arlo, four for immediate!" yelled the man who held Ripley, bringing her out of the shaft.

"We got the order a minute ago!" said the man on the left, who typed on the panel. Amanda and Lina recognized him as Arlo.

"B, C, D, E are a go!" said the man by his side. Arlo turned around and walked towards the group. The respective pods opened up like coffins.

"NO!" screamed Amanda, still refusing to give in to the man's grip. Arlo picked up a white gun from his belt and shot Ripley in the chest with a tranquilizer.

"This should make it easier," said Arlo. He aimed at Stryker's chest and fired. As Ripley became drowsy, the guard dragged her towards the pod, where he proceeded to unstrap and position an increasingly sleepy Ripley inside.

"NO! Don't do it, Arlo!" screamed Amanda. Lina also tried to put up a mild struggle, but she was no match for the man's size. Stryker then also was taken to the pod next to Ripley as Arlo shot Lina and Amanda in one breath. Amanda looked at the small needle in her chest as she trembled with panic and rage.

As she saw Stryker close his eyes, she looked at Lina, who seemed to have made her peace with it and was looking apathetically at the floor. When she noticed Amanda was looking at her, she smiled peacefully and sighed. Amanda felt tears streaming down her face as the grip the man held on her arms seemed to go numb and her balance was affected.

She breathed in and out, trying to calm herself before fading out, and looked ahead as the man placed her in the pod and strapped her in. She then heard the entire system vibrate and a cold smoke poured from little openings that filled the entire pod's interior. Amanda felt cold as she continued to control her breathing and looked ahead to see the door close in. Her vision turned black from the edges, as the darkness grew into her central focus. She looked outside from a small rectangular window on the pod into the lab as the workers turned to the panel. She inhaled and exhaled one last time as the darkness reached the center of her line of vision.

Chapter Thirteen - //hypersleep

2042

2043

2044

2045

2046

2047

2048

2049

2050

Chapter Fourteen - 2051

Amanda's eyes popped open as she struggled to breathe in and out. Her pod's door was sliding open, and she saw a bald man sitting at the control panel. If she'd been asleep for ten years, the place surely remained intact. Soon she heard breathing to her right and figured Lina and the others were also awakening.

"Say nothing for a few minutes - it might damage your vocal chords. It is normal to feel you want to throw up," alerted the man in the control panel. Amanda identified him as an older-looking Peter. "It's not the day of, it's the day before."

Lina, Stryker and Ripley's pods slid open as well. All immediately opened and closed fists and turned their knees to each side, re-awakening and re-connecting with their bodies. Lina closed her eyes and tilted her head back as she regained her breathing.

"Apart from the questions that are racing through your mind at this moment, there isn't one which will appropriately answer everything that's changed while you were gone," said Peter. "Know the world is at war - which is the main reason why I'm overriding the system to get you out of here a day before."

Amanda cleared her throat and started asking back, in a raspy voice:

"I'm sorry, I could care less about my voice right now: you're here without clearance?" she asked.

"We all know about his plan," answered Peter. "Every Firm worker. You've got us on your side."

"You know about the exposure? Is he still planning it?" asked Amanda.

"His plans are intact and a go - the select few who know about the radiation are ready to self-destruct. He's molded us to oblige and as much as we don't feel any rage towards him, for some reason..," he said, hesitating. "A great deal of us are secretly refusing. I am only here through the combined work and efforts of a select group of us that are overriding the system while he's gone."

"It's good to know some people here have come to their senses," said Amanda. "Is Arlo with him?"

"Yes. The entire launch for the time-warping is on standby, fully ready. We have 24 hours to stop him," said Peter, getting up from his chair to undo the straps of the sleeping pods.

"Who's part of your group? Who's with us?" asked Amanda.

"Ironically, all of us are from the restricted areas. In some ways, working for a decade towards our demise gave birth to a sense of vindication within ourselves – during the entire process, we struggled, alone and together, to understand why we were there. Knowing we were working to achieve something that would be our demise brewed something within us that has resulted in my standing here, now, asking you. There has to be something we can do," answered Peter, as he successfully unstrapped Amanda.

"What happened with the Europa mission?" asked Lina.

"Oh. That was the start of everything," answered Peter as he unstrapped her. "Marine and microbiological forms of life confirmed, as predicted. But what should've dawned a newer, better conscience and understanding of humanity has truly been the gateway for the situation we are in today."

"What situation is that? What happened?" asked Lina, again, free from the pod and stretching herself alongside Amanda.

"Well, there are civil wars raging in every major city across the globe," he answered as he unstrapped Stryker, who still remained silent. "Many small religions have fallen - many have risen. But all around it generated conflict from an awakened mass who refused to accept that teachings from the world's major religious groups maybe weren't so true. That announcement fundamentally switched the way mankind perceived itself and its place in the universe - shook up every existing religion in the world, you could say," he explained as he unstrapped Ripley, who also listened intently. "Christians, Muslims, Hindus, Jews, Buddhists, Spiritists, you name it. There wasn't a single group unaffected by this discovery."

"What did that do to Oswald?" asked Amanda.

"He thrived on it. In fact, we handled over seventy operations in the last nine years, where we either worked as the supplier or the bridge between two groups in search of firearms and weapons. We also were responsible for supplying multiple chemical elements for terrorist groups planning nuclear attacks. Some happened. Some didn't. We watched him fuel the fire," he explained, looking at all four standing in front of them. "You must feel weak. Here, take these cocktails." He handed them four flasks with three pills in each, floating in shocking pink water. "Everything you need to take after a long period of hyper-sleeping." All four opened the flasks and drank the fluid.

"We don't have much time, though," said Peter. "We've been reuniting at your childhood home, Amanda. Ironically, it's always been unsecured and since we're restricted-level workers, we're not really missed during the night. We must go. It's not safe to stay here, overriding the systems and the audio and video feeds for so long. The entire Firm is on pins and needles about tomorrow and we don't want to draw any attention towards ourselves."

All four agreed with Peter as they recollected themselves from the drowsiness and absorbed the amount of information that had been thrown at them.

"Is everyone okay?" asked Amanda to Stryker, Ripley and Lina. All three nodded a Yes with their heads and Amanda asked, "Is everyone just as disoriented as I am?"

"That's a common side-effect after hypersleeping," answered Peter.

"Yeah, I feel like it's not dawned on me yet," said Stryker. "That it's been ten years."

"We must go," said Peter, making his way to the shaft. "You'll have a few minutes to wind down in the shaft. Just please walk here now because we're only truly free from risks when we're inside the house."

Amanda, Lina, Ripley and Stryker walked towards the shaft as they pulled through the numbness in their bodies. After all five had entered, the shaft doors closed and started moving down.

"I see not much has changed in a decade," said Amanda.

"There hasn't been time for any redesigning - ever since the Europa crew landed back, Oswald changed. The Firm's sole purpose became perfecting this machine. Which I understand is also an incredible accomplishment, but the radiation used to fuel it... ends us," said Peter.

He stared ahead without addressing any of the four. His expression had changed - he'd aged and seemed exhausted.

After a few moments, the shaft doors opened and they once again found themselves in the dark corridor that led to the outside door of Oswald's old lab. They walked past it in silence for what seemed like a minute until they found themselves in the open field between The Firm's entrance and Amanda's childhood home. It was a cold, star-filled evening and as they crossed the field, they saw a room in the house had the lights on. The house in itself hadn't changed much, and

Amanda felt strange, walking back to it decades later. After a minute, they got inside through the back door, landing in the kitchen, and immediately heard footsteps coming down the stairs. Amanda looked around the house, which still seemed cozy and welcoming, still with all the furniture, dusty but intact.

"You got it! I'm so glad you did it!" said a familiar voice. Lina then recognized him as Carlos. Sarah came after him and three other men and women, whose names they didn't know yet, also emerged in the kitchen.

"I thought you weren't on the restricted levels," said Amanda.

"Oh, both Carlos and Sarah were transferred a while after the Europa crew landed back safely," answered Peter. "These are Josh, Sam and Lucy," he introduced the other three.

"Okay, so now that we're here, what can we do?" asked Amanda.

"Well, there is a reason why we brought you out," said Carlos. "But you may not be too happy with it."

"First of all, we should move into the living room. It's far more spacious for us to discuss this," suggested Sarah. They obliged and made their way to the next room. As she walked around, Amanda was astonished, finding everything to be in the same spot as she'd remembered. Her home truly hadn't been touched and the timeless quality it now had felt comforting to her. They all sat around on the couches and Lina asked:

"Please tell us what your idea was." Sarah, Carlos, Josh, Sam, Lucy and Peter looked at each other, as if waiting for one to step up and announce something.

"The entire operation is on standby, and we're a crucial part of the restricted areas," began Sarah. "Together, we can hijack the operation."

"Tonight," added Carlos. This time, it was Lina, Stryker, Amanda and Ripley's turn to stare at each other, confused. Amanda then asked:

"What do you mean exactly by hijacking?"

"Well," said Sarah. "Oswald would only expose the world to the radiation as the craft warped. But that's a control programmed by us. The only way to stop him is if the four of you warp to Gliese tonight," said Sarah.

"You'll leave him behind on Earth and he won't pull the trigger if he's here," added Carlos.

"We can have the entire operation up and running during the late hours of tonight, before dawn. With the radiation unused, through Orbit we can convert it to energy, enabling us to program the spacecraft to warp back one hundred hours exactly after it reaches Gliese. We can get you there and back," said Peter.

"It's the only way to use the extra energy for good," explained Sarah. Amanda, Lina, Stryker and Ripley looked at the six Firm employees flabbergasted.

"I understand it might be too much to take in after you've awoken from a decade in hibernation," said Sarah. "But what may seem extreme and sudden to you is, in fact, a plan we've had in the works for a decade. Peter got you out of the pods tonight because of it. Please."

"What about my father?" asked Amanda. "He'll end you as soon as he lands here tomorrow morning!"

"We are aware of the consequences that will be thrown at us," said Sarah. "but we'd rather blame it on a malfunction of the system than face certain death as we pull the trigger when he warps. Since the spacecraft is sealed and built to stand extreme levels of radiation, he strictly demanded that the exposure take place as the craft loads. It's his insurance, in a way. Because of the massive amounts of energy required to fuel this, the entire Firm's power will certainly go out as soon as the craft launches. That is why if he's here for the launch, we'll have no choice but to pull all triggers - and then we can't really even hide from anything," he sighed. "We will have answers for anything you need to know. Like I said, this has been over ten years in the making. "

"You have absolutely nothing to lose. The spacecraft's programming cannot be changed - you will warp back exactly 100 hours after you land," assured Peter.

Amanda and Lina looked at each other and immediately smiled as their eyes locked. To them, it was already a done deal - it would only take some more time to convince Stryker and Ripley.

"We're in," announced Lina, nudging Amanda's shoulder. "You had me at hijacking," she then looked at Stryker and Ripley, who as expected had their eyes bulging out of their skulls as they stared at Lina.

"What are you talking about?" said Stryker. "I will not be the first person to be warped seventeen light-years away from here!"

"In all fairness" interrupted Peter. "Over the last twelve years, we've run countless experiments and tests on this. You will safely warp away: that I can guarantee. You may not land as smoothly as you'd like - but you *will* get there."

"I see it as the opportunity of a lifetime" said Lina. "And we get to ruin Oswald's plan. Isn't that what we were aiming for all along?" asked Lina.

"Yes, but not on these terms! Can we survive for a hundred hours in an alien environment?" asked Stryker. "As inhabitable as it is, listen to yourselves!"

Ripley nodded her head in agreement with everything Stryker pointed out.

"Yes, this is overwhelming to me, as well. Who would pilot the ship, for instance?" asked Ripley.

"I'm perfectly prepared to do it" said Sam, who still hadn't spoken. "I'm the only one from our field that will travel with you."

Sam was a scrawny-looking man in his mid-30's, with puppy eyes and young features.

"I'm sorry, I'm not sure I know you enough to completely throw my life into your hands," said Stryker.

"Stryker, what the fuck did we discuss during our sessions?" said Amanda. "The two of you can stay behind if you want. Lina, Sam and I are going,"

Sam then got up from the couch and picked up a large black board and placed it on the table. He turned it on by clicking a button on one end, revealing it to be a TV screen. It lit up, emanating light from the center and in a split second, it projected a three-dimensional hologram of a miniature version of the spaceship in front of them. They looked at the design of the craft, which looked like a big zeppelin attached to a large ring that encircled it.

"This is the ship," pointed Peter. "You can see that it doesn't look very similar to what you'd expect. It's entirely built to get you there safely, not to look impressive. Oswald was very, very strict about this."

"The ship itself floats in a "bubble" of normal space-time that will float along the wave of compressed space-time, the way a surfer rides a break," explained Josh, who had been silent up until now. "The ship, inside the warp bubble, will go faster than the speed of light relative to objects outside the bubble. The drive works by using a wave to compress the space-time in front of the spaceship while expanding the space-time behind it,"

"What will we eat? How would we even survive for four days and four hours?" asked Stryker.

"Oh wow, impressive math, Stryker," Amanda cut him off, sarcastically.

"There's an entire module inside the ship designed for comfort, closets with changes of clothes, your beds and enough food to sustain you for more than a week. You obviously don't have to worry about that," answered Josh. "Sam will control the heating, so even if you land in a freezing landscape, you'll still be safe inside the ship. It's the perfect small home, designed to travel light years in deep space."

"Think about it from a different point of view, Stryker" said Amanda. "Ever since I knew what his true plans were, I've had the urge and desire to go to Gliese, as well. If it's possible, then obviously I want to do it! And we are certainly far more worthy of discovering it than my father and his team are,"

"You can *assure* us we'll be back in exactly one hundred hours?" asked Lina.

"We wouldn't have risked ourselves by taking you out of hyper-sleep if we couldn't," explained Sarah. "That's the part we're looking forward to the most because we get to use the energy he'd be using to destroy humanity to bring you back - you can even bring anything from Gliese you want with you, as long as it's in the ship. Please consider it. It's the chance of a lifetime."

"It would be if this wasn't Oswald Rose's lovechild," said Stryker. "But it is obviously the right thing to do," he continued, looking at Ripley. He held her hand and then said, looking up: "We're in."

"Can we override the panels in the restricted areas again?" asked Amanda. "There shouldn't be any evidence that we ever went."

"Yes, we'll do it quietly through the night. We'll strike when no one expects and we'll leave the scene untouched and untraceable," said Peter. "Any other option assures our demise, so we can't take any chances there. Oswald's plane is set to land back in Keflavik at 7. He'll be flying, on his way here, as we do it,"

"It won't take long, though - as we said, all systems are on standby. We just need the four of you to be as prepared as you can," alerted Sarah.

"We've been preparing to act ever since we joined this place," said Amanda. "And that monster silenced us for a decade. I'll be glad to finally fire my shot against him."

"But what about when we come back? Close to five days from now we'll be back and Peter mentioned Earth's changed in the last ten years," said Lina. "We'll come back and start hiding from Oswald forever? He will come after us. We're about to ruin his master plan,"

All ten remained in silence for a few moments. Amanda then answered: "But if we don't do this, there won't be a next week, even. This is our only option of delaying the damage. If what he wants is for us to come back, then we have to come back with something that makes us untouchable. If we bring back something with us, it'll be of enough value for him to come to us without ordering his men to kill on sight,"

"How much did it change, exactly?" asked Lina. "What happened in the last ten years?"

"Well, he fueled the fire" said Peter. "As the first protests and strikes erupted reacting to the confirmation of marine life in Europa, we noticed an increasing amount of activity in Combat Training and Programming as Oswald began creating operations designed to frame certain groups... leaders of demonstrations and high-profile political targets as he planned hits for hire," he explained.

"Because he could act invisibly, he framed each of three major hits on the opposite party. The first target was the leader of a liberal activist group which was blossoming in the United Kingdom shortly after the Europa announcement. His death was framed as caused by a religious conservative group, so, obviously, chaos broke out."

"Now, however," Sarah cut Peter off, explaining, "that was a low-profile target compared to what would come next. So, no-one really spoke out or pieced together how he was, in fact, playing dominoes. As the protests in the United Kingdom turned to war, he heightened the situation by mass-manufacturing firearms and weaponry and making them easily accessible, turning protests and demonstrations into domestic terrorism."

"Some people used it for the wrong purposes," continued Peter, "not that there was ever a good one, I think. Six years ago, the second and third strikes were almost simultaneous, when he intricately planned the Vatican bombings, which was seen as the liberals' payback attack. The Vatican bombing didn't kill the Pope, who wasn't there at the time, but blew up an entire wing and murdered the Camerlengo."

"That was enough to start war in Europe" said Sarah. "And the third strike followed the day after as we handled the hijacking of a London plane headed to New York City. The world watched in terror as the plane was re-routed and crashed through the United Nations headquarters. Europe and Asia united to fight against the Americas as we watched the start of World War III."

As soon as Sarah finished her sentence, there was silence for a split second in the room. The explosive sound of shattering glass and a loud thud that shook the entire home shattered the silence. Every piece of furniture or object jumped as the glass shattered and all ten covered their ears and faces as fast as they could. After the explosion, they heard the engines and beating rotors of helicopters above, as each shone a bright spotlight that rotated around the dark room, searching for faces.

"They're onto us!" screamed Peter. "Let's use the shaft!"

"There's a shaft here?" screamed Amanda, over the sound of the helicopters. As soon as she'd asked the question, all six workers were already on their way out of the room, heading for the door on the stairs that led to the basement. A robotic voice Amanda was so familiar with then echoed all over the woods, alarming in a grating tone:

"COME OUT OF THE HOUSE! ALL TEN OF YOU ARE ORDERED TO SURRENDER NOW!"

As she saw Sarah and Peter open the door by the stairs, Amanda, Lina, Stryker and Ripley rushed to it as fast as they could. They ran down the stairs on their way to the basement of the house, except at the end of the stairs now stood a metal door. Sam opened it and soon all ten squeezed themselves inside a shaft.

"You've built a shaft here?" screamed Amanda. The sound of the helicopters seemed slightly distant, one level down.

"There's always been a shaft here. It was the only thing Oswald altered in the house," answered Peter, coming in last and closing the door. The sound of the helicopters faded completely away. "We've programmed it to take us straight to the restricted areas. Once we're in, we'll use the enhanced security system to lock ourselves in for as long as we can."

"We can override the systems in fifteen minutes, but the entire engine takes some time to load," said Sarah. The shaft then started moving and Stryker asked:

"How did they find out about us? This fast?"

"Someone must have been alerted by something or noticed you were gone," said Sam.

"My father hasn't landed back in Iceland yet, though, has he?" said Amanda. "That's our only advantage, then, if we're safe inside the restricted areas,"

"You must dress yourselves in the suits designed for the passengers as soon as the doors open. Don't worry about safety, we'll take care of sealing ourselves from them," alerted Sarah.

The shaft came to a halt after a few moments and immediately Peter placed his hand on the door, ready to push it open as soon as it unlocked. A few seconds later, all ten found themselves on the first floor of the restricted area. This level was undeniably larger than the third and fourth, which Lina, Ripley and Amanda had accessed. Stepping onto a round platform, immediately Lina, Amanda, Stryker and Ripley noticed a gigantic grey hole in the center of the room. The spacecraft they had just seen miniaturized was there, with the silver circle attached to the zeppelin horizontally instead of vertically. The platform circled the entire hole and on its far end led to a tech station with a spiral staircase in the middle, accessing the second level.

Sarah, Carlos, Peter, Josh and Lucy immediately ran to the staircase, while Sam stood behind with Lina, Stryker, Ripley and Amanda.

"This is it" said Sam, as they lingered for a while, amazed by the spacecraft in the room. Sarah, Carlos, Peter and Josh sat down on the control panel on the tech station, right next to the staircase, as Lucy made her way up.

"It's the size of a submarine," said Amanda. The entire spacecraft was porcelain-white and the central door had the shape of the Firm's inverted triangle.

"Lock systems are on!" yelled Peter from the control panel. "Go get dressed, now!"

Sam looked at the four and said: "Come on, it's on the next level up," All five then made their way to the spiral staircase to access the second level. Once inside it, Sam led them to a glass chamber which included an infinite number of suits stacked up to the ceiling. There was a big metal door at the end of the room which all four assumed led to another part of the restricted rooms. The white suits seemed like standard spacesuits at first, but as Amanda unfolded hers, she noticed it was much lighter than expected, as was the helmet. All five got dressed and Sam added:

"We're safe inside here for now. Reach the third button down on your chest when you've worn it so you can power it," After a couple of minutes, they made their way to the stairs and heard loud thuds coming from the metal door.

"OPEN THE DOORS! NOW" said Arlo's voice from behind the metal doors. He banged a couple of times first, aggressively, and then a louder final thud as he fired a shot against the metal doors. Lucy, who had been sitting on a computer close to the metal doors, jumped in fright. All five rushed down the staircase and Amanda warned the other five, who were frantically typing on the control panel:

"Arlo and possibly many other men are already on the metal door upstairs!"

"What's the system loading percentage, Sarah?" asked Sam.

"We're at 70%, but the ship is still loading," she answered. "Go and board already!" she said, pressing a different button on the panel. The entire room was already vibrating with the loading engines on the ship, and a high-pitched sound came from below as they watched a metal bridge come out from the platform, connecting to the tip of the inverted triangle of the ship. The triangle then lit up in a light-blue light and slid open, touching the tip of the bridge.

"Let's go in!" said Sam, proceeding to the bridge.

"This is it," said Amanda. She could feel her heart beating out of her chest in awe, excitement, and adrenaline.

She looked at Lina, who had the same psychotic look on her face, since it was obvious all the wheels in her mind were spinning out of control with feelings and emotions. Lina smiled at her and answered back, "This is it," They then made their way to the ship, following Sam. Stryker and Ripley still hadn't moved from the place they had been standing. As they watched everyone type, click and discuss on the panel, he looked at Ripley and said:

"There's a part of me that wishes I was just sitting there like them, loading the system, helping out. I don't know if I can do this, Ripley."

"Look at me, Stryker. We can do this. You said it yourself. We'll do it because it's the right thing to do," She held his hands and looked deep into his eyes through their helmets. A loud thud came from upstairs and soon after, the sound of multiple gunshots.

"Lucy!" screamed Peter from the control panel, looking up at the spiral staircase. As he did it, Lucy's bloody body was thrown down the stairs, dead. She fell three steps next to Stryker and Ripley, who screamed in panic. All five Firm workers who typed at the panel looked at Lucy's body, lingered for a few seconds and immediately went back to typing, without expressing much emotion. Even Peter, who had screamed her name in tension, now went back to the panel, expressing no other reaction.

"100%!" screamed Sarah. "Go, Stryker, go, Ripley!"

"The craft will warp in two minutes!" screamed Peter.

Stryker and Ripley ran to Amanda, Lina, and Sam's side, who had also halted their way to the craft as they stared at Lucy's cold, dead body on the floor. Amanda and Lina knew that if they'd gotten to Lucy, it was because the metal doors had been opened, and as she connected the dots, she saw Arlo's feet emerging from the second level, slowly making his way down the stairs. She immediately turned around, grasping Lina's arm, and made her way across the bridge. Sam followed close behind, and Stryker and Ripley started to run in their direction, too. As soon as she reached the spacecraft's door and stepped on the inverted triangle, Amanda heard a gunshot and looked back as she heard Stryker's voice scream: "NO!" As she turned around, she heard another gunshot.

Arlo, who was now halfway down the stairs, had shot Ripley in the chest twice. Ripley fell to the floor, and Stryker held her in his arms, screaming her name.

"RIPLEY!" he screamed.

"Get in the craft! One minute!" screamed Peter from the control panel. Arlo then fired a shot in the panel and more men fully armed come down the stairs, following Arlo. Peter looked at Arlo and, as he turned around, Arlo reached the end of the stairs, raised his right arm and fired a shot in the center of Peter's forehead. Peter fell down to the floor, dead.

"We're ready to launch!" screamed Sarah and Amanda looked down to see the triangle's door closing, inclining her body back. Sam immediately entered the ship, followed by Lina, and Amanda looked at Stryker and screamed his name:

"COME, NOW!"

Stryker looked at Amanda and then at Ripley, who he still held in his arms. He let her go as he looked at Arlo to see him firing a shot at Sarah and an increasing number of armed men coming down the stairs. Stryker ran to Amanda's side, crossing the bridge and looking down at the grey hole below them. The entire circle beneath them was now filled in a blue, smokey light that seemed to be generated from the core of the spacecraft. Stryker crossed the bridge as fast as he could, as he heard multiple gunshots being fired at him.

Amanda reached her hand out for Stryker to hold, and he jumped over the inclining door, grasping Amanda with one arm as they fell inside the spacecraft. Amanda got up from the floor as she continued to hear gunshots being fired and looked through one window inside the ship to see Carlos and Josh shooting at Arlo and his men in the panel. Arlo fired a shot in Josh's chest and Carlos hit a button on the panel and then looked at the ship. His eyes and Amanda's locked for one second and he nodded his head to her, confirming their job had been completed. Arlo then fired a shot in his head and he fell to the ground.

Amanda heard the doors of the spaceship shut beside her and lost her balance as she felt the floors vibrate. She turned around to take her first look inside the spacecraft. She found herself in a small but wide white room. Lina, Stryker and Sam also had their arms stretched open, trying to maintain their balance. The walls had a row of twenty chairs attached to them and there was an opening at each end to the other rooms. Immediately, they made their way to the chairs and sat down, attaching a metal safety lock to their chest to hold them in. The structure continued to vibrate and the circle that enclosed the craft started spinning around it. Every two seconds, they would see the metal ring sliding down from the windows with increasing speed.

"Sam" called Amanda, staring ahead. She was shaking uncontrollably, and so were Lina and Stryker. "Can Arlo stop the system?"

"I wouldn't worry about Arlo," said Sam. "There's nothing he'll be able to do. And there's no turning back for us now,"

All four held a tight grip on the arms of their seats as they felt the entire structure's vibration increase exponentially. With no time to process what had happened in the last ten minutes, they exchanged glances for reassurance and tried to remain calm.

Then, from below came the deafening sound of what seemed like a gigantic trumpet and the blue, smoky light that

Stryker and Amanda had spotted brewing in the hole beneath them came up over the windows of the craft, covering them. Amanda's heart thumped as she locked eyes with Lina, feeling as if the spacecraft was plunging into an endless abyss. Both girls gripped the handles of their seats tightly and screamed as loud as they could, staring at each other in panic. They could feel the entire zeppelin dropping at an increasing speed as whatever seemed to stand below them wasn't there anymore. Amanda's insides froze as a deep chill spread through her chest and her heart pounded harder and harder, thudding against her chest. At any second, they could be extinguished from the face of the universe and be forever forgotten in this abyss. Was it working? Were they travelling at a speed faster than light? When would they stop dropping?

Sam remained silent by her side, staring ahead as the ship dropped. Outside, all they could see through the windows was the endless blue smoke, which now seemed like vertical chopsticks in all shades of blue racing each other. Sam then reached for a button on the end of his arm chair and pressed it. His seat immediately turned around and he was gone from sight.

"What? Sam?"

"Press the button!" said Sam from behind them.

Amanda, Stryker and Lina reached for the button on the arm of their seats. They pressed it and felt the seat turning around 180 degrees, leading them into an oval room with a control panel and a porcelain screen for each, a few centimeters away from their seats. Sam's screen was already lit up and a million logs loaded on it. He turned around and said:

"We're halfway there. I'll pilot it as soon as we leave the warp,"

"You should've told us it was this big of a drop!" yelled Amanda. After dropping for more than a minute, the sensation itself became familiar. From inside, they remained intact, merely reacting to the vibrations and movements of the ship. However, there was an immense pressure pushing them down, which seemed to stick them tied to their seats as no one would dare to make any sudden movements.

Amanda and Lina closed their eyes, wishing for it to end as soon as possible, as Sam typed away on the panel, apparently unaffected by the steep fall. Then, the pressure came to a screeching halt - and there was silence for two seconds. Stryker, Lina and Amanda opened their eyes immediately. You could hear a pin-drop in the room as only the erratic, panicked breathing of Amanda, Stryker and Lina filled the room.

"Are we dead?" asked Stryker.

"Get the button. Let's check the windows," whispered Lina. All three pressed their buttons and their seats turned around. For a split second, they noticed the windows weren't filled with blue, but white smoke. As soon as the seats were back in position and they focused on the white, the spacecraft plummeted once again. Lina, Stryker and Amanda screamed in shock and panic, and Sam yelled from the opposite row:

"I can't get the propulsions to work!"

"What does that mean?" screamed Amanda.

"We're out of the warp, but we're falling!" yelled Sam.

"SAM!" screamed Amanda.

"DO SOMETHING!" screamed Lina. The craft was being pulled down to the ground more aggressively, causing panic as it often jolted to the left or right because of the high pressure from the thrusts.

"I can't do it! It's completely broken!" yelled Sam.

The ship continued to plummet and then collapsed against the ground. It penetrated the ground, as they'd collapsed against something but hadn't stopped moving - and then all four realized they had landed in water. The windows now changed to a greener blue and immediately they knew they were sinking in an ocean. Amanda, Stryker and Lina hit the buttons and turned around again. Amanda immediately addressed Sam:

"We're sinking!"

"Yes, we are," said Sam. A loud thud came, and the ship came to an immediate halt.

"Are we at the bottom?" asked Amanda.

"Hopefully we haven't landed somewhere very deep." said Lina.

"We've successfully arrived at our destination!" said Sam, smiling. Amanda frowned her eyebrows and asked:

"Successfully? We've sunk to the bottom of the ocean!"

"Yes," said Sam, "but I can get us to float."

All three heard the good news and breathed a sigh of relief. Amanda turned around to look at Stryker and saw his eyes filling with tears as he stared emptily ahead. Amanda reached for his left hand and held it.

"Hey," she said. Stryker gazed at her as the first tear fell from his water-filled eyes.

"We're here."

"Yeah, but Ripley's not,"

Amanda looked deep into Stryker's eyes and gave him a half-smile. "We'll make 'em pay." She said, gripping his hand tighter. Stryker smiled back and slightly nodded his head forwards. Sam continued to type frantically on his control panel. Lina turned to him and asked:

"Can I... walk around the ship now?" asked Lina. "When can you get us to float?"

"Yes, by all means," said Sam, without taking his eyes off the screen. "I'm working on it."

Lina undid her safety locks and stood up on the floor of the craft. She walked around the oval room opposite to the one they'd launched on. There were no windows on this side of the ship, but ten double-bunked beds attached along the wall. In the center of the room, there was a spiral staircase very similar to the ones from the Firm that led to the lower level.

"Lina, seeing that we're deep in the ocean, will you search for an opening close to the last row of beds?" asked Sam. "You'll see what I mean there."

Lina looked around the spaceship and saw that between the last row of beds and the mobile wall that held the seats, there was a large handle pointed down. She walked over it and pulled it to reveal a glass window the size of Lina's body.

"Oh my God," said Lina, as she immediately stared at the sight in front of her. She could see they had crashed just on the edge of a big, rainbow-colored coral reef that overlooked a large fence on the ocean. Below them there was a horizon of the whitest sand she'd ever seen and above her, the greenest, most transparent water she could think of. But what amazed her the most was the infinity of colors and species she immediately saw in front of her, circling the craft. Lina observed an array of dozens of small and medium-sized fish congregating in front of her, showcasing their diverse shapes and colors, which led her to realize she had arrived in a thriving and dynamic ecosystem. They seemed indistinguishable from the marine life she'd known on Earth. She raised her hand to touch the glass as she saw one particular group of green fish, seeming to head in her direction, but they dove away as soon as they spotted her. She then looked to her left to see an odd-looking anemone swimming close by, as each time she moved, an inner green glow seemed to shine in her core. Lina felt hypnotized, staring as the glow turned on and off, and her attention quickly shifted to focus on another group of sea creatures next to her. On the ground of the coral reef, there were a couple of transparent, silicon-like starfish trying to float from the sand. Lina kneeled down to look at them closely.

"You should see this immediately," said Lina. "I feel like I've opened a window to a dream," Amanda stretched herself as she got up from her seat, and Stryker undid his safety locks as well. Sam typed on the computer and asked:

"Is it everything you hoped it would be, Lina?"

"It's... incredibly Earth-like," she answered.

"Why wouldn't it be?" asked Sam. Lina remained silent, staring at the ocean wildlife in front of her. She then looked at the fence in front of them, which seemed to lead to a ten-foot drop.

"You have to be really careful once we float because we're just on the edge of a big drop here, Sam," warned Lina.

"This is incredible," said Amanda, approaching Lina and touching the glass. "What's the water temperature outside, Sam?"

"5°C. Perfect conditions for life to blossom,"

"Can you believe what we'll find here?" said Amanda. "Do you have any idea how much of a step forward for mankind this is?"

"What exactly did they come back with on the Europa expedition, Sam?" asked Lina. "If our alibi is to extract something of value to bring back, we should know how much we can improve upon that expedition."

"Yes, you see, but the thing is, the world doesn't know we're here, do they?" said Stryker, breaking his silence. "How will we get them to believe us?"

"We'll figure something out," said Amanda, reassuringly. Her blue eyes seemed to light up to an even brighter color as she gazed at the endless green ocean in front of her. "We should get to shore before thinking about collecting anything."

"Speaking of that... " said Sam, "here we go." The ship shook one more time on the ground of the coral reef and a few species that were closer to the glass window immediately reacted and swam away. Then Amanda and Lina saw white smoke rising from below and the ship rose.

"You may wanna sit down for this," warned Sam. The ship jolted up and Amanda and Lina fell to the floor.

"A little late on the heads up, Sam!" said Amanda lying down on the floor. The ship continued to rise and then halted as they reached the surface. Looking through the window, they saw a third of it was still filled with water but the other two-thirds showcased a beautiful sunset sky which shone in shades of orange and pink. Amanda and Lina looked at the open sky and instantly had any remaining suspicions about their location put to rest. In the center of the fading afternoon sky, there was a gigantic blue planet in a neighboring orbit, with four thick white rings encircling it.

"That's Gliese 581D. It seems when we look east, we can see C, as well," said Sam. "We're just near the shore, hang on." The ship then moved again, this time to the side.

Stryker approached Lina and Amanda, who were sitting down on the floor and sat down next to them to stare at the open sky as Sam drove the ship to the shore. For a couple of minutes, all three remained silently staring at the neighboring planet in front of them. They couldn't express their feelings, so they wordlessly agreed to find amusement at the moment while they calmed down and reminisced about home. As they thought about Ripley, they coped with their grief in their own ways.

The ship stopped and Sam announced: "We've reached the shore."

Lina, Amanda, and Stryker sat in their chairs and pressed the buttons, turning around. They now faced the triangle door and looked through the little windows into where they had arrived.

"What's the reading on the atmosphere, Sam?" asked Amanda.

"It's 11°C outside, air is 75.09% nitrogen, 25.95% oxygen, 0.83% argon, 0.039% and a reading which barely scratches the surface to register carbon dioxide, almost null. This is very, very similar to Earth. This is unbelievable," said Sam, staring at the panel.

"We don't need the suits then, do we? What about the gravity?" asked Amanda.

"No, you don't. 8.80 m/s^2. Slightly lighter to walk on than on Earth," answered Sam. "I am shocked by these readings. I can't believe I'm finally staring at these stats," said Sam, excited. "Can you believe it? We're really on a Super-Earth!"

Amanda looked between the small windows and saw they'd landed on the shore of a seemingly deserted beach. Close to them, she saw the sand led to dozens of massive trees similar to palms, which served as the entrance to a deeper forest behind them. To their right, the beach seemed to continue, but she wasn't able to tell exactly where it led from inside the craft.

"What do we do? Do we go out?" asked Lina.

"There doesn't seem to be anyone out there," said Amanda.

"We need to be able to defend ourselves somehow," said Stryker.

"Defend ourselves against what?" asked Lina. "I'm not going out fully armed."

"Look, after all I've been through today I don't feel like this is the hardest of challenges" said Amanda. "I'll go out, then."

"I'll go with you," said Lina.

"You're both going out unarmed? That's insane!" said Stryker.

"Look, if we see anything suspicious we'll come back immediately," said Amanda. "Sam, breach the door."

Sam looked at Amanda for a second and then looked back at his panel, clicking open the entrance door. The triangle again lit up and slid down. Amanda and Lina walked towards it and both women removed their helmets before stepping out. Amanda breathed in the smell of the unknown land in front of her as she stepped down to touch the sand. Lina followed closely behind and then jumped from the ship's door to the shore.

"It does feel slightly lighter to move," said Amanda.

"The air is as clear as a summer breeze," said Lina. "I can't believe we're here," she said, as both girls looked around to get a full view of the sight in front of them.

Amanda and Lina stared in wonder at the alien beach in front of them, as they listened to the sound of each wave crashing. The ocean seemed endless as they looked ahead into the fading, orange sky, bathed by the greenest ocean they'd ever seen. The neighboring planet seemed gigantic compared to the Moon, as if at any moment they would collapse into one - but there was no concern in the air, nor any preoccupation. There didn't seem to be any living souls or presences near them, although they could hear the chirping of what sounded like birds nearby - Lina and Amanda felt the wind blow through their hair and closed their eyes to take in the moment, filling themselves with pride and accomplishment for having succeeded in such a life-threatening situation. Any previous danger or anger seemed inaccessible and unimportant at that moment - what stood in front of them would only be cherished by their eyes, so Lina and Amanda happily obliged.

When Lina opened hers, she looked at the far distance and saw something she couldn't have seen from inside the ship: at the edge of the beach, there seemed to be a sort of construction above the water. Resembling a small island, she saw small pillars on top of it and noticed the place seemed to be accessed through a sandbank.

"Do you see that, Amanda?" asked Lina, pointing to the horizon. "At the far end of the beach, it seems to go on, doesn't it?"

"You're right - it does," said Amanda, focusing on the place Lina pointed to. "There are a dozen columns there! Hurry, we have to show this to Sam and Stryker now!"

Chapter Fifteen - Gliese

Amanda and Lina went back inside the ship and immediately warned Stryker and Sam about the pillars placed at the end of the beach. Knowing someone had built and placed those columns there was already a breakthrough which demanded instant preparation and regrouping. All four then walked towards them, but Stryker and Sam remained fully armed under their suits. They walked for what seemed like twenty minutes until the columns became clearer as they approached them. There really was a sandbank leading up to this floating platform, and as soon as Lina had her hunch confirmed, she picked up her pace. Once she got closer, it became apparent that, indeed, it was a construction on an oval island, ringed by light-gray stone pillars. In the center of the island, there was a smaller column with something colorful engraved on it.

"It looks like there's really something in the middle!" warned Lina, walking ahead of the other three. "Maybe a map engraved on the stone?" she guessed, walking as fast as she could. She reached the sandbank and, as she rushed towards the platform, the group heard running water.

They looked up to see water pouring from the top of each column. In a matter of a few seconds, a few drops increased to shape an entire wall of water behind the pillars, as if they'd just ignited a switch to turn on a waterfall.

From the water, Lina, Amanda, Stryker and Sam then flinched as they saw creatures emerging from the edge of the sea, gripping onto the platform. At first, all they saw were slimy, gray arms until the creatures' heads emerged, and they noticed long, silky, wet, blonde hair shining in the sunset sky. The four individuals stood still and observed the resemblance between those creatures and their own human physique, with heads leading into shoulders and torso - one emerging next to each pillar.

Lina and Amanda heard Stryker and Sam reach for their guns, but as the creatures resurfaced, Amanda put her arm out to block them as she observed the sight. They had their eyes closed and were naked, with only their hair covering almost the entirety of their bodies. Apart from the gray coloring of their skin, Amanda and Lina hadn't noticed anything exceptionally alien about these apparent water-nymphs' bodies. However, once all of them opened their eyes, they stopped fearing whatever harm could come from this situation. The beings had big, golden, bulging eyes, two or three times as big as a human's.

Lina stared deeply into their eyes as the two groups remained in silence, standing a few meters away from one another. And then Lina stepped forward.

"Lina, don't!" whispered Stryker.

The nymph who stood the closest to Lina also stepped forward. Stryker, Amanda, Sam and Lina looked at it in awe and the nymph approached with another step. Lina closed her eyes and breathed in, then stepped forward as well.

Listening only to the sound of the waterfall in front of her and concentrating on the landscape they found themselves in, Lina walked fearlessly towards the unknown being. Once she stood only two feet away from it, she inched her hand to touch his. The creature stared with its golden, bulging eyes deep into Lina's, then at her hand. She noticed standing close their skin seemed silky and smooth – these beings had a certain glow and ethereal energy emanating from them that reminded Lina of fairy tales from childhood, where she'd heard about mermen, elves and magical creatures. For some reason, she didn't fear any of this. Seeming to comprehend and understand Lina's pure intentions, the being reached out his gray hand and touched hers.

A soothing, lyrical female voice spoke to her in her mind.

"Welcome, Earth."

Lina's eyes widened as she heard the woman communicating through her by touching her hand. She smiled at it and asked:

"Who are you?"

"We are the *Andromedae*. We fly below the waters."

"How can you speak my language?"

"*Soon you will understand*. This is one way we can speak."

"We are visitors that mean no harm. We cannot return home anymore."

"You must journey to *Eternae*, through *Anyara*. The stellar door. You are not here by coincidence, for there is no coincidence in the universe - only the inevitable."

Lina looked at the nymph, confused.

"Do you have a name? I am Lina. What are we here for?"

"Uyara. You are here to learn. This has been planned since the Beginning."

"What can we find on *Eternae*?"

"We shall help you to reach your destination. You will need to swim with us."

"What is the stellar door?"

"It is a doorway present in every world in the universe – but its discovery hasn't dawned on Earth yet. Soon it will - it is part of why you are here."

Lina blinked a few times, attempting to take in everything Uyara said. She looked back at Amanda, Stryker and Sam for a split second to see them staring at her, flabbergasted.

"We're all hearing it, Lina," said Amanda. Sam and Stryker had an expression of utter confusion on their faces.

"But how can we?" asked Sam. "How can this be?"

"This goes against...everything we've studied or known," whispered Stryker, but Lina noticed the nymphs could understand him.

"You will *soon understand* more about conscience," answered Uyara, and Lina understood all beings present in that place were listening to their communication.

All five nymphs behind Uyara then walked towards her and Lina. Amanda reacted to this, making her way towards Lina as well. Soon after, Stryker and Sam followed her.

"May we cry with you?" asked Uyara to all of them. No one answered, as the question had thrown them off their guard. Unsure of the meaning, Lina asked:

"We don't... *understand*?"

"But *soon you will*," answered Uyara. She then took both Lina's hands. Amanda, Stryker and Sam were now by her side. Three nymphs then took Amanda, Stryker and Sam's hands and the two that remained walked towards each other and stood behind them.

Lina, Amanda, Stryker and Sam held hands with the water nymphs and felt their hands warm theirs. Lina looked at Uyara and locked eyes with her. She stared at Lina with a warm, almost concerned, look in her expression. Her golden eyes seemed like a spiral galaxy that Lina could get lost in, daydreaming for hours. Uyara's eyes filled with tears and she noticed the other three were crying as well, simply by looking at them.

The two entities positioned behind them proceeded to sing a melody that none of them grasped the meaning of, but it possessed a tranquil, spirit-raising harmony that promptly gave her goosebumps. Both sang in a high, melodic key that sounded as if this hymn had been created specifically to journey through notes and tones, as their voices soared through the afternoon breeze of the green sea around them. Even though she couldn't understand the meaning, she looked over at Amanda, Stryker and Sam to see that they, too, shared a similar reaction – the energy in their voices evoked so much emotion and freedom that, despite not knowing the words they felt obliged to respect and feel.

The four nymphs that held their hands opened their eyes to look at them while the other two continued to sing the mystical lullaby. They inclined their foreheads to each of them, and Uyara's voice whispered through their minds once again:

"Your mind, on ours."

Lina obliged, understanding she had to inch hers closer as well. She tilted her head forward and, as soon as her head connected with Uyara's, her mind exploded in racing, vivid images.

She saw a colossal forest from above, and immediately recognized it to be from Gliese, not Earth – this was an older, richer ecosystem. Then she looked ahead to see she was standing on feathery, golden-winged eagles. When she looked up again, they weren't in the rainforest anymore: in front of her stood an enormous, purple, emerald palace on top of a steep, rocky mountain. She was so high in the sky she saw the palace's entrance only began above the clouds that surrounded her.

Then, she was pulled back - back to the water temple.

"You saw Eternae, and the Sensorial Palace" said Uyara. "You must journey there to reach the Stellar Door. It is the only way to get back to Earth. Now you must swim with us."

Uyara then stood up and turned her back to them, and so did the others. She walked a few steps away from them and crossed the waterfall. The other nymphs followed and soon Lina, Amanda, Stryker and Sam went as well. After wetting themselves by crossing the wall of water, they found themselves at the end of the platform, with the infinity of the Gliesian sea ahead. There wasn't a lot of space to walk on, and Lina knew they couldn't hold their breath underwater for long. She looked at Uyara and reached to touch her, but as soon as she moved her arm, she froze at the sight that formed close to her.

From the depths of the green sea emerged another creature, but this time it wasn't humanoid. A gigantic dark-blue lizard-like water creature emerged in front of them.

"I'm going to *shit*!" yelled Stryker, as he saw the monster rising from the water.

Lina looked at the creature, who had a long neck and large black eyes. At first, her heart raced apprehensively in her chest with the possibility of an imminent attack, but she soon realized that the creature, much like the nymphs, was only daunting to an uninitiated mind - she noticed it had four flippers, a short horn in the middle of its forehead, and a heavy shell on its back, speckled with blunt knobs. She no longer found the creature menacing, as soon as she realized it could transport them on its back. Uyara's voice then said:

"This is Placo. Do not fear him; he is a loving creature – he will take you safely across the seas as we swim alongside you."

Placo then swam closer to them and bowed his head to them. Lina, reacting to the creature's act of trust, immediately felt an empathy towards him and was the first one to reach out to touch his shell.

The nymphs jumped into the water one at a time and Lina successfully grabbed onto one of Placo's knobs and sat on his back. Amanda followed her, and then Sam. Stryker went in to reach for one of the knobs but missed and fell in the water. Placo, noticing his final passenger had failed to board, looked back at the swimming Stryker and submerged his head, lifting Stryker onto him. Stryker, petrified at sensing the creature's head touch him, shook uncontrollably as he was raised from the water. He grabbed onto a knob and finally succeeded in boarding the creature's shell. He looked at Amanda, Lina and Sam, smiling nervously, and said:

"I don't understand how you can be silent."

"Aren't they mesmerizing?" asked Lina. "What beautiful, rational beings."

"I never envisioned in a million years this is how first contact would go," said Amanda, grabbing onto one of Placo's knobs as the creature glided away. The nymphs swam alongside them, leading the way.

"I feel like everything we know is a lie," said Sam. "We must be *so* primitive. How can they communicate through telepathy..."

"Soon you will understand," answered Uyara's voice in their minds. She was leading the pack, swimming far away, yet she could still comprehend them.

"And they read thoughts, as well!" said Sam.

"It's astonishing to me the peaceful energy that just exudes out of them..." said Lina.

"Yes...I don't know why we trust them, but we instantly do," added Amanda. "They seem like water angels...," she said, looking behind to see the temple becoming smaller and more distant as Placo glided across the ocean. It would soon be nighttime, and the sky now shone in a strong shade of purple. The neighboring planet was even more visible ahead of them on the horizon, and the purple sky now shone in billions of little white glowing stars above.

"Can you believe what we're doing at this exact moment?" asked Stryker. "We are crossing an alien *ocean* alongside a group we've just come across, the first contact between rational races to ever happen to mankind, yet we're here and it feels... almost *normal*." The ocean was silent and, despite the increasingly cold temperature, they still weren't uncomfortable.

"It makes me wonder, now that we know it's not only us... how many first contacts have actually happened," said Lina. "Stacking up against all the civilizations and rational beings in the entire universe... were we the first to uncover the truth that we are not alone?" She asked. "Because looking at this endless sky above, I'm pretty sure we're not..."

"You are one of the first from your galaxy," answered Uyara's voice again. "But there are too many galaxies for even us to count." All four then looked up wonderingly, and Lina said:

"I never, ever thought in my wildest dreams I'd ever witness this - to touch, see, and smell another world... it still seems impossible to me. I can't believe this isn't a dream."

"I cannot wrap my mind around the stellar door they mentioned," said Sam. "Assuming it truly exists, we must find it and journey back now that we know it exists. Now that we know there are rational, thinking beings here."

"Do not rush, for you still haven't seen Gliese..." said another voice. This time, it wasn't Uyara's, but belonged to the nymph who swam next to her.

For what seemed like an hour, they journeyed across the ocean on Placo's back, often exchanging glances with each other, smiling to reassure their well-being. When night fell, the cold felt unforgiving.

"We are halfway there," said Uyara. They understood it to mean they had to withstand the freezing temperatures, so they breathed in and out and tried to warm themselves as much as they could. A few seconds later, they noticed the nymphs moving erratically and Placo picked up the pace of his gliding. Uyara then dove and resurfaced behind them. She stared at the empty sea and they noticed some movement in the waters.

"What is that?" asked Stryker, holding onto Placo tightly. All three looked at Uyara's line of sight. Placo glided even faster away, and the other five nymphs then swam to

Uyara. The movement in the waters next to Uyara turned into waves and an enormous water snake appeared, hissing in rage.

"Oh my God!" screamed Lina and Stryker in terror together.

The snake was twice as big as Placo, and opened his mouth to reveal hundreds of blood-thirsty, sharp pointed teeth. Immediately, it ducked to attack Uyara, but as it reached for her, the nymph who had spoken to them last carved a dagger in its neck. She'd thrown it using another, different device, similar to a bow. Lina felt one of her feet drop from Placo's shell and she felt herself falling as they heard the creature protest in pain. Sam grabbed her arm and pulled her up again, and all four turned to look at the battle as Uyara shot another dagger in the creature's forehead. Placo swam away as fast as he could, apparently terrified of the beast.

The snake hissed in pain and then stopped moving, falling dead on its side and sinking into the dark ocean below.

"We are safe now," said Uyara.

"What was that?" asked Lina out loud from Placo's back.

"It was a *Najink* – malicious sea snake. But there is no need to fear now."

Placo then slowed down, and all four glanced at the dark waters along the ride, alert for any suspicious movements in the distance or near them. The appearance of the snake had distracted them from the increasingly cold temperatures – and when they forgot about any potential peril coming from below, they started to grit their teeth and shiver again, as each breath they inhaled felt colder and let out more steam when exhaled. When it seemed like the temperature would become an actual problem, Uyara spoke:

"We are here."

They looked ahead to see they were approaching shore. Lina, Amanda, Stryker and Sam smiled, relieved and shook off the cold as best they could. As the destination approached, they squeezed their eyes to make out in the dark night what awaited in the distance - and saw glowing green lights coming from inside the dense vegetation. They seemed to be heading to the entrance of a forest.

"Is this *Eternae*?" asked Lina

"This is the land before it, but we shall meet them here," answered Uyara.

"Meet who?" asked Lina

"The *Plethoreans*" answered Uyara. She then reached the sand and stood up on her feet, walking towards the woods. They seemed dense and vastly unexplored from outside – who knew what kind of wildlife lurked and thrived in such an atmosphere –so, as all four let go of the thorns and fell in the sand, they remained still, awaiting for an action from the nymphs.

Uyara then looked up and howled, or at least that is what all four perceived her to be doing. The long, mournful cry lasted for some time and as she stopped, they saw some shadows emerging from outside the trees and bushes.

A tall, muscular man appeared. He had long, thick black hair and his skin was as white as snow. His entire body was covered in black engravings of drawings and symbols, and he immediately walked towards Uyara.

He mumbled and screamed at her in a raspy, throaty voice, and as he approached them they saw this being was twice the nymph's size, much more built and athletic. His muscles bulged from his white skin and the contrast of the black engravings, coal markings all over his body, gave him the energy and presence of a warrior.

Uyara answered back in the unknown language, in a much lower and calmer tone than the man expressed. As he answered her, they noticed him also lowering his tone as Uyara apparently painted the picture of their situation.

"So, we should be looking at a *Plethorean,*" whispered Stryker by Lina, Amanda and Sam's side.

"I cannot believe my eyes..." whispered Lina.

"They seem like two completely different races of living beings – the Andromedae are essentially designed for marine life and the Plethoreans, judging by this man, are beings of the forest,"

Uyara and the Plethorean continued to communicate with each other. The Plethorean would often move his arms around and seemed more articulate, whereas Uyara remained still and spoke with a soothing tone.

The Plethorean had turned around and started walking back into the woods. Uyara then stepped forward and followed him, instantly communicating telepathically to them:

"You must follow us now."

Lina and Amanda obliged and started walking in Uyara and the Plethorean's footsteps. Stryker and Sam looked back, still in the same place, to see the other four Andromedae bow their heads to them and then retreat back into the water.

Stryker and Sam then also started walking, glancing at Placo to see the creature distracted nearby, trying to catch a group of small fish.

As they reached the edge of the forest, Lina and Amanda were immediately surprised, once again, by the vivacity and variety of colors and plants present in front of them.

They looked ahead, entering the woods to see luminous petals of silver shining in the nearest flowers in front of them. They found themselves inside a botanic wonderland, instantly recognizing a familiar, earthy scent drifting down their nostrils - very similar to the smell of a rainforest on Earth. The forest's splendor was soul-nourishing, and below the silver flowers they saw bulgy, golden mushrooms growing under a tall hollow tree. Before them lay a labyrinth of wood and foliage, the density and variety of which made it remarkably easy to lose one's bearings when venturing deep into the woods. While the tall trees appeared ancient and primitive, the thriving ecosystem was evident from the harmonious sounds of birds, bees, frogs, and other creatures, some of which may have been entirely new to them. Lina looked back at Stryker and Sam, who had entered a few seconds later than Amanda and Lina, and then looked ahead to see Uyara and the Plethorean already gaining distance, brushing past bushes and plants.

They followed an earthy trail into the jungle and, as they walked, Lina and Amanda curiously explored and took in every inch and detail of the alien environment they were in: the smell and temperature were very similar to being in a rainforest on Earth, but being a planet multiple times larger, everything in Gliese seemed denser, bigger and more powerful: they walked past enormous yellow and purple mushrooms the size of a human's body and past a field covered in glowing, imperial bromeliads, and saw hundreds of small fluorescent bugs flying, gathering nectar above the bromeliad's flowers.

After some time, they reached a gap in the dense jungle to find a circular, open area filled with tall, elaborate brown huts that seemed to be made of clay. In the center, they saw a bonfire burning in a dazzling shade of green and yellow, and many other Plethoreans circling it. They held hands and sang a melody very different from the Andromedae's song. This melody was harsher, syncopated and monosyllabic.

"Om Im Ra, Om Im Ir, Om In Ur, Om In Eternea!"

Lina, Stryker, Sam and Amanda continued following Uyara and the Plethorean, who headed straight to the fire. Once they got closer to the center of the open field, all the Plethoreans noticed their presence and stopped, turning around in silence. The only sound you could hear was the crackling of the flames. The first Plethorean then yelled a long sentence which none of them understood, speaking to his people. Amanda and Lina looked at each other to ask if either had translated anything and as Lina shrugged her shoulders, they looked back to see a few Plethoreans now staring straight at them.

Two broke from the primary group and walked towards them.

"Is this supposed to be happening?" whispered Stryker through gritted teeth.

Uyara looked back at them as the two Plethoreans approached them and Lina and Amanda noticed them to share similar engravings on their bodies. All Plethoreans seemed muscular and intimidating and all four couldn't help but flinch in suspicion and tension as the beings got closer.

When they stood only a few feet away from them, they stopped and bowed.

"We are Illi and Illia" said the two Plethoreans, also telepathically. Their voices echoed in their minds and as they looked up, it became apparent they were female and male. Illia was very muscular, but had more delicate traces on her face than Illi's, who had some cuts and scars visible against his white, pale skin. *"We shall guide you through Anyara until you reach Eternae"*

"This is a small Plethorean village at the edge of Anyara's eastern forest" said Uyara. The other Plethoreans walked towards them, as well, forming a circle of eyes staring down at them.

"But - I don't understand," said Amanda. "Why are you helping us? Will we really be able to go back to Earth?"

"Before you leave, you will have the answers to your questions. Our plan is not to reveal them to you, but to help you reach the ones who will," answered Uyara. *"For now, you must trust."*

Illi and Illia stood up and reached out their hands. Illi gently took Lina's right hand and Amanda's left hand and turned around. Illia took Sam's and Stryker's soon after and then led them as they passed Uyara and the Plethorean, and walked towards the bonfire. The other Plethoreans opened up space around them and circled them.

A female Plethorean appeared, holding what seemed to be an open coconut in her hands, with a shiny, silvery liquid inside. Illi and Illia led them to her, and she reached her hand in the coconut to wet them and then touched Sam's face. Lina's heart skipped a beat when she saw the Plethoreans didn't have opposable thumbs. All five fingers were the same size and the middle finger had a thicker bone, while the other four served as opposable flaps. She touched Sam's face and drew an intricate, elaborate engraving on his forehead, nose and cheeks. Humming as she painted, she soon moved on to Stryker, repeating the procedure.

"Savann's the tribe healer. Her enchantments shall protect you against the harms of deep east Anyara" said Illi in front of them. Savann then touched Lina's forehead and as she did it, Lina could swear she felt a jolt of energy burst through her spine. Savann hummed and bobbed her head to the sides as she painted Lina. Once Savann moved on to Amanda, Lina asked Illi and Illia:

"What would the possible threats in deep Anyara be, exactly?"

"Anyara is the largest forest in the Eastern hemisphere of Gliese. It will differ from your usual experiences, so you must prepare, for the only way to cross Anyara is through its heart."

Savann finished painting Amanda's face and Illi and Illia took their hands, leading them away from the bonfire and inside one of the tall huts. They found themselves in a small, but reasonably wide, room. The walls were made of bamboo and the floor was covered in straw.

"*You shall rest tonight and we will begin journeying at dawn,*" announced Illia before she and Illi left the hut and they were alone in it.

"So, tonight we'll sleep in a nest," said Stryker, looking at the room in front of them.

"We're on another *planet*, Stryker. I could use some rest." said Amanda, already stepping on the straw and adjusting herself to sit down.

"Me too. I was afraid we'd start crossing the forest tonight," said Lina.

"This entire experience is so atypical and unexpected, I'm having a hard time associating *reality*," said Sam, also sitting down.

"If I were to assume what would happen, I would've imagined being stranded for four days near the deserted beach...," said Stryker. "I never, ever thought we'd be communicating and depending on *two* races,"

"Well, you should have considered better possibilities," said Amanda. "Neither one of them is that different from us. Any good-hearted being would try to help like they're doing to us,"

"Yeah, but we wouldn't be able to - we're not nearly as evolved," said Lina. "They talk to us through the power of their minds! Except, until now we haven't seen a shred of technology."

"This planet is three times as big as Earth. I'm assuming we've landed somewhere far from their civilization," noted Amanda.

"I hadn't considered that," said Lina. "Do you think maybe the people they meant, then, the ones they're supposed to take us to…"

"I assume they are powerful beings, very different from the Andromedans or the Plethoreans. As evolved as they are, they are still very primal and lead a borderline mystical life, depending only on nature and the ocean. I think this shows we've landed somewhere much more evolved than Earth. Their level of awareness is through the roof - they can listen to us from a distance and seem to be immediately devoted to aid our quest as soon as they're told we're from Earth," said Amanda. "You saw it."

"What does that mean?" asked Lina.

"It means that it seems as if we've been *expected*," answered Amanda. "It doesn't mean I'm *scared*, but it surely means we have absolutely no control - and being this powerless leaves me on edge," she admitted. "I'm amazed. Don't get me wrong. But feeling like a needle in a haystack is daunting. Assuming our theories are correct, we'll just never be the same - what will become of us if we reach Earth again?"

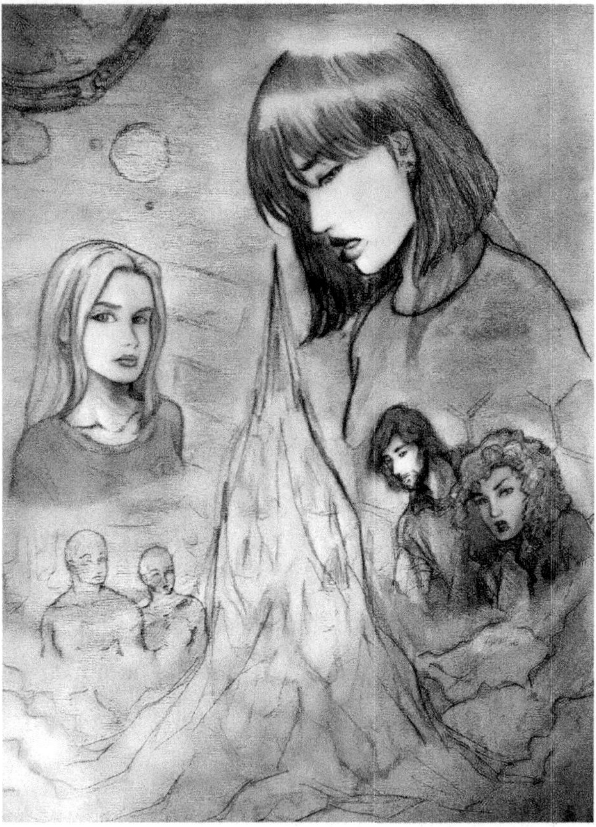

Chapter Sixteen - Plethoreae

"We must journey now," said Uyara. All four opened their eyes to see Uyara, Illi, and Illia standing inside the hut. Despite the uneasy sleeping conditions, all four of them slept like babies through the night because their bodies and minds were exhausted and overwhelmed. Amanda sat up as she opened her eyes, and Lina and Sam stretched next to her. Stryker remained sound asleep. Illi and Illia each brought another coconut, this time filled with a red, almost pink substance inside.

"Each of you must eat one Hukko. It is a treasured aliment which will provide all the strength and nutrition necessary for the journey." All four drank the liquid, which Amanda found tasty and sweet. She lightly kicked Stryker with her leg and he woke up, immediately connecting the dots and picking up his Hukko to drink.

"You will be guided during the first half by creatures that are unknown to you," said Uyara.

"What creatures?" asked Lina, curious.

"Once you're finished with your Hukko, we ask you to please step outside." Soon after, Lina, followed by Amanda, was already done with her fruit and out of the hut.

It was now daylight and the brightness outside instantly overwhelmed Lina and Amanda. They covered their eyes at first and slowly opened them up to notice how vivid each color from the forest seemed. At the center of the tribe, in front of the ashes of the bonfire, stood six winged creatures. At first, they seemed like massive birds to Lina, but as she focused on them, they found their muscular bodies and yellow fur to rather resemble a tiger. These creatures were double the size of Earth's tigers, but both Amanda and Lina found them enchanting, not frightening. One of them licked his gigantic paws and the other five sat around.

"Gigantic, winged tigers," Lina said. "I can't believe it."

"They are Cerberuses. These are the six most docile of them," said Uyara, stepping out of the hut with Illi and Illia.

"Oh, my God!" said Lina, walking towards them excitedly. "Can I touch them?" she stood her hand up and one of the Cerberuses locked eyes with her. They had silky, shiny yellow, white and golden fur and the longest whiskers Lina had ever seen. His wings were closed, but Lina could see their size and proportions from the sides. He stared at Lina with his big, blue feline eyes for a few seconds and inclined his face up to smell her hand. She stepped closer, and the creature licked her hand with his coarse, purple tongue. Lina shivered slightly and then smiled, walking closer to pet the massive, winged beast.

"They shall aid you through the air straight to the Palace. You will no longer have to cross through Anyara's heart," said Uyara.

"What is the Palace? Why won't we cross the forest anymore?" asked Amanda.

"These creatures brought with them orders from the Center to escort you safely to the Palace. You shall all discover Anyara, but at a later time."

"And what is the Center?" asked Amanda.

"The Center is the hierarchy of Gliese. We have coexisted peacefully under their care over the last ten of our centuries. They are the ones who will uncover everything to you. Upon detection of your arrival, they have asked the four of you to reunite with them presently. It seems the plans for Earth differ from those of others...," answered Uyara, smiling at both Lina and Amanda. Knowing all four to be listening to her words, she finished her sentence, smiling at Stryker and Sam, who joined in coming out of the hut. Amanda looked at Uyara, and smiling, thanked her.

"There is no need for that - this is our duty. Now you must travel the skies."

Amanda looked ahead at Lina, who listened in while caressing her Cerberus and then walked towards the next animal. Stryker and Sam also each chose their companions, and Illi and Illia hopped on the remaining two.

"Aren't you coming?" asked Lina to Uyara, who still stood in front of the hut.

"My duty is over. But we shall reunite soon. Good luck," she said. All four then mounted the Cerberuses, then glanced at Uyara and waved her goodbye. The Cerberus stood up and Lina bowed her head to thank Uyara.

"What are those creatures flying up there? They don't look like Cerberuses," said Amanda, pointing up at the sky. Lina looked up to where Amanda pointed to and saw one of the giant birds flying towards them. She noticed these winged creatures didn't have any fur, but a crimson leathery, pebbled appearance.

"They are Kratens," said Uyara.

"They look like Pterosaurs," said Amanda as a Kraten landed near them.

"What, a flying dinosaur?" asked Stryker, as all stared in amazement at the creature. Uyara walked towards the Kraten and caressed its long tail: The creature responded by lowering his long beak in a movement that approximated a bow.

"No, a Pterosaur. They're extinct on Earth but aren't classified as dinosaurs," said Amanda. "Of course... I can't believe I excluded this possibility in my mind," Amanda looked back at Lina and Sam. "Do you have any idea what this means? Deep in these woods there are not only new, alien creatures, but extinct ones as well,"

> *"Kratens and Cerberuses are two races of creatures that dominate our skies. They are of great aid to us, and it has been this way for a long time."*

Uyara smiled at them, and the Cerberuses stretched their wings. All four stared at the animals behind them as they opened two enormous, white feathered wings - so massive in musculature and strength that on the first flap came a loud sound of an entire current of wind being pulled forward. They flapped their wings again and jumped up. Lying down on its back, Lina opened her eyes after multiple flaps to see she already stood a few feet above the ground. Amanda, Stryker and Sam already flew slightly higher than her and her Cerberus flapped his wings strongly, inching forward as they rose.

Reaching up, she could see the Gliesian morning sun shining west and the neighboring satellite covering most of her line of vision, already glowing in the sky like a nearly collapsing blue world. As the Cerberus flew higher, she saw Anyara's forest cover most of the east and the ocean they'd crossed with Placo and the Andromedans to the northwest. The creature seemed to fly effortlessly, gliding through currents of wind as all six Cerberuses intertwined their sequence in the endless morning sky. Lina breathed in the air that blew in her face as deeply as she could, trying to capture the sensation and emotion of the moment as she stared at the scenic landscape all around her. They seemed to fly east, crossing above Anyara's green carpet of wildlife.

Lina looked back to the south, as she hadn't had the chance to glance at the entirety of Gliese before. She saw a mountainous valley of sharp rocks that seemed like an endless stone labyrinth. The group travelled through the skies, crossing Anyara's forest for what seemed like an hour. Then, as the woods seemed to reach an end, leading into a mountainous area very similar to what Lina had seen to the south, the Cerberuses inclined their bodies upwards and all of them held on tighter as they followed the steep rock to its surface. Looking up, Lina couldn't see where it led, as the massive stone wall in front of them was so tall it crossed the clouds. As they reached them and flew through the white vapor, Lina saw an enormous purple construction slowly coming into vision from within the mist. All six Cerberuses cut through the clouds and Lina looked down to see everything below covered in white. To her right, Stryker hugged onto his Cerberus with his entire body and eyes closed, and to her left Amanda, Sam, Illi and Illia glanced at each other reassuringly: a construction the size of a cathedral, entirely covered in amethysts that glimmered against the sunlight.

"This is The Palace," said Illi's voice. *"We have safely arrived."*

The palace stood on top of the jagged mountains and was accessed by a staircase the Cerberuses took them to. As they landed, Lina, Amanda, Stryker and Sam dismounted from the winged tigers and Lina caressed hers, thanking him. Illi and Illia remained on top of theirs and spoke to them:

"We shall leave you now, but if you ever need us, call us through this Xun." He handed them an object shaped like an egg, with four holes in its center and one on the top. Sam, who was closest, took it from Illi's hands and thanked him, bowing his head. He walked towards Amanda, Stryker and Lina.

"It's like an ocarina, or a whistle," noted Stryker.

"It is a special item which you must hold dearly. Play any note and we shall find you, in time," said Illi. He bowed his head and so did Illia, as the Cerberuses flapped their wings, turning around to take off. All six dove beneath the clouds as they disappeared from sight. A few seconds later, they stared at the clouds ahead and the neighboring planets in the sky above, as they saw they were truly alone for the first time since they'd left the spacecraft.

Amanda took the Xun from Sam's hand and analyzed it.

"Should we just... go in?" asked Stryker, looking at the staircase in front of him and the Palace's entrance.

"I think so," said Lina, taking the first steps. Stryker and Sam followed her and Amanda finished examining the object and placed it in her pocket. She then went up the stairs as well, as all four reached the tall, oval purple doors. Looking at the amethysts closely, Lina reached out her hand to touch the massive doors, since there were no apparent handles to push them open. Once she touched them, she heard them slowly creak and the enormous entrance slowly opened to reveal the inside of the colossal palace.

Chapter Seventeen - The Palace

Upon entering the room, the sound of their footsteps echoed on the marble floors. The doors slid open to reveal a round, elegant space with intricately designed walls and floors in shades of gold and bronze. Circling the entire floor were paintings of intertwined silver lines, much like a DNA structure. The lines only divided themselves when each reached one of five oval doors at the end of the room. The palace was supported by colossal bronze pillars and was a cathedral-like structure on the inside. In its center stood a floating golden circle, the size of their spacecraft, inside a transparent fluorescent tube connected from floor to ceiling, which emanated the same iridescent light as a soap bubble. Despite the magnificence of the entrance room, Amanda instantly focused on the only thing she couldn't wrap her head around as she focused on the incomprehensible texture of the fluorescent tube - unable to define how or why a golden circle would float inside it or what exactly the protective cylinder was made of.

Lina, Amanda, Sam and Stryker walked around the room, some enthralled by the entire structure, some following the silver intertwining lines. Amanda approached the center tube and started to walk around it, identifying the golden circle as a miniature of Gliese. She found it curious that walking around the tube would make the surface seem to change colors, exactly mirroring the effect of iridescence from a butterfly wing or a luminescent sea shell. Yet she couldn't comprehend what element that was, and imagined it was non-existent on Earth. The golden circle inside floated effortlessly and seemed to rotate extremely slowly. She noticed the planet Gliese was divided into fewer continents than Earth, as an entire half of the planet was an ocean, while the other half was almost entirely land - and the gigantic, unified mass had the shape of a star.

Lina followed the golden lines on the floor to the first of the five oval doors. There were no handles, just like the front door of the Palace. She looked around to see the other four doors, each connected by a silver, bronze, white and black line, respectively, to see none of them had handles either.

"Welcome to the Palace, Earth," echoed a male voice from nowhere. All four looked around, seeing no one. *"You will find me by the door,"* said the voice.

All four turned to look at the front door and saw a tiny figure in white garments. As he approached, she saw him to be a fragile-looking, humanoid old man. He held a pointed golden cane and moved slowly, but calmly, towards the group.

"Who are you?" asked Lina.

"I am very pleased to welcome you, Earthlings. I am sorry to refer to you that way," he said with a tender tone. Despite his old age, when he spoke, he seemed vivid and energetic. Differently from the *Andromedans* or the *Plethoreans*, this man seemed to be human and spoke to them using his voice. "This is The Palace. You may wonder why we have brought you here."

"We are wondering how we'll ever get home, why all of you are helping us and why everyone here is able to speak our language," said Lina.

The man smiled at her kindly and continued: "Earth has been studied and watched closely since the Beginning. Speaking your language is the easiest of tasks. You will find that we are all helping you because it is not a coincidence that any of you are here, with us, on Gliese," he said, walking around the room. "And yes, you shall go back, but you shall *come* back when you are ready - and you shall learn now. Will you follow me, please?" he asked, heading towards the first of the five doors. He knocked his cane on the floor twice and the doors breached open.

"You see, the universe is far vaster and more elaborate than you, Earthlings, perceive it to be," he said as he entered the room in front of him. "But all truths, all evolution, must come slowly." Lina, Amanda, Stryker and Sam followed the old man into another round room. While this one appeared to be empty, it was still designed intricately, with the golden line becoming a spiral on the marble floor. He turned around when he reached the center of the room and looked at Amanda.

"Will you join me, please?" he asked. Amanda immediately walked over to him. When she reached him, he hit his cane twice on the floor once more and the lights in the room dimmed, darkening the ambience. The old man breathed in and then lifted his cane, encircling Amanda with it as if protecting her with an invisible force. While at first she didn't comprehend his actions, she noticed a spark coming from the tip of his cane and looked up to focus on it. She followed the cane's movements and noticed it wasn't invisible; a shimmering fluorescent light appeared with each stroke.

Amanda suddenly felt light-headed, and the man stopped to look at her. She couldn't understand if she'd become dizzy from focusing on the moving cane or if he'd actually done something to her: but soon the light-headed state turned into a blissful, joyful feeling of peace and, as she looked at her body she couldn't believe what she was seeing. From head to toe, she saw her body glowing with a purple, indigo light. She reached out her hand to see the glow and noticed it encircled her body like a line of protection.

"This is the color of your aura," said the old man, and he immediately glanced at Sam, inclining his head for him to join him too. Sam walked to the center, and he lifted his cane again. Lina walked to Amanda, looking at her, speechless. Amanda looked at her arms and then at Lina, saying:

"Lina, are you seeing this?"

"Yes, yes I am," she said, looking at a glowing Amanda in front of her. Soon, Amanda's light wasn't the only in the room as the old man finished circling Sam and his body, too, shone in a white glow. The old man turned to Stryker and Stryker joined them, and Lina marveled, watching Sam and Amanda studying the light that shone from them. After a few seconds, the man finished with Stryker and turned to Lina. He turned around her, lifting his cane and Lina, too, saw the glowing curtain coming from the cane. She looked at Stryker, who began letting out a green glow and back at her body as the man finished dancing around her.

"An indigo, a choral and an emerald soul... indeed you are *special*," said the old man. Lina looked at her body to see it beginning to glow, as brightness emanated from her skin.

"A golden soul..," said the old man, looking at Lina. "What a team!"

"What does that mean?" asked Amanda, still fascinated, looking all around them.

"A choral soul is a soul harbored in the vibration of peace... an emerald soul is the *luckiest* in the universe," he said. "The indigo soul brings forth *change*... and the golden soul is *light*."

"I'm... I'm not sure I understand," said Lina. The old man knocked his cane twice on the floor again and the light faded from their bodies.

"It is not gone, it is merely going back to your core - you see, they weren't meant to be visible," he said, turning around and making his way to the door. They followed him as he stopped in front of the second door and hit his cane on the floor again. The doors opened and he went inside another room, also circular, but this time with a big, black circle painted in the middle and ten smaller circles encircling it.

"Will you step to the center, dear... I will love to see this done to a golden soul," said the old man, looking at Lina. Lina walked towards the middle of the room and stepped on the black circle. She looked up to see the beautiful shapes of the stone ceiling and looked down again, unsure how to proceed.

"What should I do?" asked Lina.

"Look around when the mirrors rise," he answered. The elderly man tapped his cane on the floor once, causing small circles to open up around her. Inside were long glass cylinders. The cylinders were all in the same shape and they rose from the floor until they reached Lina's line of vision. She found herself surrounded by the objects, unable to get out. Her reflection in the cylinder was different from what she saw in each mirror, causing her heart to skip a beat. With a quick turn, she saw herself change from herself to a man, a small girl and a monkey. She turned around quickly back to the mirror where she saw her reflection, scared of the faces she'd seen.

"What is this?" she asked, her voice trembling.

"There is no need to fear. These are all you," he answered. "In this room, you can see all of yourself. As we walk around here," began the old man, "I can see a boy on the first one, which is the mirror of your past life. You were a boy before... with traits very similar to yours. In the second mirror, where we can find your true essence, we find a fragile, beautiful young girl. How *fascinating*. Your warrior-self is a strong, muscular man from another of your past lives... Your animal is the *monkey*. If you would turn around, please, so you can unlock your other mirrors..,"

Lina breathed in and slowly turned around. She saw the boy as she turned left and recognized they had the same eyes. As she looked back at her reflection, she stopped fearing it, and identified herself beneath all changes. She immediately felt a familiar sensation seeing her other half: she identified that boy to have been the main guiding voice in her mind during her entire life. She turned around to look at the little girl, associating instantly her innocence and unstoppable drive to be coming from her. Then she looked at the warrior. As she locked eyes with her reflection. she recognized the strength she'd felt during any moment of her life in which she'd been challenged or required to pull through. She turned around to look at the monkey's reflection and turned around a bit more to reveal the sixth mirror, which had the reflection of a rabbit.

"Fascinating!" said the old man. "Your spirit animals are the rabbit *and* the monkey. It is rare to find two animals in one being, let alone two that reign in the vibration of *perseverance*...," Lina then turned around the other four remaining mirrors at once, but was disappointed to see her reflection on all of them.

"What's wrong? Aren't there supposed to be more?" she asked.

"I assume your other reflections will only be unlocked by your subconscious once you become older..," answered the old man. He knocked the cane on the floor twice and the cylinders withdrew back into the floor capsules.

"What do these mean, though?" asked Lina, as her body reappeared in the center of the mirrors.

"Every trait of your personality and who you are is determined by what comprises all yourselves," he answered. "It shall still take a long time for Earth to master the secrets behind consciousness, but the first step starts with you,"

***

They walked into the third room, which was again empty and round. As they gathered in the center, the old man said:

"My name...if you wish to know, is Synthious. Watch your step," he said, knocking his cane twice on the floor. Immediately, all four felt their bodies floating up from the ground.

"This is a gravitationally altered room," announced the old man as all four looked around to find their bodies floating in open space, effortlessly inclining horizontally. "And it is made to represent other dimensions."

"Other dimensions? So there really are higher dimensions?" she asked, curiously, instantly reminded of the visions from her near-death experience.

"There are *nine*," answered the man, floating alongside them. "And the main reason why you are here is because Earth is slowly advancing from the third to the fourth," he said, as Lina flipped on her back, twisting in the air. "But this is not the purpose of this room." He started singing a note and extended the last tone as the vibration in his voice showed them something their eyes had never encountered before.

"*Do-ooooooo*" he sang, and the vibration coming from the note magically shaped a transparent circle in his mouth, which grew as he extended the note. As he said "o" the vibration increased to all sides as if given life and as he stopped singing, they saw an entire iridescent shape as a horn from his mouth. All were unsure of what they'd seen, so Synthious continued:

"La-aaaaaaaa" a fluorescent glowing stream appeared from his mouth and ascended up and down, forming a shining wave in front of them.

"Si-iiiiiiiiiiiiiii" the high-pitched tone again vibrated into a shining line that then circled, this time like a spiral in front of them. "This is the wonder known as visible sound. In higher dimensions, melodies have colors and songs become visual drawings of energy and harmony."

As they floated around the room, each sang their own harmonies and melodies to play along with the visible energy that burst from the vibration of any singing. They played with the shapes, sizes and different intensities and Lina noticed the four of them seemed like kids in a playground. She looked at Synthious, who smiled proudly with closed eyes.

After a few moments, Synthious turned the gravity back on and they left, walking into the fourth room, which was an exact replica of the previous three. Synthious led them to the center and knocked his cane once and from a small opening in the floor appeared a thin gray needle with a lightning tip. As the lights went out, the lighting tip burst in a fraction of a second into a full hologram that filled the entire room. All around them stood, in green neon, a holographic representation of the universe. They hadn't ever seen technology so complex and elaborate, as all around them shone a spectacular visual simulator of billions of stars, galaxies and constellations.

"Telescopium, Taurus, Pegasus, Draco, Eridanus, Ursa Major, Cancer, Aquarius and the *Milky Way*" said Synthious, and as he mentioned each constellation's name they lit up all around them. "These are the constellations - with the names Earth has assigned to them - currently in the process of evolving dimensions,"

"Where are we?" asked Lina. "Gliese and Earth. They're very close to each other from this perspective, right?"

"*25844687, 450909119*" Synthious mouthed each number and the holograph zoomed in immediately, approaching a constellation on the northeast part of the room. Soon, an exact replica of Earth and Gliese appeared in front of them.

"From a universal perspective... they are close neighbors," said Synthious as they stared at the rotating holograms of the two planets. He walked towards the Gliese hologram and touched the planet with his small hands. As they saw the planet they were in and its star-shaped land, Synthious pointed to the highest of the five directions in which the land was spread through and said: "This is where we are. The stellar door will open up not far from here, at the edge of the ocean. As you can see, there is still an infinity of Gliese for you to explore,"

***

They walked out of the fourth room and, standing on the door of the last remaining opening, Synthious stopped and turned around to look at them:

"Before you head in, you must know that this room will lead you out of the Palace and into the Center. It is time that you meet and you understand why you're here. Apart from everything you will hear, keep in your hearts that it is your destiny to be here. In sight of the storm ahead, you will be wise to channel that energy to pull you through it,"

"Storm?" asked Amanda for all four of them.

"What you are being taught here are essential keys towards your success upon your return to Earth," said Synthious. "But the Earth you'll return to is at war. It will be a dangerous, perilous place and it is essential that you restore it to what it once was. It may seem daunting or confusing now, but I assure you *soon you will understand*," he said, smiling tenderly. He knocked his cane on the floor and the last remaining door opened up. They entered the room to find it finally differed from the other four as half of the floor was a water tank and the walls around them were not made of stone, but of glass, overlooking the clouds and the open sky from their altitude.

"Wow" said Amanda as they entered and stared out the glass windows. The room was breathtakingly beautiful and overlooked an entire, mountainous Gliesian valley.

"Now if you enter the water tank, it will lead you to the Center," said Synthious.

"Enter the water tank? What do you mean?" asked Amanda. "There's no way out."

"There is a way out, yes, from below. You'll dive, crossing a passageway that connects to the city."

"But we can't hold our breaths for very long!" said Lina.

"That is the benefit of the fifth room," said Synthious. "Enter the tank and you shall see."

All four looked suspiciously at the water tank in front of them. There didn't seem to be any openings or passageways, but maybe they would only be visible once they submerged. Stryker approached the tank first, and then Amanda and Lina followed him. Sam continued to watch as the three of them entered the water tank without hesitating, and Amanda submerged her head underwater. A few seconds later, Stryker did the same, but quickly after came up again and asked:

"I don't understand. What's supposed to be different about this?"

"I believe she has already figured it out," answered Synthious, and Stryker and Lina looked at Amanda, who was still underwater and diving even deeper. Lina felt as she swam, her feet couldn't reach the floor of the tank, so she looked down to see there didn't seem to be one at all. Amanda continued to dive even deeper and Lina asked:

"How deep is this?"

"It goes to the opposite side of the mountain. More than a mile,"

"How is she breathing underwater for this long?" asked Stryker, looking down at Amanda's swimming silhouette becoming smaller with each second.

"The waters are rich in perfluorochemical molecules," answered Synthious. "She's diving below as she breathes an oxygen-rich liquid. Many of Gliese's oceans and rivers are filled with it. That is why our marine-life is so vast,"

As she heard Synthious reveal this, Lina immediately dove and swam, opening her eyes underwater to see the inside of a vast, transparent tunnel that seemed to go on forever. At first, looking down and diving even further below seemed like a daunting task, but she took her chances and inhaled the oxygen-rich water. Water rushed up her nose and throat, causing fear, but she didn't choke or drown. Instead, she exhaled and saw water bubbles come out of her nose. A body cut through the water and Sam appeared on the tank while Stryker floated next to her, coughing uncontrollably as he had an opposite reaction to the breathable fluid. He shook his legs and Amanda imagined he was having a hard time concentrating on properly inhaling it without choking.

Amanda dove up to the surface and looked at Synthious, positively surprised with the invention.

"You must swim through the tunnel until you reach the Center. You shall be escorted there to meet our Galactic Council."

Amanda looked at Lina, Stryker and Sam and asked them:

"Did you breathe it? I can't wrap my mind around it"

"Yeah, we did. It's surprisingly smooth in the lungs," answered Lina.

"Will we see you again?" asked Stryker to Synthious. Synthious looked at them for a while in silence and then nodded his head reassuringly. The four of them floated for some time and then swam down the tunnel.

Lina began swimming down in breast strokes with Amanda by her side and Sam and Stryker just behind. While descending through the glass, it took some time for everyone to synchronize their strokes with their breathing, as she felt confused swimming deep down without worrying about oxygen depletion. Ahead, all they could see were endless blue tides - so instead, they guided each other by staring below, where the glass showcased the descending rocky valley. They felt as if they were swimming in a liquid sky overlooking the world below them as they continued to cross the massive cylinder. They gazed at the blue waters for what felt like three or four minutes, and then noticed the glass bending horizontally, creating a pool on the ground.

After swimming for another minute, they entered the larger area and saw the surface above. They swam to it and breathed in with open mouths, exhaling the fluid through their noses. On either side of them, they saw a lake that appeared to be in the center of an oasis. In front of them stood a palace with a long glass tunnel leading up to it. As they turned around, however, they gasped at the vision in front. A few miles from them there was a different type of stone labyrinth, as they saw different constructions, as tall and jagged as the valleys, in different shapes and sizes. Initially, it appeared to be a complex and rugged mountainous region, but it turned out to be a metropolis with buildings that had gravity-defying designs, far more intricate and geometrically daring than any structure on Earth. An entire alien city thrived in the desert, and by each building there were dozens of little flying rectangles floating around, barely visible to the naked eye - but their choreographed movement made them glimmer to their sight.

"Can you believe what we're seeing?" asked Stryker, looking around to see all other three just as flabbergasted as he was, floating while staring at the horizon.

"An entire living organism in front of us...." said Sam.

"I was right," said Amanda. "They are all much bigger and more evolved than we thought."

Chapter Eighteen - Utopia's Puzzle

One by one they got out of the lake and walked to the edge of the desert to get a closer look at the city nearby. The atmosphere on the Gliesian afternoon was warm and dry, so their drenched clothes weren't as much of a bother as they could be - and Amanda, the first to reach the edge of the desert, looked up at the sky, focusing on something the others failed to see.

"There's something approaching us," she said, gazing up. She pointed northwest and they immediately stared at the orange Gliesian sky above them - but saw nothing.

"I don't see anything," said Stryker, twirling his soaked shirt.

"There *is* something coming, indeed," said Lina as she reached Amanda. "I see it now."

"It's flying towards us!" said Amanda. Sam and Stryker reached side, and the four of them spotted the flying craft. After a few seconds, the flying object became bigger as it approached them and they saw it to be like a flying car. The white craft flew effortlessly through the air, without a helix or visible propellers - nor was it possible to see who or what sat inside it because of Gliese's sun reflecting onto it. As it continued to fly towards them, they gasped when they saw the craft magically split into four smaller parts. The four flying white compartments descended and landed in front of them. Each had a glass door that slid open to reveal a white, cushioned seat. There was nothing else inside, and as they looked at each other confused, a voice came from each pod and they heard an ethereal, soothing female voice call each of their names. "Amanda", said the first pod to their left. Amanda looked at it in disbelief, but started walking towards it. "Lina" said the second. Lina walked towards it, examining it and asked:

"Do you think this will take us to the Center?" she answered as the third pod said "Stryker".

"I think so," said Amanda, as the fourth pod called "Samuel".

"Well, let's see it then," said Stryker as all four entered their circular pods and sat down. The glass doors closed behind them and the four craft lifted onto the air, propelled by an even less identifiable energy from inside, as Amanda touched the glass window, seeing the craft rise in the air. The pods turned around and sped away across the desert below them. They headed straight towards the city and flew at high speed, as Lina, Amanda, Stryker and Sam sat inside their respective compartments, trusting the unknown rides. As the city grew closer, they were able to see the pods apparently heading to the top of the nearest tower, the pointed building nearest to them.

Below them, endless miles of orange sand painted the horizon to their sides, and the only visible view was the approaching city in front of them. The first building was also the tallest, and they noticed as they approached the last floor of the construction that it seemed to be a transparent oval dome, made of glass and attached to the building by a single room in the center. As the pods approached the tower, a familiar face became visible where they would land.

"It's Uyara!" said Amanda, alone in her pod, but looked around to see Stryker and Lina looking at her through theirs, also noticing Uyara's presence. She stood next to a Cerberus, alone on the top of the building, awaiting their arrival. The pods slowed down once they were above their goal and descended vertically, exactly as they had landed before them on the lake. The doors opened, and all four rushed out to greet Uyara. As they got out, they could see she stood behind a big, golden and silver door, very similar to the Palace's entrance. This one had the same design of intertwining lines on each side, coming together in the middle.

"*We meet again, dear ones,*" said Uyara's voice in their minds, her soothing tone soaring through their hearts and minds. She looked at them with a kind, welcoming expression on her face.

"Uyara!" said Amanda and Lina, together. Amanda then continued: "Is this the Center?"

"Yes. You shall go through these doors and you shall meet the Galactic Council. The Council comprises a vast confederation of civilizations from various planets, galaxies, and universes collaborating towards the harmonious coexistence of all life. As a high-level governance body, the Council sets precedence, protocols, and conditions of behavior regarding planetary exploration, first contact, new membership, and trade relations among its member planets. Because of you, Earth shall now join the Council. Inside, you will understand everything that is in your destiny to achieve."

She turned around and approached the metallic doors. Her Cerberus went round in circles and lay down beside the entrance. Uyara touched the right door, and both slid open. They entered a circular area, similar to a courtroom, with a center bench where five beings sat. As they stepped in, they were immediately taken aback by the absence of a ceiling above them. In place of the open Gliesian afternoon sky, or intricate ceilings as in the Palace, stood an enormous night sky, so real they could swear that by crossing the doors they'd switched to nighttime. There were white porcelain rows that overlooked the bench to each side, and the entire room was magically lit by the brightness emanating from the multitude of stars above them.

"Our dearest welcomes, all four," said the bald male figure sitting on the top spot. His skin was a mixture of green and grey and his face had human features, except for an enormous forehead. His eyes were big and bulgy, similar to the Andromedae's, and he was the only one wearing a bright red garment. "You are safe and not in any danger; we have long waited to share this day with you. I am Chairman Bartheus for the Galactic Confederation."

"We have the greatest expectations for Earth" said an earthy, throaty voice from the male on the spot below the Chairman. He wore the same silver garment as the others, and his skin was white and pale, much like a Plethorean. "First contact has always been planned to be shared between Earth and Gliese - simply not as fast."

"Which is the main reason why we have brought the four of you, standing in front of us, to this planet," said the Chairman. "If we intend to thrive together to achieve transition, we must start."

"Is there anything you would like to add, dear?" asked the female who sat on the other side below the Chairman. She looked very similar to him, with a big forehead and no hair, but her features were much softer and more feminine. All four failed to respond immediately. Amanda then understood the cue and stepped forward, asking:

"Why are you aiding us? We didn't come here for this," she said, listening to her voice echo in the middle of the wide council. All five beings focused on her as she spoke, listening in silence. Amanda felt a jolt of nervousness spike through her body as she finished, hoping she hadn't offended them.

"Oh, but you did!" answered the Chairman. "You just didn't know it. There are many forces which you won't yet comprehend in the third dimension. But you were always meant to come here for this, not by accident - there was always something pulling you to this, and these forces are incomprehensible to you just yet. Rest assured, there is no coincidence to this, Amanda. The four of you were already born with this event set in your destinies, and as always, it is only unlocked in due time. But this experience and achievement, it is yours - and *always has been*."

"But..," said Amanda, trying to piece together the best possible questions as she heard her mind's engines racing with thoughts and assembling the revelations. Before she could speak, she heard Lina's voice cut through the silence.

"But why, then? What did you mean by transition?" she asked.

"As it is with every planet in the universe, it is now time for Earth and all life on it to transition through a higher dimension. It is time to ascend. Earth shall now join an infinite number of planets, but only a smaller percentage in this galaxy is vibrating on a higher level. Ascending planets bear no war or chaos, at least not in the sense you're accustomed to."

"Well, I think it's not time yet," replied Amanda. "Earth is a long way from that, I'll tell you that much!"

"But that is where you come in," said the Chairman. Lina, Amanda, Stryker and Sam exchanged confused glances at each other and then back at him. The Chairman then continued:

"You shall leave this planet with a gift. Much like Earth, Gliese already thrives as an ascended planet - we have been watching you for centuries."

"But... you're evidently more evolved than we will ever be. We could never foresee this planet to be such a vivid, alive organism. Why wait for us to come here, then? Why didn't you come to us?"

"Well, but that is the most crucial part of it," answered Bartheus. "You needed to see Gliese and experience it for yourselves. To even grasp the concept of another living world, it is essential that you - *the aliens to us*, are brought here, and by your own terms. Everyone is an alien somewhere," he answered. "You needed to want to come here, you needed to create the expectation and search for it, fueled by your strength of hoping, and only your hope."

"This enables your mind to comprehend the concept... whereas, if we'd shown up in your living environment, your home, our goal would never be fully understood. We'd be seen as intruders, misunderstood by the aggressive mass of afraid minds," complemented the man next to him.

"Soon, we shall have the four of you ready to travel back through our stellar door for Earth's new age to dawn," said the female.

"We understand there are complications," said the Chairman. "In order for you to blossom into the woman you are today, with your mind-set and endless energy designed to move your world forward, it had also always been in your destiny to grow weary and resentful of a polar opposite energy, whose genius disabled his perception of the universe, giving him narrow-scoped, greedy objectives, which made you question power."

"You mean my father," said Amanda, instantly associating the Chairman's words with the face of her despised creator.

"Yes," said the Chairman. He paused and then continued: "We are also very aware of the conflicted state Earth is in. Starting today until the opening of the stellar door, you shall train to achieve your highest potential. There are still many secrets and teachings for you to learn and grasp until you become who you are destined to be,"

"Most importantly, why did you say in the beginning first contact wasn't expected to happen this fast? What sped things up?" asked Amanda.

"We must admit there was a certain... underestimation of our part in many of Earth's origins. You are, indeed, capable of achieving spectacular accomplishments - in the Galactic Scale you are the earliest planet in the Milky Way to break faster-than-light traveling, with only two centuries of technology. You being here is proof of that."

"How many more planets with technology are there? How many more living planets in the universe, like Earth and Gliese?" asked Lina.

"The number of living planets in the entire universe is close to the number of planets in your own galaxy, the Milky Way, as a matter of fact - rounding up at about *ten trillions*," answered the Chairman. "All purposely located far away from each other, until life evolves and the neighbors find each other."

"Every time the Interplanetary Bond is broken... that is, when a singular living planet's population that comprehends their place in the universe and understands that they are not alone, overwhelms another which still does not, the two planets' vibrations are always raised from the third to the fourth dimension. All planets, all across the universe, start as you did: fellow Earthlings staring at the sky, as thinking beings form groups that will later develop into societies. You have proven how Earth is worthy of becoming a member of the Council," said the Chairman.

"Now that your world faces the aftermath of the truth, the reactions are always varied - war becomes common. You are not the first planet, nor will you be the last to discover this, as all across the universe, in the farthest of regions, there is life blooming and discovering itself," said the female.

"You... you mentioned a gift," said Lina. "What kind of gift do you mean?"

"You shall train to become your higher selves before the stellar door is upon us," answered Bartheus. "This training will aid you upon your return to Earth. Only once you've achieved completion and understanding shall you be able to truly fight and make a difference in war. You will be given invaluable weapons that are the keys to raising Earth's vibration, the keys to the enlightened future that lies ahead for all of you, and us. Only one of you, however, shall truly evolve. Do you believe you are capable of enduring this task?"

Amanda, Lina, Stryker and Sam were visibly excited by the Chairman's announcement, finding the knowledge and notion that they'd be taught lessons during training riveting.

"There shall be risks and danger, but in order to bring peace to your world you must enlighten it. Do you accept your destinies?"

Lina, Stryker, Sam and Amanda switched glances and, knowing her group's will to thrive, Lina stepped forward once more to speak.

"I must say something" said Lina. "Please understand how much information we've been given in the past days... try to see things from our point of view," she began, stepping forward. "I never thought I'd be standing in a world like this, so far away from home, and communicating with intelligent beings, much superior to my race. Ever since we've known each other, all we've known... was us," she said. "Yet out of all the people that could have achieved this... out of every mind and conscience that would've backed down, feared, given up or doubted themselves, we have not. I can tell you as much as my body is shaking with adrenaline and a few sides of me still doubt any of this is truly happening, we have pulled through. And we're here and *this*," she said, raising her hand to her mouth to point out her voice, "this *communication*, this answer coming *from me*, is happening. It is here," she paused and smiled. "We are in awe, but more than glad to oblige."

She looked back to see Amanda, Stryker and Sam smiling at her encouragingly. She turned around again and stared at the Council. The two members who sat on the lower seats began speaking to the other three members in an unknown tongue. After a few seconds, there was silence and the Chairman spoke:

"So it is. You shall now begin your training."

The council's doors burst open again and Uyara announced that they should follow her outside. Once they stepped out, they saw the sun setting behind the horizon, filling the sky with a darker tone of orange - and all four of the Cerberuses who had led them to the Palace had re-joined Uyara's. Each Cerberus seemed to recognize their former rider, who greeted them by petting their fur as Uyara's voice again soared through their thoughts:

"We must journey to the heart of Anyara," she announced, mounting her winged tiger. All four did the same and soon they were taking off, as each feline took off into the sunset. They flapped their wings as they rose from the ground and flew through the Gliesian towers and skyscrapers.

"What is this city, Uyara?" asked Amanda from her Cerberus, as the group left the central building and started to cross the town.

"In your language it would be the city of Titanizze," answered Uyara, as the Cerberuses flew close to a line of flying pods. As they approached them, Lina curiously looked at each pod, trying to spot a glimpse of everyday life on Gliese. The tall towers and buildings around them could pass for an Earth-based city any day if it wasn't for its intricate design and gravity-defying shapes, as each building around them reflected the sunset in its windows and metallic structures, giving the entire city a sense of faded elegance. They flew through the megalopolis, cruising through flying craft above and below them. As she glimpsed each living being inside their compartment, she saw many seemed to share the same race as the Chairman.

"Who lives in this city?" asked Lina as she looked all around her, taking in as much detail as she could. Amanda and Sam did the same, but looking at Stryker she saw him again struggling to feel safe on his Cerberus.

"Mostly Vargans. That is, like the Chairman," answered Uyara. *"More than half of the living rational beings on Gliese are Vargans. They are a peaceful society that has co-existed in harmony for centuries with all other races,"*

"But what distinguishes the Vargans from us, humans? Is there a government, with politics and law?" yelled Lina, curious. Uyara continued to fly ahead, without answering for a few seconds. Lina saw her Cerberus flap his wings as they continued to cross the city of Titanizze. Uyara then looked back at Lina and smiled at her, kindly.

"Vargans no longer need to be ruled by a government. This is the way it has been for centuries. Virtues and beliefs are shared and followed, but to fully comprehend how our world functions, you must wait until your training is completed," answered Uyara. Their crossing continued as they reached the end of the city and began flying above a forest. They flew for what seemed like ten minutes more, and as the fading afternoon turned into the bright, vivid Gliesian night, their Cerberus descended onto an open field in the middle of the woods. The winged creatures then started to land and touch the ground, and as they got ready to dismount, they saw a wooden hut close to their location. The small hut was built

like a cabin but, as with most Gliesian constructions, had a shape very different from what would be built on Earth. The round cabin seemed fragile and rusty, and as all four began dismounting their Cerberuses, they saw a tiny man coming from inside the hut.

"Synthious!" yelled Amanda, surprised to meet the Palace's guide again.

"How delighted I am to see you again so shortly after we met," he answered, smiling. Lina, Amanda, Sam and Stryker walked towards him, and Uyara's voice spoke to them again. As they heard her speak, Lina turned around to see Uyara still standing on her Cerberus.

"Synthious, I have yet again safely delivered them to you. I assume you will begin their training immediately?"

"Yes, I will. Farewell, Uyara. You have done well," answered Synthious. He turned around and entered the hut, signaling with his head for the group to join him. Amanda, Lina, Stryker and Sam nodded their heads and thanked Uyara, and as her Cerberus began flapping his wings, they turned around to follow Synthious inside the small cabin.

They entered the wooden hut and found themselves inside a tiny, but welcoming room, lit by a fireplace in the end. The room felt warm in contrast to the chilly night of Anyara's woods and was divided into two, with pools of water on each side. A wooden platform separated the two sides, and they all stared confused at the small pools, unsure of their purpose. They saw the pools were only a few centimeters deep and spotted a balcony at the end of the room in front of the fireplace. Synthious immediately walked towards it and all four followed him.

On the balcony stood two big and oval glass flasks, each filled with a liquid in a different color. The first one was purple and the other was a very strong shade of green.

"Your training starts with the first potion. It contains a chemical element only present in Gliese, which will open your heart's walls for a wild rush of emotions that will flood you with joy. Once an organism is exposed to this element, it is forever changed - your hearts will be set free. Only by experiencing it shall you comprehend," announced Synthious. "The other potion will be taken once the first one is in full effect - a few hours later, tonight. This liquid will boost your mind's potential to its fullest and cherish your soul. It will improve the production of what you call DMT in your brain's pineal glands. What will happen tonight will change you forever."

Synthious took the first flask from the table and gave it to Amanda. Amanda held the bottle and, before she could do anything, Synthious added:

"One big sip. Your brain shall be the judge of how much is enough for you."

Amanda looked at Synthious and then at the glass in her hands. She looked at the purple liquid inside and smelled it, but it didn't have a scent. She then closed her eyes and took one big gulp, passing the glass to Lina as she swallowed it. The taste was metallic and bitter, and she frowned as the taste filled her mouth. Lina drank her sip and passed the drink to Stryker, who sighed before drinking.

"It tastes like I've eaten a melted robot," said Amanda, coughing. Stryker and Lina both frowned and as Stryker passed the drink to Sam, Sam asked:

"I'm afraid I can't... drink this,"

"But you *must*," said Synthious.

"No... you don't understand. I'm not a regular human being. My brain's judgement centers have been altered by neuroscience and it's been nearly two decades since I've last felt emotion,"

Synthious looked at Sam intrigued, apparently unaware of his condition.

"You're the one who needs this more," he answered. "You must *trust*,"

Sam looked at all of them reluctantly, and breathed in, thinking deep. "Very well," said Sam, proceeding to drink the fluid. Unlike Lina, Amanda or Stryker, he didn't flinch or show disgust, swallowing the liquid and then looking back at his companions apathetically.

"I would suggest we now head outside," said Synthious, turning around and making his way across the wooden platform.

"Synthious, what are these water pools?" asked Lina as the group followed the elder man.

"Well, this is where you'll rest!" he answered blatantly. "See the inclined sand banks near the end? You will rest your heads there and rest in these waters. These are therapeutic thermal streams that come from a fountain in the northern hills. These waters will heal your bodies from toxins and cleanse your auras during the training days."

Synthious looked at the group to see each had a puzzled or confused expression on their faces. "You seem surprised,"

"It's just that, us from Earth, we don't, well, sleep on water. I've never slept in water before," answered Stryker.

"Well, but this is not Earth," answered Synthious, turning around and exiting the hut. As all four caught up with him, they walked around the empty open field while breathing in the pure air of the forest.

"I feel like I need to pinch myself every few minutes" said Amanda, looking up at the sky. Synthious turned around to look at them and asked:

"Tell me, Amanda, do you feel anything yet?"

Amanda remained silent for a moment, staring at the night sky above them emptily. Lina noticed her eyes were filling up with tears. As they stood in silence looking at her, the sounds of the forest became more audible, and crickets, howling and hoots from the expansive ecosystem all around them sounded closer and louder. Standing by Amanda's side, Lina saw her blue eyes glisten with the reflection of the starry sky and immediately understood the reason for her friend's lament. She felt as if their entire journey had been coming back to them in a matter of seconds, and whether it was because of the effects of the potion starting or a genuine and random emotional outburst, Lina couldn't help but feel overwhelmed by the resurfacing feelings.

"I cannot put it into words" said Amanda, as she blinked and one tear fell from her left eye, dripping down her cheeks.

"You must *try*," said Synthious.

"I feel as if I'm more aware that nothing was ever in vain," she began, with a cracking voice, "and that if something ever felt purposeful, it's my life. I feel good, I feel blessed..."

Synthious then looked at Lina, who looked back at him, also teary-eyed, and answered, smiling:

"I feel thankful for finally feeling part of something bigger than myself. It's been the strength that has pushed me forward and made me take every step here. I longed for this feeling for my entire life."

Synthious then looked at Stryker, who quickly took off his shirt and unbelted his pants. All the others looked at him confused, and Stryker stripped off his pants and underwear, running stark naked around them, screaming in excitement.

"I feel no fear anymore! I feel like I can take on the world!" he screamed with open arms, running naked through the empty open field.

Amanda and Lina burst into laughter as more tears fell from their eyes and a surging sensation of well-being and ecstasy poured through their veins, imbuing their every move and action with understanding, patience, and love. Lina and Amanda felt as if all of their troubles had been lifted from them - and the place where they now stood wasn't an alien, dangerous environment, but a comforting, fantastically wholesome, safe place. They felt their minds being lifted as their resurfacing worries about Oswald, The Firm, Earth's war and coming home became irrelevant. Synthious looked at Stryker with a contented expression on his face, and turned to look at Sam as Lina and Amanda did the same. Sam stood motionless, staring ahead with a painful, grieving expression on his face. He fell to his knees and Amanda and Lina watched as the emotionless warrior they'd come to know tugged at his chest as he started to cry. He held his chest with his right arm, seemingly clutching at his heart, gripping it as if he felt pain - and Lina and Amanda walked towards him. They each knelt by his side and Amanda touched his left hand, looking him in the eye.

"I...," he sobbed, barely able to put his thoughts into words. Lina and Amanda felt surprised by his outburst - they'd never seen Sam show any emotion, much less ache in front of them. He mumbled as he cried and continued: "But... half of me has been asleep..,"

"Open yourself up to every sentence and voice that soars through your mind," said Synthious, looking at Sam.

"Feel it, Sam," said Amanda, as she held his hand. He then stopped and closed his eyes. After a few seconds, he smiled. He opened his eyes and looked at them with a joyful, hopeful expression.

"I have never felt more complete in my life," he said, smiling at them.

"Very well, we should start with it properly, then. I'll bring the second potion," said Synthious as he walked back inside the hut. After a few seconds, he came back holding the glass of green liquid.

"Once you drink this," he warned, "you shall experience the universe,"

Chapter Nineteen - Visions of Anyara

At dawn, Lina awakened and sat up in her water bunk, dressed in simple garments discovered within the hut, evocative of colonial times. They'd chosen not to soak their own clothes while trying out their therapeutic pools. Lina hadn't slept well through the night, finding the idea of resting her head in a sandbank while keeping her body drenched for hours strange - so she got up before the other three and made her way out of the hut.

She squeezed her eyes as she stepped into the sunlit woods, listening to the welcoming sounds of the wild forest grow louder all around her. By daylight, the woods that surrounded the hut seemed even more vivid, and Lina was immediately distracted by the wilderness surrounding her, staring befuddled at the vibrant, powerfully beaming colors of Anyara's trees, plants and flowers. Lina closed her eyes and inhaled the scent of the woods, feeling a deep, resonating inner peace. She was enchanted by the blooming violet and pink petals of the flowers to her left, and walked towards them to see multiple flickers of light from what she later identified as creatures similar to glow worms or fireflies, flying in circles above the flowers. She squeezed her eyes to see the bugs properly, as they would flicker and disappear to the naked eye each second, glowing in an even sharper and brighter tone of fluorescent blue.

"He's here!" said Amanda's voice from the hut's entrance. Lina looked back to see Synthious and his Cerberus landing close by as Amanda watched and switched her gaze to inside, talking to either Sam or Stryker there.

Lina walked towards the group and soon Synthious greeted them, offering each a Hukko to drink and supply them with the vitamins and nutrients as Stryker and Sam joined the group.

"Is this all you eat?" asked Lina as she finished drinking her own.

"Of course not," answered Synthious, "but this is mostly what your Earth-based bodies can digest for the time-being. Very well, we shall begin. Today's challenge is mostly the opposite of what you went through yesterday. Follow me."

He turned around and made his way to the back of the cabin, entering a gap in the bushes and following a thin trail of grass inside the woods. All four followed the elderly man, walking through the narrow path and looking all around them as they began their trail to the depths of Anyara. Their line of vision was mostly filled with tree branches and occasional glimpses of bigger, wider paths - but as they heard the sounds of a waterfall, they understood the trail outside the hut led specifically to the cascade, not out into the wilderness. They shortly reached the end of the path and emerged at the top of a colossal green, emerald rock that overlooked an open space, entirely surrounded by waterfalls. The water streamed down endlessly, fading into a central pool of vapor, and the sound of the collapsing curtains of water was loud and aggressive, like a never-ending roar.

"Below the rock that we stand on, a hundred meters below us, streams Anyara's purest river," announced Synthious. "The stream flows to a fountain nearby, but the water is deep and there are no dangerous creatures in these fresh waters."

Amanda, Lina, Sam and Stryker each stepped closer and looked around, amazed at the steep drop below them.

"You can feel the ground vibrating from the strength of the water," noted Stryker.

"Why did you bring us here, Synthious?" asked Sam.

"Your task is to jump," answered the man, calmly. All four turned to look at him, thrown off by his announcement.

"Jump? Down this *pit*?" asked Amanda, shocked.

"The waters are deep and flow calmly to the fountain - the only thing you must overcome is your fear of falling. It is a crucial part of your training and you will do well in proving your worth. There is no attachment to the physical body that should prevent you from enduring such a challenge. It is possible, it is safe. Your mind is all that says otherwise. Only then will your brains be perfectly adapted."

"Adapted to what?" asked Amanda.

"*Soon you will understand*," he said, coyly. There was a sensible, ominous tone to his constant mentions of adaptation. Amanda felt uneasy - but Stryker cut through her thoughts, screaming by her side, changing her focus too quickly to act then.

"There are no rocks below? Nothing on the river? I can't see properly down there because of the vapor!" said Stryker.

"It is safe. Only deep, fresh waters," answered Synthious. "The challenge is on."

Lina inched her head to glimpse the fall below them and immediately shivered at the vision, retreating in fright.

"You can control that. I taught you and Stryker how to control this," said Amanda, looking at Lina concerned. Sam seemed fearless, stepping out into the edge of the emerald and looking down, then saying:

"Now this is insanely brain-powering. I can't wait to do it." Sam had a smile on his face and Amanda and Lina looked at him as he stepped even closer to the edge, the entire circle of waterfalls in the background as his figure reached the tip.

Stryker looked at Amanda with a bold, brave expression on his face - assuring her he'd be up to the task, as well. Lina breathed in nervously and Amanda suggested:

"What if we jump together?" she asked. "That would make it easier wouldn't it?" she looked at Stryker, then at Lina.

"I'm in!" yelled Sam from the edge of the rock. His voice was barely audible through the sound of the crashing cascades of water below them. Amanda looked at Lina, who nodded in agreement.

"Very well," said Synthious. He inched his cane to their right, pointing towards Sam and the edge, looking down silently.

As Lina walked beside her towards the drop, Amanda closed her eyes and stepped forward as well, knowing Stryker would follow close behind. She breathed in and out for a few steps, trying to clear her mind of whatever attachments she still had for her physical body or her life - concentrating her thoughts on already drifting in the river, safely streaming towards the fountain. The drop - which no matter how much they tried to ignore seemed to get bigger and more fatal with each passing second - grew in their line of vision as they approached the tip of the large emerald, and Lina looked at

Sam, trying to ignore the increasingly huge whiteness below her. Sam looked at her and reached out his hand, which she held immediately. She closed her eyes as she brought her body closer to his and reached out her other hand for Amanda to hold. As Amanda held it, she looked at her to see Stryker already by Amanda's side, and all four reunited at the tip of the stone. The wind blew aggressively and their bodies got wet with the tiny droplets of water pouring from all sides.

"Are you ready?" asked Amanda, through gritted teeth.

"Yes!" answered Sam and Stryker, and Lina looked at her, nodding reassuringly.

"I'm ready," said Lina.

"On the count of three," said Amanda. "Let's hold each other's hands and we'll each jump in the direction in front of us, right?"

"Yes," said Sam by her side. Lina and Stryker remained silent and Lina closed her eyes as she heard Amanda count:

"One, two, three" she said, and Lina immediately screamed as she felt Stryker and Amanda reach for the impulse by her side and she imitated them, with panic and fear rushing through her veins. As she felt the bodies next to her incline forwards and jump, she closed her eyes and propelled her legs from the ground, jumping as high and as strong as she could - immediately letting go of everyone's grip. For what seemed like ten to twenty seconds, she felt an intense propulsion pulling her body downwards as she plummeted down Anyara's waterfalls, closing her eyes throughout the drop. She only felt her mind re-ignite as she noticed her feet, legs and then torso cutting through the deep river below as she shot through the surface like a gunshot.

Lina felt her body submerged deep and immediately reached out her arms trying to halt her diving - she opened her eyes and mouth swallowing big gulps of water as she frantically began reaching for the surface, coughing and counting only on her last few seconds of oxygen. She swam up as fast as she could, reaching her arms up for the surface as she felt her heart thud against her chest like a loud drum. Her hands cut through the surface and she inched her body upwards in one last burst of energy, reaching for air. She breathed in as she swam in a pond with the river's course in front of her - following its course just as peacefully as Synthious had described. She turned her head back to see the surrounding waterfalls, searching for her friends. Amanda and Sam swam nearby, already surfacing, and Stryker's hands cut through the waters to Lina's left. Lina swam with the river's flow and they followed the stream towards the fountain, getting out of the river as soon as they saw Synthious walking alongside the shore.

"You may not sense it anymore, but you could only endure such a task because of yesterday's elixirs," he announced. "Your bodies and minds are now free of fear," he said, looking down at the ground as he walked.

"Where are you taking us now?" asked Lina, drenched from head to toe. All four instantly began following Synthious, but had no clue where they were headed next.

"To the temple, where you shall receive your gift," answered Synthious, without glancing sideways.

***

Chapter Twenty - Through the Stellar Door

After marching through Anyara for half an hour, they began walking up a steep rocky road inside the woods. As they went up the path, they saw the climb led to a mountain with a temple at the top, similar to the one they'd seen when their ship landed on the deserted beach, but more intimidating. This temple was noticeably larger but still shared the same Greek style, with a dozen long, white pillars guarding the entrance. Lina realized the mountain they were climbing onto was the first behind a chain of rocky valleys, as Anyara seemed to disappear into the background as they climbed the path.

"It will soon be time for you to head back to Earth," announced Synthious as they followed.

"What?" asked Amanda, curious. "But what about our training?"

"After both elixirs and the waterfall, it's time for you to receive your gift. After it is with you, there is no reason why you should remain in Gliese..." said Synthious. "You are needed back on Earth presently,"

"We haven't even discussed what we'll be going back to," said Amanda, glancing at Sam and Stryker. Lina, who walked a few feet ahead of Synthious and the group, stepped back as she heard Amanda finish her sentence.

"I agree," said Lina, now looking at the group. "I mean, what should we do? Oswald's going to be out for blood."

"Should we go back to the Lair and into hiding?" asked Stryker.

"He'll want payback for what we've done. We took away his masterpiece," said Sam.

"I am well aware of all those things," said Amanda. "But Synthious, you said during all our lives we've been watched and guided over by higher powers - which we'll never understand, apparently. Aren't there any words of wisdom you're supposed to share with us?"

"Your quest will be aided by the gift you'll receive as soon as we reach the top," said Synthious, placing his cane forward before each step. "The rest you must unravel yourselves as the challenges are presented to you."

"Well, that's very easy to say," said Amanda. "I don't see anyone else being tasked with ending a world war while being hunted by a cold-blooded army."

"Patience," said Synthious. Amanda sighed and then continued debating:

"I think we should find him," she said, with a firm, strict tone in her voice. "I'll kill him myself."

"He's your father, Amanda," said Lina. "I think, given the moment, you'd choke."

"No, I wouldn't. I'd also certify beforehand so the gun won't jam," retorted Amanda, as soon as Lina had finished speaking. "He *needs* to die. It's the only way to make sure there won't ever be any other surprises - because with him there's always a plan. I told you. He's had time to think and we haven't. He'll be out after us and we should give him exactly what he wants."

"But he will try to kill us, Amanda." said Stryker.

"Not if we kill him first,"

"Are you serious? I mean, what are the odds we're going against here? We can't take him on by ourselves!" answered Stryker, his voice trembling.

"You shouldn't worry about this. As you have so smartly noted, you have always been watched and guided by higher, divine powers," said Synthious. "Your task is to bring forth the dawn of a new age of consciousness upon Earth. Once you go back, no one will want to hurt you... but only when you cross through the stellar door will you understand why."

They reached the top of the climb and all four turned their heads from their master to the temple, catching their breaths from the tiring uphill path.

"Welcome to the temple of Eternae."

The temple was accessed through a central staircase, which Synthious immediately began climbing. The group followed him and once they entered the temple, they found there was no ceiling. The inside of this place seemed in ruins, as rays of sunlight burst through every gap on the vine-covered walls. Looking up, they could see Gliese D, the neighboring planet, beaming in the afternoon sky, even closer than they'd become accustomed to.

"Once the sun is down, the stellar door shall open inside this very space" said Synthious, reaching the center of the old temple. "This place may seem like it's past its prime, but, like most of what you'll find in life, its appearance is in contrast to its efficiency. You are standing on sacred grounds. Inside this temple, three millennia ago stood the man who proclaimed the freedom of our planet in a battle fought with similar goals and purposes to the one Earth faces today. This period was known as the Rain Wars."

"So this is why you exist and thrive in a society so advanced and far from us. Uyara said there's no money, no government, no laws! Your society is three thousand years ahead of us in terms of development!"

"That is not entirely correct, for everything evolves in different paces - Earth's technology is vastly superior today to what ours was three millennia ago," answered Synthious.

"Your people are developing faster than anything the Council expected or predicted. We have control of earthquakes and tsunamis, and many of us have visited Earth in passing, but our antimatter-fueled starships can also make us invisible. Our planet only speaks mostly one language today, the *Melliaro*, where on Earth you still have many. There is a greater attachment to the physical body on Earth, however, which is what brings us here today. Your people need to be set free from fear, like you were. But not all can experience what you have, and not all can withstand such revelations - such a journey, as you know, was chosen only for the four of you."

"But how will we ever prove our story to the world?" asked Amanda. "I don't see a way we could ever pull this off."

Synthious then turned around, and they saw behind him stood a tube which they hadn't spotted walking in, glowing in the same iridescent glow they'd seen in the Palace. They noticed looking up that the glow covered the entire temple as if surrounding it as a protective bubble or dome, and where the ceiling should have been shone a layer of the magical substance, protecting the ruins like a flickering cloak. Depending on their position, the cloak seemed invisible, so, as they noticed the magical surroundings, all four twisted their heads slightly to the sides and squeezed their eyes to fully comprehend what was in their line of sight.

"You must touch this cylinder with one of your hands," said Synthious. "Your gift shall be given then."

Amanda focused on the glow emanating from the tube and stepped forward.

"All I have to do is touch it?" she asked.

"Yes. Place the hand of your choice inside it." Amanda reached out her hand and touched the glow, penetrating the surface to sense its gelatinous texture in her fingers. She felt it drip through her arm and cover her entire palm and fingers.

"Very well, now take it out," said Synthious. Amanda withdrew her hand from the cylinder and looked at it, covered in the fluorescent liquid. Lina walked towards Amanda and touched the tube as well, and Stryker and Sam awaited their turns.

"This is the single most valuable substance in all of Gliese" said Synthious. "From now on, through touch, you will communicate deeply with each living being in the universe. You are now forever blessed as you are *heightened*,"

Lina looked at Amanda as both women gazed at their own right hands, watching their skin glow from the shiny substance.

"You must think of something you want to tell each other," said Synthious to Lina and Amanda. Lina locked eyes with Amanda and immediately thought of the mental images she'd stored in her mind from her visions. If she could somehow transfer these recollections to Amanda, she'd know both had truly shared similar trips. She then focused on her thoughts and reached out her right hand to touch Amanda's shoulder. As soon as her skin reached Amanda's, she felt a jolt of energy spike through her body and Amanda opened her eyes wide.

"You really did see it," said Amanda, flabbergasted. She looked down and then at her hand. She thought about the day she decided to run away from Oswald as she ripped off the wires he'd strapped to her chest and fell from the chair in his private lab. She concentrated on her memories and touched Lina on the center of her chest, aiming for her heart. This time, Lina was flooded with images from Amanda's younger years. She saw Amanda falling from Oswald's experiment chair and running away alone. She saw helicopters rising from the woods and recognized the place to be where The Firm now stood. Amanda's images and memories flooded through her mind and Lina looked at Amanda to see she was crying.

She looked deep into Lina's eyes and her grasp lingered as she flooded Lina's mind with every detail she could remember about her past and what motivated her to become estranged from her father, leaving him to move to Chicago and eventually meet Lina and Stryker. Lina understood her friend as she saw tears stream down Amanda's face in what was extremely unusual behavior for her - but Lina saw Amanda was crying tears of relief as she could now transfer accurate depictions of painful recollections through to someone, and the experience was strangely cathartic - as she lifted her hand from Lina's chest, sighing, Lina opened her arms wide and hugged Amanda tightly.

"Thank you," whispered a tearful Amanda to Lina's ear, her voice shaking in a vulnerability Lina hadn't seen before.

"This is *incredible*," said Stryker's voice in the background as Lina and Amanda broke their embrace. "This is the ultimate truth-teller."

"Yes," said Sam. "There's no way to fake an image or memory, to pass through something that never existed.

"One by one, you shall be enlightened," said Synthious. They heard a mechanical noise in the distance and looked up to see their spacecraft floating above the temple's fluorescent coat. The ship began to descend and cut silently through the iridescent shield, landing in the center of the temple.

"How... how did you fix our ship?" asked Amanda, baffled by the sight of the craft.

"It was broken! We had no way of warping back!" said Sam.

"You have been told time and time again this has been in the works since long before you arrived here. Fixing your ship is the least we could do to send you back properly," said Synthious. The group began walking around the ship, and the inverted triangle doors slowly opened up.

"But where will we get the energy to power it? There's no fuel left," asked Lina.

"The stellar door will guide you through. Your fuel is the same door every Gliesian spacecraft uses for faster-than-light travel. As we've said before, taking you back was never an issue. Our concern lies in whether you'll succeed in your tasks once you're on Earth."

"But, where is it then? The stellar door?" asked Lina, scanning around.

"It stands right above us, in a magnetic field that extends over two hectares. In due time, your planet's technology shall unveil the passageway that exists in between every auroral zone. Once the cold sets in and day turns to night, the sky above us becomes a passageway into the universe. You shall arrive back in Earth's northern lights without trouble. Your journey back home is what we can gift you. But as soon as you land back, you must be mindful. Your race's destiny lies with you."

"But what about here? We've come to this amazing planet and all we've gotten was a brief trip. I wish I didn't have to go back, or that I at least knew I'll visit Gliese again someday," said Amanda. Lina headed inside the ship, and entered the craft to look around.

"You must carry that longing with you," said Synthious. "It may just end up bringing you back someday. You still have a long life ahead."

"How can we be sure?" asked Amanda. "Many people back home want to end us."

Synthious smiled and let out a small sigh, saying: "You Earthlings really want to cling to certainties. Fear not... it shall unravel by itself."

"Thank you, Synthious," said Amanda, as she saw Stryker and Sam walk towards the craft as well. Synthious closed his eyes and nodded his head to her. Amanda began walking towards the ship and Synthious announced, looking at the group:

"Whoever pilots the craft must set the engines for take-off exactly an hour of your minutes, from now. The course is already programmed to warp back to Earth's respective auroral zone, the one aligned with this opening. Take-off upwards for exactly seven thousand meters."

Sam listened intently to Synthious's instructions, stopping dead in his tracks before entering the ship and turning around to further discuss how to pilot the craft through the stellar door. Amanda walked past him and entered the ship, reaching for her seat.

"I plan on sitting down and waiting until we're there," she said. "If we have to do it, I don't want to linger here. Let's just go before I change my mind about coming home."

She sat on her seat and began sealing the safety locks as Sam entered the craft, announcing:

"Okay, are we ready to do this? We can go home!"

"I don't see why you're beaming. Absolutely zero parts of me want to return," said Amanda.

"Why not?" asked Stryker.

"Well, have you considered what we're going back to? It's not exactly home to me."

Sam sat on the seat by her side and began turning on the control panel. From inside, the spacecraft seemed intact - they didn't know who had fixed it or been inside it, but ever since they'd left it on the beach, days before, Amanda had given up hope of returning home.

"I didn't think they'd do this; I mean, that they'd even be able to fix a spacecraft!" said Amanda. "I guess I just thought we had some more time left. Can you believe the amount of wonders, locations, creatures, and places to see and discover here? Why should we return to war?"

"I agree," said Lina's voice from the opposite side of the room. "But I have to tell you, everything's been so rushed I haven't had time to rest or associate anything. Can we do it? Can we actually walk up to people and... *touch* them?"

"There are *too many* things to discuss," said Sam. "For now we should focus on getting home safely."

He clicked on the panel and the craft's door slid back inside, closing. He set a countdown for fifty-nine minutes and began calibrating the engines through the control panel. The ship vibrated once more and Sam said, excited:

"It's really working! The propulsion levels are through the roof again! I can't believe they fixed it!"

After an hour passed, the sun went down on Gliese and the spacecraft rose from the ground.

Chapter Twenty-One - Reign of Fire

Once the craft had risen seven kilometers from the ground, the entire structure shook violently from the sides and Amanda stared through the tiny windows to see Anyara below them and the dark purple night sky on the horizon. Then, as Sam stabilized the propulsion and they floated around for a moment, the ship was jolted upwards by something below them. They began rising again, and each one held a tighter grip on their seats. The craft then stopped moving and plummeted. Looking through the windows, Amanda saw they'd been engulfed by the same blue lights that surrounded the craft during their first trip.

"We must be inside the warp bubble already" said Sam, noticing Amanda staring outside.

The ship continued to fall and Amanda closed her eyes, reminded of the unpleasant sensation of a never-ending drop, breathing in and out, trying to clear her mind from worry or panic. After a few moments had passed, they looked through the window to see the blue energy around them seem to turn green.

"Please let this be over soon" said Amanda as they continued to drop. The fall suddenly halted and all four looked around, confused.

"We're back" said Sam, hitting a couple buttons on the panel. Amanda saw the green energy's color was extremely reminiscent of Earth's northern lights, and asked:

"Is this the aurora all around us?"

"Yes, yes it is!" yelled Sam excited, and Amanda unlocked her safety belts and ran to the windows to get a closer look at what was below them.

"Amanda, don't get up yet, it's not safe!" warned Sam.

"It's snow, guys! There's ice below us! Have we landed in Iceland?" asked Amanda, looking through the tiny glass windows. She saw the craft floating up in between a spectacular show of northern lights surrounding them, with the snowy white mountains on the horizon below.

***

"If you want my opinion, I say we seek shelter somewhere until we figure out a way to end him," said Amanda, sipping her tea and placing the mug on the table. They'd walked a few miles after landing the craft in the snowy mountains until they found a small village with wooden cabins and entered the local coffee shop.

"This is *Egilsstaoir*, a small village seven miles from *Eiðar*," spoke the waitress with a thick Icelandic accent. "Where are you headed?"

"Then we're not far from Hallo Woods at all," said Amanda, ignoring the waitress's question. Stryker and Sam ordered some coffee as Lina asked Amanda:

"So what do you think now you know we're not that far from The Firm?"

"I don't know," answered Amanda, sipping her tea once again. There were half a dozen other customers sitting on tables nearby and theirs had a window that looked outside into the snowy Icelandic fields. Amanda stared outside wonderingly and continued: "Stranded here in Iceland it's as if the world's the same. This place is so isolated from everything... can we just take a moment to acknowledge the fact we're sitting safely in a warm place, back *home*? I can't think properly today."

"Yeah, tell me about it," said Stryker. "I keep thinking about Placo, Uyara, the Cerberuses..."

"How many days has it been, exactly?" asked Lina, intrigued.

"Hell, I'm not even sure of that," answered Amanda. "We need to find some place where we can rest for the night."

"I think this is a bed and breakfast, as a matter of fact," said Stryker. "Want me to check?" Amanda nodded and Stryker got up and walked towards the counter to talk to an elderly man who was counting bills of Icelandic krones. The waitress came back with their coffees and Lina looked up to talk to the woman.

"We've been.... away, without being able to communicate or see any news for the past week. Did anything... important happen?"

"I'll tell you this, we are certainly lucky to live here" answered the waitress. The woman was in her mid-40s, wearing jeans and a red snow coat and chewing gum. "I think Iceland, Africa and Australia are the only safe places left to go to! We get news everyday of new bombings in the Americas and more and more deaths in Europe and Asia,"

"But the last big attack was at the UN, right?" asked Lina.

"Yes, yes," answered the woman. "But there are thousands and thousands of deaths every day... the suicide rates have gone through the roof."

"We can stay here overnight. The second floor's got two spare bedrooms," said Stryker, arriving back at the table.

"You're not from here, are you?" asked the waitress. "I'm Bibbi Boken, by the way - and I'm sorry to ask..."

"We're from Chicago," answered Amanda. "But I grew up here. Why do you ask?"

"Well, it's just that we've gotten more and more visitors from abroad - people are popping in from all over the world, running away from the chaos. I was just curious, that's all. Is there anything else I can get for you?" asked Bibbi.

"We want the house's specialty. We haven't had a proper meal in ages," said Sam. Bibbi nodded and turned around, walking to the counter to place their order.

"I get what's happening now," said Amanda, "now she's said masses are running away from the major cities. Our society's always perceived and understood itself through multiple contexts. The confirmation of marine and microbiological life in Europa changes most of these contexts drastically, and they come from an undisputable source. What I'd suspected about the sleeping masses was right - a sizeable chunk of the population is simply in denial."

"But what does it change, really?" asked Stryker. "We've been to Gliese and back. We know more than these people could ever cope with. Yet we're standing here and talking like the rational, thinking beings we are. Nothing's really changed, has it?"

"Yes, but we don't depend on faith or count on higher powers to get through the day. More than half the world isn't as fortunate as we are, and *these* are the enraged ones," answered Amanda.

"They need to see what we saw. The ability we've been given is what's going to bring this to them. I truly believe that if you take the proper time and care for each person, they'll get it, because it's the truth. They're fighting and warring because they refuse to accept a stamp on their foreheads that they were wrong this whole time. That most of their beliefs were fiction. It's offensive because it's harsh and it's a delicate matter... perhaps the most delicate of all."

"The world's been told the universe is far vaster, far more alive than we'd ever imagined, but they're taking that from marine and microbiological life forms. What if the world really knew the truth? The truth that we share? It's not only marine life, we've contacted rational, thinking, evolved beings that thrive peacefully in an apolitical society without laws. How would they handle that?" asked Amanda. All four remained in silence at the table, sipping their drinks.

"It's always been in the odds. We've just turned a blind eye to it."

"What did I tell you about conformity when we first arrived in the Lair?" asked Amanda. "Bear with me here. When you stack up our race against Gliese, you can't help but think of us as vermin."

"Don't say that, Amanda. It makes you sound like your father," said Lina. Amanda arched her eyebrows and asked back:

"Are you being serious? There's an obvious difference. I don't want to destroy any of the vermin, I want to help them! I want to be like freaking Mother Nature to them!" she said, laughing. Lina and Stryker laughed as well, and Sam opened a half-smile. A few moments later, Bibbi returned with their dinner and they relished a home-cooked meal, without speaking much until everyone finished. After a few minutes, Lina and Amanda made their way upstairs to sleep, and Sam and Stryker went for a walk around the village to burn off their coffee high. Lina threw herself on the first bed in her bedroom, soon feeling overwhelmed by sleep.

"Maybe we should touch Bibbi tomorrow morning and see what happens to her," said Amanda, unfolding her sheets. Lina saw her vision turning black and her eyelashes felt heavy.

"We'll do that. Try to get some sleep..." she whispered back, lapsing into slumber.

Lina opened her eyes and her line of vision was pitch black. She breathed in and felt the texture of cloth circling her lips and nose and immediately panicked when she realized she was hooded. Her breathing became erratic, and she began moving her body around, feeling her hands strapped to the arms of the chair and her legs tied to the base. She frantically began twirling and turning her body, trying to move around or free herself somehow.

"No need, sweetie, no need," said a man's voice in the background. Lina immediately froze as she heard the man's somber tone and remained silent.

"Where am I? Lina? Stryker?" said Amanda's voice whispering beside her. Her voice also seemed muffled.

"Amanda, *I'm here*" whispered Lina.

"I'm here, too" said Stryker to Lina's right.

"Me, as well" said Sam's voice also to her right.

"Yes, well, isn't this a very happy reunion indeed," said the man again. Lina felt someone pull the bag from her head and she found herself inside an abandoned cathedral. Oswald sat on a marble chair and had his feet up on a desk, in front of the altar, which was composed of four coffins adorning the raised dais. He wore a black tuxedo and light came from the ceiling and behind the stained glass windows set into the walls. A large bronze crucifix hung above the sanctuary, and the floor had several rows of pews. Lina looked to the sides to see her three friends tied up alongside her, staring up at Oswald. Four Firm guards stood behind them, holding a tight grip on their chairs.

Amanda looked at Oswald with rage and spat on the floor.

"Now what?" she yelled, fixating her sight on her father. "You really thought I'd let you go through with it? I'd let you sail away to Gliese and destroy what you left behind?"

Oswald gave a half-smile and remained in silence for a few seconds, staring at them ironically.

"You took something from me. You took everything I've worked to achieve during my life. Your motives are irrelevant to me."

"Well, that brings me back to my first question," said Amanda. "Now what? What, you're going to kill us? Look at what you've done to Earth. You've fueled a fire you can't control anymore, haven't you? You never expected your plan to backfire, did you? Tell me Daddy, did you scream, throw a fit? How many times have you thought about putting a bullet through my head since then? It truly doesn't matter what you try to do. I'll be forever *grateful* that I took this away from you," answered Amanda, smiling back at her father sarcastically.

Oswald punched his desk and screamed, enraged: "I'm going to end you, Amanda. I want to see you smile a few hours from now. Should I start by recalling my obliviousness in accepting a hacker into my facility?" said Oswald. "Stryker Pendarvis, would you look me in the eye?"

Stryker raised his head and stared at Oswald, visibly nervous.

"By hacking the center panels you overrode the visual and audio feeds, didn't you? We knew your group was up to something as soon as all you began to do in the feed was *sleep*. Were you proud of yourself for achieving that, Stryker?"

Stryker hesitated for a few seconds and then answered back: "As a matter of fact, I was, yes."

"Sam... my own Sam," said Oswald. "How could you betray me?" Sam looked at Oswald with angst, yelling:

"How can you question that? You sentenced our group to literally work on something that would kill us."

"I fixed you so you wouldn't behave this way."

"It seems you forgot to rip out one last inch of self-worth," answered Sam.

Oswald got up from his chair, opened a drawer in his desk, and retrieved a small silver gun.

"Allow me to correct my mistake, then," he enunciated, walking alongside the desk and then making his way towards the group. All four flinched at the sight of the weapon and Lina felt her heart pounding against her chest. She tried to move her hands and legs but failed, noticing her skin burning red from the friction. Oswald approached Amanda and Stryker's chairs at a slow pace, and upon reaching them, he gradually lifted his arm and aimed his gun at Stryker's forehead. He then turned towards Amanda and ultimately directed his aim towards Lina. Lina felt her head thud against her chest and as she opened her mouth to speak, Oswald turned and fired a shot in the opposite direction. She heard Sam screaming and inched her head to see the bullet had gone through Sam's thigh as he screamed in pain, looking at his bleeding gunshot wound. Sam's chair rocked forth and to the sides as he writhed in pain. Oswald let out a sinister laugh that echoed through the cathedral's walls.

"You're sick!" screamed Amanda enraged. Oswald looked at his daughter with an expression of disgust and switched his focus to Stryker.

"You see, I don't truly wish to take your lives away instantly," said Oswald, smiling and focusing his gaze on him. Stryker breathed nervously and his entire face was drenched in sweat. "But it bothers me you have such ease in standing up to me with your prized talents."

Oswald placed his gun on top of Stryker's left hand and stared at him silently.

"No, no, don't do it, please" begged Stryker, trying to move his hand away from the gun, centered on the back of his hand. Oswald pressed the cold metal against Stryker's skin, forcing his hand down.

"Shouldn't I?" asked Oswald, without moving an inch. He twisted his head to the sides and asked: "Or should I?"

"No, no, no, no you shouldn't---"

Oswald opened his mouth wide for a full smile and pulled the trigger. A second loud gunshot erupted through the area, and Stryker screamed in terror.

"Fuck! Fuck! *Fuuuuuuck*!" screamed Stryker as Oswald turned around. He looked at his hand and tried to move his fingers, but was filled with unbearable pain. The gunshot had gone straight through the center of his palm, and Stryker screamed as he looked at it.

"Let's see how fast you can type those feeds away, now" said Oswald, walking back to his desk. Lina heard the guards giggling behind her as they watched Sam and Stryker cry and scream in pain.

"Those wounds won't kill you, they'll only begin pouring out your blood." He turned around, sitting on his desk and picking up a handkerchief from it to clean the firearm. "I'd like to see these floors covered in red."

"Don't you get it?" screamed Amanda. "What will this bring to you? Is this bringing you joy?"

"Oh, very much so," answered Oswald.

"And that's your plan? To keep increasing the body count? It's over, Oswald, you're not going anywhere. You're not getting away from Earth. Is this the Earth you want to live in? Hurting us won't bring your energy back."

"You're right, it won't. But no one takes something from me and walks out unscathed. Guards, tie the straps."

The guards behind them turned around and began going through items stacked in the row of seats behind them. They heard the noise of clinking metals and ripping plastic, but no matter how much they turned their heads back, they could not see exactly what items the men held in their hands. A few seconds later, they walked back to their chairs and began gluing wires to their necks and heads. Oswald picked up a sharp, small knife from his pocket and Amanda saw the blade's reflection shine.

"What is this?" asked Amanda. "What are you going to do to us?"

"I will merely attempt to perfect you, that is all" said Oswald. "I believe there's a lot to gain by ripping out every emotion from you. Of course, there's one asset here who's become expendable, since perfecting him clearly wasn't enough to ensure the proper behavior from his part," said Oswald, focusing on Sam. The guards glued and strapped multiple wires to his body, and Oswald walked back to his desk and retrieved a remote control from the drawer.

"My plan for you is considerably shorter," said Oswald, smiling and walking towards the group again. He pressed a button on the remote and Sam screamed, as the wires tied to his body began buzzing and electrocuting him. Oswald pressed his finger firmly on the button, pointing it at Sam as he watched him fry and scream in suffering. As he screamed, Amanda saw Oswald's stare turn cold and noticed he looked at Sam with a sick lust in his eyes. Oswald took the knife and began cutting Sam's chest, slicing the blade down his torso slowly, opening up his mouth to a wider smile with each passing second. Sam's loud yell echoed across the room for a few seconds and then he stopped, leaving only the buzzing sounds in the background. Sam's body became motionless and his head fell to the side, dead.

"You killed him!" screamed Lina, feeling her eyes fill with tears of rage and horror.

Oswald looked at Lina, raised his eyebrows and asked: "Well, yes, but there wasn't any use left for him, was there?"

"There's no reasoning with you," said Amanda. "You're evil and you accept it. I refuse to believe we're father and daughter."

Amanda looked down as the guards continued to place wires on her, Lina's and Stryker's bodies and saw a few of them were twirling around the chair's bases. She lifted her feet and stepped on two wires, pushing them to the ground and holding them down with her foot.

Oswald looked at Stryker and seemed to notice something bulging in his shirt's pocket.

"What's this that we have here?" he asked, reaching in to grab the item. He retrieved the ocarina they'd gotten from Illi and Illia and looked at it curiously. "Is this... a whistle of sorts? Did I invent it?" he asked sarcastically. Oswald blew the whistle and a few notes of a high-pitched melody soared through the cathedral. Oswald then looked at the item again, saying: "Is this of any value to you?"

"What does it matter to you?" asked Lina, breaking her silence.

"It *speaks*!" said Oswald, opening up his arms and staring at Lina. Amanda looked at Stryker's hand to see blood dripping through the chair's arm to the floor, forming a small puddle from his open bullet wound. Stryker looked at her and saw her staring at his foot. He then looked at hers and saw she held a couple of wires with her foot. She subtly elevated her upper body from the chair, bringing the seat along with her, and proceeded to shift the chair's feet onto the cables, intending to sever them on resuming her seated position. She repeated the process a few times, disguising her movements as slight twitches of discomfort and reluctance as the guards glued the final wires onto them. Amanda looked down to see she'd successfully ripped the insulation from the wires.

"What's your place in this?" asked Oswald, focusing on Lina. "I know about you. This is not even your fight. You're just a background player... with no redeeming qualities."

Amanda dragged the foot that held the wires to the right and Stryker caught her, whispering:

"I get it. The blood combusts the wires, right? Like salt water."

Amanda nodded and Stryker lifted his left foot from the straps as much as he could, dragging the wires towards his puddle of blood. The second he succeeded and the wires began short-circuiting, Oswald turned his head and caught them, screaming:

"What are you doing? Take that out of there!" he ordered to the guards.

In a fraction of a second, the wires combusted and they saw a stream of electricity flash along the wire, landing on the central hardware towers, where one guard typed frantically, trying to shut down the panel. In a matter of seconds, the wire caught fire and the flames expanded onto the rows and pews behind them. The guards began running away from the fire and Oswald looked around the cathedral, following the spreading flames. Amanda, Lina and Stryker began thrusting their bodies and chairs forward, trying to jump out of the ring of fire forming around them.

"You brought this upon yourselves!" screamed Oswald, reaching for things in his desk drawer in a rush. "I'll see you in Hell!" he yelled as he picked up his gun again. A couple of guards ran past him and kicked down a door to their left. Oswald turned around and jumped down from the altar, running toward his bodyguards. Lina, Amanda and Stryker frantically tried to raise their chairs from the floor as much as they could. Lina coughed from the smoke coming from the flames behind them, and Amanda felt the scorching heat from the flames as sweat dripped down her forehead. She heard Stryker beginning to cough to her right, and the flames reached the walls to their sides. The flames crackled loudly and objects behind them crashed on the floor.

"Somebody please help us," whispered Amanda as she cried in desperation and panic. Despite their efforts to break free from the straps, Lina, Stryker, and Amanda struggled to maintain composure as they coughed and gasped for air, with Amanda's blood pressure dropping as she looked up to the sanctuary. Her sight became blurred and her balance dizzy and behind her erupted the loudest thud yet - as if an entire wall or block of concrete had fallen to the ground.

Amanda coughed uncontrollably as she inhaled a deep breath of smoke, and felt her body beginning to feel weightless, preparing herself for the worst. She let her head fall and closed her eyes. Then she felt two large hands gripping each shoulder, holding her tight. Her body was lifted up along with the chair and her vision turned to black.

Chapter Twenty-Two - Bells of Heaven

Amanda opened her eyes slowly, twisting her lids at the extreme brightness outside. She covered her face with her hands and breathed in, coming to again. She looked down at her body before looking up again and saw that her body was protected inside a glass case that started at her shoulders. Amanda looked up to see a multitude of Vargans floating above her in empty space, wearing white gowns. She lay inside a gigantic oval white and black room, being kept horizontal by a glass pot. Above her, Vargans typed, clicked and processed intently on large screens that surrounded the entire dome above her. She looked to her sides to see Lina and Stryker lying beside her, deep asleep inside their glass compartments. The entire room vibrated while the beings effortlessly floated around above her, going about their work.

"You've awoken," said a familiar voice below her. Amanda looked toward the voice to see Synthious floating in her direction.

"Synthious! Where am I?" asked Amanda. A few Vargans noticed her awakening and glanced at her, then spoke in an unknown language to each other.

"You're in one of our anti-matter spacecraft. It seems we've severely underestimated the dangers of this aggravating situation."

"Wait, you've come to Earth, then?" she asked, confused. Lina opened her eyes and began scanning around the room, landing on Amanda.

"Where are we?" she asked. Amanda looked to her right to see Stryker had also awakened.

"As I said, you have been safely rescued by us. Your Cerberus heard the whistle of the ocarina from far away, as soon as we'd reached Earth."

"But why did you come here a day after we left?"

"We had severely underestimated the situation regarding one volatile element. The Council asked us to step in to aid you in eliminating this threat."

"Yeah, well, that's the second time I've heard you talk about underestimation," answered Amanda.

"We are advanced, but not perfect - we are forced to intervene in many events, and this is one," answered Synthious, raising his body up to float above Amanda. "This man is your father, I've been informed - he's chosen a dark, insidious path for his life. Many of us had high hopes for him, since he's been the driving force behind achieving faster-than-light travel on Earth... but it seems as if Earth shall only begin awakening once we cut evil at its root."

Synthious clicked on a blue button at the center of Amanda's glass pod, opening it.

"How can we take him down, though?" asked Stryker as Synthious floated towards him to open his pod.

"You'll find many of us have traveled to aid you. If you'll escort me out of the healing chambers, you'll find our best Andromedae, Plethorean and Vargan warriors outside."

"Yeah, but they've got heavy ammo. I'm talking big guns," said Stryker as he got out of his pod, stretching his arms.

"We have weapons as well. But we don't shoot guns," said Synthious.

"Well, what do you do, then?" asked Stryker.

"We fire to dematerialize."

"Thank you for saving us," said Amanda, sitting up as Synthious moved to free Lina.

"Thank your Cerberuses, who took each of you from inside the ring of fire," answered Synthious. "They are outside, and will be glad to see you."

The group got out of their pods and floated towards an opening that led to a corridor on their right. As they entered the gap, the gravitational field from the corridor activated and they felt their bodies being dragged back, pulled down to the ground. The ship appeared to be silver or white, with walls made of porcelain. Amanda followed Synthious down the long hallway once her feet touched the ground. They passed through oval glass doors that led to other rooms and compartments on each side, walking a straight path towards the exit from the ship. Finally, they reached a round glass door at the end and walked outside.

The sun was about to set in Iceland, and they stood on top of a mountain. On the horizon nearby they could see Hallormsstaður's woods and Amanda immediately walked towards the edge of a cliff nearby, to get her bearing.

"We can see The Firm from here," said Amanda, looking down at the steep fall below her. In the distance, she could see the roof of her house and The Firm's enormous dome to her right, a few miles away from where they stood. The wind blew past them in a cold rush and Amanda was reminded of the familiar sense of isolation and solitude she'd usually associate with Iceland, as she looked at the landscape in front of her, seeing no trace of living beings nearby.

"You haven't looked behind you yet," said Lina, and Amanda turned around to see Gliese's magnificent spacecraft in front of her. The ship had the form of a thick frisbee and seemed to be half the width of The Firm's dome. Amanda noticed the afternoon sunset casting an orange glow on the craft's polished white surface, causing the glass entrance door to reflect the sun's rays. Uyara emerged from the side of the ship and then Illi and Illia walked out, followed by Savann.

They walked towards them and more and more Gliesian beings emerged from behind the ship.

"Uyara! Illi and Illia!" yelled Amanda, walking towards them. "Synthious, you're all here!" said Amanda as half-a-dozen Cerberuses emerged alongside the Vargans, Plethoreans and Andromedans. Then, they looked up to see dozens of flying Kratens, flapping their wings in an area behind the ship.

"*We are here to aid you in this battle,*" said Uyara's voice in their minds. There seemed to be fifty warriors around them, and Synthious knocked his cane once on the mountain's rocky ground. Amanda, Lina and Stryker watched in awe as everyone's arms seemed to burst with light, seemingly out of nowhere. They then saw the beings raise their arms into the air and they could see the light coming out from the center of their palms, not their arms. Each Vargan, Andromedan or Plethorean raised both arms in the air and had a tiny ball of light shining at the center of their hands.

"This is how we *fight*" said Synthious, walking towards the front of the group to face Amanda, Lina and Stryker. The lights grew strong and burst from their hands onto the sky above them, like a hundred lanterns had been turned on and pointed at the clouds. Grey clouds above them dissipated and all around them rain poured as the lights seemed to evaporate the haze, as if shining light onto the darkness. The hundred rays of light persisted, and Amanda,

Lina, and Stryker observed the grey clouds disappearing, leading to a wide, open orange sky.

"Our guns are sources of light, which we place in each hand. These rays dematerialize anything that's in front of them. If we aimed this at a solid object, like a tree, or even a person, the ray would go through you and you'd die without even feeling or sensing the lethal hole left across you," announced Synthious. "This way, if we have to kill, we aim at the heart and the being falls dead instantly, without knowing."

The Cerberuses circled the group and made their way towards Amanda, Lina and Stryker. All six winged tigers sat around them, greeting Lina, Stryker and Amanda with the tip of their nose as they watched the lights displayed above, continuously opening up the night sky.

Amanda smiled confidently and closed her eyes, sensing the raindrops collapse against her skin. Even with eyes closed, she could see the beaming in front of her pointing up. She looked to her left, down at the cliff to glance at The Firm's dome one last time. She then looked back at the group as they retrieved their weapons and switched off the lights, nodding reassuringly to Synthious.

"But if we do this, you'll be exposed. They have cameras and video feeds all around them in a tight security system. You'll have to kill everyone that sees you," noted Amanda.

"We are aware of the circumstances," said Synthious. "Again, there are two paths. What shall happen remains to be seen."

***

"We'll cover them from each side, then," said Lina, mounting on her Cerberus. A few hours had passed and the entire group had reunited outside before heading out to battle. Synthious had given each a dematerializer, which they'd placed on the palm of their left hand and it was already pitch black outside. Lina would take Uyara and the Andromedans to the lake near the entrance and Amanda would head inside with Illi and Illia, hunting for Oswald. Stryker and the Plethoreans would approach from the center, expecting The Firm's security to tackle them as they crossed the open field. The Cerberuses would aid any who were injured, transporting them back to the ship and Synthious would lead the Vargans in the surrounding mountains to dematerialize the dome that covered The Firm so they could infiltrate from the air, landing on the top floor.

"Dahr dar imanns nar! Dahr dar immans nei!" screamed a group of Vargans and Plethoreans to their side.

"What is that?" asked Amanda to Synthious, who was talking to Uyara next to the ship's entrance.

"They're chanting for war," said Synthious. "Dahr dar immans nar, dahr dar immans nei means... Free from the vessel that contains me, we move because we must," answered

Synthious. "They're liberating their attachment to their physical bodies since we know this is a battle fought not for us, but for higher powers. You *must* keep that in your mind."

Amanda mounted on her Cerberus and saw Stryker by her side, already ready to take off. Then, the commotion that came from the soldiers turned to silence and all beings turned their focus to the group.

"We are ready when you are," announced Synthious. Amanda looked around and breathed in, concentrating on what she could do to find Oswald once inside The Firm. She saw the Kratens descending from flight and their respective Plethoreans and Andromedans mounting on them.

"This is it" said Amanda, looking to her right and left to check on Lina and Stryker. Both nodded reassuringly and smiled back at her. "Now that we have them, we stand a fair chance of succeeding. All we've done comes down to this."

"We have to cut the head off the snake," said Lina, with a firm tone to her voice.

"I'll do this not only for me, but for Ripley and Sam as well," said Stryker.

Amanda breathed in and closed her eyes. She opened them after a few seconds and yelled, addressing the entire army.

"We must destroy that facility! It's done nothing but bring evil, death and destruction upon us!" she screamed.

Then, all Vargans, Andromedans and Plethoreans answered back to her, in a shout:

"HOY WEY HO!" and they raised their right arms into the air.

Amanda and her Cerberus stepped forward a bit and Amanda yelled her call to battle:

"For Earth! And for Sam and Ripley!" she screamed, raising her fist in the air, as her Cerberus began flapping his wings to take off and the army in front of them roared back "*HOY!*" and began mounting on their Kratens and Cerberuses. Her Cerberus rose into the air alongside Lina's and Stryker's, and Synthious, Illi and Illia and Uyara took the remaining three winged tigers. The wind seemed to get even colder as they flew up, and Amanda looked around and smiled at the surrounding sight, as the army took to the skies and they began flying in The Firm's direction.

Lina guided a flock of flying Kratens to her left while heading towards the lake. Meanwhile, Stryker led his pack to descend and land first. Amanda continued flying forward as her Cerberus flapped his wings against the chilly, Icelandic air. Once she saw herself flying above the open field that led to the entrance of The Firm, she signaled for the winged tiger to descend and she looked around to see the three separate groups in the distance, disappearing in the background, becoming smaller as each took up their position silently.

Then, all around them, The Firm's alarm blasted into the night, as the grating, robotic sounds signaling a perimeter breach repeatedly echoed through the deserted fields.

"WARNING! PERIMETER BREACH! MULTIPLE UNKNOWN ASSETS APPROACHING! MULTIPLE UNKNOWN ASSETS APPROACHING!"

A multitude of lights shone in the distance and Amanda watched as Synthious and his pack began attacking the Firm's glass dome by attempting to dematerialize the protective glass. As the jolts of light collapsed against the glass dome, Amanda watched the glass crack on each side. A dozen more lights appeared, and the army attacked in full force from above until finally the glass shattered into thousands of pieces and a deafening crack announced the explosion of the massive protective dome while the alarm continued to blast repeatedly.

As soon as she saw the bubble had been crashed, Amanda signaled her Cerberus to change course. The creature touched the ground for momentum and flapped his wings in the direction of Synthious's army. They flew into The Firm's top floor, where a dozen Kratens had already landed. Andromedans and Vargans dismounted and headed out with glowing white lights in their palms. After a few seconds, Amanda landed on the last floor and immediately recognized the corridor that led to what was once their dormitory. By her side, a handful of Vargans and Andromedans had already arrived and Amanda signaled for the group to follow her as she made her way towards the shaft.

As she began walking, she saw two doors burst open in front of her and multiple armed Firm guards erupted out of the rooms. As soon as Amanda glimpsed their firearms, she reached out her arm and looked instantly to her right to see two Vargans doing the same. They immediately beamed at each guard, aiming for their heart. As the guards turned around from the door to spot the invading group, some immediately began firing as they aimed their beams at their bodies. The Vargans hit two of the ten guards, who immediately fell to the floor. Amanda panicked as she heard multiple gunshots being fired around her.

She threw her body on the floor, aiming her palm at the legs of the eight remaining guards, seeing two other guards falling with smoking holes through their chest. Amanda hit a guard's leg, and he fell to the floor, firing his rifle in all directions, screaming in pain. She looked up to see one of the guards had his aim on her so she instantly placed her palm in front of her body, aiming for his forehead. As the man targeted her, the beam hit his head, and he fell to the floor, dead.

An Andromedan fell by her side, dead. Amanda glanced at him without moving her aim and felt enraged at the sight. She looked back to see three other guards down while the remaining two aimed their shotguns at her once more. A Vargan fell by her side, dead and as Amanda aimed for a guard's heart, she threw her right hand across the floor to reach for the dead man's rifle. As she hit him with the ray in her hand, she switched her focus to the other one as she raised her right hand, picking up the rifle. She took it in both hands and shot the guard several times in the chest, screaming in rage as she fired the bullets. She looked back to see the remaining Andromedan and three Vargans still standing, and a dozen Kratens flying above in their direction. Amanda breathed in and continued to make her way towards the shaft.

***

As the Andromedans approached the lake, their Cerberuses descended and they jumped onto the water when the alarm went off. Lina landed near the shore and dismounted, looking up at the Firm's building without its usual surrounding protection. Uyara landed beside her and spoke through her mind:

"You must hide, Lina. Fly alongside your Cerberus above us, you'll be safer that way."

Oswald's lab door burst open as an infinite number of armed guards emerged from The Firm's entrance, led by Arlo. Lina looked to her right to see the group of Plethoreans arriving near Amanda's childhood home and ran to mount her Cerberus as she watched the two impending armies march to the center of the open field. Her Cerberus took off flying as

Lina saw the Andromedans camouflage themselves in the lake, as the Firm's army passed without noticing.

"Open fire!" yelled Arlo from the field.

In a fraction of a second, Lina looked to her right again as she heard shots being fired. The lake's blue waters then burst into light as the Andromedans revealed their location and turned on their rays, blasting them at the guards. Then, the Plethoreans also deployed their rays, as the first rows of the Firm's guards began to fall dead on the ground, unable to defend themselves from the crossfire.

More and more guards emerged from the Firm's entrance - however, as the first rows fell, more and more guards would come out to replace them. Lina looked around to notice the Firm's army seemed to double theirs - and she signaled her Cerberus to fly above Oswald's lab and land on its ceiling, above the door where the guards appeared from. The creature landed on the ceiling and Lina dismounted. She turned on the ray, crouched down, and aimed for the guards below, keeping herself hidden from view.

She successfully blasted around a dozen who made their way out, but after a few seconds, she noticed the stream of soldiers finally seemed to end. Leving the door open, Lina waited for the right moment to jump from the ceiling and enter the Firm's dark entrance corridor as the guards made their way out onto the field. With no-one in sight, she quickly began running down the corridor, looking for the first available shaft.

***

The Andromedan and the three Vargans accompanied Amanda across the corridor until they reached the shaft. As she saw the closed doors in front of them, she looked up to where she knew the camera was for the video feed. The Vargans mumbled something in *Melliaro* which she couldn't understand, but Amanda focused on the camera above her and began speaking:

"I know you're there. Take me to you. I've come here to end this."

The shaft's doors remained closed for a few seconds, and when Amanda sighed thinking her plan had failed, she heard the engines moving and the metal doors slid open. Amanda turned around to address the beings behind her.

"I have to do this on my own," said Amanda, closing her fingers in a tight grip where her ray rested. She saw a group of Kratens land a few meters away from them and signaled with her head for them to join the others. She then turned around and entered the shaft, without thinking twice.

The shaft's doors closed in front of her and the elevator moved, descending. She closed her eyes and breathed in deeply, trying to concentrate on firing the ray at her father as soon as she spotted him. After a few seconds, the shaft stopped descending and halted as the doors slid open.

Amanda found herself inside Oswald's office once again, the black stone walls reflecting each polished golden object and collectible from the room. Amanda walked out and immediately saw her father sitting in his chair, looking straight at her, a guard on each side. Amanda looked around the room as she began reaching out her hand to aim her ray, but was left distracted and confused by the sight. In the center of the room stood a hooded person wearing The Firm's uniform. The shiny triangle badge shone on their bust as Amanda identified the person as a woman.

"It seems you've brought some new companions back with you," commented Oswald. "Fascinating!"

"Who is this? Who is she?" asked Amanda, looking at the woman in the chair. She had her legs and arms strapped, much like they'd been the day before.

"This?" asked Oswald, ironically. He had a naive expression on his face, which only fueled Amanda's rage. "You're not the only one with surprises, it seems," he answered.

Oswald smiled slightly and got up from his chair. He walked towards the hooded woman and pulled the cloth from her face. Strapped to the chair, breathing, stood Ripley. Amanda brought her hands to her mouth in shock as she felt her heart jump in her chest.

"Ripley!" she cried, and Ripley looked at her with a scared, wary expression.

"You have to get me out of here," said Ripley, with a trembling voice.

"But... but you were dead," said Amanda. "She... she was..."

"Many people died as Arlo tried to prevent you from hijacking my ship" said Oswald, smiling. "But when we found Ripley her heart was still beating, and her wounds hadn't been fatal... You see, if you try to harm me, then I'll explode her into tiny little pieces."

Amanda closed her eyes and breathed in, trying to calm herself. In a fraction of a second, she raised her arm and aimed at the guard on her father's right, hitting him straight in the head. The guard fell dead behind Oswald as her father's eyes widened in shock, then looked at her enraged, screaming:

"What is that? What have you done?" He screamed, with his face becoming redder and a vein bulging in the center of his forehead. Amanda quickly switched her beam to the guard on his left, hitting him as he picked up his weapon and Oswald stood up, reaching for his pocket. He walked towards Amanda as he retrieved a remote device in his hand with three white buttons.

"Now, your friend will die," he said.

Amanda closed her palm and pointed her hand at Oswald.

"Drop it or I'll beam you. I can dissolve a hole right through you in a second," she said, feeling her anger rising as her heart pounded against her chest.

Oswald raised his eyebrows and then stretched out his arms, raising his hands in the air.

"If you beam me, I'll press the button," he announced. "Let's talk,"

"There's nothing to talk about. This is where it ends," said Amanda. Oswald sighed and answered:

"Amanda, why do you hate me so? Why is it your battle to stop me?"

"Because I'm the only one who can," she answered, flatly. "I've recently found out there're bigger plans for your so-called ant-hive. You think of yourself as omnipotent, but the world is not your chessboard."

"My team and my finances say otherwise."

"They're not your team," answered Amanda, feeling tears of rage beginning to surface. "You've corrupted them, you've messed with their heads. That's what you do to people. But it turns out you don't get to call the shots anymore."

Amanda quickly glanced at Ripley, who stared straight at her. Ripley whispered:

"Kill him."

Amanda looked back at her father to catch him slightly inching his thumb towards the first of the three white buttons in his hand. Amanda immediately opened up her palm and a beam of light hit Oswald on the neck. Oswald immediately ran for the shaft, screaming and holding his neck. Amanda ran to Ripley as she saw her father turning around to aim a tiny silver pistol at the both of them. Amanda attempted to grab Ripley's ropes, but halted when Oswald turned around. Instead, she lifted her left hand and directed another beam at him. He threw himself inside the shaft as the beam cut through his thigh and he fired a shot in Amanda's direction. At first thinking she'd dodged it, Amanda fell to the floor screaming in pain as she felt her left arm being ripped open by his bullet.

"Amanda!" screamed Ripley, jolting her chair forward as Amanda fell to the floor and the shaft's doors closed as Oswald got away.

Amanda screamed in suffering and reached her other hand to hold her shoulder, as she looked at the bloody wound to see the bronze bullet on the floor.

"Through and out," whispered Amanda in relief, catching her breath and trying to ignore the burning and aching coming from her arm. She breathed in and closed her eyes, reaching her right hand for Ripley's ropes right after. A few seconds later she reached her other hand and began undoing Ripley's straps and knots.

"Are you okay?" Ripley asked.

"I should ask you that" said Amanda, breathing erratically.

"Your arm's bleeding... bad," said Ripley. "We need to get out,"

Amanda glanced at her arm and then back at the chair as she continued to free Ripley.

"My arm's gonna have to wait," said Amanda as she finished untying the last knot in Ripley's legs and her friend stood up. Amanda got up from the floor and reached for Ripley's back, untying her hands.

"Are you healthy?" asked Amanda. "How did he keep you here?"

"I've been kept in solitary ever since you warped. But it took me a couple days to come to again. I lost a lot of blood, but I'm fine. I guess I can't even begin to ask you what's going on,"

"We're taking it *down*. We went there and back, and we've got an army you'll never believe. Tonight we are taking him down, so we need to find him. It's strictly about him and these walls, he's the root of evil. He needs to go down *tonight*," answered Amanda as she finished untying Ripley's hands. Both women ran to the other of the four shafts in Oswald's office and entered.

"Where will we land?" asked Ripley. "Do you have any way to control them?"

"No, I don't" said Amanda as the shaft's doors closed behind them and the elevator rose.

"So there's no way of telling where we'll get out," said Ripley, as the elevator continued to move up.

"That's how it is with us," said Amanda, holding her bloody wound trying to contain the blood loss. "Each moment we're just hoping for the best."

"I love how you're in your best mood during chaos," noted Ripley. Amanda smiled slightly and the shaft's doors opened, leading them out onto the top floor again.

"Yes!" said Amanda, immediately running out, sticking her hand out. "Ripley, stay behind me."

She looked down from the metal platform onto the lower floors and saw Kratens and Cerberuses flying below, as Plethoreans and Vargans infiltrated each corner below them. In every direction she'd see bursts of iridescent light and the firing of gunshots. She looked at Ripley, who stared down the platform with her.

"They've spread throughout the entire facility," said Amanda.

"That's good, right?" asked Ripley. A Kraten landed behind them, with a Plethorean mounted on it. Ripley screamed in terror.

"That's a dinosaur!" yelled Ripley, grabbing Amanda's arm and losing her balance in fright.

"It's okay," said Amanda. "Look up," she said, and both women looked up to see a Kraten- and Cerberus-filled sky, as Gliesian warriors flew across in all directions. "That's our army," said Amanda. A Cerberus then landed beside them and Amanda recognized him as hers. She ran towards him and caressed his face, and he answered by licking her cheek. Amanda mounted on him and signaled Ripley to join her.

"Won't it eat me?" asked Ripley, standing up reluctantly. "They're... so beautiful..."

"It won't eat you. Sit behind me," answered Amanda as she reached out her hand for Ripley to hold. Ripley took it and mounted the Cerberus with her, and soon the tiger began flapping its wings and looking up. They took off and Ripley held Amanda's stomach tightly, whispering over and over, "Oh my God", as the creature rose in the air and ahead of them they saw the battle taking place in the open field below them. Multiple beams and gunshots were being fired, and Amanda looked down to see Lina standing on top of Oswald's ceiling.

"Lina!" screamed Amanda, but Lina didn't hear her. Then Amanda heard mechanical engines and looked ahead to see a black helicopter surfacing through the woods, near Oswald's laboratory. Amanda signaled for the Cerberus to fly towards it and Amanda immediately began firing beams at it.

"That's him!" she screamed as the Cerberus took off towards it. Amanda continued firing beams onto the helicopter's glass window, and as the Cerberus flew towards it, Ripley said in her ear:

"Now!"

Amanda aimed at the approaching helicopter and fired a beam into the glass window, shattering it to pieces. Oswald looked ahead in the cockpit to see both women and the creature flying towards them. The Cerberus collided head-on with the helicopter, jamming its paws in the gap where the glass window had been and causing the helicopter to crash. Amanda held a tight grip on the creature and aimed with her right hand on the helix, firing a beam at it. The helix exploded and flew to their right, as Cerberus jumped from the helicopter and took off, flying to the left.

Amanda closed her eyes, concentrating on holding tight to the winged tiger, and looked back to see the helicopter plummeting to the ground, black smoke coming out from where the helix once stood. Oswald jumped from the helicopter and a few seconds later opened a black emergency parachute. The helicopter crashed against the woods, collapsing above the trees as a loud explosion came from below.

Amanda signaled for the creature to follow Oswald as he descended into the forest, and the creature reached the man a few meters before they hit the ground. Oswald looked at them and, for the first time. Amanda saw a frightened expression on his face. His eyes widened and, as he opened his mouth to speak, Amanda reached out her right arm and fired a beam into his heart. She fired another beam in his head and his head tumbled forward as his legs reached the trees and his parachute slowly descended into the forest.

Amanda looked at her father's body being dragged slowly down to the ground, and Ripley gripped her shoulders reassuringly.

"You did it," she whispered, as the Cerberus flapped its wings, taking off towards the lake.

Amanda looked emptily ahead, as if the world had turned to slow motion, concentrating on knowing she'd completed her task. The Cerberus landed near the lake and only when the creature reached the ground did Amanda feel a rush of relief flow through her. She looked to her right to see the Gliesian army had taken down most of The Firm's guards: Andromedans sneakily fired shots from the lake and the Plethorean army had gained ground and stood very close to the Firm's entrance. At the end of the first row of Plethoreans, stood Stryker. As she landed, he looked at them and his expression turned blank at the sight. She saw he stood in front of Arlo's dead body, and he ran towards them as Amanda and Ripley dismounted the Cerberus. Amanda noticed Stryker had an expression of utter shock in his face, and as he reached them, his eyes watered and he cried.

"How?" he asked, looking at Ripley's entire body as if she was fragile and would break into pieces at any moment.

"Wait until you hear the best part" answered Ripley, smiling.

"What?" Stryker asked, glancing at Amanda, confused.

"Oswald's dead. I shot him with their beam."

***

Amanda, Lina, Stryker and Ripley stood in the rocky landscape overlooking the field and *Hallormsstaður's* forest below. The Firm's building stood in ruins, without its glass bubble and smoke coming out from multiple floors. The sun rose on the horizon behind the Gliesian spacecraft, and the group looked at the army in front of them as they gathered after winning the battle.

"We must part ways before dawn. Our task here is done - yet yours still isn't," said Synthious, standing in front of the group. Many Plethoreans and Vargans who had been injured were being taken inside the craft and a few agitated Cerberuses and Kratens flew around them. "The root of evil has been destroyed. If enlightened one by one, Earth shall now be well on its path towards ascension."

Amanda looked at Synthious and smiled. She then asked:

"But, what are we supposed to do now, Synthious? There are far too many people on Earth: we'll never reach them all. Not alone and with no help."

Synthious stood in silence for a few seconds, and Uyara, who stood close by, near the group of Andromedans, turned around and spoke to them.

"Each person enlightened is an awakened being, aware of the truth. Each person enlightened is an ally. They themselves will help you carry on your job. Before you know it, you'll have reached the globe. You must trust. However, one of you shall come with us. We need a female human to aid us on an even greater quest. Once it is done, we shall bring you back to Earth safely."

The group looked at each other for some time, and quickly figured out what Uyara had meant.

"Wait, I'm staying?" asked Stryker. He paused for a moment, frowned and looked at Ripley. "Well, I can't say I'm unhappy, seeing as I'd like to spend some time with Ripley," he said, holding her hand. Ripley smiled at him. "How could I stand any chance of enlightening anyone, though?"

"Always remember you're being guided and protected by higher powers," said Synthious. "Take all you've learned with you, and you shall succeed. There is no way to know where the winds of destiny will take you. As you help Earth evolve, the future in which Earth and Gliese co-exist may not be a too distant one. You're the ones who came to us, after all," answered Synthious. He then inched his head forward to greet them and turned around, walking towards the craft. Uyara walked towards Stryker and Ripley and held his hand. She looked deep into his eyes in silence and spoke to him:

"May you know it is all a journey. May you flow through it with the greatest of ease," said Uyara, and she turned around. As she turned, she glanced at Amanda and spoke to them.

"When you're ready... you're expected at the ship,"

Amanda, Lina, Stryker and Ripley faced each other and smiled. The four of them held their hands and closed their eyes, feeling the icy winds of Iceland against their skin as they felt the heat coming from the horizon's rising sun.

The ground vibrated and they heard the craft's engine loading. Amanda took a couple of steps back from Lina, Ripley and Stryker.

"As soon as it's done they'll bring you back. You heard him," said Lina to Amanda.

"You can do it, Stryker," said Amanda. "Start with whoever you can,"

"I'll do my best," said Stryker. "Please don't stay too long away,"

Amanda smiled at Stryker and then turned around, beginning to walk across the ship's bridge.

After a few seconds, she was safely inside and Stryker, Lina and Ripley watched as the doors instantly shut in front of them. He looked at Ripley and hugged her.

"You know we can do it," whispered Ripley as Stryker held her in a tight embrace.

The Gliesian antimatter craft began rising into the air. No wind came from it, nor any loud noises that announced its presence - it merely lifted into the air and glided above them, flying towards the ruins of the Firm. Both watched the ship as it glided silently away from them. As soon as the spacecraft reached The Firm, they saw it jolting upwards and disappearing above, as a tiny fluorescent drop fell from it, like a shooting star. The glowing stream descended onto The Firm and Lina, Stryker and Ripley were thrown from the air onto the ground as the entire Firm's structure exploded as if it had been hit by a nuclear bomb. A gigantic curtain of smoke and fire burst through the air in the distance and the trio stared at the destruction, feeling a cathartic emotion spread through their lungs.

Chapter Twenty-Three - The Beyond

Amanda's palms grew sweaty as she stepped onto the platform leading to the first module, and the bright lights at the ship's entrance blinded her instantly. It took her some time to put in perspective the objects and beings around her, as she struggled to focus and maintain her balance while trying to follow Synthious's small but swift steps. This first module's entrance was a long, purple and brightly lit corridor with length-long white light stripes that guided you to each turn or shaft. At first, Amanda was startled by the overwhelming purple that surrounded her on the walls and ceilings. But soon, she felt a comforting vibration from the saturation of color. The ship was cold, yet cozy - what surprised her most was the feeling of security that burst through her as soon as she heard the doors shut behind her. The entire structure seemed to slightly vibrate, as Amanda noticed a soothing, yet intense humming sound to her left. Judging from her entrance position, she assumed the sound came from the center of the ship, presumably where the core energy was located.

"It won't be long now," said Synthious after they'd skipped the first corridor. "Lift-off is best experienced in the room I'm taking you to."

Amanda looked around, barely making sense of Synthious as she tried to take in as much as she could from the ship now that she properly had the time to look around. Her brain was still puzzled by the realization of the presence of peace - just a few moments before, it had been done. It was finally over. And now she was about to take off to Gliese once more.

"That's *Nitro*, mind you" -- said Synthious, looking back at her as they reached an oval glass door.

"What? Nitro?"

"It's the first of many pieces of utmost important information we are about to give you. Our planet is not named Gliese, nor has it ever been. Nitro. *We are Nitro*,"

Amanda raised her left eyebrow and licked her lips, surprised by the information. "I knew that was not the real name. It just hadn't occurred to me to ask."

Synthious gracefully smiled at her, then walked onto the glass-like substance, which Amanda soon realized was actually a liquid. He glided through to the other side unscathed, and Amanda followed suit. The liquid glass came towards her and she closed her eyes just before it touched her face, but opened them when she realized she had succeeded.

"It won't blind you," said Synthious. "It's *eerah*. A substance we are rich in."

She looked at Synthious and then registered the room they were in. The round room was both spacious and purple, with see-through windows offering views of the valley below and *Hallormsstaður* Forest in the distance. A starry, dark blue sky and full moon above heightened her sense of adrenaline as she prepared to blast off towards it. The room reminded her of the spaceship they'd used to first arrive in Nitro, although this room alone comprised the entirety of their previous ship. There was a long, U-shaped porcelain seat overlooking the view in the center, which Amanda assumed was their version of a couch. No one was in the room but her and Synthious. She looked at the small master and asked:

"There aren't any safety precautions before lifting off?"

Synthious looked at her sternly and reached the porcelain seat. He climbed it and sat on it, facing Amanda. He held his cane in a tight grip, looked down to the floor and said:

"This room has its own gravitational pull. It's our only and best one to enjoy the view as we take off. As the team readies for it, we find ourselves here because you and I need to have a little chat," he said in a serious tone. This was the second time she'd seen Synthious take this approach before delivering new information. She watched him breathe in and out for a few seconds, only listening to the humming sound coming from the rooms to her side.

"You may wonder why I have only called upon you to journey back with us, and not the others."

Amanda shrugged her shoulders in disbelief, let out a small laugh and said: "Well, that's the first of many things I'm wondering."

"You see, Nitro stands as one of the few dozen hierarchies in the known galaxy to possess our numbers. We have excelled at every chance to change for the better. But the planet you briefly visited in days past is not entirely without its faults - for we are unfortunately facing an increasingly darker peril and, mind you, we find ourselves in this ironic situation..."

"Which ironic situation?" she asked, intrigued. Amanda was trying to follow through Synthious's line of thought, but wasn't sure she knew where he was going with this.

"That I, as High Councilor for the Nitroan Council should need the help of an Earthling. Take no offense," said Synthious, looking from the floor straight into her eyes, and then smiling kindly.

"I'm not sure I can do that just yet," said Amanda, frowning. "What could you possibly need from me?"

Synthious raised his hand to the side and tapped the couch he sat on twice, indicating for Amanda to join him. She obliged and as soon as she sat down; the couch turned around to the side to have them face the glass window, and, consequently, the scenic view from below. As she gripped the couch while it turned, Amanda could sense the ship's smooth purple floors beginning to vibrate with more intensity.

"Life in Nitro is not the same as it has been before. And because you are not from Nitro is exactly why I must ask for your help,"

"But in what, exactly?" asked Amanda. "What could possibly be enough of a reason to take me away from Earth again?"

Synthious immediately stopped dead in his tracks and looked at Amanda, petrified. His bulging, wide-open eyes stared vividly at her, as if she'd just said something that had broken his entire being.

"Do you not wish to discover more?" he asked. "I was under the impression that you would have that drive in you."

Amanda frowned and answered: "It's not that. I do… have it. I just haven't had time to breathe."

Synthious's gaze calmed and he said, "I understand." He paused for a few seconds and then went on: "But I ask for your help now only because it is a matter of utmost urgency."

"You can tell me. I'll help if I can."

"The energy cores of our solar system's planets are stored in secret locations throughout each planet. These energy cores are responsible for sustaining all life on the planet and keeping the gravitational pull in its place. A dozen satellites orbit each planet and all twelve represent a key component in sending the energy in and out. They prevent the nearby stars from going supernova. But they have been tampered with. Life on Nitro and in our system is not the same, and the Council can only do so much to prevent our population from discovering their world is slowly perishing. We've delayed the process as much as we can in order to decrease any suspicion from our people, but the cracks are slowly beginning to show. There are sand and thunderstorms raging all across the ten continents. The frozen lands have spread throughout continents that were once tropical… turned to frost."

"What's happened with the energy cores?"

"The K'zaars have been replaced with fakes. It's been close to three jens, which is our measurement of years. That would be close to five Earth years. We cannot keep this from the people any longer,"

"How would I be able to do anything?" asked Amanda, puzzled.

"We have noticed your drive, your passion. You've been selected by the Council from your friends as the one with the best chance of successfully aiding us. You see, you can help us because during this time we have been able to track down which of our enemy planets are the most likely to have infiltrated and stolen from our world. We are sure that it is one of three suspect planets. We are just unsure of which one, because it would involve accessing each. That is impossible to us Nitroans since each of us would be blown to pieces as soon as we crossed the Frontier."

"The Frontier?"

"These are *lifelong* enemy planets. The Frontier is a station orbiting each living planet in our galaxy. The Frontier can detect unwanted beings from a distance and will instantly blast any enemy vessels heading towards them. If the Frontier misses us, we'd still perish when going through the atmosphere, since there is another sensor which detects the frequencies from our registration chips. Every Nitroan has a registration chip in their spine. It's inserted at birth. We have designed a special vessel able to bypass the Frontier, but we need you, an Earthling, to join four other alien races to form a team able to infiltrate each of these three planets, as you'd go undetected through both Frontier and the atmosphere sensor. You'd be able to access these worlds and find which one has our K'zaars. You can reveal which of them has decided to start a war…as it is too great of a risk to face the end of our ten-century long peace."

Amanda breathed in and closed her eyes, and instantly asked him the first question that popped into her mind:

"How long until the ship takes off?"

"One minute."

"If I don't answer in one minute, I have to go against my will?" she asked. Synthious frowned and looked at her as if she'd asked him to commit a crime.

"Amanda," he paused, visibly upset by her question, "Have we ever forced you into action?"

"No, I don't suppose you have. It's just that--" he interrupted her as if he hadn't finished speaking:

"If you don't agree within a minute, this ship will not take off. I am merely offering you the chance to explore, and, with that, to make a difference. We need you. I speak for all Nitroans were they to learn their fate. This conversation is being held in utmost privacy and it deals with urgent matters,"

Amanda looked at the view in front of her and stared as the forest's green carpet of leaves turned orange with the fading sunlight in front of them - and she felt a sense of melancholy in knowing this is where everything had begun. She'd taken control of everything in her life, but knowing this decision had been thrown at her so suddenly forced her to do what she hated the most. Something she'd grown accustomed to do more than anything: postponing her peace. She recalled how life's opportunities are often unexpected, and traveling through space to alien planets with Nitro's protection gave her a new adrenaline rush - an unbelievable feeling she never thought she'd encounter in her human life. Amanda felt her blood boil, gripped her seat, and looked forward firmly.

"Take us away," she said, looking straight ahead. She closed her eyes and took a deep breath, analyzing her emotions and attempting to identify the associated feeling. It had been a while since she felt such a thrill without a specific goal in sight, but she was eager to explore. Once she decided, Amanda felt revitalized.

Amanda's hands gripped the seat tightly as the ship vibrated and lifted off the ground, mimicking the motion of a lifeboat on water. The pulsating vibration indicated levitation, and Amanda's heart sank as they descended into the abyss, feeling a cold rush of air through her chest. She glanced sideways to Synthious, who had a tender smile on his face and then immediately back at the gigantic open view's trees like a speeding train.

She looked ahead, flabbergasted, as the ship rocketed upwards and into the sky above, reaching for the big, bright blue sky with the preciseness of a bullet. The ship seemed indestructible, with no sense of danger or struggle, and Amanda's brain couldn't fully comprehend it. Despite the extreme intensity pulling them backwards, everything appeared to be projected on the screen in front of her. She stared at her hands, then outside, then at Synthious in a rhythmic cycle. After some time, a new sensation spread through her mind and she surrendered to something bigger than herself. Tears filled her eyes as a sense of insanity took over, knowing how unbelievable it would sound to anyone but herself. She laughed uncontrollably as a tear fell.

After a few seconds, Amanda looked at Synthious and saw him give her a confused look. Amanda laughed even louder, placing her hand on her forehead to compose herself while gazing at the ever-changing blue sky. The sky resembled an endless, deep blue ocean that Amanda felt she was sinking into. A mix of fear and excitement overwhelmed her as she traveled back and forth in the Firm's capsule to Nitro. She had already experienced this before. The intensity of the events was truly getting to her - she hadn't had time to sit down and assimilate just how insane her life had become. She was setting off into the stars for the third time, yet her mind was only fully grasping it now. She closed her eyes and looked down, calming herself down.

"When you feel you can speak again, I shall make this even easier for you. We would never ask for your help without giving you the best weaponry and protection we could offer. You are truly about to embark on the journey of a lifetime. You are a warrior, Amanda, and you have become a hero."

"Well...," she breathed in and out once more, eyes still wide shut. She then continued: "If you say so,"

"You can look now. I understand it can be too intense to watch a launch for the first time."

Amanda opened her eyes slowly and looked up to see they had already reached space. Endless glistening pearls of brightness were thrown in every direction imaginable - she had never seen such a multitude of stars.

"May I ask how it is you're feeling, Amanda?" asked Synthious.

"I feel... exhausted, to be honest. Is there any way I can rest? I still have a thousand questions to ask, believe me. But all I need right now is to just lay my head for a while... I need to be alone. Even if it's just for an hour,"

"Very well. We can give you as much time as you need. It will take us twenty hours to reach Nitro."

"Why does it take twenty hours? Our trip didn't last that long."

"You accessed our planet from a stellar door. That is a rare occasion, like balloons being used for transport on your planet. We are on our way to it through common, regular interstellar travel. Our ship's power can take us around a light year per hour. A stellar door dematerializes anything inside its sphere and rematerializes it in Nitro. You were safe because your ship protected you," Synthious smiled and asked her: "May I ask what relaxes you the most? The atmosphere that would help you in your recovery more than any other."

Amanda thought for a few seconds and then answered: "Quiet, clear blue water on a summer day."

Synthious smiled again and hit his cane on the floor of the ship twice, then uttered a sound Amanda couldn't recognize. The lights in the room cleared, brightening up the space around them and the chair they sat on turned, having them face the open room ahead. Amanda looked at the floors, which began flooding with water from all directions, much to her surprise. Her eyes widened with confusion as she noticed the water climbing up the wall, forming a big blue wave that Amanda realized was just an illusion. As she stood up, a wave spread out in two directions - a larger one on the floor and a smaller one that grew as it filled the walls with crystal-clear blue water. Amanda witnessed the movement of every wave with clarity, but her mind refused to accept that the water was not real. As she looked down, she saw the waves crash onto her feet, revealing a vast expanse of yellow sand and seashells behind her. Amanda inhaled the fresh, breezy aroma of a tropical beach, feeling a sense of peace and relaxation as the sound of waves hitting the shore filled her ears.

"I will leave you alone with your thoughts. When you are ready to know more, we'll introduce you to the group and tour the rest of the ship. Say "I'm ready" and I will return."

"So you can listen in to whatever I say in here?" asked Amanda.

"Yes. Why?"

"Sometimes I talk to myself when I'm alone."

"Speak up as much as you need," said Synthious. He walked over to the *eerah* door and crossed it, disappearing from her sight. Amanda closed her eyes and breathed deeply as she knelt down in the fake sea below her, adjusting her thoughts.

Amanda thought about the place she stood, rushing back into outer space, heading to Nitro to fight for a quest she knew little about. She tried to comfort herself because it was normal to feel this divided, as she fought back her thoughts which questioned if this hadn't been too abrupt of a change and if she still had her purpose in her. Amanda knew if she didn't fight for a purpose, she wouldn't feel the drive that usually allowed her to focus and be successful on any challenge. She needed to want it. She needed her wish to conquer back. This was a new challenge - a new perspective needed to be created, since Oswald isn't the primary target anymore - there's nothing left for her to avenge. She knew the reason she stood on the ship was completely because of her nature - how could she ever crawl back on Earth, sit on a beach and rest knowing *this* is what she could do with her life?

Unfortunately for her, Amanda felt this time she had chosen the right path. This is what the Amanda who brought down The Firm would do - this persuasive, persistent and audacious side of her she'd only gotten to know since she'd invited the gang into her Lair. Amanda breathed in and out and felt the rush of memories unfold in her mind - she saw the Nitro hills and the Palace from above, remembering the rush of flying across the Nitro skies aboard a Cerberus - she remembered Shirley back at the Lair and wondered what she was likely to be doing at this time - then the shootout at the Firm where Arlo tried to kill his way into the ship - and Amanda opened her eyes to the sound of the crashing waves around her, and lay down on the floor, as if pretending to float. She stretched her arms as she lay down, floating above the mirage below her. She lay on the floor and watched her left arm move above the endless blue water. Above the water, an open window revealed the infinity of the cosmos.

"I'm ready," she uttered, peacefully. She smiled to herself and slowly got up as she realized the lights in the room immediately began to light up. The waters turned into the purple porcelain walls and floors once more and the illusion was gone within a fraction of a second. Gone were the crashing waves and back was the humming, soothing sound of the ship's core vibration. As soon as she was back up on her feet, she saw Synthious emerge through the *eerah* door once more, but this time, another being came on his trail behind him, and then another one. The duo looked like two Plethoreans if it weren't for their skin color - these beings a grey, almost blue appearance as opposed to the pale white skin of the Plethoreans, but they shared the same muscular build and tone. Immediately, she noticed they focused their gaze on her - and their appearance, which would initially startle or intimidate you at first sight, was completely misinterpreted in her mind, as they instantly gave her the warmest of smiles. Amanda noticed that, much like anyone else from Nitro, these beings, too, were harmless, regardless of their first impression. Their big, bulging black eyes turned into half-moons as they smiled at her.

"Would you like to know who will set off with you on your journey first or would you like to know more about your quest?" asked Synthious.

"I want to know everything I still don't know about the three planets. And I want you to sell me on how I can properly take them on," said Amanda. "Assure me."

"Very well. You should come with us, then. Rest assured, you'll be pleased within minutes, and far more relaxed. That is, once you get to know your fortress," said Synthious, and he then began to walk towards the east exit of the room.

"My fortress?" asked Amanda.

"Yes, the Belladonna. A fortress for the skies if there ever was one. Come, Amanda. We are close," he announced as he and the two Plethorean-like beings set off through another eerah door, glancing sideways at her briefly for her to follow them.

Chapter Twenty-Four - Alienized

Amanda was led to a separate module of the ship by Synthious and his two helpers - she followed them through the ship's corridors, and Amanda focused on every aspect of the ship she laid eyes on. As she walked through the corridors, the crowds thinned and the space seemed to shrink. Passing the Plethoreans, guards, and other beings, she sensed she was being guided to the central hub where Synthious would reveal more information. Instead, Amanda was baffled by the giant scope of what stood in front of her as soon as she turned left one last time - the ship's main bridge. About twenty Nitroans sat in front of holographic screens, monitoring the ship's path, typing on a plain desk that glowed blue with their touch. The holograms displayed rapid algorithms that appeared to be beyond Amanda's familiarity, as if the machines were being controlled by a hack rather than the Nitroans. However, their stillness and silence showed Amanda they had complete control over the situation. Synthious made a signal for his guards to halt and they stood behind the workers, watching them silently.

Amanda was distracted by the Nitroans, but eventually noticed the big glass opening in the center of the room that Synthious wanted her to see, which caused the Nitroans to make a surprising noise. They all seemed to moan in relief at the same time, uttering a high-pitched *"yeeee"* as they gazed up to announce their arrival home. Nitro stood in front of them in all its glory, shining as a beacon of life amid the dark, endless space around them.

Amanda realized this was her first actual glimpse of Nitro in its entire scope. Amanda identified five enormous terrains, which she believed were split into multiple quadrants or continents. These were parallel to each other and very wide horizontally, with oceans at either end. The upper land was the biggest and had an icy pole much bigger than Earth's.

The Nitroans then began communicating with each other, as if exchanging coordinates on how best to prepare the landing - but Amanda comprehended none of it.

"We are ready to land," said Synthious. "Welcome back to Nitro, Amanda."

Amanda smiled at Synthious, and he smiled back. He then pointed towards the next room and walked towards it. Amanda followed him inside and found herself in the middle of a dark room with a center cylinder that was lit by a single light on the ceiling. There was nothing else in the room but the cylinder and Amanda was quick to look to the floor, expecting to fall into what seemed like a dark abyss below her.

"Synthious?" she asked, seeing his shadowy silhouette walk effortlessly towards the center cylinder.

"You can walk. The room has to be kept dark because of the Dimensioner. Come."

Amanda followed him and tiptoed her way to the center, praying she wouldn't fall into an unseen hole.

"Stop worrying, Amanda. You are safe," he said.

"It doesn't work that way," she answered. "It's not a switch."

"It should. Maybe it will soon," he said, pausing in front of the cylinder. Amanda could now see it held multiple square boxes, and the light expanded to illuminate Synthious. Amanda walked into the light and looked at the table in front of her. The boxes were bronze and seemed to have no opening - nothing was encrypted on them, either. They seemed like random gold cubes. Amanda glanced at Synthious and he walked around the table, stopping at the opposite end to her. He turned his back and said:

"These will be your companions."

Two other lights lit up on the far left and on the far right of the room to reveal two doors, which opened instantly, revealing other beings were in the room with them. One was a man dressed in a black suit, with long black hair and pale skin. He looked very much like he was from Earth, as did the woman to his left. She had long blonde hair and was dressed in an orange suit seemingly made of multiple layers of what seemed like sea shells. They looked confused and startled, but as the doors opened, they immediately stepped into the darkness and made their way towards them.

"These are Sev and Cai," said Synthious. "They've been selected alongside you to aid us in your avenging of our K'zaars. Unlike us Nitroans, they won't understand you."

The three of them screamed in pain simultaneously, as something seemed to bite their thighs suddenly. Amanda felt a burning sting on her leg and all three of them looked at each other as they touched their legs, suspicious of their reactions.

"You've now been inserted with our universal translators. It'll sting for a few minutes but it'll soon be over. Otherwise you could not understand or communicate with any beings that are not from Nitro. You're now able to speak to each other and understand yourselves fully."

"So they're not from Earth?" asked Amanda.

"No! We don't come from Nitro, either," answered Sev.

"Where do you come from?"

"I come from Austacya. It's in this galaxy, except on the far end, by way of the Pluster," answered the man in black. He had a deep, throaty voice.

"I don't know what any of those are," answered Amanda.

"The Pluster is my solar system, located at the far end of this galaxy. I'm an Austacian,"

"And I'm from C3K. It's in the Hylia galaxy," said Sev.

"The Hylia galaxy is your Earth's Ursa Major, Amanda," Synthious paused for a few moments and began walking around again. "I've already discussed with each of you the reason why you've been summoned here,"

"Were both of them on Earth with us during the battle? How am I meeting them only now?" asked Amanda.

"They were in Nitro and were just sent up to the ship as we arrived inside the system. Cai and Sev have been on intriguing journeys, and you may find you've got more in common than you'd think once you've become acquaintances," answered Synthious. He walked away from them and into the dark corners of the room, fading from their line of vision. Only his voice echoed, and the trio listened intently.

"Below you are dozens of Dimensioners, the most powerful tool ever created by us. It may not seem powerful at first, as it is certainly not a weapon, nor is it able to inflict any harm. But the Dimensioner's true functions don't lie in the obvious - and that's where all of its glory lies,"

Three of the boxes on the table then burst open with a crack, revealing transparent Y-shaped items.

"These are the Dimensioners. Pick them up and place them on your forehead," said Synthious. "A Dimensioner enables you to expand your perception even further. You'll be rulers of energy - these items safely detect energy levels and identify auras."

Amanda was reminded of the time in the Palace when Synthious mentioned about people's vibrations and ruling energies. She'd always wanted to expand on it, as the technology present in Nitro fascinated her - and this seemed to be her chance.

"You'll have to explain it more," said Amanda. Sev and Cai had already picked up theirs and placed them on their foreheads. The Dimensioners adhered themselves akin to leeches and upon proper attachment, the central component, which linked all three legs, became alight with a green radiance. Amanda looked at the item in front of her and reached in to get it as Synthious continued:

"It is crucial that you know where danger lurks in this journey - this will enable you to sense whether you're being told a lie or the truth, whether someone has evil and negative thoughts and vibrations towards you and also a first-hand initial diagnosis of anyone's aura as soon as you meet them. You'll need to get acquainted with the colors to understand the being's respective vibration. It will all be taught to you in

Garrien, which we are descending upon as we speak. Garrien is the historical Nitro city which was two centuries ago responsible for being the main hideout of the Nitro warriors during the Rain War. It is a magical and mythical land, an underground plethora of blooming lifeforms. For two nights, you'll live in Garrien as the final preparations are made for your departure towards the first suspect planet."

Amanda affixed her Dimensioner onto her head, initially feeling a tight grip that eventually relaxed and became slightly soothing. She experienced a brief electric shock from the Dimensioner, which she quickly disregarded as it was only uncomfortable and redirected her attention to Synthious.

There was a loud thud and the ship's vibration came to a halt. The humming sounds were gone, and there was complete silence in the room.

"We've landed. It is time to uncover Garrien," announced Synthious.

****

Amanda, Sev and Cai were guided out by Synthious, and during the walk out Amanda took the time to introduce herself properly to Sev and Cai. Cai's skin was very white and gave him a somber appearance - Sev was the complete opposite. She had big, full lips and innocent blue eyes.

"I'm Amanda," she said, standing in the middle of the two and switching glances to both. "It seems we'll be a team from now on?"

"I have had little luck with teams" said Sev, smiling. "But I suppose this could be different."

"Do you two know each other?" asked Amanda.

"No," answered Cai. "We met just before we entered the room, before being zapped onto the ship."

"Keep in mind," said Synthious, interrupting them, "that as soon as we're out of the ship, your Dimensioners will start working. The first being you meet will already have their details announced on your minds. I shouldn't have to tell you you're not supposed to reveal any information the Dimensioner gives you, correct? All Nitro beings are aware of them, but the ones you'll meet on your voyage are not. And you'll find most beings don't appreciate being stripped of their mental privacy."

He stopped and they saw they'd reached the door that led outside.

"Are we already in Garrien?" asked Sev to Synthious.

"Yes, you are."

The doors of the ship opened to reveal a wide, open green field ahead. Amanda covered her eyes for a while as the sudden brightness affected her vision and she saw that Synthious began heading outside. A series of uncontrollable events occurred, starting with Amanda's realization that Synthious had not walked out of the ship and had instead fallen into an unexpected abyss. She saw Sev and Cai reach out to look and, as she looked at Sev and Cai she saw both of them had already seen what was below them.

Sev looked at her and then at Cai, as if bidding farewell, and then jumped, disappearing out of Amanda's sight. Amanda quickly stepped outside, placing her hand on the ship's door. A gust of wind blew through her face as she gazed at the open fields of Nitro. Adrenaline surged through her when she saw a massive tunnel below them that led underground. As she looked at Cai to see if he was planning on jumping before her, she saw him step out and jump without looking at her. Amanda saw him drop with ease, as the bodies seemed to slide through the visible opening, gliding smoothly downwards.

Despite this, Amanda still didn't feel secure, as she recalled the waterfall jump and how Synthious and Nitroans had greater control over their bodies, making seemingly crazy moves seem ordinary. She focused on her breathing, closed her eyes and tiptoed to the edge. She took a deep breath of the cinnamon-scented Nitroan breeze and convinced herself that returning was a significant achievement and the correct decision.

Amanda felt a freezing jolt shoot up her stomach as her brain acknowledged the free-fall. A fraction of a second later, she felt her back hit the tunnel, and she began gliding down. She had put as little thrust into her jump as the others, so she immediately opened her eyes once she knew she was safely on her way down. She saw herself sliding down the tunnel in what seemed like an almost vertical position, falling fast for who knew how many meters. Nevertheless, her body relaxed, and she noticed openings on the ground ahead, revealing a variety of plants and animals beyond the fences. Amanda quickly passed through the openings, realizing she was descending into a subterranean city made up of possibly hundreds of floors.

Between the vines and plants, there were living beings, smaller than an Andromedan or a Plethorean. They appeared to be similar to elves.

Amanda kept falling, counting over forty stories in the first minute. As time passed, her attention shifted from her unknown destination to the growing community visible through the fences. The tunnel stretched horizontally and Amanda felt her body incline. She continued to slide down, holding her hands in her chest as if speeding through a water park - but this was much harsher. Her body jolted to the sides a few times, and she was amazed to see a stream of water forming behind her as the tunnel shifted to a horizontal position, guiding her downward. The water current increased and Amanda looked at her feet to see her destination: she was heading straight into an underground lake. She shut her eyes and shot through the water like a cannonball, increasing in speed until she crashed into the pool, feeling her heart thump against her chest like a drum. This was her worst nightmare:

any alien creature that was water-bound could be an inch away from her, and there was no chance of escape in time. To save Sev, Cai and Synthious, she needed to find the courage to open her eyes and see if she could help them.

Only then, Amanda noticed the water didn't feel cold at all, neither was it tepid. The water felt as if she'd been thrown into a soup pan. Amanda emerged from the water, gasping for air, and found herself in a beautiful hot spring. She had been hiding her embarrassment as she swam to the surface. Cai, Sev and Synthious were floating close by with a relaxed look on their faces. Amanda looked around and saw that the spring was in the center of a cave, with pearly stalactites on the ceiling, as Synthious smiled at her. The waters below were the whitest and most transparent Amanda had ever seen, reflecting the shining diamonds above. The warmth and smoke felt cozy and purifying, and Amanda breathed a sigh of relief.

"Welcome to the best way to access Garrien," said Synthious. "We can stay here for some time, but I suggest as soon as you're ready, we pick up and go. There is much to see and too little time. A feast will be held tonight and you must be ready."

Amanda observed Cai and Sev enjoying the newly found hot spring, and they seemed familiar with each other, exchanging looks of pleasure, making Amanda feel as if they had known each other for a while. She tilted her body backwards to float in the water, relaxing her mind to assure herself she was in a safe place and began thinking about Sev and Cai. These were not beings from Earth - it wasn't the same as being on Nitro with Stryker, Lina and Sam. They were aliens - but absolutely nothing gave that away. They both looked like regular humans, maybe slightly detached as Cai seemed to show a predominant apathy - but Sev had a tender energy in her and both seemed as misplaced as her. Regardless, Sev and Cai seemed to be focused on enjoying what Nitro offered - which only helped Amanda in freeing herself from constant, multiple controlling thoughts.

"So, this is Garrien...," said Amanda, feeling her body become pleasantly numb as she floated in the spring, staring at the mystical stalactites above.

"No. This is *one* entrance to Garrien. You're lying in the Waters of Heyn...don't float for too long or you'll fall into deep sleep before you know it," answered Synthious, and Amanda heard his voice becoming more distant and then looked up to see the master leaving the pond.

"I don't want to sleep!" said Amanda, immediately standing up and swimming in his direction.

"I do," said Cai, proceeding to mimic Amanda's floating.

"If you fall asleep here you won't wake up for days," said Synthious.

"Never mind," answered Cai, instantly getting up and heading towards Amanda.

Sev was already on her way as well, and Amanda stepped out into dry land.

"We're soaked, Synthious."

"The way up will dry you. We'll pass through multiple vapor tunnels. Come, the Garriens must have already finished preparing your succulent feast," he turned around and walked towards the cave stairs.

"Why is it we're always *rushing to some place* when in Nitro?" asked Amanda. "For once, I would love to actually spend some time in a place like this, without worrying about leaving."

Synthious's steps came to a halt, and he turned around, staring deeply into Amanda's eyes. Amanda felt uncomfortable as he stood in silence for a few seconds, merely focusing his gaze on her, as if trying to decipher her entirely.

"What?" she asked. Synthious then blinked a couple times and shifted his focus, now looking at Sev as he answered:

"That is an interesting thought, Amanda. Be wary of those. You'll have time to feel adjusted now. You'll spend the night before leaving."

"Oh, that's good. I think all three of us could use some rest before setting off."

"Is there anything the three of you wish to ask before we head up?" asked Synthious.

"Yes," said Cai.

"How much of a chance do we stand of surviving the task ahead?" Amanda felt a punch in her stomach as Cai asked this, and was reminded this was quite an appropriate question, one she had given little thought to - after all, Synthious had asked them to infiltrate three enemy planets, and Amanda's biggest undercover experience was breaking into The Firm. This hardly seemed like an easier target - and she felt the butterflies setting in.

"Inside The Belladonna, there is no chance of demise. It's our safest and most powerful craft - your peril lies once you step out into each of the three planets. But our firepower is incomparable - and we'll be monitoring you closely. Be mindful of danger and focus on your purpose and I don't see a reason why any of you would come to fail," answered Synthious.

***

Garrien did, indeed, feel inviting and celestial - all across the vine-covered walls there were many unusual plants and flowers, blooming in colorful shades. The air felt light and safe - and there were no alarming sounds in the background. Garrien was filled with bees, insects and birds all co-existing in harmony - everywhere Amanda looked, she saw a stair which led to another level. The Garriens moved about their day in red and green garments, evocative of Earth's fictional Santa Claus's helpers, while Amanda, Sev, Cai, and Synthious explored what felt like a vast botanical labyrinth, a serene and wondrous city. The Garriens appeared unfazed by their presence. They had climbed six levels when Amanda asked Synthious how much longer they'd have to walk.

"Not to sound like a spoilsport here, but my legs will give in any time," said Amanda. "I'm doubting whether Earthly beings have as much muscle tone on their legs."

"Fear not, we're a level away from our destination," said Synthious. They reached the seventh level, which was by far the most crowded so far, as Garriens walked around carrying tools, boxes and many objects, transporting them from one level to another.

"May I ask what function these beings are performing?" asked Cai.

"Garriens are responsible for manufacturing many of Nitro's weapons and tools for construction. The hot springs lead to a multitude of mines with many minerals and rocks which enable them to live a wealthy life providing materials for the planet," answered Synthious. "But that's not all they do. Some Garriens dedicate their lives solely to gardening, agriculture and nutrition. At this moment, you'll see they're rushing back and forth because they're all working on the final preparations for the Belladonna. Every single Garrien today is dedicating their time to you."

They walked past the Garriens and onto the last flight of stairs. The Garriens had a subtle, peaceful expression on their faces - and Amanda relished the discovery of beings that were so eager and happy to engage in their usual routine schedule. Nitro seemed hectic and different, but here she found similarities to Earth - these alien beings adored their day-to-day lives, seemingly taking pride in the quiet and ethereal forces of nature. Most of all, Garrien felt safer than any other place she'd been to this far.

Synthious led the trio up to the eighth floor, where Amanda quickly spotted a massive wooden block serving as a table, surrounded by smaller wooden stools. A bowl was placed in front of every stool, indicating the start of a big feast. Half-a-dozen Garriens stood at each end, chattering and preparing something.

"They always seem busy," said Amanda.

"It's because they are," said Synthious. Then, Synthious raised his voice and spoke up, drawing the attention of every Garrien present: "We have arrived!"

The Garriens opened their eyes wide and, from each extremity, one of them left their group and walked towards them. Amanda noticed both Garriens seemed to be female, as their features were softer and more delicate, with longer, silkier silver hair flowing. As both of them made eye contact with Amanda, she felt her brain zap and a green color surrounded the Garriens - a voice sounding exactly like her conscience emerged in her mind, saying *"cleared, peaceful being"*. Initially, Amanda found it strange, but then realized Synthious was glancing back and forth between her, Sev and Cai, and she remembered this was the first time their Dimensioners were giving off their signals - the first beings they'd effectively shared eye contact with. The Garriens reached them and, much to Amanda's surprise, she also understood them, although they spoke in their native tongues.

"What wonderful creatures you've selected, Synthious!" said the first female Garrien, who seemed younger and livelier than the other. "They seem to emanate so much potential," She looked at Sev, Cai and finally Amanda, smiling at each. Amanda was startled as she opened her mouth, realizing Garriens didn't possess teeth - merely greenish gums. Initially finding their smile off-putting, Amanda realized their eyes gave off the complete opposite impression, as they seemed to be filled with kindness and genuine joy. "You may call me 37." She pointed at her fellow Garrien and introduced her as well, saying, "This is 70."

Amanda frowned and looked at Synthious confused. Synthious then answered. "Garriens don't have names. They go by numbers."

70 looked at the trio and then began speaking: "The feast is ready. May I ask how long we have before our guests take off?"

"They will take off tomorrow morning," answered Synthious. "Is the Belladonna ready?"

"1 to 35 are putting the finishing touches," answered 70, smiling as well. "It'll be ready by dawn."

"Good," answered Synthious, taking a few steps towards the gigantic wooden table. He signaled for the trio to sit down and immediately 37 and 70 turned around and walked back to their groups. Amanda, Sev and Cai looked at each other and then joined Synthious, sitting down for the upcoming feast.

Much to Amanda's surprise, within minutes the Garriens began setting up the food on the table, but the food was made only of baked, cooked and fried insects. There were crickets, cockroaches, worms, beetles, caterpillars, termites and many dead bugs. She felt her heart sink to the pit of her stomach and looked at Sev and Cai, who seemed to have no reaction whatsoever to the unusual choice of dining. Amanda breathed in and out and saw one of the Garriens was serving water. She drank an enormous glass of water and felt her head zap slightly. She wasn't sold on these Dimensioners as the others seemed to be - she could do without these unusual zaps. Amanda tried to calm herself down, breathing in and out, and then served herself a plate of what seemed to be the least cringe-inducing insects. She closed her eyes and listened to Sev and Cai chewing away by her side - then, without looking at her plate, she picked up her first bug and dined.

Chapter Twenty-Five - The Belladonna

Amanda held her stomach as Synthious led them up to the Belladonna. She knew it had been a nutritious meal, but she couldn't help reminding herself what she had just chewed and tasted.

"So, we'll spend the night inside the Belladonna even though it's not yet ready for take-off?" asked Cai, seemingly unfazed.

"The Belladonna is a living organism - it'll feed you and provide you with all that's needed for living during your task."

"May I ask which planets we're visiting?" asked Sev, who had grown bubblier after dining.

"As soon as we're inside I'll give you a detailed explanation of your trip," said Synthious. "Remember, our entire planet is counting on you."

They climbed three more levels of stairs until they reached a steep corridor which seemed to go up for another dozen levels. The tunnel was lit with torches on each side and reminded Amanda of a rustic version of the Firm's corridors. "The Belladonna is at the end of this path."

"I would also like to ask what made us stand out to you," said Cai. "Although I'm not one to pass judgement, we hardly seem like the fittest or strongest of trios."

"We don't search for physical strength," said Synthious. "All three of you excelled in many aspects which are crucial in turning you into the selected three. We Nitroans pride ourselves on tenacity, perseverance and persistence. I believe, as you share your journeys with each other, you'll find out you have much more in common than you think."

Amanda walked with her companions for a few minutes until she saw an opening at the end of the tunnel. As they emerged, she realized it led to a vast open field. It was still daylight outside, and they seemed to have gone all the way back up to where Nitro's spacecraft had landed. Amanda compared the vast open field to a football stadium, and this section of Nitro appeared more Earth-like than any other. The stunning mountains in the distance provided a breathtaking backdrop for the view, but what caught Amanda's eye was the enormous structure in the middle of the grassy field. The wind blew the same strong current as before - and Amanda breathed a sigh of wonder as she got her first glimpse of the Belladonna.

Belladonna was a silver octagon, composed of two main X-shaped floors, which were already the size of three or four Garrien levels. The lower X was thicker and larger than the upper X and she saw an opening which she assumed to be the entrance between the closest two legs. The vessel resembled two colossal stars, one atop the other, surpassing in both grandeur and complexity the other Nitro vessels. Its vastness was such that one could easily lose their way within it for hours. The vessel exhibited polished edges that gleamed under Nitro's afternoon sky. Amanda surveyed the entirety of the ship, while its grandeur left Sev and Cai equally awed, as they stood observing it in silence with widened eyes. Dozens of Garriens walked in and out of the ship, hustling to complete their work in time.

Synthious began walking towards the entrance of the craft and the trio followed. They rushed past the Garriens and entered the ship. Amanda was left baffled by the sight: the Belladonna wasn't a regular ship. Inside, it seemed like an entirely different place.

"This is the main bridge," said Synthious from behind them, and Amanda noticed the elder master hadn't stepped in. The Belladonna's main bridge was an oasis, with a patch of sand in the center and dozens of palm trees circling it. Streams of water flowed in various directions, branching into numerous pathways and corridors. The tropical ambiance was interrupted only by the walls, which adhered to Amanda's expectations. A central panel with hundreds of small, colorful buttons, a large opening in the center, offering a view of the outside, and a holographic image of a serene female face at the center. As the trio stopped to focus on the image of the woman, Synthious announced what they were staring at:

"She is the *Belladonna*."

The woman smiled at them peacefully, speaking in a high-pitched but throaty voice:

"Hello to all. My reserves are at 94% capacity. I will soon be ready to set off on our voyage."

The fragrance of a tropical beach permeated the entire module, which halted Amanda in her tracks. She was astounded by the contrast between the intimidating, high-tech walls and the peaceful floor. It felt as if two entirely different ambiences were put together for no apparent reason.

"I don't understand," said Amanda. "This is a private, artificial beach."

"We have always prioritized safety - you felt at home inside the Belladonna. The main bridge is a beach, yes, but the Belladonna is an oasis of life - journey through any corridor and you'll find forests, waterfalls, deserts and snowy lands, all artificial and created in order for the three of you to feel at home. The ship itself is a living organism, and will answer directly to any of you when asked."

In order to get to the sand island, they had to step by half-a-dozen circular rocks or they would get wet - Sev and Cai headed out, jumping from one rock to the next and onto the sand. Amanda followed as she heard Synthious speak behind her:

"Now, if you excuse me, I must set off. The ship will teach you all that is needed to know about the Dimensioners, the planets and your journey. You merely need to ask. I am needed in Anyara."

Amanda was confused by Synthious's statement, and looked back at the ancient leader.

"Already? You're not joining us?"

"I never said I would join you."

"I'm aware of that, but I expected you to at least guide us out. There's still a lot we don't know."

"That is what the Belladonna is for," Synthious smiled to Amanda with a kind expression on his face, and continued: "Trust me, Amanda. When have we ever failed you?"

Amanda hesitated for a couple of seconds and then smiled back.

"Very well," She said. "Thank you for everything, Synthious. I hope we can do you and Nitro proud," Sev and Cai turned around as well, also thanking the elder master.

"I am sure you will deliver and exceed expectations on your quest. It is the flow all three of you have been in ever since your journeys began. Use tonight to get to know one another. The galaxies await you," he said as he blinked and smiled once more. He turned around and proceeded towards the open field behind them. There, he joined the line of Garriens who were constantly entering and exiting the ship with various objects and apparel. Amanda stared as Synthious headed out, and a few seconds later she could not tell him apart from the Garriens.

Amanda turned around and stepped onto the rocks, making her way towards Sev and Cai.

"Let me tell you, all that's missing is a couple hammocks!" she joked, but Sev and Cai looked at her confused. "Hammocks!" she insisted, but neither of them responded. "You hang them between two palm trees, then you lie down on them to rest? There are no hammocks on your planets?"

"You mean a *burga*?" asked Sev. Amanda frowned and dismissed her, changing the subject.

"Never mind. Should we get to know the rest of the ship or ask the Belladonna all we need to know first?"

"I want to see the desert!" said Sev. "Can you believe the scope of it all?" she said, spreading her arms and looking around joyfully.

"We should ask the Belladonna for immediate instructions. I know I'll feel safer that way. This is no joke. We're safe here, but we won't be as soon as we land on the first planet," warned Amanda.

"Belladonna," said Cai, immediately turning around to face the prompter with the woman's figure. "Please instruct us on our first destination."

The Belladonna smiled at them peacefully and began speaking:

"Your first destination is a planet in the Specter Galaxy, named *Kratik*. It is a snowy paradise, and the first suspect planet on the list, located exactly 105.2 light years away. It will be a two-day trip with our current engines set to maximum potential. You'll be required to wear pressure suits to withstand the freezing temperature."

The ship's voice was ethereal and soothing, and Amanda instantly felt a sense of security beginning to grow on her.

"Regrettably, we lack any data on the K'zaar's potential location on the planet. Nonetheless, don't be disheartened, as we have approximations for the other two. This is the only planet where you'll have to search entirely by yourselves."

"So, the hardest quest comes first," said Sev. The Belladonna didn't answer, but blinked slowly as if in silent agreement.

Chapter Twenty-Six - Kratik

Over the next few hours, Amanda, Cai & Sev watched as the Belladonna took off from Nitro and up into the infinite sky above as they dove head on for their first quest. The trio spent most of their time soaking up the Belladonna experience, as if the ship was a world of its own and not just a spaceship. A network of white corridors suspended by gravity allowed the entire structure to seamlessly traverse between atmospheres. As if reassuring themselves that the ship was a lifetime home, they headed straight to their bedrooms and bathrooms, and their expectations were exceeded with each room they entered.

The bedrooms were in a circular room with floating waterbeds and a silk-like carpet that felt like stepping on cotton clouds. Amanda and her new friends walked around their new space with ease. Open porcelain chests filled with colorful clothes were placed next to water fountains at opposing ends, creating an ethereal ambiance that could soothe even the most energetic hearts.

The bathrooms resembled Garrien's hot springs. Amanda was tempted to spend a relaxing hour in the lavender-scented vapors, but her attention was quickly drawn to the Belladonna chamber. Here, they could request an infinite number of foods, fruits, and drinks. They left for Kratik. Whatever they craved, the ship could provide.

It was with the greatest of spirits the trio rejoiced and got to know one another as the Belladonna set off towards Kratik. Amanda's stories from her past uplifted their moods, giving them a child-like feeling of happiness. To Amanda, some of what Sev and Cai told her sounded like fantasy or fiction, blurring the lines between reality and imagination. Cai's anecdotes about his people's society made her realize there was no clear definition of incest in Austacya.

The trio's underlying sense of wonder and gratitude always remained regardless of their conversation topic, showing their eagerness to arrive on Kratik. Much to Amanda's surprise, the two-day trip passed by like a flash as she woke up in her waterbed the following day to find Cai next to her. Amanda got up straight away and followed Cai onto the bridge, only to find Sev already standing there in her sleeping clothes.

The trio stared through the Belladonna's bridge onto Kratik, a seemingly lonely, icy world. The white planet seemed devoid of life, save for a solitary green continent situated on the far right. Belladonna settled into orbit a few hundred kilometers above the surface. The space below it was filled with hundreds of tiny moons - seemingly a cruder version of

Saturn's rings. The moons were drifting around the planet at a very slow speed.

"Belladonna, we have to land on the green patch of land. Do you copy this action?" ordered Amanda.

"I do," answered the Belladonna. "But before you head out, you must put on your suits. The atmosphere is capable of inducing rapid freezing within seconds, if not properly addressed."

They could see three folded black suits, and Sev walked towards the objects to pick up their garments. Cai stood still, staring outside as if trying to solve Kratik merely by looking at it.

"What is it, Cai?" asked Amanda.

"The green patch seems oddly out of place. I don't understand how it can sustain its natural cycle of life, seeing as it's surrounded by a mass of frost and ice." He looked to the right and could see the sun from that system was still orbiting the right side of the planet. "However, it is still daytime on the green land. We should land immediately,"

"Belladonna, are we invisible?" asked Amanda.

"My settings for invisibility are on. I do not believe we can be detected," answered the ship.

"Good. I order you to land!" said Amanda. Immediately, the ship pulled them down, and the trio held onto whatever they could find in order to keep their balance. "Not that fast, Belladonna!" yelled Amanda, gripping the metal bars as tightly as she could. The Belladonna slightly eased the pull downwards and continued to descend.

Sev held onto another bar at the end of the bridge, also holding their three suits in her hands. As the ship landed, she threw Amanda and Cai their garments, and both picked them out of the air while still holding onto their positions.

"We are too sloppy!" said Amanda.

"It doesn't seem to be our fault," answered Cai.

The moons differed vastly from Earth's: most of them were potato shaped and only one to two miles in circumference. Amanda noticed they were hugged in a close embrace with the ice planet, only a few hundred thousand feet from the surface. They could see through the ship's windows the ship penetrating the atmosphere and descending upon Kratik's grey clouds. A few moments later, the glacial mountains of the planet appeared on the horizon. Then, without delay, the Belladonna landed on its phantom surface, leaving them breathless.

"Is this it? Did we land safely?" asked Amanda. Looking out onto the planet, the ship stood perfectly still, overlooking the grassy fields.

"Yes," answered the ship. "We are in Kratik."

Amanda, Sev and Cai expeditiously adorned themselves with their space suits, while Amanda discovered that the material responsible for its black color was also the one that provided insulation - the entire suit was composed of a velvety fur, denser than chamois, unlike any texture she had experienced before. She caressed it a few times and noticed she was inadvertently delaying her actions because she felt extremely anxious. Her stomach and lungs felt cold and Amanda breathed in and out once again, calming herself down. Sev and Cai were ready to head out and Amanda finished suiting up, then joined the duo.

"How can we find the K'zaar? How long can we stay outside?" she asked the duo, unsure any of them had a proper answer.

"We shall explore for as long as it is needed. The Dimensioners should alert us if we're close to a K'zaar. As the atmosphere in this part of the planet isn't as cold or snow-filled, I assume the K'zaar should be close. The energy in it would not be sustained had it been stored in the icy depths. The K'zaar is fueled by heat. However, at the first sight of peril, we must head back immediately. Keep in mind we have landed undetected, and the Belladonna is invisible, but we are not."

"Under no circumstances should we part ways," said Sev. "I really, really don't like the cold." She frowned and sighed.

"Belladonna, are there any signs of life nearby?" asked Amanda.

"No. I have not picked up any intelligent signals since we entered orbit."

The trio looked at each other suspiciously.

"This is a life-bearing planet, isn't it?" asked Amanda.

"It seems the bigger cities are in the southern hemisphere. We have landed on the northeast continent," said Cai.

"So the living beings go about their lives in the extreme cold?" asked Sev.

"Yes. Kratik's intelligent life is not composed of humans, neither are they carbon-based," answered Cai. "I believe most of them are like Nitro's Plethoreans, in that their skin is thicker to adapt to the surrounding environment. I could be wrong. What I know is that they are not friendly," said Cai. "In any way."

"How do you know so much about Kratik, Cai?" asked Sev.

"My planet shares a similar atmosphere to Kratik. It is not uncommon for Austacyans to hear about Kratik's legends when growing up," he answered. Amanda was fazed by his lack of emotion - Cai answered every question as if being prompted a questionnaire.

The trio heard the Belladonna's openings unlock and instantly turned around to head out into the icy alien planet. Amanda kept reminding herself of every re-assuring thought she could find, but felt the tip of her fingers turn cold as soon as the ship's hatch opened up. An intense rush of icy wind burst through the opening, and as the ship's doors opened, the current only increased. However, the ship had safely landed inside the green area. The trio stepped out onto the ground of Kratik, turning heads to each side to take in all they could find.

Were it not for the imposing, snow-capped mountains in the distance, Amanda could have mistaken their landing site for another part of Nitro, or even Earth. The nearby hills were lower, and there were wide fields of red flowers that bore a remarkable resemblance to poppies. The air, however, didn't match the summery landscape - it was cold and even through the suit, Amanda could feel it lowering her temperature.

"We should look cautiously from up that hill," suggested Cai. "If we duck onto the higher one, there is a chance we could see far into the icy fields."

"It's too cold," said Sev. "Why is it this cold if it's so sunny here?"

"I don't know," answered Cai. He walked towards the closest and tallest hill, and Amanda looked at Sev.

"Try not to focus on the temperature. Hopefully, we won't have to be here long."

Sev nodded, and they both followed Cai, who was already a few steps away from the hill. As he reached it, he ducked and crawled up slowly. Soon after, Amanda and Sev repeated his actions, following Cai to the top of the hill.

"The area which is covered in grass and filled with life seems to be shrinking by the minute," said Cai.

"What do you mean?" asked Amanda.

"Look," said Cai, pointing to the east. Upon reaching the summit, Amanda and Sev beheld a multitude of towering, pointed mountains in the distance, and below them the flourishing green fields. The sky above them was blue, but there were dark, grey clouds all around the snowy fields - and they seemed to be heading towards them.

"Focus on the exact divide between the grass and the snow," said Cai.

Amanda focused her gaze and, sure enough, Cai was right: the colorful fields seemed to be shrinking. In a matter of ten seconds, Amanda was able to notice a significant reduction in the green portion of the land, as the white fields around seemed to surround them and consume all life around like a fast-spreading virus.

"We'll still be able to stand here once it's all snow, though," said Amanda. "This is what these suits were made for!"

"Yes, but the snow seems to be spreading fast. I'd give it a full hour before this is entirely frosty. I believe that is the natural cycle of this ecosystem - it's late afternoon and the snow takes hold during nighttime,"

"So, during the morning it clears out again?" asked Amanda.

"I'm not sure, but certainly a part of it does," answered Cai.

"This means the K'zaar is in a cold place after all," said Sev.

"Yes, but the question is, how?" asked Cai. All three stood in silence, staring ahead. By now, up to four or five meters of grass had already been devoured by the ever-growing cold. Amanda heard strange noises coming from behind them, but before staring back, she looked at Cai and Sev for reassurance - surely, they'd heard the same, as the trio exchanged a quick glance filled with fright and insecurity. Sev opened her mouth to speak, but there was no time left - suddenly, Amanda felt a brutal thud in her neck. She fell to the ground as she felt her body collapsing fast and her line of vision was engulfed by blackness.

Chapter Twenty-Seven - Frost

She could feel her arms becoming numb, as if her blood wasn't properly circulating through her veins. Amanda's body was filled with pins and needles, and she felt dizzy as she tried to open her eyes, realizing she was hanging vertically. She couldn't lift her arms and initially thought it was because of feeling anemic, but then realized her neck and legs were also paralyzed. Though feeling immobilized, Amanda could still adjust her wrists and ankles to ease the discomfort. Once she accepted her inability to escape, she observed her surroundings.

She noticed the ground trembling slightly, covered in unseasonal cracking of ice and stirrings like ever-growing vines. It was as if the earth and frost were slowly awakening from a long frozen state. At any moment, it seemed the ground could give in - so Amanda kept looking around and, as she looked up, she found herself in the immense ruins of what seemed like an old colosseum. The sphere was circular and ten times larger than the biggest football field on Earth. It was made of grey and black rectangular blocks, with missing pieces for support. Through the gaps in the missing blocks, she could behold the night sky, with countless stars shining above in the vast darkness. However, any attempt to escape her restraints and reach the sky would require running and climbing, with the colosseum's inward-curving structure resembling a sealed dome that was once a colossal cave. She'd certainly fall before reaching the first of the missing blocks, so Amanda attempted to look to her sides and see if she was being held along with Cai & Sev. As she did so, she felt her neck ache with such agonizing pain she almost let out a scream. She closed her eyes to take the pain in, trying to fight it off, to no avail. A cold rush of wind blew through her body like a never-ending jolt of adrenaline, and Amanda realized then just how cold the atmosphere was.

"Amanda," said a soft, faint voice to her left, and she recognized it as Sev's.

"Sev?" she asked back. She couldn't see her, and it seemed as if her voice was coming slightly from behind - and then Amanda heard approaching sounds of steps and metallic tinkling. What she saw next befuddled her at first - Cai was brought in front of her by what seemed at first like four beings covered in white fur. The creatures, resembling Yeti, moved like apes and appeared to be twice the size of humans. They were bound to metallic X-shaped structures, with an unknown, smoky, electrical substance tying their neck, ankles, and wrists. Amanda gasped as the beings moved away from Cai, revealing their true nature: they were not four but two, with a fence dividing their double-headed bodies. Instead of noses, there were snake-like fences in each head and their eyes looked like big, bulging black plums. Amanda was shocked by the disgusting creatures and their aggressive behavior, as she realized the danger they were in.

"Kratikans," said Sev's voice from behind her.

Amanda didn't respond - she stood in silence as she didn't consider it wise to dialogue with these creatures - she felt no desire to interact with them, although she knew her reluctance was pointless. Unfamiliar with the species, she didn't expect Sev to have knowledge of them. Despite this, she paid close attention as the Kratikans turned their heads towards them and stumbled towards Sev.

"You are invaders," said the Kratikan to their left, but only his left head spoke. Then, the right head continued: "You must be terminated."

Both his voices sounded more like throaty growls than a regular, deep voice. There was no tone, just a grating growl which formed words, as if they lacked vocal chords.

"We are not invaders," answered Sev immediately. "We received authorization to land here."

"No authorizations were given by the Grand Vizier," answered the left head of the second Kratikan. "We wish to fry you," said his right head.

"What?" asked Sev, raising her voice slightly. "If you do that, there will be severe consequences," she said in a threatening tone.

Amanda remained quiet, wondering if Sev would expose their plan to save the K'zaar and whether she would ever disclose their undercover mission for Nitro. Then, the first Kratikan stumbled towards Sev and pulled her forward, pulling her into Amanda's line of vision. Amanda glanced at Cai, who seemed to be deep asleep, showing no signs of awareness. As she saw the second Kratikan approaching her, her heart thudded against her chest, and when he stood in front of her, his black eyes stared through her as if he could read her soul. At first, her gaze fixed on the left head, and her Dimensioner alerted her to the danger by announcing the words *"rejection, primal killer"* - a purely malevolent creature. Then, he placed his immense, ape-like hands in the structure that held her, and Amanda gasped as she believed with all of her senses he was about to gut her. However, the Kratikan twisted her, and Amanda was given a vision of what stood behind her.

She was horrified and wanted to turn back immediately as the view in front of her was shocking and beyond her control. The opposite side of the colosseum was a gut-wrenching nightmare of dead, disfigured and mutilated bodies. There were up to a thousand bodies hanging from the snowy soil to the last block of the colosseum, almost a kilometer above her head. Amanda had never seen such a multitude of bodies before - each body had been gruesomely mutilated. The floor was littered with intestines and organs that had fallen from the suspended bodies and lay in a heap, while a pool of dark red blood stood in stark contrast against the snow. Amanda surveyed her surroundings and beheld an assemblage of creatures from diverse species, including Plethoreans, Andromedans, humans, unidentified species and even Kratikans, all subject to a common destiny. The colosseum was a chamber of torture, and Amanda immediately feared not only for her life, but for Sev and Cai's - and had not even a single faint hope of attempting an escape, as the energy chains held her tightly and wouldn't let her loose even if she tried to throw and twist her body around with all of her strength.

"Sev!" she screamed, deciding to end her silence - certainly staying quiet would only assure her rapid demise, so she screamed Sev's name at the top of her lungs to show the Kratikans she was there, alive, and manifesting - she knew there was no way to reason with them, but maybe she could trick them with words or negotiate some sort of redemption or surrender. There had to be a way - this wouldn't be it, they had just reached Kratik, just begun exploring their first planet. As she screamed, she let out another shout, this time in pain, as her Dimensioner jolted up and shocked her head to a point she felt her head spin. The violent shock came as an unwanted bonus, as Amanda thought what else could go wrong. She felt her body being turned around aggressively again, and stared deep into the Kratikan again. This time, she looked at his right head, and to her surprise, the Dimensioner alerted her again, echoing the words: "*cleared, primal being*". Amanda widened her eyes in surprise as an idea shot through her mind like a speeding bullet, but remained silent, so as not to let the Kratikan read into her expression.

Amanda had noticed before that, as the left head said a rational order, the right head would immediately respond with a wish for action - they didn't seem to share the same traits or personalities, especially after a different alert from the Dimensioner. She wondered if their brains were segmented, and the rational-thinking brain was the left head, leaving emotion solely reserved to the other. If her hunch was correct, Amanda knew she could twist them around and have both sides turn on each other. She could confuse them with words.

"We are not who you think we are," she said immediately.

"Where do you think we come from?" she asked the Kratikan. Both heads stared at her in a deep focus. Amanda could see Sev was only pulled towards Cai, and the other Kratikan also turned his attention from Sev to her, walking in her direction.

"You are trespassers. It does not matter where you come from," said the first Kratikan's left head. The right head then completed: "You have betrayed the rules of Kratik."

"I can tell you it does," said Amanda. "You turned me around. I saw all of them," she said, referencing the bloodbath behind her. "They are not as important as we are. If you value who you answer to, you should wait before you...fry us. If you attempt to go on, you must be entirely sure we are disposable. And you are uncertain of that because you don't know who we are. If you fear consequences, I assure you you cannot kill us. We are protected, see?" she looked up, attempting to draw focus to their Dimensioners.

"Yes, we can. There is nothing special about you," answered the left head of the first Kratikan, who seemed to take offense at Amanda's questioning. The right head then turned around and looked at the left head, whispering: "But we do not know who they are."

The Kratikan's left head then turned around to face his right head, and they talked to each other.

"It doesn't matter. The Grand Vizier has allowed exceptions to no invaders," said the left head.

"But we cannot be sure there won't be repercussions. We captured them routinely. They should contact the Grand Vizier first," said the right head.

"That would only waste our time. These are obviously human beings from either the Specter or the Cluster galaxy."

"If they are indeed regular beings, then we shall proceed in frying them as usual. But it wouldn't hurt to confirm. I, for one, have never seen beings sporting those things on their heads. They glow," said the right head, referencing the Dimensioners. "It could mean resistance to the frying circuits,"

The left head then turned around to look at the other Kratikan, who stood beside him, looking for another opinion. Amanda knew her plan was working, and her hunch seemed to be correct - but that still didn't mean there was a way to escape. The Vizier certainly would order their instant executions, and she knew she was only buying them time.

Through what seemed like a fracture in the Kratikan's vests, spoke a harsh voice uttering a command:

"No such thing as harboring trespassers! Terminate now!"

Immediately, the Kratikans pulled out a sharp blade from their garments and pointed it at Amanda.

"Amanda!" said Sev, watching the Kratikans hold Amanda down, ready to puncture her gut.

Amanda's eyes widened, and she panicked. There was no way out and this was her end, and there were only seconds to come to terms with her demise.

Then, Amanda saw the left head of one of the Kratikans explode into little pieces, as it blew up, throwing guts, brains and blood all around them. Amanda's face was covered with the Kratikan's black blood, and a few seconds later the other Kratikan's left head also burst apart, as if a bomb had been placed inside it. The right heads screamed in shock and pain, and the first threw the blade on the floor as it screamed in agony, falling to the floor. Amanda looked ahead to see Cai had awakened from his sleep and had fired his brace onto each left head. Amanda sighed in relief but her peace didn't last long: the other Kratikan's remaining right head seemed to think Amanda had been responsible for the explosions and ran towards her, pointing the sharp edge at her heart. She closed her eyes before the blade sank in hoping for a quick death, but was again surprised when she felt her feet spring up from the ground and she noticed she had been freed from the machine.

"Hello, Amanda," spoke the Belladona's voice in her mind. "It's time you learn the Dimensioner's true functions, which are always activated at the point of death. From this point forward, your energy sources have been activated to full potential and the Dimensioner is working alongside your brain in a state of complete unity. This is the first demonstration, the Soar."

Amanda felt the winds of the colosseum all around her, and opened her eyes to see she was floating almost on top, looking downwards at a shocked Sev and Cai. "In order not to fall in the next three seconds, you must utter the second command: Flight,"

Amanda immediately screamed "FLIGHT!" and the tip of the Dimensioner's Y which stood closer to her forehead began to descend down her face, as if it was a snake coming out of a cave. The tip of the Dimensioner continued to grow alongside her face as she felt the cold metal press against her skin, reaching her chin, then her neck and chest, her waist-line and proceeded to descend her legs and knees, until it settled on her feet where it expanded onto two sides for her to place her feet. It was as if the object had become an extension of her body, becoming a crozier she could hold on to. As the impulse from her jump subsided, she noticed the Dimensioner was now allowing her to float effortlessly in the air, holding her up with the greatest of ease. "Point it towards the direction you wish to fly to," said the Belladonna, and Amanda breathed in and out before reluctantly pointing it slightly to her right, only to speed through the air a few meters away. Amanda gripped the Dimensioner's extension with all of her strength, terrified she could fall at any second.

"If you wish to communicate with Cai and Sev, you can now reach them with your mind. You must only find their presence below you and it will be transmitted."

Amanda held the crozier up, halting again in mid-air as she closed her eyes to focus on the third function. She felt

Cai & Sev's presence and focused on the energy she felt whenever she spoke to them.

"Can you hear me?" she asked without uttering a word.

"We can," answered Cai from below them. "Yes" said Sev. She noticed they didn't speak loudly, but the sound they uttered was enough to turn the Kratikan's attention to them. They were now ceasing their incessant screaming of pain and seemed to survive normally without their left heads. Amanda knew she'd have to be swift and create a diversion of sorts in the shortest time possible - and, surely, the Dimensioner spoke to her again.

"There are two other functions available. The sonic punch can be activated from the floor. To descend, merely lift your feet slightly from the tip of the crozier, pointing them up," Amanda obeyed and instantly the Dimensioner lowered to the ground. Amanda inched her feet higher and the speed at which she plummeted increased. She held them down again and jumped from it, still holding the object tight with her hands. She felt as soon as she reached the floor that it contracted again: it left her feet, her legs and sprang up, becoming a small head accessory again. As soon as she landed, she heard Sev scream in panic as she saw the Kratikan try to stab Cai, only to have Cai free himself from the machine as well and spring upon the air. Then, it hit her: all it took to activate the Dimensioner was reaching the point of death. The other Kratikan would do them a favor in trying to kill Sev, as she would also activate her Dimensioner and they could escape. The logic seemed to hit Sev, too, as she instantly saw her calling the other Kratikan:

"Hey, you useless ogre! Kill me if you have the courage!" she screamed, and Amanda saw the Kratikan run towards Sev. Amanda tiptoed in their direction, as cautiously as she could. Cai's Dimensioner extended from the Soar to Flight as she looked up and saw the Kratikan aiming for Sev's heart. Amanda followed the Belladonna's instructions and held her hands together, channeling all her anger and rage into her aim. As she felt her hands tingle with energy, she screamed with all of her strength as she pushed her arms back and then let them go in the air. A thin, silver-like shade of energy emanated from the tip of her hands and jolted towards the Kratikan. The line of energy traveled across the field like a speeding bullet and hit the ogre with the strength of an anvil. The Kratikan screamed in pain and had his body thrown across the Colosseum, crashing against the floor aggressively. The other Kratikan watched as his companion was thrust across the field, visibly shaken and afraid of Amanda. She looked up to see Cai descending and Sev extending her Dimensioner into the Flight mode. They began to immediately communicate without uttering a single word.

"Should we kill the other heads?" asked Cai.

"They seem to be nicer. I'm not sure they deserve to die," answered Sev.

"Either way they'll come for us eventually if we do nothing," said Amanda.

Cai reached the ground and ran to Amanda's side. He positioned himself to perform his Sonic Punch, quickly mastering it before Amanda. His energy bolt blasted through his hands and hit the other Kratikan with greater intensity than Amanda's, knocking him down and away. Not long after, Sev descended by their side and the three looked at each other.

"Where should we run to?" asked Sev as Amanda looked all around the Colosseum searching for a way out.

"That way!" she yelled, this time forgetting about the Dimensioner's functions as she was too excited to contain herself. The structure in the center of the mutilated bodies had an opening at the bottom, which the three ran towards without being seen by the Kratikans.

"They didn't see us! They're searching, look!" said Cai, pointing back as they ran, to show the two Kratikans confused, looking all around them to find the trio. Somehow, they couldn't see them.

"The last function has been activated," voiced the Belladonna. "You will be invisible for a full minute. To activate this from now on, you must utter the word

"Transparent." Be aware, this function is only available once every 24 hours. Use it wisely."

The trio understood why the Kratikans couldn't see them and picked up their pace, running as fast as they could towards the Colosseum's fence exit. They reached it half-a-minute later, and the opening was too narrow for the three to pass through alongside each other. Cai led the way, followed by Amanda and Sev. The fence seemed to lead to a sort of corridor, which was dimly lit except for the light at the end, leading to a way out.

Chapter Twenty-Eight - The Other

The trio emerged from the tunnel and found themselves in the open fields of Kratik, surrounded by a forest of thorn-branched woods. The trio looked at each other in disbelief as they all thought up ways of cutting down the branches. The sky overhead in Kratik was clear, and Amanda was struck by its unfamiliarity. She could not distinguish any of the constellations, nor could she locate the Belladonna. The suits felt heavy despite being light, and relying on the Dimensioner's powers was the only way to navigate through the icy night air with low energy levels. She was uncertain how long they had been captive, and realized that none of them had eaten before their journey, showing their lack of preparedness for the unforeseen circumstances.

"These branches may be poisonous," alerted Cai. "Kratik is known for these forests, and it's best to avoid the poison at all costs."

"Can you cut them down with your brace?" asked Amanda. "Where did you get that brace, anyway? It sure came in handy back there!"

"It's a regular warrior weapon of every Austacyan. Its effect is like a sharp razor or knife, and it can reach up to thirty meters away from my aim. But I don't think they break apart these," he said, looking at the thorns. The branches were thick and dark, and it was impossible to cross by ducking and crawling through, as many thorns seemed to emerge from the ground up.

"Idiots! We can fly above them!" said Amanda, yelling again as she came to the idea. "How didn't we think of this before?"

"I don't think any of us are entirely familiar with the Dimensioner's functions yet, seeing as they were presented to us only a few minutes ago. But yes, that seems like an efficient solution," said Cai, apathetically.

They simultaneously uttered the word "Flight," and their Dimensioners grew from their foreheads across their bodies. A few seconds later, they leaped into the air to survey the thorn woods. Amanda held her Dimensioner tight, and they could see Kratik's icy mountains on the horizon, looking ahead to see a couple of mountains they instantly recognized as the hills they were captured on. Their attempt at an escape didn't last long, though - the trio stared down, baffled, as they watched the spiky woods grow from beneath like vines that had somehow come to life and were springing up towards their direction.

"I can only assume it's their natural defense system," said Cai, looking down at the forest and to each opposing end, trying to find an escape route. The woods continued to expand and grow below, reaching their feet in less than ten seconds and springing up across their line of vision. The vines didn't attack them or expand outwards - they only seemed to form a barricade of defense against any trespassers. Something was setting off their presence, and those life-forms could detect any incoming predators. Before they could turn around again to face the Colosseum, Amanda felt a tug at her arm and screamed in pain - one thorn had ripped her suit and left a deep cut in her right arm, which she couldn't touch or hold suspended mid-air, as it would cause her to fall from the Dimensioner. As her arm throbbed in a burning pain that seemed to increase with each passing second, Amanda heard Cai's voice to her left saying:

"Look! The Belladonna is active! Someone has boarded it!" he announced, and the trio turned to see their ship in the distance, far from the Colosseum, turn its engines and lights on. They had little time left, otherwise Kratik would become their permanent home.

"We have to reach it now!" screamed Sev. They all floated in mid-air, far enough away from the branches that they wouldn't reach them anymore, but even further away from any chance of escape.

"Where should we turn to? We can't reach the ship from here!" said Amanda. "These woods make up almost the entire area!"

"Yes, but not all of it," said Cai. "There has to be a way through, or out."

Cai inched his Dimensioner even further up and started rising again, this time at the fastest speed they'd been to. Amanda and Sev quickly followed, as did the branches. The polar wind blew through Amanda's suit aggressively as if she was speeding up on a motorcycle, except there was nothing touching the floor and instead of travelling horizontally, she was going up. She didn't dare to look down - Amanda had to stay in control. There was no time for the faintest thoughts of self-doubt to cross her mind.

After ascending for what seemed like almost an entire kilometer, Cai threw a sonic punch, which seemed to disable a few branches from growing. The punch's intensity was such that a few roots and thorns cracked and fell to the ground below, so Sev began to copy his actions. Amanda threw her first punch, aiming at the same spot as they created a clearing. Sev soared through the openings, with Cai and Amanda following. They blasted off sonic punches as they crossed through the woods. Amanda would aim down to prevent any roots from reaching them as Sev and Cai threw them horizontally, opening up the way. Amanda screamed in agony as a second thorn pierced her bruise, causing her arm to throb with pain. Blood trickled down her shoulder as she hoped the crossing wouldn't be too long. Her punches were failing in strength as her own body twitched in a strange reaction to the bruising.

The trio reached the end of the woods and descended immediately. Amanda watched as Cai and Sev stepped down from their Dimensioners onto the ground, but she wasn't her usual self. Something was wrong and growing - her vision was becoming blurry and she couldn't hold her body up. She stepped down and fell to her knees, with her Dimensioner retracting as Sev and Cai looked back at her, worried.

"Amanda!" said Sev, running towards her and kneeling down beside her. "What's wrong?"

"I don't know. I feel drained," she answered, struggling to transfer her thoughts into words.

"We have to reach the Belladonna," said Cai, reaching the duo. Amanda's suit was ripped and her arm felt cold as she saw the ship in the distance. The hills and Kratik's surface were completely covered in snow.

"Do you think it'll damage the oxygen?" Sev asked Cai, referring to the rip.

"The helmet has a separate seal. But we can't stay here long or there won't be a ship to go back to."

"Go," said Amanda. "Let me lie down here and you can pick me up with the ship," said Amanda. "I can't walk now."

"But we can carry you," said Sev.

"But then I'll be dead weight and will surely be an easy target to whoever's hijacking the Belladonna," said Amanda. "You two are fine. Cai, use your brace and kill them. They're likely more Kratikans,"

Cai looked at Amanda without answering for a few seconds, merely staring deep into her, as if contemplating his decision. He then nodded once and turned his back immediately, rushing towards the ship. Sev stayed with Amanda, looking at her in a state of panic.

"Sev, help Cai. It's a regular walking distance from here. I can do it. I just have to go slowly."

Sev lingered for a few more seconds and stood up as she announced: "We'll be here in no time."

She took off in order to aid Cai. Amanda saw the two fade in the distance as they ran towards the Belladonna. Amanda focused on her breathing and tried to regain her balance. She successfully stood up slowly, and as Sev and Cai disappeared from her sight she heard the Belladonna's voice in her mind:

"Amanda, you've been poisoned by a Nekro. I have an infinite supply of Uzcarias in my garden chamber, which provides you with an instant elixir to extinguish the poison from you."

Amanda looked around at the desolate Kratik, only seeing the snowy mountains around her. She didn't want to look back at the thorns and the Colosseum, so she looked forward and focused on reaching the Belladonna with each step. Her arm was now numb with the freezing temperatures and affected by the poison. She stumbled on her path and fell to the ground again.

"Amanda, you can do it," she said to herself. Amanda was reminded of everything that had been thrown at her ever since Oswald's set-up back on Earth. She saw flashes of Lina, Stryker and Ripley at the Firm and then felt her sense of joy arriving at Nitro for the first time. During the Firm's battle to take over the company, she focused on the rush of adrenaline and the sense of completion that came over her that night. Despite being poisoned, Amanda stood up and was surprised to see a flower growing nearby in the snowy grounds of Kratik.

"Could this be...an Uzcarya?" she asked, talking to herself. "How would a flower survive in this atmosphere?" The flower was black and thick, with golden petals blooming against the darkness of Kratik's freezing night. Amanda summoned all her strength to reach the flower, but was terrified when she saw that it was growing rapidly. The root grew so forcefully that it knocked her down again, this time onto her back. Much to Amanda's terror, she gasped in shock as she saw the flower had turned into a gigantic reptile. Its scales were black and green and the petals had turned into golden, blood-thirsty teeth as the creature stared at her with red, bloodshot eyes.

Amanda screamed and tried to get up, but her legs were giving in. She crawled away from the being, who would surely attack her.

She could feel her breathing becoming erratic and her vision turning even darker - it seemed as if the snow had cracked and she'd fallen deep inside a lake, and the waters during the night were pitch black. She couldn't see the lake's bottom or find a place to swim to. Despite her sensor's warning of low oxygen and deep water, she was terrorized by the creature's sudden dive and the crushing sound on her right.

Amanda struggled to keep afloat, flailing her arms and attempting to lift her legs, but the heavy suit and limited vision made it impossible. She relied solely on her helmet for protection and to sustain her breathing. She blinked, looked around, and focused on the black waters, but found no guidance. Amanda swam up slowly and a few seconds later she felt her hands reach something - frozen snow. Her heart was racing so fast that she could hear it like a loud drum inside her suit. She punched the frozen snow but it was as hard as concrete. Horror flooded her as she saw the golden scales of the creature through the water; it was coming towards her effortlessly, leaving her with no escape. She punched the frost grounds above her relentlessly, screaming inside her vest as she knew there was no way she would escape - this was it, this was the end.

Amanda's breathing became erratic and her oxygen levels dropped as she struggled to inhale. With one final punch at the ground, her body gave out and she blacked out, gasping for air.

Chapter Twenty-Nine - Pleiadians

Amanda's vision was blurred, and it seemed like something was blocking her breathing - she saw flashes of Cai and Sev's rushing faces as they ran towards her and then back multiple times, but she couldn't tell her location. She felt her body numb as if it had become absent from her, fallen asleep on a type of paralysis that blurred her focus in a way she struggled to overcome. Once she understood she was able to move her head, she tilted it lightly to the side and felt her heartbeat against her chest as she realized she was standing in a pool of blood: her own blood. This wasn't mere paralysis, this was bad. Amanda lost her vision and felt her soul slipping away, her thoughts became foggy and she had no sense of self or location. She was gasping for air and felt a desperate fear of losing control. Amanda fought with all her strength to focus her sight, but to no avail. She was consumed by darkness, her mind fading as her eyelids closed and her strength depleted, leaving her in blackness.

    Amanda was terrified on awakening in Kratik, but to her surprise, she was safe in a peaceful forest inside Cai's favorite chamber. She let out a scream of anguish as she stood up. The sound of chirping birds and a flowing river surrounded her as she stood among tall, leafy purple trees with Cai & Sev by her side. Cai was holding her body up, and Amanda regained strength in her legs to stand, holding onto Sev's shoulders as they helped her take hold of her balance again.

"The Uzcarias cured you from the venom," said Sev, and Amanda noticed she held a handful of black flowers in her hand, shaped like long straws of wheat.

"It was a matter of seconds before their elixir got a hold of your bloodstream. But a few moments later it would've been useless," said Cai.

"What venom?" asked Amanda, although the deep throbbing cut in her arm reminded her she might already have the answer.

"You were cut by one of the thorns. As I suspected, we were dealing with one of Kratik's poisonous thorn forests. The liquid in the tip of a thorn first sends people down a rabbit hole of dementia of their biggest fears as the body fights the takeover, but it ultimately fails as it conquers the heart and kills any living being in a matter of less than an hour after stinging," said Cai.

"Unless you've got these," said Sev, happily raising the flowers to show with a smile, "and it wasn't long before the Belladonna told us about it, but for some reason you didn't listen," she continued, with a concerned look on her face.

"I believe the poison had taken over much of Amanda's nervous system by then - there was no way for her to distinguish reality from delusion anymore."

"I did hear it," said Amanda. "And the flower I saw in my mind as I heard it appeared in front of me, but then it turned into a massive snake as I tried to reach for it."

Cai then let out the greatest sight of relief Amanda had ever seen, as he laughed at her answer, seeming genuinely calmer now he saw she was sane.

"So I'm okay now?" asked Amanda.

"It will take some time for you to feel perfect," said Sev, "but we are safely on our way to the Pleiadians."

"Our second planet," completed Cai. "It's a four-day journey."

"How so?" she asked, confused. "We failed miserably at Kratik. How can we move on to the second one? We didn't find the K'zaar," Immediately, Amanda frowned as she saw Cai and Sev beaming with excitement - even more so than before. They had been overjoyed at her question, and Amanda was left floored at their answer.

"We did," said Sev, smiling from ear to ear. "We've stored it safely on the bridge. Are you okay enough to come see it?"

***

A silvery, glowing porcelain eye shone in the center of the bridge, protected by a circular glass dome. Amanda figured instantly it was the K'zaar.

"A group of Kratikans just like the ones who kidnapped us were boarding the ship to hijack it," said Sev, with a cheerful grin on her face, "but Cai and I got here in time, as the Belladonna wouldn't answer them. They were carrying the K'zaar, wanting to take it someplace else. It was almost too easy, really," she said, letting out a relaxed laugh. "Cai's brace does wonders, as well."

"I didn't even know you had that brace before you botched that Kratikan's head," said Amanda.

"It has an infinite range. I must admit it has proven useful in many situations," he answered.

"And that's not all" said Sev. "The Belladonna tipped us off about a chamber on the left hemisphere that is filled with firepower. You wouldn't believe the weapons they have there. We can take down armies from now on."

"What chamber is that? I want to see it!" Amanda said, excited. "And then we have to make a quick stop at the Galley. I'm famished."

Cai and Sev had overtaken the prisoners and saved Amanda. The two of them had saved their entire expedition from total doom. Amanda felt light at the news - she couldn't recall the last time she'd woken up to actual good news. She realized she was craving for some stability as each day seemed to be slipping out of her control. Things had been exaggerated for a while, but Amanda was only now experiencing the consequences of her actions. Her usual self was accustomed to taking control of the situation and manipulating it to her advantage. As unfamiliar and alien as the place was, Amanda cherished the time spent with Cai and Sev as they, this time, had been the bearers of change. She had grown fond of these beings - and felt they offered her as much protection as ever. It felt like a burden to have thrown Ripley, Stryker and Lina into chaos and stripped them of their control, always being the spur of their actions and decisions. There was now a sense of unison, a sense of forming a team that felt new to her. This wasn't Amanda leading the way - this was a group of three individuals sharing an equal passion for a quest.

    The four days passed by like hours, and they seemed to spend each day in an entirely different chamber of the Belladonna, relishing the marvel of all their ship had to offer. The Belladonna was a work of art, its world-building characteristics dazzling and admirable. After awaking each day to eat in the Galley, the three had created a routine of spending what they assumed were their afternoons rolling around in the dunes of the desert chamber or swimming through the rivers of the forest they'd baptized as The Uzcarias Woods, later settling down in the hot springs. They'd check the bridge every once in a while, since the Belladonna kept in contact with them whenever they asked how much time they had left until arriving at the Pleiadians or to simply ask if there were any incoming planets, as they would rush to excitedly sight-see any neighboring systems and stars. The Belladonna seemed to be taking a clear route, as their closest moment to peril was having to tilt away to evade an incoming asteroid field.

The Pleiadian system arrived before them like an oasis. The main solar system was an endless array of colorful worlds, and they watched in awe as they soared across multiple life-bearing worlds. This system was teaming with life and the planets grew exponentially in size and colors. It felt like the most unique place Amanda had ever seen - this surpassed Nitro, and they hadn't even landed in their destination yet. Against the dark and vast backdrop of endless, shimmering stars, arriving at a solar system felt like reaching a milestone. The group was headed to the final planet, the Pleiadians. The group eventually observed from the Belladonna's bridge the approach of the Pleiadian planet, which boasted six radiant golden rings in its orbit. The rings appeared to safeguard the vibrant globe, which resembled an enlarged version of Nitro, featuring several spherical continents scattered throughout its expanse.

"Pleiadia," said Sev beside Cai and Amanda as they watched the Belladonna enter its orbit and plan for landing. "In C3K we'd hear endless stories about here, like a legend we never got to know was true."

"You won't have to take the same approach here," announced the Belladonna. *"The Pleiadian civilization is a Type I civilization and they will welcome you with open arms, no matter your business. They are the only known planet to be this advanced, surpassing Nitro. Its beings differ from what you're accustomed to, be warned. They are not part of the Galactic Council."*

"Why not?" asked Amanda.

"I do not possess that information," said the Belladonna. *"They are the only system to be this advanced and not part of either the Council or the Senate."*

Regardless of the information provided by Belladonna about the distinction in Pleiadian culture, upon crossing the orbit, it became immediately apparent that they were headed towards something completely unprecedented - the cities appeared to be situated not on the ground, but above the clouds. Amanda saw a multitude of floating empires; cities that were so shiny and precious they shone like purple emeralds against the Pleiadian sun. Every city had the most awe-inspiring skyscrapers that seemed to reach almost into outer space, all in a mixture of silver, gold, and purple. The clouds appeared akin to white sheets extending across the horizon, so expansive that one could almost disregard their distinction from the planet's surface.

"Which city are we heading to?" asked Cai to the Belladonna.

"I am not headed anywhere. I am being guided by a force stronger than me ever since I entered orbit. This is the Pleiadians. Remember these beings are far beyond any comprehensible grasp. Most of their culture will baffle, but fear not - their system is so peaceful they've ascended into an almost entirely harmonious existence ages ago. You shall see."

The Belladonna was not flying at its usual speed, but rather it was gradually approaching a platform located at the border of one of the floating cities. Amanda observed that the ship was being pulled in by what was unmistakably a designated landing area for starships. Before they could sense it, the ship had landed and the Belladonna announced its platform was being opened by the same unknown force. They were even more surprised as the platform descended, and upon inhaling the pure, calming air of the Pleiadian planet, their physical forms experienced a magnet-like pull, being forcefully extracted from their comfort zones. Cai, Amanda and Sev began to soar horizontally out of the ship, reaching for each other, side by side. The trio instinctively clasped hands and proceeded towards the magnificent central palace. Nevertheless, the experience was daunting, and they felt helpless, even though they knew that no harm would come to them. It was as if they were being dragged to meet gods - nothing was in their control and they had never stood in front of such an ever-growing and approaching monolith.

They glided with ease across the landing strip, and past a platform that connected to the city. Amanda gazed into the vast expanse, endeavoring to cherish the moment as she observed the clouds on the horizon and attempted to discern any hint of existence below the shroud - though it remained entirely concealed, with solely the god-like civilization drawing near with each passing moment.

Amanda stood in the middle of the trio, feeling the warmth of Cai and Sev's hands as the wind blew against her skin like a caressing summer breeze. Rather than halting at the imposing golden monolith, they were effortlessly drawn inside, traversing a tunnel illuminated by shimmering lights that gave the impression of flight - suspended in a kaleidoscope of hues, with no visible floor beneath their feet as they journeyed through the glass conduit towards an obscure end. The tunnel then twisted up and Amanda knew they were heading towards the top of the central tower: their bodies turned horizontally and they continued to soar above, like their souls were being lifted out of their bodies.

At that point, Amanda felt a new sense of safety spread through her - she felt as if she was visiting an amusement park ride, because the entire experience was too baffling and filled with wonder to feel on edge. They headed up until they saw they were reaching a bright, open end. Their bodies were drawn towards the terminus of the tunnel, with the force intensifying as they approached, as though being swept away - only to re-emerge outside once more, atop the monolith. Amanda failed to grasp their location, because there was no platform visible on top of the tower - it felt as if they had just entered an invisible dimension. Not only that, but she was shocked to find her body was floating: there was no gravity, yet there was a gravity-like pull in the movements. She could drag herself up and down and move where she wanted to, but it felt like flying. There was no rational explanation for it, and a few seconds after noticing their bodies were free from the force that had led them to the top of the tower, she noticed a few meters away from them stood three beings on top of an altar. Upon noticing them, Amanda couldn't believe she hadn't seen them before - their energy was subtle but captivating. The three had long, silver and gold hair that reached their feet, and they were tall, with beautiful features. Their sexuality was indiscernible - there was an androgyny to their breath-taking splendor that left the trio visibly breathless. The Pleiadian trio extended their hands, signaling for them to come forth, and Amanda, Cai and Sev instantly soared towards the god-like beings. They were naked, but their genital parts were covered with their long, silky hair, and their skin seemed to glow in a white light, as if their aura was strangely visible.

"Amanda. Cai. Sev," said three harmonious voices in their minds. They extended their hands towards the Pleiadians as well, and the instant they touched them, Amanda felt a rush of ecstasy jolt through her body. Once more, they were drawn towards the Pleiadians, but this time it was not a mysterious force, but their own desire as they felt an unexplainable urge to touch and hold these entities. As they hugged, each inch of skin that touched the Pleiadians seemed to fill them with relief, joy, and an almost sexual feeling. Amanda felt her body and mind surrendering to the irresistible energy emanating from the Pleiadian's body, which encouraged them to surrender more and more. Amanda felt all the stress and worrying leave her as her entire body touched the being. Suddenly, a rush of images and memories flooded her mind - her past was flashing before her eyes, and she saw herself as a child, growing beside Shirley, then becoming a neurosurgeon, waking up from her coma, infiltrating the Firm, crash-landing deep in Nitro's sea: the Pleiadians were getting to know all of her through touch.

Then, the contact was gone: the Pleiadians let go of their bodies and they floated a few meters away, finally locking eyes with the beings: they had big, yellow pupils, and looked at them with a look of serenity.

"We do not hold any K'zaars," said the main Pleiadian, who stood in the center, his voice echoing through their minds like a symphony.

"Nitro and we share differences," said the Pleiadian who Amanda had hugged. "We are aware of the reason as to why no one from their system has visited us in this quest - we comprehend the purpose of your being here."

"However different we may be," completed the third Pleiadian, who stood the farthest from Amanda, "this occasion is too special for you to leave empty-handed: it's been a long time since we've had three lifeforms from three different planets visit us at once. It is our pleasure to welcome you. We offer to purify you and your soul before you leave."

"What do you mean?" asked Cai. The three of them had sensed all of them had already been purified - none of the three fully understood the offering from the Pleiadians.

"You have already been given the answer you sought - there is no K'zaar. We saw in your minds there are two left for you to encounter...they must be on your final destination, the third planet. That is an answer we cannot give. But it would be unwise and impolite of us to send you back so instantly - we are offering you to unravel more of us."

The Pleiadian's offer promised tranquility and wonder. As soon as the trio accepted, the Pleiadians shared a different insight - this time, flooding Amanda's mind with wisdom from their alien system. Upon learning about their evolution, she discovered that the Pleiadian beings were unique in that they possessed both male and female sexual organs that could reproduce on their own. The Pleiadian society maintained peace by punishing negative thoughts and hurtful expressions with their nail sensors. Each finger represented a handicap of sorts which measured the length of their life - once all apparels had been used, the Pleiadian being would perish out of lack of vital, positive energy. At a funeral or passing ceremony, she witnessed mourning Pleiadians who functioned without money and instead valued energy as currency, where equal contribution to good was considered wealth. Their routine consisted of waking up and offering back to their society in whichever way they found suited them the best. There were beings who saved inferior lifeforms, purified equals, nourished mother nature, mentored infants, cleaned the atmosphere, and rewarded good deeds with food, comfort, affection, and luxury.

There was a longing in the Pleiadian beings to experience physical freedom that surpassed all other necessities - a common ritual was a group meditation in which they lifted their physical bodies from the ground - Amanda saw the population of what was likely an entire Pleiadian city floating above sea-level while sitting down with arms outstretched, all with closed eyes and sharing the same frequency of peace. Any act of violence was unacceptable - although it had been centuries since any Pleiadian had ever felt the urge to act on impulse or harm another physically. They considered their bodies as vessels, special shells meant to use electric vibrations and elevate whatever they received into a superior, purer, and better form. Amanda felt as if she'd been given the key to the secrets of the universe - she knew, instantly and instinctively, that it was a matter of a natural process of evolution: every civilization, at some point, had looked up at the sky in wonder, to wonder. Time moved at a constant, and in the blip of the radar that a civilization seemed to come to be, grow and reach the point the Pleiadians had, it took centuries. Centuries that were merely seconds in the universe's scale, yet knowing they were possible and real, being at the Pleiadian system made it seem like it wasn't far away - she felt her own body evolving as her brain was flooded with the precious information being offered by these alien beings.

The experience became more and more dreamlike with each passing second; she felt her senses had been numbed and her worrying and anxiety washed away, but reality was being experienced in a sort of mental trip: Amanda found herself beside Cai and Sev floating down the tunnel once again, and she didn't recall saying goodbye to the Pleiadians. When they descended through the tunnel, they found the alien trio was already expecting them at the exit. They were taken cloud surfing in order to reach the place where they would rest their body and minds for the day. Cloud surfing consisted of boarding an apparatus that could have been a function of the Dimensioner: much like a surfboard, these transparent items were made to balance your vessel as you soared to your desired destination. Amanda's body was climaxing with ecstasy and joy, and moments later all she could feel was the immensely inviting breeze blowing through her hair as she soared through the passageway that had led them to the monolith and then down, crossing the clouds.

The Pleiadian trio followed and the six soared through the white clouds of the planet in an almost child-like experience: there was laughter and no fear, a sense of unison and completion that Amanda had only experienced before with psychotropic drugs. It felt too unreal to believe - they would dash through clouds with cotton-candy textures, and Amanda would exchange glances with Sev and Cai as they relished what had become a gift: it was as if the Pleiadians had drugged them with eternal happiness.

They dashed through endless clouds, flying up and down until the Pleiadians signaled for them to descend further in order to meet their destination. Below the clouds, Amanda was shocked to find there wasn't a terrain, nor any land - but an infinite, almost transparent blue, paradisiac sea. The Pleiadian trio didn't hesitate, and crossed the waters, diving straight into the sea as if it was just another cloud. Amanda, Cai and Sev looked at each other dubiously for a short while and then did the same, only to be left in awe once again by what was surely the most incredible sight offered to them yet.

Amanda felt the purifying energy of the water as it crashed against her skin. They rode their cloud surfing boards through the vast sea and discovered a breathable underwater world. They saw an immense civilization of large circular domes that looked like UFOs. It was a city teeming with life that lay right before their eyes. The domes were circular and large and held on the sea floor by massive platforms. The metropolis thrived peacefully underwater with endless lights, moving objects and submarine ships passing by above and below. While following the Pleiadian trio towards the central dome, Amanda pinched herself and breathed in the water as her board cruised the seas, with Cai and Sev in front of her.

It felt like everything she'd experienced in Nitro regarding her sense of awe and wonder had been turned up to an extreme level - this was even more of what was once already unbelievable to her, and she entered the central dome, passing through a portal of liquid glass she was sure was made of *eerah*. They entered a salon filled with Pleiadians, and it all seemed to be made of marble - there were endless corridors to run through, and the dome was transparent from the inside, with the infinite blue and green sea filling their sights wherever they looked, like a liquid sky.

The Pleiadians ignored the outsiders as they followed the alien trio to a separate chamber. They were instructed to lie down in cryogenic pods. No head zaps, no worrying, no nervousness - they complied and lay down as each Pleiadian activated the pods and a golden liquid began to fill them.

"Rest," said the three Pleiadians in unison. Immediately, it felt as if the liquid, which filled half of the pod had a sedative effect on them - their bodies didn't have to move, because they didn't want to. Amanda, Sev and Cai felt drowsy and their eyelids started to close. They were unsure if it was a dream or reality, but they knew the beings wouldn't harm them. As Amanda's eyes closed, one thought occurred in her mind as she recalled the Pleiadian being mentioning a big difference between their ways of living and Nitro's. If her body wasn't in such a state of climax and relaxation, she would surely feel tempted to ask what the difference was. But for now, it wasn't apparent and didn't seem to matter. Amanda's eyes closed and opened again in a matter of a second, but she knew hours, maybe days, had passed by, because everything in front of her had changed.

Chapter Thirty - Home?

She was standing on the Belladonna's sand dunes, and there was no one around her, nor any recollection of how she had gotten there.

"Cai? Sev?" Amanda called, but there was no answer, only the blissful lack of sound from the desert all around her.

"Belladonna?" she then called, and the ship immediately answered.

"*Yes?*"

"Where are we?"

"*We have just arrived on the third planet,*"

"What? Where are Cai and Sev?"

"*You are my only passenger,*"

"They didn't board with me after we left the Pleiadians?"

"*No. The same force that pulled me down to the landing strip took hold of me. I, too, have been drifting asleep as my systems were down soon after landing. I have just woken up, like you, to find we are on the third planet. I cannot tell you how you boarded the ship, either, for I do not have any recollection.*"

Amanda rushed to the bridge to talk to the Belladonna eye-to-eye and look at the planet they had landed on. She ran past the corridors, and was astonished at the sight that filled her eyes when she reached the bridge. Through the ship's windows she could see the grey, older, simpler buildings of a grey, populated city. This was Earth, and they were standing exactly above her building.

"I can't believe it" she said to herself, eyes widened. The sky was cloudy, as if a storm was approaching. Amanda stepped down from the Belladonna's bridge immediately and looked back to see the ship barely fit in her roof. She couldn't believe she was back home - nor could she find a reason why it had happened. The air was cold and dreary, like most winter days. She wondered how long she'd been away from Earth - by her counts, it had been close to a month since she'd set off to Nitro, but she knew this was not how time worked once you've travelled light years away. Step by step, she reached the edge of the roof and looked down at the streets of Chicago. There were no cars in the street apart from the parked ones in the sidewalk, so she figured it had to be very early morning. She turned her back and walked towards her building's stairs, making her way down to the Lair. As she descended, she thought about Shirley - was she home? What about Stryker, Ripley and Lina? She would have to get in touch with them immediately. A few seconds later she found herself in the corridor that led to the ballerina painting, and she turned the knob to access her hiding home. The Lair's walls opened to the side, revealing the immense ballroom where her entire odyssey had begun. The lights were on in the kitchen, so Amanda rushed past her tech gear, the mirrors and the sofas and went straight inside it, searching for Shirley.

"Shirley!" she called, but there was no answer. Instead, she found a note on the fridge with Shirley's handwriting on it.

"Dear Amanda, seeing as I can't contact you for the life of me, I've gone into hiding in my country home. When you get this, call so I can come back and know you're okay. Love, Shirley"

Below the note, Amanda read a phone number and immediately went back to the ballroom to call her. She sat in her armchair and called Shirley's number, but after multiple tones no one picked up. Amanda was alone in her home. She breathed in, taking in the surrounding strangeness. She'd always felt safe up there, but this time something felt out of place - so she turned on the news channel, but there was no signal on the television. All she saw was static and grating noises, as if it had broken. Amanda sat back in her armchair and called Stryker's number, who also failed to pick up. She then tried Ripley and finally Lina, but no one answered. She got up and walked around the room, thinking aloud.

"Someone's got to see that huge ship parked on the roof - or someone had to have seen it landing!" she said to herself. "Poor Shirley. It's been a month since we've destroyed the Firm by my counts, but to her it's gotta be even longer! We left here months ago."

Amanda then rushed to her tech center and turned on her computer. The screen lit up and she looked at the date: it was 2052. A year had gone by.

"We woke up from cryo in 2051. How can a year have passed?" As she said the words and the questions filled up her mind, Amanda jumped in her seat as she heard the phone ring. She ran for it and picked up, and Lina's voice echoed through the speakers.

"Amanda! Is that you?" said Lina's muffled voice, and Amanda noticed immediately she seemed out of breath and nervous.

"It's me. I'm home. Where are you?" she asked.

"It's not good, Amanda," she whispered. "They can't find out I'm talking to you. Stryker…"

"Who? What are you talking about, Lina? What happened while I was gone?"

"No!" screamed Lina. Amanda could hear the commotion and knew they had found Lina.

"What happened is that you missed," said a cold, low voice on the phone. Amanda froze as she felt shivers run down her spine as she recognized the voice as Oswald's.

"What are you doing alive?" she yelled, getting up from her seat, raising her hands to her hair and walking in circles. He couldn't have been alive - she'd shot him. She knew she'd killed him.

"Things don't work out the way you expect them to," Oswald answered. "If you want us, come find us. We're in the Halo Woods," announced his menacing, throaty voice. Immediately after, he hung up. Amanda pulled back her hair with her hands, arms outstretched, looking all around the Lair.

"How can I get to Iceland? How can I get to Iceland?" she asked herself. Then, she was reminded of the gigantic ship parked on her roof.

"Belladonna," she said, directing the command to the ship. "Can you fly?"

"*Of course. I was built to fly,*" answered the Belladonna, with her soothing voice as if nothing had been going on. Amanda had thought of the ship as a person, and it took her some seconds to comprehend how oblivious the Belladonna was to the situation.

"Can you find the coordinates on this planet to a country called Iceland?"

"*Yes.*"

"How soon can we lift off?"

"*In ten minutes,*"

"Is your firepower from the index chamber loaded? All kinds of weapons ready to go?"

"*Yes.*"

"Prepare for take-off. We're leaving as soon as I get to you," she said, feeling something drip on her shoulders and then in her nose. Amanda touched the liquid and saw it was bright red.

Amanda then looked up, and fell flat on the floor in shock. Pinned to the ceiling of the Lair was Stryker's body, barely hanging on. His body had been stapled with what seemed like big, thick nails. Amanda noticed a gigantic pool of blood behind her armchair, and wondered how she hadn't spotted it before. Someone had been there, someone had found the Lair - and immediately, she knew she wasn't safe anymore. She looked up at him, trying to see if there was any life left in him, but his body was pale and his lips were dark, eyes opened wide as if he'd been killed in shock. Amanda turned on the Dimensioner's soaring and flew up to reach for his body, as the blood dripping from his puncture wounds came from being stapled onto the ceiling.

As she approached him, she couldn't help but fight back her tears - she didn't know who had done this to him, but it surely had to have been Oswald's doing. She reached the nails and pulled them out one by one until his body was suspended in mid-air, hanging only from the pins in his arms. Avoiding eye contact, she balanced herself with the Dimensioner, pulling out the last two nails from his arms simultaneously. Stryker's body fell on top of her, and she grabbed him with one arm as the other gripped the

Dimensioner. She then lowered herself to the floor and, as she reached it and knelt beside his cold, dead body, Amanda wept.

"How could they have done this to you? Why?" she cried, holding Stryker in her lap. His motionless figure seemed as if he'd been dead for days, maybe even weeks - she reached for his eyelids and closed them, feeling the tears stream down her face. It was unusual for her to feel, but Amanda knew the rage that came from those tears - these were tears of hate. She picked up Stryker's body, which was heavier than she expected, and stumbled her way onto the stairs that led to the roof. It took her a few minutes to walk up the stairs while holding him up, but she would never leave him alone - the least she could do for him was give him a proper send-off. As she opened the door to the roof with her elbow and her legs, she saw the Belladonna already gearing for take-off, its lights beaming on and off as the ship vibrated. She reached the platform and walked up inside the ship, reaching the bridge and laying Stryker down on the first sandbank of the tropical beach.

"Who are you carrying?" asked the Belladonna once they were inside and the platform was closing in behind them.

Amanda looked up at the Belladonna's face, who seemed genuinely concerned for Amanda.

"This is a hero," she answered, without hesitation. "Take-off, Belladonna. We have business to avenge."

"As you request, Amanda,"

***

The Belladonna soared through the Atlantic Ocean towards Iceland, and Amanda watched the seas from the bridge. She didn't have the strength to look back at Stryker's body, but she did it anyway multiple times during the journey. Each time she did so, it fueled her with rage and the need for revenge. Oswald couldn't be alive. It was impossible.

"How long until we get there, Belladonna?" she asked, anxious. She'd walk in circles around the sand dunes and wash her face with the salt water. Beside her were two of the most powerful rifles she could find onboard, and they would shoot to dematerialize.

"Ten minutes. Where should I land?" answered the ship.

"Search for the Halo Woods. It's a big forest right next to Keflavik. He's somewhere deep in there, hiding. Still no sign of Cai and Sev on any of your chambers?"

"Negative. They have vanished. I am sorry I cannot find an explanation for you,"

"It's fine. Just give it all you've got to get us there as fast as possible,"

The Belladonna continued to fly above the ocean, with the immobile endless blue below them as Amanda looked up at the gray sky, hoping to see land at any moment. Along with the powers the Dimensioner had given her and her firepower, she knew Oswald was no match for her. He couldn't harm her.

Amanda spotted a green patch of land after a few minutes and they flew over Iceland, past inactive volcanoes and patches of ice. It wasn't long until they reached a gigantic forest which Amanda knew to be Halo and the ship began to descend. Amanda picked up the rifles and loaded each of them, placing one on her shoulders and gripping the other one firmly as she'd aim to shoot as soon as the platform opened up. He could be anywhere inside Halo and she needed to have that shot. She thought about Lina and Ripley, wondering if they were still stable and fine. If he wanted to talk or try his chances at any sort of bargaining out of the situation, which Amanda figured he would, then it would be smart of him to have kept both women alive.

The platform slowly slid down and Amanda closed her eyes to concentrate one last time before heading out. As the familiar icy breeze of Iceland brushed past her skin, she inhaled the air deeply and used the sense of purpose that filled her to head out completely focused. The Belladonna had landed on a patch of land in the middle of the woods, and she knew her house and the Firm's ruins weren't too far away from there - She had hiked through that same spot with Lina before infiltration.

Amanda stepped out into Halo Woods without looking back at Stryker's body or the Belladonna, feeling vindicated and certain of her goal. She could feel her pulse beating faster and her rage fuming inside her. It was still daylight and the forest seemed inviting and peaceful - so Amanda used her sense of safety to draw out the path she thought was the right one, carefully making her way through the trees and branches in the direction of her house. She stepped on the damp grass and fallen leaves without looking down, when suddenly the Belladonna spoke in her ear.

"I have received an incoming signal from an unknown source."

"What is it?" she asked back at the ship.

"The male specimen goes by the name of Oswald and has instructed me to tell you to walk ten minutes to the west."

Amanda froze in her position, wondering how he would be able to contact the Belladonna. How did he send a signal, how did he know how to find her? The questions kept piling up in her mind as the voices in her head made her confused. There were too many questions building upon other doubts - and Amanda lost her sense of control. Still, she immediately headed west, speeding up her steps now that she knew where she was headed. She let out a loud scream as her Dimensioner buzzed in her mind, with a shock that was so powerful she felt as if her brain would explode.

"Belladonna" Amanda asked. "Why does the Dimensioner still send out these awful brain shocks? I should be fully adapted to it by now."

"I am not allowed to divulge that information," answered the Belladonna flatly.

Amanda closed her eyes and sighed, for a moment considering ripping out the device from her forehead.

"I shouldn't," she thought to herself. "I need the abilities to end Oswald." Amanda kept on walking, crossing the forest as the sun set on the horizon behind her. After some time had passed, she noticed she was being led to the ruins of an abandoned building, which she knew used to be a children's hospital. The more she walked towards it, the more she acknowledged the horrible state of the hospital - the walls were cracked and the large glass doors from the entrance were broken, leaving the shattered pieces scattered across the floor. It seemed as if the building could fall in. She hesitated before entering until the Belladonna confirmed she'd reached the correct spot.

"You must reach the last floor," she said. *"Good luck, Amanda,"*

Amanda grew increasingly suspicious of the ship's behavior, but decided to try to silence all the questions in her mind as she made her way inside the children's ward to find absolutely nothing, except for ruins of what was once a busy hospital and the stairs that led up to the other floors. Compared to the rest of the building, the stairs were in the finest condition - she aimed her rifle straight ahead as she began walking up, alternating between looking back, down and to her sides, always on the lookout for anything to jump at her or for Oswald to appear. Amanda climbed each step slowly, but picked up her pace and began to run up the stairs as Lina's screams echoed through the walls of the hospital:

"AMANDA!!!" She screamed, and then there was silence. Amanda's heart jumped and she climbed two, three, four, five floors in a matter of seconds, finally reaching the sixth and last floor. She was surprised to find a large empty room like the Lair, but with Lina and Ripley tied together on the floor and Oswald sitting in a chair, looking out the window at the forest below.

Oswald turned around from his chair to look at Amanda as she locked eyes with Lina and Ripley. They seemed exhausted and their clothes were filthy. Lina's eyes were filled with tears and their mouths had now been gagged. Their hands were tied together, immobilized.

"Welcome, Amanda, to the beginning of your true journey. And the end of what you know to be your reality," he said, standing up. Oswald raised his arm and Amanda saw he also carried a gun. She let out a loud scream as, before she could think again, he immediately fired a shot at Ripley and then at Lina. He fired into their heads and both fell dead to the ground in a split second, their bodies disposable as trash.

Amanda fired a shot at Oswald, screaming in terror and rage. The ray of light beamed from her rifle and, much to her shock, was deflected by an invisible shield that seemed to have been formed around him, ricocheting across the room like a blind shooting star. Amanda's eyes widened in shock at the knowledge her firepower could not end him, running towards Lina and Ripley's bodies as she sobbed, mustering up the strength to ask him only one question:

"How? How are you doing this?" she cried, reaching Lina's dead body and caressing her cheeks as her body turned cold.

Chapter Thirty-One - Judgement Day

"They are not dead, Amanda," said Oswald. He looked at her daringly and Amanda froze with his deep stare. "Tell me, do you feel invincible?"

Amanda stood there for some time, staring back at him without uttering a word. Oswald then went on: "You should. You've earned it. Hold on to what's left of your heart."

Amanda frowned and looked at Oswald sideways. She gave him a suspicious look and exhaled, saying: "Get to the point, Oswald,"

"You'll need your heart."

"I haven't needed it for some time now," she answered.

"You're about to find out how alive you can still feel," he said, and then smiled from ear to ear. Immediately, Amanda was stunned as she saw the wooden walls behind him seemed to give in - the panels disappeared one by one and Amanda opened her eyes in shock, stepping forward as she looked at the wall behind Oswald in disbelief. Two, four, eight, ten, twenty panels vanished, allowing the extreme brightness of daylight into the room. Amanda looked at Oswald and saw he hadn't flinched - he remained still, yet staring deep into her eyes with a sinister smile on his face. Amanda felt a rush of fear jolt through her unlike anything she'd experienced before - the loss of control within an increasingly chaotic situation had always been her worst nightmare. In a matter of seconds, the entire apartment wall disappeared into thin air and the elusive force continued to grow all around them, as an intense rush of wind filled the room and Amanda heard Oswald scream by her side:

"Congratulations!"

A loud explosion filled the room and Amanda threw her arms up, trying to cover her face from the increasing wind as she noticed the floors erupted from below, as if being summoned up by a hurricane.

The wind blew with such strength Amanda struggled to maintain her balance - she felt her heart beat faster by the minute as she wasn't even settled on what to do - there was nowhere to run and no one to turn to. Through closed eyes, she could feel an intense brightness increasing outside - and Amanda opened her eyes in the middle of the pandemonium. She saw Oswald was pointing his gun towards her. Without missing a beat, she tried to turn back as he fired a shot that reached her full on the chest. Amanda fell to the floor, collapsing as the darkness engulfed her vision. On the instant she did so, the wind, the explosions, sounds and chaos all around her came to an immediate halt.

***

Amanda could feel her body suspended vertically and immediately had a flashback to Kratik - but this wasn't it. The air was warm, and she didn't feel as locked in. Still, she knew her body was pressed against something stronger than her. She could hear commotion everywhere - whispers and giggles and sounds of voices all around her, but her eyes were closed shut. She knew she was awake, but she didn't want to move - she was too terrified to open her eyes. Opening them would mean announcing to whatever stood in front of her she was awake - and she wanted to take in the courage to do so slowly. She could feel her head was suspended, facing down and she avoided moving her neck or making any slight motions - she assembled the feelings in her body, assuring herself she was okay. Amanda wiggled her toes inside her shoes, and they moved fine. She could feel her arms outstretched and her fingers, and she could breathe properly, although she carefully inhaled with her diaphragm to not let her chest expand.

Small, quick breaths were all she needed - there was a sense of dread and doom in her as she knew she'd find herself somewhere she didn't want to be - still, she kept her location a mystery to herself. She pressed her eyelids against her closed eyes, and licked her lips slowly, swallowing her saliva.

Everything in her body seemed fine - the wound from the bullet didn't ache or burn, nor did it seem she'd taken any major fractures or injuries - but the sounds kept on increasing. She felt as if she were on stage as the headliner of a festival, and she knew it was a very public place - there were thousands, maybe millions of voices echoing around her, from all directions. Amanda breathed in and out, and used what was left in her to pull her face up with one move. She opened her eyes, and the multitude of voices instantly gasped, followed by silence. What stood in front of her, where she stood, was too much to take in. Still, she stared ahead, her head raised, announcing her awakening.

    She was being held on top of a gigantic dome, maybe ten times the size of Kratik's colosseum, with a transparent glass platform below her that connected to each opposing edge of the circular stadium. Meters away from her stood Synthious, and behind him, millions of beings, probably all from Nitro, as she saw Andromedans, Plethoreans and a majority of Vargans in the blurred horizon, sitting in the benches of what was certainly the biggest, most majestic stadium she'd ever seen - and she was the main attraction. Behind the visible rows of beings, there were more rows, and Amanda couldn't see where it ended - all she could see was a sea of empty faces staring at her, like a billion ants, with their gaze focused on her platform. The stadium was lit by red and white lights, which circled the entire diameter of the dome.

Above them, the Nitro sky shone in its usual orange shades, and a storm seemed to be heading their way. She around her to see a bifurcation in the center of the stadium: she wasn't the only one being held for the show. To her right, Cai stood, also awakening. And to her left, Sev moaned as she reluctantly came to her senses as well. The trio was being held at the exact center of the massive stadium, dangling dozens of meters in the air, their arms and feet held by chains. The stadium rose in an uproar of voices and cheers as they saw all three had awakened. Amanda's eyes widened as she saw Synthious slowly making his way towards her. Amanda's breathing was erratic and her heart was pounding louder than a drumbeat. When she looked up, she saw the circular sphere holding the three of them connected on top by many colorful wires and cables that writhed like snakes searching for prey. There was a particular dance in the way the wires were moving, as if they were sensing or feeding off of their energies. Wherever Amanda looked, the wires followed. The floor wasn't visible from their line of vision: they were standing too far up to see what was down on the ground, and all she could make out of it was a cloud of fog that seemed to cover the ground like waves.

"This has been planned for a very long time," said Synthious, without blinking.

"Welcome to your destiny, Amanda," said Oswald, emerging from the end of the platform where Synthious stood, as every single being from Nitro screamed in an uproar, as if they were witnessing a deity.

"I was never back on Earth, was I?" asked Amanda.

"No, you weren't," answered Synthious. The stadium then lowered their cheering once again, listening in closely to the dialogue. Amanda focused on everything surrounding her - she had never felt this threatened in her life. Her sweat dripped across her forehead and her fingertips were freezing as her entire body was drenched in this rush of fear and impotency.

"You were here, in your final destination. The simulation of reality offered by the *final* stage of your journey."

"What...my journey?" asked Amanda.

"Your journey is complete.," said Synthious.

She could feel the tension rising and she needed answers - these beings had never offered her anything but well-being. She found it hard to concentrate on one idea as her mind replayed every detail where she might have misunderstood any motives. In silence, she looked for a solution, a reason for missing what she believed she should've predicted - how was this possible?

"You have reached the end of our biggest, most notorious and prestigious event - you are the official winner of the Ascension. And before you ask... it is time for you to know the answers."

The cables and wires above her head seemed to spring to life, clutching at her head like snakes that had captured their prey. They clung to her head like leeches and immediately Amanda saw flashes of images in her mind - these wires were sending signals into her brain, signals that were forming memories or visions.

Images began piecing together in her mind and Amanda could tell she was seeing the Council - the same one she had visited with Stryker, Lina and Sam a few weeks back. It wasn't as if her body was present, though - she knew she was merely a witness to a scene, watching the unfolding of an event that had already passed.

All Council members were sitting in the same position she had seen upon her visit, but the room seemed more crowded and filled with discussion. There was commotion on every table, and Amanda saw multiple races debating between themselves in the Nitro courtroom. Amanda noticed Chairman Bartheus was missing from the benches, but saw him speeding towards his companions a few seconds later, seeming out of breath.

"The Galactic Senate has brought to us the most urgent matter," he said, and his companions sat up on their benches, allowing him to continue speaking. "A Type 13 planet which wasn't in the running for the Event has achieved a breakthrough discovery. They know one of their moons can harvest life."

"Are you talking about Earth?" asked a female Plethorean who sat in one of the top rows.

"Yes. Their solar system indeed has an ocean teeming with life, named Europa. They plan to send an expedition there soon. They will break the bond in a matter of years."

"But Earth isn't even in the running for the Event," retorted the Plethorean.

"Well, now it is. We cannot allow a planet to discover alien life by themselves. Earth is now a front-runner for the event," said Bartheus.

"This, indeed, ultimately urges Earth to bypass all other planets in the queue" said a third Chairman, this time a regular Vargan.

"I propose we dispatch moles immediately," announced Bartheus. "This is the last year of preparation. The other two planets, Austacya and C3K, already have infiltration in full gear and are moving successfully,"

"Not only that, they have already found their beings who tested positive for sylph. A man for Austacya and a woman for C3K,"

The Council stood in silence, but Amanda could feel they were stunned by Bartheus's news. There seemed to be no negotiation left - their silence was a matter of consent. Amanda was puzzled by the last sentence when her surroundings suddenly blurred and transformed like a kaleidoscope of images injected into her brain's visual cerebellum as she spun through a vortex of shapes.

The intertwining images again took shape and form, and Amanda found herself in an open field, which she immediately recognized as Iceland. Not only Iceland, she was standing on the exact spot where her house would be built and subsequently, The Firm - the lake gave it away. She knew that lake better than she knew most places. It was where she spent the happiest moments of her childhood, splashing around with Shirley. The sky was blue and there was a summery breeze in the air, unusual for the cold temperatures of Iceland. Two figures began walking in her direction, but they weren't looking at her or past her, but talking to one another. Amanda recognized them as Synthious and Oswald. They shared the same robe, a worn-out garment which was old and very messianic in appearance. Synthious carried his usual cane, but Oswald also had one. They walked alongside one another, and as they approached her, Amanda could hear their conversation.

"This is where this planet's institution will rise," said Synthious. "The ships will carry all the gadgets and weaponry, with their arrival planned for tomorrow morning. By next week, you'll have your lab. As the years pass, you'll witness the growth of your empire."

"What about the sylph testing and research? I will need to assemble a team."

"Your team will grow exponentially. Remember how invisible the operation must be. This is your first Ascension event. If operations don't go smoothly, it spoils everything," answered Synthious.

"The Council and the Senate are keeping a close eye on this? At any moment, if I need to contact you, will I be able to?" asked Oswald.

"The Council and the Senate are dedicating their entire efforts to watching every move that happens on Earth, on Austacya and on C3K. The first 100 test subjects have already been sorted by the first wave of moles. You'll meet them next week. Wonderful Earthly beings, I've heard. With the utmost potential," said Synthious, calmly as ever. "The humanoids that will be delivered next decade will be indistinguishable from true Earth beings - and they will answer to you and only you. Remember, this is your operation. It is your goal to find whoever tests positively for sylph, Arrien. You are a worthy Cerrian. Your similarity to Earthly beings is uncanny. I am confident there isn't another capable of enduring such a long task. This will be your life for the next decades,"

Amanda frowned as she heard Synthious call Oswald a name she'd never heard before, and then assign him to an entirely different race. Her mind was spinning, but her thoughts were being placed. As she focused on their conversation, the images in her mind blurred again and she knew she was being transferred through experiences yet again. Another vision began forming amidst the chaos of shapes and sizes in her sight, but this time, she found herself in an almost familiar place. Her vision brought her to the children's ward she had just been in, except this was when the institution was in its prime.

There were dozens of children, perhaps exactly one hundred, lying on multiple beds with wires attached to them. All of them looked healthy and well, but were in a deep sleep. Amanda gasped when she saw herself as a child in the second row, sleeping innocently. Oswald stood in a corner of the room, and Amanda was even more shocked to find Uyara, out of everyone, standing next to him.

"You found her," said Uyara. "It was long overdue. The Austacyan and the C3K woman are in more advanced stages of development to tolerate sylph,"

"Yes. She's the only one. But another subject also showed signs of tolerating the chemicals."

"Who?" asked Uyara.

"Lina. Both Lina and Amanda tested positive. But Amanda passed it with flying colors. In fact, her body already began producing more of it as if it were routine. But she's an orphan. Her parents were killed in a plane crash when she was an infant. We found her in an orphanage, and we only found her because the Dimensioner alerted us of her different colored aura."

"You are aware your designation has doubled from now on, then? As your Firm rises, you will have to father her."

"She will grow to loathe me," said Oswald. At this point, Amanda didn't know where to hold onto. The overflow of information that was being sent into her mind was putting her in a state of trance - she was only a witness to the onslaught of information and revelations being offered to her. She stood still, frozen in time and space, merely watching.

"This is the way it's been for thousands of years" said Uyara. "Over 100 planets have ascended because other beings have been put in the same position you are at this moment. This is their puzzle to solve. Do not fail. Stand your ground. The smaller fraction of planets without their sylph leader have succumbed to genocide and extinction. You must nourish them. You must indulge them. Otherwise this planet will pay for your undoing," said Uyara, and she turned away from Oswald, walking past the sleeping children and disappearing from the room. As Amanda watched Uyara leave, she saw Oswald collapse to the floor, sobbing. She could almost feel sorry for him - and the notion that he wasn't her true father made her feel less enraged. Before she could put her thoughts together, the images blurred again, and Amanda was flooded with shapes and sizes of all colors as the kaleidoscope shaped back into the Colosseum.

She heard the popping of the wires leaving her forehead, as if they had been glued together. Amanda's eyes were opened wide, and the crowd cheered in unison.

"The three have been offered the answers!" said Synthious loudly, addressing the millions around them. He looked like the main host of the weirdest celebration Amanda had ever been on. The crowd roared in approval, and Amanda looked to her side to see Cai and Sev just as stunned as she was. Apparently, the three had been offered the same visions, of the same happenings, each from their own planets. Amanda felt another head zap from her Dimensioner, screamed in protest and asked, screaming:

"What the hell is sylph?"

Synthious looked at her tenderly, but his look offended her. It was as if he stared down at an animal, an inferior, ignorant being. Then, with his soothing voice, he answered calmly:

"Sylph is what happens to you when it is time to evolve," he answered. "It is a universally present substance in all higher life forms. Sylph is a fluid which unifies the brain's sides and gives beings, like you, Cai and Sev, who test positive for it, enough tenacity, maturity and emotional intelligence to expand your universes. It is what enabled you to handle this discovery."

"Its main functionalities, however," Oswald interjected, walking towards Cai's platform. At this point, Synthious and Oswald were addressing the entire trio:

"...are others, such as the ability to discern truth from lies, complete control over rational and emotional thinking and later in life the ability to communicate through thought and touch. Beings with sylph are the highest known beings in the universe, including the Pleiadian system."

Oswald walked past Cai and then Sev, reaching Amanda. He looked Amanda in the eyes and asked:

"Don't you see it, Amanda? You never had meningitis. You were never sick. You were merely reacting to the last, final dose of sylph injection. One in each decade, with the final and strongest dose being what put you in a coma. The moment your journey began."

"Three planets," said Synthious. "Three races who tested positive for sylph, three candidates. Everything was made to observe the actions, thoughts and will of the first universal Earthly, Austacyan, and C3K being, and those alongside you were not equal soldiers, but competitors who had failed in areas you succeeded. That is why you stand here with us, not them."

Amanda's jaw dropped to the floor as she realized she had failed to notice that, above their line of vision, flying square drones circled the dome. Inside them, there were nine beings: she recognized, inside three of the nine boxes, Lina,

Ripley and Stryker. The other six were dear members of Cai and Sev's entourage, as they called their names out-loud, seemingly also noticing the drones at the same time as her.

"The Earth you visited was merely a simulation," revealed Oswald "Your entire journey was divided into seven odysseys. The three of you succeeded in each of them, but only one of you was chosen by the Galaxy to ascend. It's been an event that took decades, but the time is now."

"Every ten arns, a Type 3 planet evolves to a Type 2 planet through the insertion of this scenario, which allows you, alien lifeforms, to experience the art of first contact," said Synthious, looking at the trio.

"But you left my planet in war! Because of your Firm, Earth is facing its third World War! That's what made us hijack the ship!" Amanda yelled, feeling betrayed.

Oswald let out one of his sinister, superior laughs. But this time he didn't send out an evil energy, he merely seemed to marvel at Amanda's apparently faulty point of view.

"All that happened inside The Firm was part of the show. There was no way wanted fugitives could travel from Chicago to Reykjavik. My theater was responsible for making you believe there was no other option but to hijack the ship, thus fueling your quest and thirst to find Nitro. Earth was never in a growing war once you woke up from cryo; it was all information fed by Firm employees to fuel your need to escape. We selected the candidates, and as you slept for a decade, we set the stage. The Firm's employees were humanoids controlled by us. You must understand, there is no higher entertainment to us, than seeing the different reactions in each world," he smiled.

"All of us possess sylph" said Synthious "but you were the first for Earth. Cai was the first for Austacya. Sev was the first for C3K. Only when a planet's being successfully adapts to sylph is a civilization ready for contact, for it is a pattern in evolution which, through your existence, has now officially started on your planets. Whenever each of you has a child, it will be the first Earthly being born already fully adapted to sylph. Once he reaches maturity and starts reproducing, all your children will be like him as well. Within millennia, every being from where you come from will be as evolved as us, Nitroans, or even the Pleiadians."

"Your illnesses were a collection of side-effects to an aftermath of your bodies accepting the final dosage of sylph, opening up your brain lobes to see the visions you had, as we watched intently, rooted for you and chose through popular vote our desired outcomes for many parts of your entire journey," explained Oswald. The crowd was silent and seemed to relish Amanda, Cai and Sev's astonished expressions.

"Before we crown the winner, leave your feelings out of it. Use the sylph that runs in your veins to think properly," said Synthious. "The winner will be welcomed as an official member of the Galactic Council. This will provide infinite benefits to life on your planets, since it will be officially the baby-member of a network of more evolved civilizations spread across the galaxy, who will gladly share technology advancements, infinite cures for diseases which are still fatal on Earth, the beginning of implementing what will be eventually a money-less society and many, many more. Ever since the Rain Wars, we have followed this model, and it has never failed us."

"You left my friends with a goal of enlightening our planet as I left them behind," said Cai.

"Yes! You gave my friends an ability, and you told me I was coming back with you because of a quest!" said Amanda. Sev nodded in agreement.

"That only meant they had been eliminated from the contest," said Synthious. "Thought transferring through touch is not something that exactly requires sylph. But then the three of you set off on your journey as you visited Kratik, the Pleiadians, and your final destination: your own planet. Surely you must know there are more effective ways of ascension and enlightening than to have three regular beings touch one another, one by one. It would take forever!"

"So Kratik, the Pleiadians, the version of Earth I witnessed - was it all a ploy? It was all staged?" Amanda asked. "There was no impending doom if we didn't retrieve the K'zaars?"

"It was all part of the Event, yes," answered Synthious. "We wanted to see how you, alien races, would react. Surely the first K'zaar would never have been found that easily. And the Pleiadians... the Pleiadians are the most evolved beings in the cosmos. They would never raise a hand to harm you."

Amanda was befuddled by disgust and mistrust. "How can you expect this to not upset us? How in your advanced ways can't you foresee how overwhelmed we feel with betrayal and rage?" she asked through gritted teeth. Amanda had tears fill her eyes, and had never cried while speaking firmly before.

"This is not a matter of sentiment. This is an opportunity," answered Synthious, "We have known you for so long by now that we love you. Have you ever felt how that feels? To truly love another, unlike romance? Of how we wish to see you in your journey and if we could, it would go on forever? It's been an even longer road for us. We've been with you for decades already, whereas you've been with us only for a few months. To us, you three are heroes. Every time your Dimensioner zapped, we were choosing the path for you. One that sent you on a road that was better than the one you'd choose if we didn't interfere. We've saved you from yourselves." -

For what seemed like a long time, there was silence. Amanda, Sev and Cai merely stared emptily into the endless rows of beings who watched them as the sky closed in on them. Despite being in the middle of a huge open-air stadium, Amanda felt as though she was trapped in a coffin because of the overwhelming intimidation brought on by the crowd and these revelations. The storm would soon reach them, and Synthious and Oswald walked in circles between the three, as if waiting for a reaction.

"Why must two fail, then? If your claim is love," said Sev, out of the blue.

"Well, because otherwise there's no point!" answered Synthious flatly. "There should be a resolution!"

"But that is an evil resolution," said Sev.

"And what is wrong with that?" asked Synthious instantly. Amanda froze - everything fell into place in her mind by looking at Synthious's expression. He'd answered Sev's question as if she had just asked him what was the point in living. This was their entertainment, and therefore their system had rejoiced in such endless peace - they were both good and evil, regular to them. Their morals weren't clouded by judgement or filled with regrets from past decisions - they had achieved a perfect society by allowing their good and bad intentions to be set free. It could be the effect of sylph, or it could simply be them - but Amanda knew she didn't share their state of mind.

"Now, for the results," announced Synthious.

Chapter Thirty-Two - Sky Gods

The crowd erupted in cheers of anticipation and excitement. Screams were heard from every direction, and every being seemed to be sitting up anxiously or moving about in their seats - this was not good. Amanda, Sev and Cai were helpless, immobile, unable to react in any way - exactly the way it had been for centuries, and Amanda knew it wouldn't change now. From time to time, she would look at Lina, Stryker and Ripley, flying about locked in the pod drones. Their expressions were even more lost than hers - to the entire Nitro population this was a matter of celebration and anticipation, but to Amanda, Cai and Sev this felt like standing on the edge of certain death.

"Although the winner is already known in the minds of all of us," announced Synthious, "it is a tradition that we follow the standing principles."

Oswald turned around and spread his arms wide open, addressing the masses.

"All those in favor of Sev being the winner, stand up!" He yelled, and immediately a few rows all around the stadium stood up, cheering and rooting for her.

It wasn't nearly enough, though, and Amanda knew that - a small fraction seemed to root for Sev.

"As it is, Sev, you have been... eliminated," said Synthious. "May a merciful light fall upon you."

"What?" screamed Amanda, Cai and Sev at the same time. But there was nothing to be done - the platform where Sev placed her feet entered the cylinder on which they stood, and her feet dangled in the air. The chains that held her right arm were broken, and she stood hanging in mid-air, holding onto the chains on her left arm. Below them, Amanda flinched at the sight of the fog that covered the ground being transformed into green flames. Seconds later, the entire floor of the stadium seemed like hell - the heat began to rise and Amanda felt as if their bodies would begin boiling in a matter of minutes. Sev screamed "NO! Please!", begging for mercy and redemption.

"It has been decided," said Synthious, smiling a peaceful grin which completely shifted Amanda's perception of him. To them, this suffering was common... it was morally approved. And then, Amanda closed her eyes as she saw Sev's left arm chain break. Sev plummeted down to the fiery inferno, being engulfed in flames in a matter of seconds as she screamed in pain and her body was burnt alive. Just a few moments later, the screaming stopped. The crowd cheered, erupting in applause and admiration. Sev was dead.

"The third place has been settled," said Synthious. He exchanged glances with Amanda and Cai, who seemed possessed by rage. He furrowed his eyebrows, walking slowly towards them with his cane. "Do not worry. She only suffered for a few seconds. Those crucial seconds were enough to set her spirit free."

"You are all demons," said Amanda. "You disgust me."

Synthious and Oswald found Amanda's revolt intriguing, and looked at each other for some time. Oswald whispered: "You know Earthlings. They still live with the notion that only good should prevail. They do not see the benefits of evil."

"Nor do any Austacyans!" protested Cai.

"Which is precisely why your planets haven't ascended yet. But you can bring forth this change," said Synthious.

"So to ascend I have to become a primal bastard, like you? I'd rather stay the same," said Amanda.

"Sylph is in your veins from the moment both of you woke from your comas," said Oswald.

"It's been a few Events since we've had candidates who protested to this level. Most had comprehended by now. Don't disappoint us," said Synthious. Amanda spat on the platform, reaching Synthious's foot.

"Why are you thanking me?" asked Synthious.

"It does not mean that," informed Oswald. "This is an action of *outrage*."

"Oh, I see," said Synthious, dismissing Amanda's action. "There are over one hundred billion beings watching you at this very moment, from multiple frequencies in multiple systems. We shall wait no longer. The time to crown the winner is now!"

Uyara, Illi and Illia emerged from the end of the stadium, walking towards Synthious and Oswald. The crowd erupted once again in cheers, apparently rooting for the appearance of the beings. Disappointment was building inside

Amanda as she realized every being she had frown attached to was involved in the secret unfolding of the Event.

"Both of you have shown exceptional behavior - it has been a very, very close race between the two of you," began Synthious. "Cai, your call to action is simply mesmerizing - you act on intuition without thinking twice, and it has aided you in all of your quests - when you came to Nitro, you almost called upon war for disagreeing with a Vargan. In Kratik, we've particularly enjoyed watching you defeat the Kratikans that held you in the Death Dome. Your apathy also falls into a category that we, Nitroans, very much see as being like us. And you, Amanda" continued Synthious, now staring deep inside her. "You were on from the moment you woke up from the coma. Your sense of purpose and your mistrust of others have led you to question things we have never seen in a contestant before - you even brought to my attention the question why it always seemed like we were giving you a tour of our planet, why you were always being led from place to place. The truth was always there, in the back of your mind. You just didn't want to believe it - but you always asked the right questions. You stood in the Council and surprised us all. You took on the Firm with an astounding grasp of the acts of revenge - but your behavior at the Pleiadians is what sealed your fate. At each of your homes, as you began to unfold the puzzle, you were being tested on the first of the seven parts of your journey. The *Wisdom* test.

Once you infiltrated your planet's Firms, you passed the *Strategy* test. The third part, as you reached our home for the first time, was the *Observation* badge. And once we'd convinced you to take revenge on those who had wronged you, you entered the fourth, the *Leadership* chapter. Upon excelling on those four, the fifth began as we summoned you back to your journeys and you entered Kratik to face your *Bravery* test. At the Pleiadians, both of you also excelled on your *Ingenuity* test, the sixth. And, finally, once you visited the simulation of your home only to have it all crash down upon you, the two of you also marveled in the final test, the test of *Strength*. All seven virtues were put to the test and you, Amanda and Cai, surprised us in each and every one of them. Before we announce the results, we salute and congratulate you."

"So, the question is ...," started Uyara, looking at both Cai and Amanda. She knew Cai was contorting himself in his position, trying to find a way to break the chains. Still, he looked at Uyara as if he paid full attention to her.

"Which one of you has done enough to ascend? Which one of you is worthy of ascending not only yourselves, but your entire planet as well? Which one of you will be welcomed into the Galactic Senate?"

Illi and Illia then soared into the air, which surprised Amanda even more - she didn't know these beings could levitate. Illi was directed towards the left side of the stadium, hanging in the air above them, and Illia to the right. Their expressions were blank, and they stood looking down upon Amanda and Cai as if this was a routine procedure.

"NITRO! The time to choose is upon us! Raise your hands and emanate your sylph rays onto whoever you choose as the winner! Illi and Illia will be your vessels! If you wish Illi, Cai and Austacya to ascend and become the winner, point your rays to him! If you want Illia, Amanda and Earth to ascend and win the Event, point your rays to her... beginning... NOW!"

What happened next changed the course of events forever. Illi and Illia glowed as the entire stadium sent out astonishing blue and green lights from their palms, each voting for their favorite. It was clear Sev was never in the running - Amanda and Cai were by far the favorites of the public. Illi and Illia seemed to receive each beam of light as if being fueled by it, like a panel that fed on solar energy. A green and blue light surrounded each of them, growing exponentially as each Nitroan made their choice.

Plethoreans, Vargans, Garriens, Andromedans and many other races Amanda hadn't yet known were partaking. Amanda and Cai saw rays of light coming not just from the beings in the stadium, but also from satellites sent out by other races across the galaxy. There were multiple systems and populations voting all at once, and Illi and Illia were vessels for the results. They both shone like gods, with outstretched arms and closed eyes as their aura grew, making it unclear who was in the lead in the close race.

"Amanda!" whispered Cai next to her. She instantly turned her head to look at him, and he continued. Everyone was focused on the energy emanation as Synthious and Oswald had their backs turned - the outcome would determine who lived and who died by just an inch.

"When I give you the command, you have to set your Dimensioner to invisibility. Then you must do whatever you can to rescue your friends and meet me outside. The real Belladonna has landed just outside the stadium," Cai quickly whispered to her.

"What?" Amanda asked, astonished. "How do you plan to-"

"There's no time. Do you understand what I said?"

"Yes, I did. But how will we be set free when--"

And then it happened. Cai had strategically positioned his arm so that his brace fired onto the chains that held his left arm. Amanda's eyes widened in shock as she heard him fire his brace once again on his feet and then release his right arm. Before Synthious, Oswald or anyone in the stadium noticed it, he was free - he immediately ran to her and fired his brace on her left and right chains, releasing her arms. Amanda immediately set her Dimensioner to invisibility at the exact moment the entire stadium gasped at the sight - they had switched their attention from the voting to their escape. As

Cai launched his brace on Amanda's feet, he also set his Dimensioner to invisibility and both disappeared from sight.

"No!" screamed Synthious.

"Disable the Dimensioners! Who is on the panel tonight?" yelled Oswald instantly.

"We can't disable the Dimensioners without locating them first!" yelled Synthious.

Amanda and Cai were standing right on the edge of the platform as they whispered their command to Soar. Amanda flew towards Synthious in the stadium while holding onto her expanding Dimensioner, as the thunderstorm darkened the atmosphere and her chains felt like heavy bandages on her wrists. She focused her rage as she flew, landing beside him without making a sound. As another thunderclap echoed across the stadium, she looked up and felt Cai's presence heading towards the gates of the rescued prisoners. Amanda yanked her chains up with all her strength and hit Synthious in the face with them, letting out a scream of rage.

She dashed towards the old master and strapped the chains on his neck, tugging them tightly with a knot. Synthious gasped for air and she gripped onto the chains, taking in every bit of juice that was left in her to strangle him. She screamed as she held onto the Dimensioner and soared up, dragging Synthious with her. The stadium watched and gasped as Synthious rose into the air being pulled by an invisible force. His little arms tried to grip the chains and set his neck free, but Amanda tightened them and pulled the knot with all of her might. Synthious's neck was cut by the chains and Amanda whispered to her Dimensioner the command to Jump, flying up in the air as she watched Synthious scream in pain. Rain poured down in the stadium as Amanda raised her arms in the air, pulling the chains with her and decapitating Synthious.

His head was instantly separated from his torso and his body divided into two, plummeting down into the flames of the stadium below. Despite the rain pouring down on the fire, the green inferno continued to burn. The stadium was filled with horror and shock as they watched Synthious die. Oswald was petrified, scanning the area for Amanda or Cai.

"Guards!" yelled Oswald, and a multitude of armed Plethoreans stormed into the stadium, as he pointed towards the cages being opened. "One of them is freeing the prisoners!"

Amanda's jump lost strength and she felt herself falling with the wind blowing strongly against her face as the raindrops crashed onto her skin like little pieces of cold glass. She called upon her Dimensioner again to use the Soar command, and held onto the crozier, pointing it towards the cages as she soared towards Lina, Ripley and Stryker. On her way, she threw a sonic punch in Oswald's direction, but missed and hit a couple of Plethorean guards who fell from the platform onto the flames.

At this point, the stadium was in full panic mode - havoc and chaos were in the air, and every being was either rushing away from the rain or in fear of being killed - there were screams and beings stepping onto each other, all trying to reach an exit. Another loud thunderclap lit up the stadium in a white light as Amanda reached Lina, but Amanda had no way to open the cages - only Cai's brace would break the locks.

"Leave them to me!" screamed Cai's voice in her mind. She couldn't see him, but Amanda almost fell from her Dimensioner as she jumped at his voice, seeming so close. Lina's lock was crushed by his brace and her cage was opened.

"I'm here, Lina," said Amanda, even though she knew Lina couldn't see her.

"Amanda!" screamed Lina. "We can control these pods! We couldn't escape from them, but we could direct them to where we wanted to go. That's why we were floating around the stadium."

A light bulb went off in Amanda's mind and she immediately instructed Lina:

"Lina, you listen to me. I need you to tell Stryker and Ripley to head west towards the enormous ship parked behind the stadium. We'll escape with it. The fact you can control this just saved your lives. I'll meet you there."

Amanda called upon Cai's mind, feeling his presence: "Warn your loved ones, they need to ride the pods to the ship." As she did so, she heard Stryker's lock break open and then Ripley's.

The rain cascaded down, making it increasingly difficult to see - Oswald and the Plethorean guards fired multiple rays to dematerialize each target. They instantly hit one of Cai's cages, and then all of Sev's. Lina, Ripley and Stryker immediately set off west, flying away from the rays as Cai reached his remaining loved ones to warn them. As Amanda watched Cai's two pods fly in the direction of hers, Amanda and Cai's invisibility shields wore off.

"There they are!" screamed Oswald. "Get them, now! Disable their Dimensioners!"

Amanda and Cai instantly pointed their Dimensioners' croziers up and soared to the skies, flying up and inching them as far up as possible.

"Belladonna!" screamed Amanda as they approached the grey, rainy clouds above. "Belladonna, can you hear us?"

"I can hear you,"

"Five incoming pods are headed your way! Open your passageway only for them to enter. We'll follow closely behind! Only the five pods are allowed access. Do you copy?"

"As you request,"

The stadium below decreased in size, as the round dome that was once so massive seemed like a tunnel of flashing lights. Amanda and Cai flew ever up, flicking left and right to avoid incoming rays. As they flew through the grey clouds, Cai announced:

"They can't see us now. Quick, we must board the ship."

Amanda and Cai turned their Dimensioners around, heading west. Within seconds, the Belladonna appeared through the pouring rain, and Lina, Ripley, Stryker, and Cai's friends were spotted as tiny figures running towards the ship. Amanda and Cai pointed their Dimensioners down and descended as the multitude of Nitroans began to leave the stadium. They touched the wet ground, running instantly towards the platform. They only had a few seconds of head start against the population leaving the stadium, away from the pandemonium. Amanda and Cai ran up the platform to find their loved ones mesmerized by the Belladonna's bridge. As soon as Amanda entered, she screamed:

"Close the platform! Seal all entrances and take off NOW!"

"*As you request*" answered the Belladonna. In an instant, the ship's platform closed in on them to seal them inside the ship as the Belladonna vibrated.

"Take off first, close the entrances later!" screamed Cai. The Belladonna's vibration intensified, and they watched as the ship rose from the ground, in a matter of seconds, surpassing the stadium's altitude and soaring up and away.

Amanda stood petrified, looking down on the planet they left behind as the massive dome once again looked smaller, but she still didn't feel safe. She watched as millions of Nitroans left the stadium and looked up. Some guards had already reached the outside and were firing rays at the ship.

"Belladonna, set invisibility now and tilt!" ordered Amanda. The ship obliged and immediately tilted to the side, evading the incoming shots and soaring into the clouds.

Cai walked towards Amanda and she felt him hold her hand. He looked deeply into her eyes and said:

"We did it."

Only then, Amanda felt her entire world come down on her - she fell to her knees and screamed in relief and horror, sobbing as she brought her hands to her face. At the same moment, she felt Lina, Ripley and Stryker touch her and embrace her, kneeling beside her. Amanda looked at her friends, alive and well, and tried to control her breathing.

"I feel like I'm about to pass out," she confessed, and Lina hugged her in a warm embrace.

"Thank you, Amanda," she said.

Amanda broke down in Lina's embrace, her mind with racing thoughts that were a mixture of shock, awe and adrenaline.

"These last minutes were the most intense and insane events I've ever witnessed," said Stryker. As Amanda sobbed, she managed a small smile as she heard Stryker's voice.

"I missed you," she confessed. "I missed you all. I had no idea. I didn't know about any of this."

"None of us knew," said Lina. "They were onto us from the beginning."

"Oswald is from Cerres," said Amanda. "The same thing happened on your planet, Cai? Why didn't we talk about it on Kratik or the Pleiadians?"

"It never came up," answered Cai. "Or maybe the Dimensioners stopped us from ever having the conversation. It's not like we suspected any of it."

"Do they still hold any control over us?" Amanda asked, touching hers. "We have to take these off."

Amanda watched as Cai ripped off his Dimensioner from his forehead, handing it to his loved ones.

"These are Aurio and Enya," said Cai. "They are my brother and sister from my planet."

Amanda ripped her Dimensioner from her forehead and stood up to meet Cai's family. Aurio and Enya seemed very much like Cai, sporting the same clothes and unusual hairdo, but seemed genuine and just as frightened as all of them.

"So now we're mere mortals. No special abilities" said Amanda.

"We're seven fugitives in a massively powerful spaceship," said Cai.

Stryker, Ripley, Lina, Aurio and Enya looked around the peaceful tropical beach known as the Belladonna's bridge. They seemed in awe - a regular reaction to the wonders of the Belladonna.

"We should head to the Pleiadians," said Amanda. "We'll be safe there. I remember them hinting that Nitro should not be trusted. I'll bet you anything they didn't take part in the Event. They just received us so openly because they're higher beings," Cai nodded in agreement and ordered the Belladonna to head to the Pleiadians. The ship had left Nitro's orbit - all around them from the ship's windows was the darkness of space, with its infinite stars glowing in the endless abyss.

"There will be serious repercussions to our choices. We rebelled against their biggest Event," said Cai. "I'm not sure Austacya or Earth will be safe. I fear their need for revenge may backfire on our planets."

"At this point I can't even believe we made it out of there alive," said Amanda.

"The Pleiadians?" asked Ripley, breaking her silence.

"Yeah, I get that both of you are incredible and just saved our lives and all, but would you care to bring us up to speed here? If you guys are lost and on edge, imagine how we feel!" said Stryker, with his unmistakable tone of urgency.

As the Belladonna soared through the pitch black darkness of space, Amanda and Cai brought their rescued friends up to speed on everything that had been going on while they were apart. During their talks, they gave them a proper tour of the ship's multiple chambers, resting on the Galley where they shared a long overdue meal. After revitalizing their energies, the team set out to the hot springs to relax as they made their way to the Pleiadian system. Amanda and Cai parted ways with the others, walking towards the ship's bridge once again.

"So what happens now, Cai?" Amanda asked as they looked out into the endless stars above through the ship's windows.

"Now we hope for help. We've begun something that could escalate into war. But it was our only option," he said, as they both stared ahead. Amanda crossed her arms and continued:

"There are too many questions still unanswered. Why didn't sylph merge our brains properly? Shouldn't we be unified by now? Shouldn't we be unable to discern the blurred lines of good and evil actions?"

"What concerns me is what lies ahead for Austacya and Earth. The ship may be invisible, and they may not track us, which leads me to think they will try to hit us where we care."

"It makes sense. It's their best hope to bring us out of hiding," answered Amanda.

"Should we just surrender?" asked Cai, bluntly. Amanda immediately tilted her head to the side, then signaled a no.

"I have another plan. We'll get the Pleiadians. I'm sure they'll buy into our struggle, they'll hear our version of the story. We stay and we fight."

"You can't possibly think the seven of us can destroy an entire Empire. They must have had some part in meddling or interference in the story, as it seems our physical bodies left the underwater pods and were taken straight to the Nitro stadium, where we experienced the altered state of consciousness that made us believe we were back at our home planets," said Cai.

"Yes, but they're different. They don't morally accept evil as a part of life. Besides, it won't just be the seven of us. If we get them to help us, the Pleiadian system, we have a fighting chance. Nitro took everything from us, now we'll take everything from them."

"The biggest question to me is what, or who, took us from the underwater Pleiadian city and back to the Nitro stadium. Revenge never turns out the way you expect it to."

"It's not revenge," said Amanda. "It's a matter of justice."

Amanda felt safe inside the Belladonna and knew Cai shared the same sensation. She felt relieved at knowing Lina, Ripley and Stryker were safe and rejoicing in the hot springs, as oblivious as they were of things to come. The ship sailed through the infinity of space, heading straight to their destination and leaving no breadcrumbs behind. Knowing they could've started something that could bring them certain doom strangely didn't bother her. She felt a sense of completion in having avenged her capture and pride in knowing they had been the first to escape the clutches of the Ascension Event. If improbability was indeed on their side, then at least Amanda knew she could hope for unexpected outcomes. So she hoped.

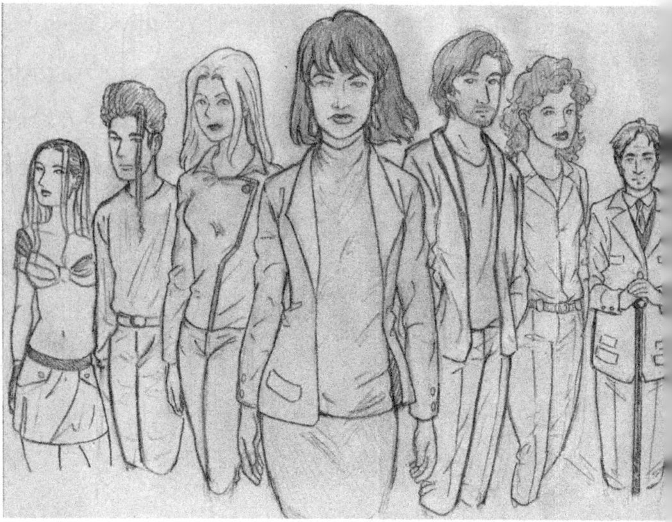

Printed in Great Britain
by Amazon